THE DOCTOR'S SECRET SON

BY

JANICE LYNN

REFORMING THE PLAYBOY

BY

KARIN BAINE

MILLS

Janice Lynn has a Masters in Nursing from Vanderbilt University, and works as a nurse practitioner in a family practice. She lives in the southern United States with her husband, their four children, their Jack Russell—appropriately named Trouble—and a lot of unnamed dust bunnies that have moved in since she started her writing career. To find out more about Janice and her writing visit janicelynn.com.

Karin Baine lives in Northern Ireland with her husband, two sons, and her out-of-control notebook collection. Her mother and her grandmother's vast collection of books inspired her love of reading and her dream of becoming a Mills & Boon author. Now she can tell people she has a *proper* job! You can follow Karin on Twitter, @karinbaine1, or visit her website for the latest news—karinbaine.com.

THE DOCTOR'S SECRET SON

BY
JANICE LYNN

MILLS & BOON

Published in Great Britain 2017
By Mills & Boon, an imprint of HarperCollins*Publishers*
1 London Bridge Street, London, SE1 9GF

© 2017 Janice Lynn

ISBN: 978-0-263-92655-2

Printed and bound in Spain
by CPI, Barcelona

Dear Reader,

While writing my last Medical Romance I became more and more intrigued by my heroine's best friend. By the end of that book I knew I had to know what her story was and give her a happy ending.

Chrissie Tomberlain has a secret she's kept for the four years since she last saw Trace Stevens—a beautiful three-year-old son. Providing medical care to impoverished and war-torn countries is Trace's life mission, but he's back in Atlanta for a few weeks and discovers the attraction between him and Chrissie has only grown with time. Trace knows he won't stay, and Chrissie isn't looking to have an affair. But when he learns her reasons why he's confronted with a past he'd rather forget.

I hope you enjoy Trace and Chrissie's book as much as I enjoyed researching and writing their story. Drop me an email at Janice@janicelynn.net to share your thoughts about their romance, about Chattanooga, or just to say hello.

Happy reading!

Janice

To my editor, Kathryn Cheshire.
Thanks for all your fabulous insight and hard work
to make my stories shine.

Books by Janice Lynn

Mills & Boon Medical Romance

Flirting with the Doc of Her Dreams
New York Doc to Blushing Bride
Winter Wedding in Vegas
Sizzling Nights with Dr Off-Limits
It Started at Christmas…
The Nurse's Baby Secret

Visit the Author Profile page
at millsandboon.co.uk for more titles.

**Janice won The National Readers' Choice Award
for her first book**
The Doctor's Pregnancy Bombshell

CHAPTER ONE

IT WAS HER.

Her hair was longer and her body a bit curvier, but the wide smile on her full lips was the same, as was the sparkle in her bright green gaze.

Not for a single second did Dr. Trace Stevens doubt the perky little blonde nurse's identity. How could he? No woman had ever caused such an intense sexual reaction in him as Chrissie Tomberlain.

Trace's lips curved.

This weekend had definitely just taken a turn for the better. A big turn. Four years ago she'd made his last weekend in the States unforgettable. He still had a few weeks before leaving again, but he welcomed the distraction.

Chrissie had been the best distraction he'd ever known.

So much so that even now, from time to time, he'd awaken drenched in sweat, with an ache in his gut that hadn't been satisfied in years.

Four years, to be exact.

Ironic to run into her because more than once he'd considered looking her up, seeing if she was single, seeing if she'd be interested in spending time with him while he was home.

Then again, this event was where they'd met, so maybe not so ironic. Still, this weekend was exactly what he needed in so many ways.

A few weeks from now, he'd go back to doing what he was meant to do in life. There were places in the world that needed him a lot more than he was needed in Atlanta, Georgia, even if his friends and family thought otherwise.

Chrissie Tomberlain hadn't spent a night away from her three-year-old son since he'd been born. So why had she let her best friend convince her that staying away from him for a whole weekend would be a good idea?

Okay, Savannah was right that Chrissie never did anything but work and take care of Joss. But there wasn't anything she'd rather do than spend time with her son, so she hadn't seen it as a problem. Spending time with Joss was a blessing she cherished each and every time she looked into his precious face, heard his sweet voice, felt his little hands pat her cheek.

Prior to Joss's birth, she had enjoyed volunteering at various charity fund-raisers around her hometown of Chattanooga. She'd done so at the huge children's cancer prevention event in Atlanta several times in the past.

But not since she'd gotten pregnant with Joss.

At the event.

By a man she hadn't seen since.

Until now.

Trace Stevens hadn't changed much from four years ago.

He was still sexy as hell and made her body do crazy, previously unexperienced things.

Made her mind go back to the night of passion of four years ago that had led to her becoming a single mother by a man she'd just met.

A man who had no idea he'd fathered a son.

Her son. Her sweet, wonderful Joss.

She swallowed the lump in her throat and prepared herself for what she hadn't really thought would ever happen.

She wasn't supposed to see Trace again.

He wasn't supposed to be here.

Yet, if she was honest with herself, wouldn't she admit that from the moment she'd gotten into her car in Chattanooga she'd had a nervous energy inside, wondering "what if" the entire two-hour drive?

What if Trace was there?

What if their paths really did cross again?

What if he still lit her body on fire with a mere glance, something no one else had ever done before or since?

There he was, standing in a tent not so unlike the one they'd met in four years ago. For all she knew it might be the exact same one if Children's Cancer Prevention Organization owned their commercial tents, rather than rented them.

A big sexy grin climbed up Trace's face as his gaze collided with hers and recognition hit.

He remembered her.

Of course he remembered her.

They'd spent an entire weekend together. A lot of it *together* together. Four years wasn't so long ago that he'd forget a weekend that hot and heavy.

Then again, maybe he had hot and heavy weekends like that routinely.

She knew nothing about the man except that he was amazing in bed and had been a fellow volunteer at the CCPO. That year, the event had done a three-day walk. This year, the organization was sponsoring a weekend of family fun. On Friday evening, they were having a welcome event and a bubble-a-thon dance party open to all participants and their families. On Saturday morning, they were having a marathon, with various levels of participation. Some committing to a five K, some to the full marathon. Others committing to various distances in between. Then, in the evening, they were having sponsored Olympic-style games for the kids.

Now, as then, Chrissie had signed up to work the medical tent all weekend. Full of nervous energy, she'd dropped Joss off to Savannah early that morning, then made the drive so she could help organize the medical station and volunteer to assist with anything else needed prior to the families and fund-raiser participants starting to arrive.

Imagine running into Trace within minutes of her arrival.

Imagine, she had.

For four years she'd imagined this moment, coming face to face with the man who'd haunted her dreams and her reality.

Yet it wasn't really as intense as it should have been. The sun hadn't stood still in the sky. The earth hadn't quaked. Lightning hadn't streaked its way to the ground. Nothing. They were just standing in a tent, looking at each other, a man and a woman with a past while the rest of the world went on as usual.

No big deal. But her heart pounded like crazy and her chest wanted to heave from lack of air.

Probably had something to do with the look in Trace's eyes when he'd spotted her that said he'd figured out exactly what he'd be doing this weekend, other than working the medical tent.

Or more like who.

Why, oh, why was everything in her screaming *yes*?

Other than her brain, that was. Her brain warned she'd best stay far, far away because to have anything to do with him would be risking everything.

He wasn't that good in bed.

She skimmed her gaze over his body, noting on closer inspection that he was slightly leaner than she remembered, more tan, too. His loose CCPO event T-shirt and khaki cargo shorts did little to hide his broad shoulders and narrow hips. His left hand was still bare of jewelry and had no telltale tan line to hint at deception. Lifting her gaze back to his face, she took in his sandy-colored hair, strong aquiline nose, cleft chin, and toffee-colored eyes that were staring straight into hers with obvious interest. His smile widened and her thighs clenched in immediate response.

He *had* been that good, but she still wasn't risking it.

She had too much at stake to play sexual escapades with Trace all weekend.

But boy, oh, boy, did the man tempt everything in her.

"It's been a while," Trace said by way of greeting when he closed the distance between them.

"Four years."

Four years. Four long years where he'd seen things he'd like to forget, and she was just the woman who might accomplish that for him, even if only for a short while.

A short while sounded like heaven after the hell he'd seen, that he'd no doubt see more of when he returned to wherever they sent him this time.

"How have you been?" he asked, studying her. Other than the change of hairstyle and the few extra pounds she carried, she looked the same as he recalled. Better even. He liked the fullness to her breasts and hips that hadn't been there four years ago.

His groin tightened.

Yeah, he liked her curves a lot.

His body's instant reaction to her nearness made him feel like a Neanderthal. It hadn't been that long since he'd been with a woman. But when he tried to think back to the last time he'd had sex, he struggled to recall exactly how long it had been.

A problem he intended to rectify, assuming Chrissie still felt the strong attraction they'd shared. Time certainly hadn't faded a thing for him.

Sex just hadn't been a priority recently. Life—life had

been the top priority where he'd been. Helping those who desperately needed help and doing what he could with significantly limited resources had been a priority. Surviving tragedy, and healing, had been a priority.

"I'm great," she answered, shifting her weight as if she was nervous.

She had nothing to be nervous about. They'd ended on good terms, or so he'd thought, after their weekend. He'd thought about her often enough that had there been anything negative he would have remembered. He'd swear he recalled every detail of that weekend in vivid color.

"That's good to hear. How's life been treating you?"

Her gaze cut to beyond him, and, ignoring his question, she said, "Sorry, but if you'll excuse me, I see someone I need to talk to." She paused, briefly met his gaze with a steely expression in her green eyes. "Good to see you again, Travis."

Travis? Ouch.

He watched her walk away, greet Agnes Coulson, a bear of a woman and the Children's Cancer Prevention Organization founder. True to how he'd just thought of her, Agnes wrapped Chrissie into a big hug, causing her to laugh as she hugged the woman back, then wiggled free.

"It's so good to see you," she exclaimed to the woman, showing the excitement Trace would like to have seen when she'd greeted him. He wouldn't have minded one of those hugs, either.

Instead, he'd effectively been put in his place.

Not that he was buying that she'd forgotten his name.

He wasn't.

She hadn't forgotten. But she wanted him to think she had. That was her way of letting him know she wasn't interested.

Which wasn't what her eyes had conveyed when she'd

first seen him. He'd have bet anything she'd felt the same excitement he had.

He knew she had.

Maybe she'd taken that closer look, seen the harshness that almost suffocated him these days, and known the best thing she could do was stay away.

He wasn't the same man he'd been four years ago. Not by far. In some ways, he was better. In some, not so much.

"You two had something a few years back, didn't you? Right before you left for Sudan?"

Trace turned to Bud Coulson, Agnes's husband. They headed up the event each year. They'd done so for the past twenty years. Their only child had been diagnosed with, and died from, a rare type of brain cancer, and they'd dedicated their lives to raising awareness and funds to fight pediatric cancers. Trace's family regularly donated to their organization. Four years ago, before he'd left for his Doctors Around the World stint overseas, Trace had done more than pull out his hefty checkbook. He'd volunteered as an extra helper, something he'd done numerous times over the years in different capacities with CCPO.

Even before Doctors Around the World he'd wanted to do more to help others than just practice medicine. Thank goodness for Bud and Agnes's influence over the years that had planted that seed that drove him to help others.

How could he not support the foundation when it was a way of keeping Kerry alive to the couple he loved so much?

"I was quite taken with her the weekend we met," he admitted, not letting his mind go to little Kerry and the guilt he always felt when he thought of her.

Instead, he let memories of Chrissie flood through his mind. He'd always wondered if the intensity of that weekend had been because he'd known he was heading into the unknown. Which he'd wanted. He still wanted even if his parents had begged him to come home to stay. He understood their concern.

Especially after the incident at the Shiara MSF hospital in Yemen.

Automatically, he placed his hand over his right lower abdomen. That one had been a bit too close for comfort, but at least he'd walked away with his life, which he couldn't say of all his colleagues.

Damn cowardly terrorists attacking a hospital. Damn that he'd walked away when so many good people had died.

"Your dad told me about what happened." Bud gestured to where Trace touched. "You should have come home to let us take care of you."

Trace rammed his hand into his pocket.

"There was nothing anyone could do." There hadn't been. He'd been one of the lucky ones. "Besides, I lived."

"I was surprised you didn't opt to come home after that," Bud mused, then shook his head. "I take that back. That you opted to stay didn't really surprise me."

"Coming home wasn't an option." Not one that he'd ever considered at any rate. He planned to live his life doing mission work. Settling down wasn't for him. A wife and kids wasn't his lot in life and he never wanted it to be.

His gaze cut to the woman still smiling and chatting with Agnes. Her hands waved animatedly as she described something. Both women burst into laughter and a deep ache pierced Trace.

"Your father would move heaven and earth to convince you to come back," Bud mused, watching Trace rather than his wife and Chrissie. "He's hoping you're home to stay."

Trace frowned. "We both know I'll be leaving as soon as I'm given my next assignment. My father doesn't understand."

Bud shook his head. "You're right. He doesn't. Not many do."

Trace's eyes shifted toward the older man. "You saying you don't? Because I wouldn't believe you. You of all people understand the need to do more than just accept things for the way they are. This organization is testament to that."

"Agnes and CCPO are my life." One side of Bud's mouth tugged upward. "Then again, at one time the Marine Corps was my life, too. I served time overseas and wouldn't trade those memories and the brothers I gained for anything. I think we accomplished a lot of good things, but that doesn't mean I'd go back. Sometimes we have to let go of one thing we care about to make room for another." He glanced lovingly at his wife.

Trace cocked his brow at the older man. "You trying to tell me you don't think I should go?"

Bud shrugged. "Only you know the answer to whether or not you should go back." He nodded toward where Chrissie and Agnes still talked, obviously catching up. "Maybe it's time you find a reason to want to stay home rather than go as far away as possible."

"Those people need help every bit as much as the kids you're raising money for," Trace pointed out, not acknowledging Bud's claim that he might have been running from something when he'd signed on to Doctors Around the World. "They're innocent victims of governments and wars they have no control over."

"Civilians are always the innocent victims of war," Bud agreed. "You do what you feel is right for you, son. All I'm saying is that there is a lot of good you can do here, too. I just think you need to keep that in mind, because I'm not convinced going back is the right choice for you."

Trace eyed the older man suspiciously. "You're sure Dad didn't put you up to trying to talk me into staying?"

Bud laughed. "I won't say he's never mentioned hoping you'd stay to me, but I'm speaking for myself."

Trace nodded. He'd figured as much. His successful

businessman father would probably fund Bud's charity for the next fifty years if he could convince Trace to stay in Atlanta.

Which would be a good reason to stay, if it didn't mean having to deal with his father on a regular basis.

"In case you haven't noticed, Blondie is looking your way."

Trace had noticed. Hard not to notice those intense emerald eyes studying him. He could feel her interest, could feel her body's reaction to him.

The same interest and reaction he was having to her.

Obviously, the chemistry they'd shared still burned hot.

So, why had she given him the cold shoulder?

Chrissie ordered her gaze to remove itself from Trace. Unfortunately, her eyes didn't seem connected to her brain.

Why did he have to be so hot? Those amazing eyes just sucked her in. Rich, warm toffee that made her want to melt.

She was melting.

No wonder she'd lost her mind four years ago. Trace was hot. Scorching, melt-a-woman-all-the-way-to-her-toes hot.

Chrissie's toes were ooey-gooey puddles in her shoes.

"It's good to have Trace back with us, too, isn't it?"

Oops. Obviously, Agnes noticed her distraction and had no compunction on commenting.

Chrissie dragged her gaze away from Trace and focused on the older woman, who was watching her curiously. Something told her the woman wouldn't buy it if she pretended not to know what she referred to. After all, Chrissie and Trace had only had eyes for each other four years ago. No doubt every volunteer there had picked up on their attraction.

"Where's he been?" she asked.

Agnes's concerned gaze went to Trace. "For the past couple of years? Yemen."

Surprise hit Chrissie. "Yemen?"

"He works with Doctors Around the World." A troubled look came over Agnes's face, making her appear every one of her sixty plus years. "He'll be leaving again soon. Unfortunately. He's home because his only cousin had a baby and the timing fell right at the end of his contract."

Chrissie's gaze went back to Trace. Yemen. She knew that was in the Middle East, but she wasn't sure exactly where. She probably should have paid better attention in geography class.

"I wondered if you two had stayed in touch while he was there and that it wasn't a coincidence you were both volunteering again at the same time." Agnes looked disappointed. "Obviously not."

Chrissie shook her head. "No, meeting Trace four years ago was nice." Nice? Ha, that was so not the right word to describe that meeting. More like naughty. "But neither of us fooled each other that our meeting was anything more. I didn't know he'd be here."

"Too bad," Agnes countered. "That boy needs someone in his life."

"You sound as if you know him well," Chrissie mused, trying not to look overly interested.

"All his life. His father and Bud go back a long way. Well," she clarified with a low laugh, "all the way back to elementary school. They were best friends. Trace was a few months older than our daughter. We'd always hoped they'd grow up, fall in love, and connect our families in yet another way." Pain momentarily aged her face. "Instead, Kerry died and Trace spends his time overseas."

"Are you gossiping about me, Agnes?"

Agnes quickly recovered, her cheeks turning a rosy pink. "Every chance I get to extol your virtues."

"My virtues don't deserve extolling."

There was more to what he was saying than what appeared. But Chrissie's own cheeks were burning too much with embarrassment at getting caught discussing him for her to over-analyze his comment.

"That's a matter of opinion," Agnes countered. "So, where are we going to put our Chrissie to work this year?"

Chrissie frowned. She wasn't their Chrissie. At least, not *his* Chrissie. But Agnes was smiling and chatting on about the medical tent and making sure everything was ready for the event kick-off.

"I'd like to do triage if that's okay," Chrissie spoke up. "It's what I did last time."

"You've been back?" Trace asked, studying her.

Agnes nodded. "Not for a few years, but our Chrissie is an angel from heaven, for sure."

Yeah, Chrissie was pretty sure with the way her insides were burning that she was from somewhere way more south.

And Agnes knew that it had been four years. Why had she left the date a little vague?

"Maybe you could take her to the triage area and show her how things are set up this year?" Agnes's question was directed at Trace.

"Yes, ma'am." His gaze locked with Chrissie's and he grinned as if she hadn't cut him off earlier. "Follow me."

His facial expression was so similar to one she often saw on her son's face that her breath caught. Her feet refused to move. Her head spun.

"Chrissie?"

Shaking her head to stop the spinning, she stepped toward him.

Three days. Three days and then she'd change charities to volunteer at ones in Chattanooga so she'd never have to see Trace Stevens again.

CHAPTER TWO

"YOU'VE CHANGED."

Chrissie's gaze shot to Trace's. Of course she had changed. She was a mother now. Not that she was going to tell him that.

Although they hadn't done a lot of talking four years ago, he had told her that he was a bachelor for life and had no plans to reproduce ever. Because of his words, and the trauma from her parents' custody battle when she was seven, Chrissie had convinced herself that Joss belonged to her because she'd just been a weekend fling for Trace.

Guilt pinched at her conscience, but she shoved it aside.

Now was not the time to feel guilty. They'd shared a wild weekend of sex that had never been meant to be anything more. He hadn't wanted it to be anything more.

Only she'd ended up pregnant.

Pregnant, and she hadn't known how to get in touch with him.

She could have contacted Bud and Agnes, could have asked for Trace's information. Perhaps they would have given it to her.

Only, she hadn't.

She and Trace had parted ways with no plans to stay in touch or ever see each other again. He'd known the city where she lived because she'd told him. Just as he'd told her he lived in Atlanta. He hadn't bothered to get in touch with her or continue their relationship in any way.

If he'd left the country, who knew if he'd even had a way of staying in touch? Then again, if he'd wanted to, he would have found a way. Chattanooga wasn't that big and tracking down a nurse with her name couldn't have been that difficult.

He hadn't, and because of that she'd never felt the need to attempt to track him down. Well, twinges from time to time, but overall she knew she'd done the right thing for her son and had even given Trace what he'd said he wanted by keeping her secret.

How Joss had come into existence didn't matter these days. What mattered was her precious little boy who was the center of her world, and that she'd do anything to protect him from the hell she'd gone through as a child. She would give him the best life possible, and that was that.

But then, she hadn't thought she'd see Trace again. Not really.

She stared into his eyes, wondering at the emotions she saw flickering there.

She hadn't known he was leaving the country, hadn't known he was with Doctors Around the World. He'd never mentioned anything of the sort to her. Something like leaving the country for an extended period of time was a big deal.

"When did you leave for Doctors Around the World?"

His pupils dilated and for the briefest moment darkness replaced the interest in his eyes. "I see Agnes really was gossiping about me."

He hadn't answered her question. Interesting. Most of the guys she knew would have made sure everyone knew they were a doctor, that they'd signed up selflessly to help others, and they'd have played that angle to the max. Four years ago Trace hadn't told her he was a doctor or that he was with DAW.

Fifteen minutes and she already knew things about him she hadn't known then.

Was that why he'd told her he wasn't interested in anything more than a weekend fling and never would be? Because he'd been about to leave?

"When?" she repeated, needing to know, although she wasn't sure why it even mattered. That he hadn't told her such pertinent details about his life just reinforced what she already knew. It hadn't mattered that she hadn't known the details of his life. She was not someone who mattered.

"The week after we met." His lips twisted as if the words triggered unpleasant memories. "I'd purposely put off my leave date until after the event so I could help Bud and Agnes and to spend a little time with them before I took off. That's why I didn't sign on to work as a physician at the event, but just as extra help where needed."

The week after... He'd left the country the week after they'd met.

"I haven't been back in the United States since. Not until a week ago."

Four years had passed and he'd not come home. For all of Joss's life, Trace had been out of the country, serving others.

"Oh."

"Yeah, oh." He reached out, brushed his fingertip over her cheek then down her jawline. "Not sure how much help I was that weekend. All I remember about those three days is you."

Her insides perked up at his admission and it was all she could do not to ask "It is?" with a silly school girl expression plastered to her face. Instead, she bit her tongue.

He'd been out of the country for four years. How many times while she'd been pregnant had she thought about him living it up in Atlanta's night life? Wining and dining some slim beauty queen while she grew rounder and rounder with his child? The glimpse of darkness in his eyes said that he hadn't been wining or dining anyone, that he'd seen things he'd like to forget, that the past four years hadn't been a bed of roses.

"Have you thought about me, Chrissie?"

She winced. Had he read her mind?

Still, she didn't want to answer his question any more than he'd wanted to answer hers. She didn't want to tell him that not a day went by that he didn't cross her mind.

How could it when Joss was a constant reminder?

When she went home, it would be even worse now that she'd seen Trace again and realized just how much her son truly resembled his handsome father. The facial expressions. The eyes. Joss was Trace's mini-me.

"Or did you forget me the minute you left Atlanta?"

His question made her sound as if she had flings all the time, as if what she'd done with him had been no big deal. Other than a college boyfriend she'd hung around with long enough for him to take her virginity and introduce her to a mediocre sex life, she'd had no other lovers. Only Trace.

There had been nothing mediocre about Trace.

But she wasn't telling him that, either.

Because he'd been so good he must have had many lovers over the years.

Had probably had many since, despite his being out of the country. Chrissie couldn't suppress her grimace.

"You know as well as I do that you aren't exactly the kind of man a woman forgets," she admitted as if it were no big deal. "Nor was that weekend the kind I'd just forget."

"Good to know." He smiled at her admission. "It was a phenomenal weekend, wasn't it?"

She crossed her arms and kept her mouth shut. She'd answered enough questions.

"But not one you want to repeat?"

Yeah, she didn't want to answer that either. Mainly because her body was like, "Yes, sign me up for an encore performance!" but her brain knew the best thing she could do was keep as much distance between her and Trace as possible.

He was the father to her son. A son he didn't know about. She needed to stay far, far away before she slipped up and said something she shouldn't. What if she said something and he pulled a stunt like the one her father had pulled?

She couldn't bear the thought of Trace disappearing with her son. Not that he would likely even want anything to do with Joss, but, still, her own father had practically ignored her the first seven years of her life and that hadn't stopped him.

Her gaze lifted to his and rather than saying, *No, I don't want a repeat*, as a good, smart girl would do, she asked, "Why do you say that?"

His expression brightened. "Then you do want a repeat?"

Ugh. She'd walked right into that one.

She studied his toffee-colored gaze, his smooth tanned skin, the obvious sexual interest in his eyes. "You do?"

"What sane man wouldn't want a repeat of what you and I had?"

There was that.

"Sex without strings?"

His gaze narrowed. "Not exactly how I'd have worded it."

She didn't let her gaze waver. "Which doesn't make it any less true."

His forehead furrowed and he did some studying of his own. She refused to look away, refused to shift her weight or show any sign of weakness.

Even if her insides quaked at the power this man had over her.

"Did you want strings, Chrissie?"

Heat rushed into her face. She was going to have to be careful of what she said. Which was why she needed to stay away. Nothing good could come from spending time with Trace.

"No, of course not." She hadn't. She'd known what they shared was just a man and a woman thrown together by circumstances and sexual attraction. "You told me you weren't the marrying kind. I didn't expect anything to come of our weekend together." She sure hadn't expected to become a mother. "No strings was fine."

A tired look came over his face and he raked his fingers through his hair. "I was leaving the country in three days. I couldn't have done strings if I'd wanted to."

Something in his tone had her insides fluttering with a bundle of nervous energy.

"Did you want to?"

Good question, and one that Trace had asked himself a thousand times in the years that had passed since he'd last seen this woman. What would he have done differently had he not been committed?

"I didn't allow myself to consider strings as a possibility." Which was what he always came back to when his mind got to wondering. Not that he would ever have settled down, but he would have liked more time with Chrissie, to have been able to let the fire between them burn out naturally.

Her pretty face pinched and her gaze averted. "Which explains why you never asked for a phone number."

Although he was sure she didn't want them to, her words conveyed that she'd been hurt. That he'd hurt her stung.

"There was no point in my asking."

"I see." Her lower lip disappeared again.

"I don't think you do." He lifted her chin and stared

into the greenest eyes he'd ever looked into. "I was leaving the country, had volunteered for a crazy assignment. Putting you or any woman through the stress of a relationship when I was over there, especially when nothing would ever have come from that relationship anyway—it wouldn't have been fair."

Her chin trembled beneath his fingertips and Trace wanted to kiss her so badly his insides ached. They were alone in the medical tent, but someone could walk in. Which didn't overly concern him. He'd seen and done too much to let something as irrelevant as someone seeing him kiss Chrissie get to him. But Chrissie was still sending mixed signals.

One minute hot, the next cold.

When he kissed her next, he wanted her to want it as much as he did, not to be second-guessing herself.

He would kiss her again. Soon. She might not want to admit it, but she wanted the kiss as much as he did. Everything in her expression, her stance, her eyes, said so.

"Well, I guess you're a damn saint, then, eh?"

There went the cold again. And the hurt.

"Far from it."

Looking away, she shrugged. "Not to hear Agnes tell it."

"Agnes is biased. She's my godmother."

Chrissie's eyes widened. Obviously Agnes hadn't told her that part.

"Her husband, Bud, and my father grew up in the same neighborhood and were best friends. Somehow, that friendship survived my father's personality all these years."

"Something wrong with your father's personality?"

Ha, now there was a tricky question if ever there was one.

"Most people would say he's near perfect."

Her eyebrow arched. "But not you?"

Not a subject he wanted to discuss any more than he wanted to discuss Sudan or Yemen or Kerry. Maybe less so.

"So, about those Braves…"

He watched emotions play across her face, but she let any further questions she had go. How many times had he closed his eyes and recalled her face? How many times when the whole world seemed to have gone crazy had he closed his eyes and just remembered everything about her?

"Yeah, well, apparently you don't recall, or maybe you never knew—" her chin tilted upward "—but I'm not a fan of baseball."

Well, no one was perfect even if in his mind she was close.

"That's un-American," he teased.

She shrugged. "Overpaid bunch of men who never grew up as far as I'm concerned."

His lips twitched. "I'll have you know those guys work hard."

She gave him an accusing look. "You sound as if you're one of them. Former player or just a wannabe?"

He laughed and it felt good. Foreign, but good. He'd not had many reasons to laugh over the past four years. It hadn't all been bad. Some parts had been wonderful. He'd been helping people who desperately needed help. But overall there hadn't been nearly enough laughter.

For all the craziness, he'd felt as if he was doing something positive in the world, had felt alive and needed.

"Nope, never been much of a baseball player," he admitted. "But I have a few friends on the team."

"On the Atlanta Braves baseball team?" She sounded incredulous.

He nodded. His father handled more than one of the players' finances, was a real-estate mogul, and prior to Trace leaving the country they'd moved in the same social circles. These days, all the parties and hoopla seemed pointless when there were people starving and being killed for their beliefs or place of birth.

Shaking off the memory, he focused on the petite blonde staring up at him and drank her in like a breath of fresh air.

Chrissie's brows pinched. "Just who are you, anyway?"

Determined that he was going to keep the past four years at bay, not think about pending decisions that needed making about his future, Trace grinned. "That's right. You forgot my name."

For the first time, a smile toyed on her lips.

A guilty smile.

That she'd pretended not to remember him was as telling as her comment about his not asking for her phone number.

He stuck out his hand. "Hi. I'm Trace Stevens. I'm a volunteer in the medical tent. I'll be working closely with you over the next couple of days."

"Not that closely."

It occurred to him that just because his life hadn't moved forward, a lot could have changed in hers.

He'd just assumed she was single, available.

His gaze dropped to her left hand and specifically to her empty third finger.

"No wedding ring," he mused out loud. "Boyfriend?"

"I'm not married." Her lower lip disappeared between her teeth. "But I date from time to time."

He let her answer digest, not liking the green sludge making its way through his veins. He had no claims on her. He never had. When he'd spotted her across the tent he hadn't even considered that she might be involved with someone else. He'd just seen her and wanted her.

Four years had come and gone. It wasn't as if he'd have expected anyone to have waited on him.

And to wait for what? A weekend fling every few years when he came home?

He had nothing to offer beyond that and never would.

CHAPTER THREE

CHRISSIE NEEDED TO get away from Trace. Quickly. Being around him made her insides mush.

"So," she said as a way of moving the conversation away from anything personal. "What can I do to help get things set up?"

"Bud and Agnes are so organized they have most everything taken care of. The bins of donated supplies are over here and are labeled. We can set the area up along the lines of what we did four years ago."

Chrissie's face heated, which told her way too much about her state of mind.

"A triage area and a treatment area?" Had her voice been several octaves higher or was that just her imagination?

"Yes." How dared he sound so calm? "We'll set one treatment area up to be a bit more private, just in case."

No. No. No. There went her naughty imagination again to places it shouldn't go. To memories of a former private treatment area where her body had been quite ravished.

She couldn't prevent her blush.

Hoping he didn't notice, or that he'd think it the result of the Georgia heat, she nodded. "That works for me. How many volunteers do we have in the medical area this year?"

The more the better. She hoped they were so over-staffed that being alone was impossible.

"Around a dozen, I think." He pulled out a list and began

reading it. "We have a couple of doctors, a couple of nurses, a paramedic, a few nurse practitioners, and a few techs, and then some med and nursing students. It should run smoothly."

"Trace Stevens, is that you?" a female voice with a light accent called out from the other side of the tent.

Trace and Chrissie both turned. A pretty brunette with long sleek hair pulled into a ponytail headed their direction. A huge smile was on her face and Chrissie wouldn't have been surprised if she'd broken into a run to close the gap between her and Trace quicker.

"Alexis," he greeted the woman, who wrapped her arms around him and gave him a big hug. "I just saw your name on the list."

Chrissie was beginning to think she was going to have to peel the woman off to get her to let go of Trace, but eventually, and with obvious reluctance, she stepped back and brushed her hands down her white shorts and turquoise top.

"I heard you were back in town—" Alexis's smile was so big and bright she could be a toothpaste ad "—and would be here this weekend, but thought it too good to be true."

"You heard right." Trace grinned easily at the beautiful woman.

No wonder. She was a Greek goddess, had a husky voice that held a light accent and was downright sexy, and she was looking at Trace with obvious interest in her dark eyes.

She was looking at him the way Chrissie had, no doubt, looked at him four years ago.

Thank goodness she wasn't looking at him that way now. Okay, maybe a little.

I am not jealous, she told herself over and over. *It does not matter that another woman is batting her lashes at him as if he is coated in chocolate and she's just come off a strict diet.*

It didn't matter. He meant nothing to Chrissie. Just a stranger she'd had an amazing weekend with years ago.

A stranger who she'd made a child with.

She grimaced. Yeah, there was that. Which explained why she couldn't bear to watch their interaction a moment longer. It had nothing to do with anything other than a natural instinct because of Joss.

"Um… I'll go unpack bins while you two catch up," she offered, not even sure if either of them remembered she was there as the woman caught him up on a few mutual acquaintances and their recent activities.

At Chrissie's words, the woman gave a horrified look. "Did I interrupt? I'm sorry. I saw Trace and had to immediately say hello and then, as always with this man, I got carried away." She winked at Chrissie as if they shared a secret. "He has that effect on women, so be careful."

Chrissie didn't need Alexis to point out the effect Trace had on women. She knew. She forced a smile, tight though it was, to her lips.

"I'll take note."

"Chrissie's immune to whatever effect I have," he told Alexis, although Chrissie had no idea why.

The woman's perfectly shaped eyebrow arched.

Chrissie frowned, but didn't respond to his comment.

Trace's gaze darted back and forth between the gorgeous brunette and Chrissie. No doubt he saw the stark contrast. It was hard to miss.

"Chrissie, this is Dr. Alexis Gianakos," Trace introduced the woman. "One of the best cardiologists I've ever had the pleasure of working with."

A doctor? Beautiful *and* smart it would seem.

"As you may have figured out from our conversation, she and I worked at the same hospital prior to when I joined DAW," Trace continued. "She's volunteering this weekend."

Will you be working closely with her, too? Chrissie

wanted to ask, but somehow managed to keep her tongue in place.

Ugh. She hated feeling jealous. Hated it.

But she was. Denial didn't make reality any less true.

"Nice to meet you," she greeted, holding out her hand and forcing the corners of her mouth upward.

The woman took her hand. Hers was smooth, strong, feminine. Well-manicured.

Chrissie couldn't help but look down at her own as she pulled away from the woman's. A bit rough, nails cropped short and unpainted, and no jewelry.

None on the horizon, either.

She'd dated, but found she quickly tired of the men who had come into her life. They either thought because she was a single mom that that meant she was easy for the taking or they didn't understand that Joss came first and always would. None had lasted beyond a couple of dates.

Her best friend, Savannah, was always pushing her to date, especially now that Savannah was so over the moon, happily married to cardiologist Dr. Charlie Keele. Just because Savannah had found the right man for her it didn't mean Chrissie had to do the same. Or that she even wanted to. She was quite happy with just her and Joss. Fabulously so.

"You're also an old friend of Trace's?" Alexis's accent came out a bit thicker than previously.

"We aren't old friends, just acquaintances who met here a few years ago."

"Ah," Alexis said as if gaining insight. This time it was her dark gaze going back and forth between Chrissie and Trace.

"If you'll excuse me, I'll get started," Chrissie said, feeling more and more awkward.

She walked away before either could say anything. She didn't want to listen to the beautiful woman chat up Trace and she sure didn't want to listen to whatever response he made to the woman's obvious interest.

Had they been an item when Trace worked with her? The woman was so beautiful that no doubt they'd made an attractive couple.

He was free to do whatever he wanted. Whomever he wanted. But she didn't want to know about it. Or see it.

What she'd really like to do was block it completely from her mind. Forever. She began organizing supplies and forcing a smile to stay on her face.

Attitude was everything and she was going to have a good attitude this weekend even if it killed her.

Chrissie was jealous.

She had no reason to be jealous, but the fact that she was made Trace happier than it should have.

Alexis was still chatting about the hospital and his former coworkers, but Trace's attention followed Chrissie to where she began opening bins with a vengeance and a smile that didn't fit. He'd already helped volunteers set up tables and chairs in their tent, so, other than however they opted to organize their supplies, there wasn't a lot more to do. Many of their items would stay boxed up until needed.

"Who is she?"

Alexis's question didn't surprise him. Right or wrong, he hadn't attempted to hide his interest in Chrissie.

"I met her here four years ago."

"You stayed in touch?"

Still watching Chrissie work, he shook his head. "I've not seen or spoken to her since until today."

Surprise registered on Alexis's face. "That must have been some meeting four years ago."

"Must have been," was all he said, then, "I'm going to help her set up. You coming?"

* * *

Chrissie was one of those people who liked event-opening ceremonies. She liked knowing the history of whatever was taking place, of who the funds were going to help, of who they had already helped. Tonight's was no exception.

Listening to Bud and Agnes talk about their daughter who'd died with cancer at such a young age, of the heart-breaking prevalence of childhood cancers, listening to how they had formed the Children's Cancer Prevention Organization and how the charity had grown, and their hope it would expand further into more cities, filled her heart with warm emotion.

She simply could not imagine something happening to Joss or how she would react if it did. Like Bud and Agnes, she'd like to think she'd deal with her grief in a way that would make the world a better place for others.

She wasn't sure she'd be able to function at all.

"What are you thinking?"

Chrissie jumped at Trace's question. "I didn't see you."

"Obviously." His gaze was on her rather than the stage where Agnes spoke. "You were lost in your thoughts."

"I was marveling at how Bud and Agnes turned something so personally tragic into something so positive."

"They are good people who live to give to others."

"Some would say a man who gave up four years of his life to help others was a good person, too."

His expression tightened. "On my best day I don't measure up to the man and woman on that stage."

"Yeah, well, I didn't say I meant you," Chrissie assured him, grateful when his serious expression lightened at her comment, as she'd intended.

There was something darker about him than she remembered. No doubt the things he'd seen over the past four years had changed him.

Was there anyone in Trace's life that made it better?

Someone who helped him deal with the no doubt tragic situations he'd encountered while working overseas?

"Is Alexis an old girlfriend?" That wasn't what she'd meant to ask when she'd opened her mouth.

"We went out a few times."

His smile was quick and too cocky for her liking. He knew she was jealous of the woman. Great.

"Which is more than you can say about me, so I guess that answers my question." Which probably only made her sound jealous and bitter and judgmental. Ugh. She should keep her mouth shut.

"What question would that be?"

"Whether or not you'd slept with her." She fought to keep the image of him with the woman from her mind. An image she'd fought for four years. She'd just never had a face to put with her thoughts of what he'd been doing while she'd been raising their son.

"I haven't."

She rolled her eyes. "Right."

"I said she and I went out a few times. I didn't say we had 'stayed in' a few times." At her continued doubt, he added, "I have no reason to lie to you."

He had a point. He owed her nothing, least of all a defense of whether or not he'd had sex with someone.

"No, I guess you don't," she admitted, trying to hide the fact that she was happy he hadn't slept with the beautiful Alexis.

"Would it matter if I had?"

Good grief. Could he see inside her head or what?

"No." But she was lying. It would have mattered. Maybe it shouldn't, but it would have. Because of Joss, she told herself. That was why she cared who he'd slept with and who he hadn't. Because she'd given birth to his child that made her more possessive, more concerned. At least, that was what she was going to keep telling herself, as she conveniently ignored the fact he'd been out of the country for four years.

Hoping he hadn't realized she'd lied and that if he had, he wouldn't call her on it, Chrissie focused on the stage.

Agnes was still speaking and Chrissie did her best to take in each word. With Trace standing so close, she couldn't focus on the woman on stage. She was surrounded by people. How was it possible to be so physically aware of one man that she could smell his spicy scent, hear the call of his body?

"I don't believe you," Trace whispered close to her ear, further sensitizing her nerve-endings.

His breath tickled her skin. She could feel his heat and would swear he'd just nuzzled her hair.

"It really doesn't matter what you believe," she said, stepping back. "I'll see you in medical."

With that she pushed through the crowd to get away from him.

But mainly to get away from her unwanted reaction to everything about him.

Later that evening in the medical tent, Trace lifted the fifty-year-old woman's foot and examined her swollen ankle.

"Yep." He glanced at her name tag on the lanyard around her neck. "Ms. Perez, you have definitely done a number on your ankle."

"I shouldn't have been quite so vigorous dancing in the bubbles, eh?"

"Apparently not." He had her turn and rest on her knees while he squeezed her calf, watching carefully as it triggered the appropriate movement in her foot. "There's no evidence that you've torn your Achilles' tendon, but you're definitely out of commission for the rest of the weekend."

The woman's face fell. "I was afraid you were going to say that. Can't you give me a quick-fix pill?"

"It's not that easy, Ms. Perez. Some things take time and rest, not a pill. I'm sorry."

She heaved her chest in frustration. "Me, too."

"Sit here with ice for about twenty minutes with your foot elevated. Later, one of the guys will drive you on a gator to your tent. Is there someone we can call for you?"

Ms. Perez shook her head. "My daughter is out of town with work and my son lives in Chicago with his wife and kids. I'm by myself."

He gestured to her leg. "You need to stay off that ankle."

"I was looking forward to volunteering in the food tent. I've not missed a year there since CCPO started these events."

"There's no way I can okay for you to serve food."

The woman perked up. "Maybe I could volunteer in a different way? One where I could still keep my foot up?"

Trace didn't want to burst the woman's bubble, but she was going to be in quite a bit of pain and wouldn't be able to put any weight on her ankle for several days. Not with the amount she'd injured the tissue.

Stepping back into the exam area, Chrissie assisted the woman in propping up her foot and then put the woman's ice pack back on her ankle. "Is there anything I can get you? We have a few magazines if you'd like, and I brought a stack of books I've finished if you want to take one."

The woman shook her head and held up her cellular phone. "I have books on this thing to keep my mind occupied for times such as these."

Patting the woman's hand, Chrissie smiled. "That's good."

The medical tent had been slow most of the evening.

Trace liked being busy, and felt restless. He was used to having more to do than time to do it.

Alexis was seeing a gentleman who had come into the tent with some indigestion. The other volunteers were not quite twiddling their thumbs but none of them were busy, either.

Trace compared it to where he'd been not so long ago, in the midst of mayhem and a war-torn country where there had been more ill and injured than hands to care for them, with problems much worse than a sprained ankle.

He closed his eyes. There were other assignments he could take with Doctors Around the World. Less dangerous places. He didn't have to go back to the places he'd gone before, but he chose to.

"You okay?"

He opened his eyes, surprised Chrissie had initiated a conversation with him that didn't have something to do with a patient or the event. For the most part she'd ignored him or given him the cold shoulder when he'd attempted conversation.

"Fine."

Appearing torn, she eyed him. "You didn't look fine. You looked like you didn't feel well."

"Had a flashback," he admitted, shocking himself that he'd said the words out loud. He hadn't talked to anyone here about the things he'd seen or done. DAW had required he go through psychological evaluation. He'd passed with flying colors, but that wasn't to say that the things he'd lived through and seen hadn't affected him. He'd never be quite the same. "No big deal."

It wasn't a big deal. Nothing he couldn't cope with.

"What kind of flashback?"

"Not one of you," he teased, unwilling to tell her the nitty-gritty details, "so it wasn't good."

She smirked. "Ha-ha. Too funny. Seriously, you turned a bit green there for a few seconds."

Maybe he'd been green at how stand-offish she was around him. He wanted to go back to the way she was four years ago.

He suddenly longed for at least a glimpse of more care-free times. Even if just a short one.

"You want to go play in the bubbles?"

Her jaw dropped at the same time her brow rose. "What?"

He gestured around the medical tent. "We're not busy and might not get another chance to catch more of the events. The bubbles are new this year. Agnes was excited about them."

The more he said, the more he wanted her to say yes. He wanted to play, to let loose and have fun. With Chrissie.

"But...we can't leave. Ms. Perez," she reminded him, looking a little panicked.

"You should go," the woman called from a few feet away, obviously listening to their conversation. "Don't mind me. I'm fine and can have one of these other folk help me out of here."

First mouthing "thank you," Trace grinned at the woman. "See, Ms. Perez wants us to go check out the bubbles. We'll share a dance in her honor."

"That would be absolutely lovely!" the woman exclaimed, clapping her hands together and obviously playing cupid. "I insist you go."

Chrissie still looked hesitant.

"Hey, Gianakos?" he called to Alexis, who had just finished with the only other patient in the tent and sent him on his way with an antacid and instructions to cut back on spicy foods. "Will you check on Ms. Perez's ankle in a few? She's got about another ten minutes of icing, then have one of the guys take her to wherever she wants to go. Chrissie and I are going to the main area for a while."

Alexis shot an envious glance toward Chrissie, then nodded. "No problem."

"Perfect. See, I'll be fine." Ms. Perez shooed them away. "You two go have a little fun."

Before she could find another excuse, Trace grabbed Chrissie's hand and led her out of Medical. "Thank you."

"For?"

"Not kicking and screaming the whole way. I needed to get out of there for a few."

She looked as if she still might kick and scream, then her expression morphed into one of confusion. "Trace, what were you thinking about back there?"

He shook his head. "Nothing important now. Let's go check out the bubbles."

Her hand was still inside his. He didn't want to let go so he held on tightly as he led them toward the bubbles. Her hand felt warm and comfortable in his.

As if it belonged there.

Without thought he lifted her hand to his lips and pressed a kiss to the top. Because that felt warm and comfortable, as if it belonged in that moment in time.

"Trace, I..." Chrissie's voice trailed off as she came to an abrupt stop and stared up at him. "You shouldn't."

She was right. He shouldn't, but he was glad he had. They stood behind the medical tent on the path leading toward the main event area. They were alone, but someone could come up the path at any time.

"Probably not." He was only home for a short while, had nothing to offer her beyond the weekend. Which was too bad, because from the time he'd seen her he'd known what he wanted, what he needed. Chrissie.

"Yes."

But her eyes said something different and that fueled him forward to say what had already been in the back of his mind, tempting his conscious thought and actions.

"We were good together. We could be good together again."

Her expression tightened.

And then he'd take off for parts unknown, for who knew

how long, before he'd be home for another few weeks' hiatus from his reality? Maybe he should let the attraction go but, for whatever reason, he pushed. Whatever it was about Chrissie seemed to be dictating his every move from the moment he'd laid eyes on her that afternoon.

"I can tell you're still attracted to me," he pointed out, as if that were breaking news.

"Doesn't matter." Her exasperation was palpable, and yet she still didn't pull her hand away from his, just kept staring at where their fingers intertwined.

"Sure, it does." To prove his point, he bent and pressed his lips to hers. Gentle, to where she could push him away with ease if she wanted to.

He hoped she didn't. Her lips were so sweet.

She didn't stop him or push him away, but he felt the struggle within her and that gave him pause.

He pulled back, stared down into her wide eyes.

Her wide, slightly dazed eyes.

Her eyes that were filled with desire so sweet it punched him in the gut.

This was why he hadn't been able to resist kissing her.

Because her kisses were addictive and powerful. He craved what being with her promised.

"You taste good, like the sweetest wine, making me want to drink until I'm intoxicated," he admitted. "Let me, Chrissie. We both know you want to."

CHAPTER FOUR

CHRISSIE STARED UP at the man who had haunted her dreams for four years. Who needed more? One kiss and she already felt drunk.

Because his kiss drugged her and made her forget reason.

She wanted to drag him back to her, to kiss him all over until they were both satiated, until the whole world subsided and it was just the two of them.

As it had felt four years ago.

"What a marvelous event," a woman's voice interrupted as she and a group of women rounded the path.

Tugging her hand free from his, Chrissie stepped back to the side of a tent.

"Absolutely. CCPO fund-raisers are always the best fun," another chimed in.

"The first day and we're already sneaking around in the shadows."

"Which should tell you something."

She sighed. "That I'm crazy?"

"That there's something between us."

More than he knew.

"That doesn't mean we should act on that something," she tried to reason, reminding herself that she had to think of Joss, not her crazy body's reaction to him.

"Should I apologize that I want you still, Chrissie? Do you want me to pretend I don't find you attractive?"

Her heartbeat thundered in her ears. "If I said yes, would you?"

He studied her a moment, then took on a slight look of remorse. "If you said yes."

Say no. Say no. Say no.

Chrissie wasn't sure where the inner voice was coming from, but the phrase beat in perfect rhythm with her racing heart.

"I know you're struggling with this, Chrissie. I see it in your eyes when you look at me. I felt it in your kiss. You wanted to let go and just feel, but wouldn't allow yourself."

He certainly had her pegged.

"My question is why?"

"Been there, done that," she reminded him.

"Was our time together so bad?"

"No, but I'd like to think I've learned a thing or two over the last four years."

"Such as?"

"Such as I shouldn't get mixed up with sexy strangers."

"I'm not a stranger."

"Sure, you are."

His brow inched upward. "You believe that?"

"Yes."

"Then we should get to know each other this weekend."

She narrowed her gaze suspiciously. "To what purpose?"

"To know each other. There doesn't have to be a purpose beyond that."

In the flickering light of the shadows, Chrissie stared at him. Get to know Trace? Why?

What about when Joss asked about his father years down the road?

Simple things like what was his favorite color and had he played sports or had any major childhood illnesses?

Shouldn't she know how to answer her son? Wouldn't it be horrible to have to say she didn't know anything beyond the fact that Trace had seemed a likable, good person, and had made her laugh and feel as if she was sexy?

He still made her feel sexy.

Every time his eyes lit on her, they shifted as if molten gold had been poured in their depths. Trace wanted her. Whatever the attraction between them was, it was powerful. The way he looked at her made her feel beautiful, desirable. It was a heady sensation.

"You're talking get to know each other as in not biblically know each other, right?" she clarified.

He chuckled. "Make no mistake, my ultimate goal is to physically 'know you' again. But for the moment, I am talking get to know each other as in not biblically."

She wanted to say yes, but knew she'd be toying with dynamite. "I'm not sure."

"It's obvious you're attracted to me," he pointed out.

"Okay, fine, you're an attractive man and I'm not blind." If not for Joss, would she even be hesitating?

"You're saying any attractive man would do?"

"That's not what I'm saying."

"Then that makes me special?"

More so than he knew.

His look of triumph made her nervous. "Are you fishing for compliments, Trace? Because, if so, you grabbed the wrong woman from the medical tent. Dr. Gianakos would be more than happy to be your fluffer."

At her comment, he grinned and shook his head. "I got the right girl and want her complimenting me. Come on, no more serious talk. Let's go have fun for a few minutes then we'll get back to work."

"Okay." This time she met his hand halfway when he reached for hers and tried not to overanalyze how amazing it felt to simply hold his hand.

* * *

Chrissie had never seen such a huge area of bubbles before.

Agnes had set up a special non-slip floor and then had machines create mountains of bubbles. Currently, hundreds, maybe thousands, of children and adults alike danced and played in the bubbles to the directions of the emcee in a bubble-a-thon fund-raiser.

"Put your right hand in. Put your right hand out," he instructed.

"You have extra clothes?"

Her head jerked toward Trace. "What?"

"Did you bring extra clothes?" he repeated, taking off his tennis shoes and raising her feet one at a time to do the same to hers.

"I'm a prepared kind of girl, but stop that," she demanded, attempting to pull her foot free and instead just helping him accomplish his goal. "I'm not going into—"

But he wasn't listening. He'd tugged her to the outskirts of the bubble floor and she was mid-chest-high in bubbles.

"Oh, my," she exclaimed, unable to resist lifting a handful of the foamy white stuff to her mouth and blowing it.

Joss would love this, she couldn't help but think.

"Put your left hand in. Put your left hand out," the emcee continued.

She wiggled her toes, letting the bubbles tickle her feet and bare legs beneath her shorts. A giggle escaped. A happy giggle. Oh, my. She didn't want to feel happy.

Chrissie frowned. What was she thinking? Of course, she wanted to feel happy. Besides, when was she going to have the opportunity to play in bubbles with hundreds of other people ever again?

Probably never.

This was fun. She was allowed to have fun.

"If we're going to do this, we're going to do it right," she informed Trace, holding her left hand out and shaking it.

"That was the plan." His grin was lethal and gave her more giddiness than the bubbles.

"I know what your plan is," she accused, trying to "splash" him, but the bubbles didn't cooperate, sticking to her hand instead and plopping back onto the sea surrounding them.

He laughed. With a wicked gleam in his eyes, he scooped up an armful of bubbles. "I'm not denying it."

"Which doesn't make it any better." Instinctively knowing what he was about to do, she took a few steps back, but only managed to plop down in the midst of the bubbles.

Laughing, he held out a hand and pulled her to her feet. She sputtered, clearing the bubbles from her face.

"You look good covered in bubbles." His eyes glittered with all sorts of mischief.

"Trace."

"What?" He gave her an innocent look. "You do. I like it."

Truthfully, she liked how he looked waist deep in bubbles, too. There were too many people around for her mind to go to romantic bubble baths, but seeing Trace laughing out loud had cracked something inside her.

Something that had been vital in protecting her from how she felt about him. How dared he break down her defenses with bubbles and laughter and talk of getting to know each other? Who did that?

Then again, nothing about Trace had ever been typical, so of course he'd use bubbles to knock down the barriers she'd erected between them. Bubbles.

No one could be standoffish when surrounded by bubbles.

"Shake your leg and be quiet," she ordered, but was unable to keep the smile from her face.

Maybe it was her inner child coming out. Maybe it was all the happy laughter around her. Maybe it was the happy gleam in Trace's eyes as he stood in bubbles. Maybe it was feeling alive and desirable and amazing because she was his focus. Maybe it was all of the above.

Regardless, she laughed and played along with whatever the emcee had going. They hokey-pokeyed through the rest of the song, then participated in a couple of the other bubble games.

When the emcee announced a bubble-snowman-building contest for kids ten and under, they made their way out.

"Admit it, you had fun."

"I had fun." No point in denying it. She was still smiling.

A teenaged boy came up and handed Trace two towels. Chrissie glanced around, amazed by the boy's appearance since towels weren't provided and they should have brought their own.

"Why did he bring us these?"

He waggled his brows. "I'm a resourceful man."

"Apparently," she agreed, taking the towel from him, and wiping off the bubbles clinging to her skin and clothes. "We weren't dressed for this."

"We were fine," he countered. "Most everyone is wearing T-shirts and shorts, except for the kids."

"Thank you."

His smile was amazing. Brilliant. Beautiful.

"You're welcome, Chrissie. Making you smile is my pleasure."

There were a dozen or so people on the medical crew. More than they'd needed tonight, but that would change with sun-up.

There were a few two-man tents at the back of the medical area so there would be medical staff close in case middle-of-the-night care was needed. Chrissie was rooming with one of the nurse-practitioner volunteers, a pretty woman in her late forties who worked with a local children's hospital and said she'd been volunteering with CCPO for the past couple of years, after one of her patients' family had mentioned how the organization had helped with expenses.

Chrissie liked hearing how the organization was making a difference out in the real world, rather than just through the testimonies given on stage at the event. Somehow, hearing Bernadette say CCPO had helped one of her patients made it all so much more real.

She and Trace had checked to make sure the medical area was still slow, then she'd slipped off to her tent to grab her toiletries where she bumped into her roommate.

"I'm headed to the shower truck to wash the bubbles off myself," she told the smiling woman.

"I'll be heading that way before the rush, too," Bernadette said, from where she sat on her sleeping bag, holding her phone. "I'm going to call home and check on my husband and kids since there's not a need in the medical tent right now."

Chrissie nodded, then left their tent to give the woman a semblance of privacy. In reality, there was very little. Yet, four years ago, she and Trace had found ways to be alone, especially at night when they'd been the two manning the slow, midnight hours.

Trace.

She'd essentially agreed to get to know him.

Ha. What did that even mean? She wasn't sure.

At least he'd been upfront that his main goal was to sleep with her again.

What a goal.

What a man.

She hung her head and took a deep breath. Why was she even fighting him?

He was right. She wanted him as much as he wanted her.

Probably more.

But she was four years older, four years wiser, four years more mature. She didn't have wild sexual flings.

Especially premeditated ones.

Then again, trying to convince herself of greater maturity right after playing in a sea of bubbles probably wasn't the most effective argument she'd ever waged.

But, oh, how she'd had fun playing with Trace.

Who'd have ever thought she'd be surrounded by bubbles, dancing and acting goofy with Trace Stevens?

She'd have bet against those odds every time.

But she didn't regret it. How could she when she'd laughed more than she recalled laughing in months? Years?

No, that wasn't true. She laughed with Joss. Lots and lots. Goodness, but that kid made her happy.

And Savannah. Spending time with her best friend and her baby daughter made Chrissie happy, too. Prior to Savannah's wedding, her friend had stayed the night and they'd giggled the night away while Joss slept.

But it was a different kind of laughter, a different kind of happy, than she felt at the moment. She couldn't explain the difference, just recognized that there was one.

Maybe it had to do with how Trace had laughed along with her, that they'd shared some magical, fun moment.

Maybe, she tried to convince herself as she made it to the bath area.

Most of the CCPO participants were still at the bubble-a-thon. There wasn't a line at the shower trucks.

Chrissie quickly squeezed into one of the tiny stalls inside the eighteen-wheeler shower trailer, rented for the event, and stripped off her sticky clothes. She let the warm water sluice over her body, then shampooed her hair, suds trickling down her nakedness.

Her mind couldn't help where it went.

Not after seeing Trace again. Not after their bizarre conversation. Not after his telling her she looked good covered in bubbles.

He'd kissed her.

She'd let him.

Craziness.

How could she have pushed him away when for the first time in four years she'd felt physical excitement? When for the first time in four years her heart had sped up at a man's touch? When her whole body had zinged with awareness? When her thighs had squeezed with excitement?

She'd wanted to kiss him back. To really kiss him back. To drag him somewhere where they were less likely to get interrupted and kiss him until they'd both been breathless.

She wanted him now, in this tiny shower stall with her, and for the bubbles and warm water to be their only covering.

She leaned her head against the wall, letting the water rinse the suds from her hair and body.

Just remembering his kiss, letting her mind go beyond that kiss to previous kisses from four years ago, had her ribcage contracting around her lungs, making her breathing labored.

She finished showering, dried off the best she could in the tiny space, slipped on fresh clothes, then headed out of the truck and over to the sink area.

She got her teeth brushed, then headed back toward the path that would take her to Medical.

"Am I seriously lucky enough to bump into you here?"

She turned slowly, her gaze colliding with Trace's. "Guess that depends on what you call lucky."

"Any time I have the privilege of setting eyes on you."

Feeling vulnerable to the emotions fizzing through her, she frowned at him in hopes of at least having a moment to catch her breath. She'd thought she'd have longer before facing him again. "I don't recall you using cheesy lines four years ago."

Her frown didn't deter him in the slightest and his grin was potent.

"Telling the truth is not a cheesy line."

"Still, I don't recall you saying such things."

That seemed to break through whatever was making him smile so intently. "If I failed to tell you how lucky I felt four years ago then I did you a grave injustice. I felt very privileged that you noticed me."

"You were hard not to notice," she admitted.

"Because I kept finding reasons to bump into you? To ask you a question? To hand you something so I could touch you? I couldn't believe my luck in meeting you that weekend."

"I wasn't complaining." She hadn't. She'd been just as attracted to him and she hadn't tried to hide it. Not then. She might as well not bother now because she was failing miserably. The hot look in his eyes warned of that.

"Do you remember that first kiss, Chrissie?" His voice had lowered even though there was no one else on the path.

"Remind me," she said to be contrary, because she knew every ounce of attraction she felt for this man was shining from her eyes like a homing beacon.

"Everyone had gone to dinner. It was just you and me in the medical tent."

"We'd stayed to clean up from a suture one of the docs had done on a woman who had sliced her arm while opening a can in the kitchen," she added.

"But the moment we were truly alone for the first time, we came together like two magnets."

"We kissed," she corrected. They hadn't "come together like magnets" until much later that night. Which had quite blown her away. She'd never done anything like that before. Never.

"We're alone right now," he pointed out. "I could remind you with more than words."

"Someone could come along."

"I'm not sure I like this older, more practical version of you," he teased.

She was older, more practical. She had to be. Did that make her boring? She bit the inside of her lip. "I'm not the same woman I was four years ago."

"Neither of us are the same as we were four years ago."

Something in his voice said life had thrown a lot of things at him during that time.

"But I am attracted to you," she heard herself say.

His smile returned. "And?"

"Apparently, we share very potent sexual chemistry."

"Is that something you encounter often?"

She almost said, *Only with you*, but caught herself just in time. She was already vulnerable enough.

"Not that often," she improvised. "What about you?"

"Not since you."

Three little words that made her heart sing. Okay, so he wasn't saying he hadn't ever experienced such a strong attraction, but that no one since her had made him feel that way. A minor, silly, little thing, but his admission made her happy.

Funny, because not for a second did she doubt the truthfulness of his words. She never had. There was something about him that she instinctively trusted, rightly or wrongly.

"You got quiet," he accused softly.

She nodded. "We're standing in the middle of a path between the bath area and the medical area. Maybe we should head back."

He nodded and stayed in step beside her. "Agnes said

this is the first year you've been back to volunteer since we met. What kept you away?"

"It wasn't fear of running into you, if that's what you're thinking."

"Don't jump to conclusions, Chrissie."

"You're right. I just didn't want you to make assumptions that…"

"Where you are concerned, I'm doing my best not to make any assumptions. Not even the ones I want to make. So, what kept you away? Family? Work?"

"Family."

"Tell me about your family."

Not likely, but she smiled and suggested, "Then you'll tell me about yours because that's all part of us getting to know each other?"

His nose wrinkled. "Okay, so you have a point. Let's talk about something besides family. Do you still live and work in Chattanooga?"

"Yes, I love my job at the hospital."

"You're a CVICU nurse, right?"

Pleased that he remembered, she answered, "Yes, I work in the cardiovascular intensive care unit." She straightened her shoulders proudly. "I was promoted to nurse supervisor a few years ago."

"That's great." He smiled. "I'd say your family must be proud, but that would take us full circle. So, I'm going to say how proud you must be of that accomplishment."

"I love taking care of patients and I always try to do my best. This time, hard work paid off."

"Have there been times in the past where it hasn't?"

She shook her head. "I didn't mean my comment that way. What about you? Tell me about working for DAW."

The medical tent was within sight and their steps had slowed.

"What do you want to know?"

"What made you decide you wanted to do that?"

"Probably Agnes and Bud's influence over the years. I wanted to make a difference. A buddy of mine had joined and convinced me that doing the same would give me a sense of accomplishment that I wasn't finding in Atlanta."

"Was he right?"

CHAPTER FIVE

GOOD QUESTION. BUT not one Trace could easily answer.

In some ways, joining had filled a need within him that had been gaping since Kerry died. In others, he now had holes where they hadn't previously existed.

Maybe life was one big trade-off after another.

"I'd do it again, so I guess that's a yes," he finally said, realizing they'd completely stopped moving. "I thought of you."

Surprise lightened the green of her eyes. "What did you think about me?"

"You know what I thought."

Her eyes rolled a little. "That we share a strong sexual chemistry?"

"Among other things."

Why he was telling her so much, he wasn't sure; it was just that he felt it imperative to be upfront with her, that anything else seemed inadequate.

"I'd never met anyone like you, Chrissie."

Her chest lifted a little, as if his admission had caused her to have to take a deep breath. "And now?"

Her question caught him off guard.

"What about now?"

She looked up at him with a fierceness that defied her petite size. "I'm trying to figure out exactly what you're doing, Trace. You've admitted your goal is to sleep with me again. Is that the ultimate goal or do you want more from me than this weekend?"

More questions that made him uncomfortable, but at least he had answers for these. Not answers written in stone, but answers nonetheless.

"I'll be back overseas soon, Chrissie. To pretend otherwise would be wrong. Anything between us would only be for the weekend."

Taking a deep breath, she nodded, as if she'd been expecting that to be his answer.

"Is that nod an agreement?"

"No, Trace, I'm not agreeing to those terms. I didn't come here looking for you, or for an affair, or for anything other than to volunteer. Despite what four years ago might have led you to believe, I don't have affairs just because one is on offer and would feel good."

"Maybe you should."

Trace's words haunted Chrissie as she tossed back and forth in her sleeping bag. She'd not gone to her tent until almost midnight, but that hour had struck long ago and her mind still raced too much for sleep to take hold.

This was ridiculous.

She needed sleep. Needed to get rest before tomorrow when they'd likely be busy all day with dehydration, heatstroke and minor injuries.

But no matter how long she lay there, sleep just wasn't going to happen. She should see if whoever was working the medical tent needed help, or maybe a few hours of shuteye while she sat up.

Taking care not to disturb Bernadette, she climbed out of her sleeping bag and slipped from the tent. There was a three-quarter moon that lit the night sky so she could easily make her way through the few small tents that were close to the medical tent.

Quietly, she entered Medical and wasn't surprised by who she saw sitting at a table, reading one of the medical thrillers she'd donated.

"Chrissie?" He stood, stretched his lean body.

"It's not what you think," she began, but maybe it was, because she'd known he'd be in the tent. Hadn't she been drawn there like a moth to a flame because of that knowledge?

"What am I thinking?" His words were soft, slow, but his eyes danced with mischief.

"I couldn't sleep and thought I'd see if whoever was working needed help." Right. She doubted she was convincing him any more than she was convincing herself. She'd come to find him.

"It's been slow. Not a single person seeking care since before you left."

She nodded, took a deep breath, and glanced around the empty tent. "I'm wide awake. You want to grab a nap? I can wake you if someone comes in."

He shook his head. "I'm good." He studied her. "Why couldn't you sleep?"

Worried he could see right through her, she shrugged and sank into the chair across from where he'd been sitting.

"Me?" he guessed.

"Probably."

"I'm sorry if I'm causing you stress."

He didn't sound sorry. He sounded pleased at her admission. Then again, he hadn't made any pretenses about his interest. Quite the opposite.

"Is there something I can do to help?" he offered, causing her to look up and meet his gaze. He lowered into the chair across from hers.

"Are you promising you'd do it?" she countered, wondering how it was possible for him to be so attractive when she knew better. She did know better. But she was there all the same.

This time he was the one who shrugged. "Depends on what you say."

Okay, so the reality was that she knew it had been him in the medical tent and that he was most likely alone. Had that been the real reason she hadn't been able to sleep?

No, the real reason she couldn't sleep was that she'd been sexually frustrated for four years.

Four years.

The cure was right in front of her. Willing and eager.

She was an idiot for coming there.

She'd have been a bigger fool if she hadn't.

"I want you, Trace."

The amusement in his eyes darkened to desire. He swallowed, slowly, and with exaggerated motion in his throat.

"Chrissie." Her name came out a bit strained.

"You don't have to say anything or do anything, but I needed to say that. I needed to tell you, because no matter how much I may think I am strong enough to fight the attraction between us, I'm not."

He leaned forward, his gaze not wavering from hers. "You're okay with us being together this weekend?"

Okay with it? Ha. No, her brain wasn't. Not really. But her body, yeah, her body would never let her live it down if she ignored what a weekend with Trace offered. But this time, they'd have to be more careful. Not that they weren't last time, but Joss had arrived nine months later all the same.

Joss.

For a moment, she considered fleeing the tent, then realized how ridiculous she was being. She was a grown woman. A grown independent woman. If she wanted to have sex with a gorgeous man who had a history of mak-

ing her feel amazing, then why wouldn't she embrace
the opportunity?

"Yes." A huge weight lifted off her shoulder at the admission. "I'm sorry I protested so much. Seeing you again
and feeling attracted to you caught me off guard."

Rather than looking triumphant, his expression was
thoughtful.

"You're sure about this, Chrissie? You understand I'm
not offering anything more than this weekend?"

She nodded. She understood quite well.

"I don't want anything more than this weekend." For the
second time in her life, she was going to let go and experience a no-strings weekend with Trace.

"Chrissie." His hands flat against the table, he leaned
forward. "You make me want to forget this whole event
and sweep you to a hotel where I can have you to myself
all weekend."

"We can't leave. Agnes and Bud need us." Not that his
words didn't tempt. They did. But she wouldn't walk away
from pulling the load she'd committed to.

"I know we can't," he agreed. "And I wouldn't leave,
but you make me wish we could be alone in a comfortable
bed in a comfortable room, with room service available
twenty-four-seven so we could take advantage of every
single moment."

She closed her eyes and imagined being locked away for
a weekend with Trace, a weekend where they had nothing
more to do than to pleasure each other. A weekend that
didn't require more than throwing on a bathrobe to let room
service in to deliver sustenance to keep up their energy. A
weekend where she had Trace to herself and the rest of the
world didn't exist.

Oh, my.

"So, now what?" she asked, knowing she had to get
her imagination under control or she'd be jerking him

across the table and demanding some of that attention right this moment.

He laughed. "I take you behind that barely private partition to my semi-comfortable cot and hopefully have my wicked way with you."

Chrissie swallowed. "Okay."

Okay. She couldn't believe she was saying okay. That she was agreeing to going behind a partition with Trace so they could get naked. No, they wouldn't get naked. They'd satisfy their needs as quietly and stealthily as possible.

That hotel room sounded more and more tempting.

"I know." He didn't clarify what he meant. He didn't have to. He was thinking the same thing she was.

Trace pushed away from the table, stood, and made his way to where she sat. He reached for her hand.

Just as she slid her hand into his, felt the tingles of awareness only he seemed capable of eliciting from her nerve endings, a noise at the entrance of the tent as someone pushed the flap open had them both looking that way.

"Hello?" a female voice called by way of greeting.

"Hi," Chrissie greeted the woman and little girl coming into the tent as she stood. Disappointment filled her that she and Trace had lost their privacy, but as she looked at the little girl her disappointment quickly turned into concern.

Trace moved forward and stooped to the little girl's level. "I'd ask what was going on, but I can tell. Does that rash itch as much as it looks like it does?"

The child nodded and scratched at her neck to prove her point.

"Sorry," the girl's mother said. "I know it's late." She gave her daughter a worried glance. "She didn't break out until we lay down. I feel guilty for bothering you so late, but she keeps getting worse and I was afraid to wait until morning."

"It's okay. That's what we're here for," Trace assured. "Come to the exam area where I can get a better look."

He flipped a switch on a propane-gas-powered light, causing that area of the tent to brighten significantly so he would be able to examine his patient more efficiently.

"It's driving me crazy," the little girl said, scratching her arms. "I itch and itch and itch."

"Don't scratch," her mother reminded her.

"But it itches," the girl said matter-of-factly.

"It will only itch worse if you keep scratching it," the mother told her as she lifted the child onto the table. "Let's let the doctor take a look so he can make you feel better."

"Hi, I'm Chrissie," she introduced herself. "I need you to fill out a couple of forms while Dr. Stevens checks your daughter and figures out what we need to do about this rash."

The woman nodded and took the clipboard Chrissie offered. After glancing over the papers, she began writing her responses to the standard questions.

"What's your name?" Trace asked the little girl, who was rubbing her arms up and down in an attempt not to scratch.

"Chloe."

"That's a pretty name. My cousin just had a little girl and she named her Chloe Jane."

"I'm Chloe Darlington." The girl rubbed more briskly.

"How old are you, Chloe?"

"Four."

Trace did a quick ENT examination, glad to see all normal findings rather than swollen tissue that might block an airway. Then he checked the little girl's rash more closely. Large, raised pruritic wheals with a pattern that only appeared on areas not covered by her clothing.

"Chloe, have you ever had a rash like this before?"

The little girl shook her head.

"She hasn't," her mother confirmed, glancing up from the form.

"Hmm. This is an allergic rash, something we call a contact dermatitis, meaning that Chloe is allergic to something that she's come into contact with today."

"She didn't start breaking out until we got to our tent tonight. She was fine until then."

"Have you used any new products today?"

"Not that we know of." The woman thought a moment. "Well, other than her sleeping bag. That's new to her as she's never camped before, but I've used it a few times in the past so it wasn't brand-new."

Trace looked at the pattern of the rash again. "What was she wearing in the sleeping bag?"

"She was in her T-shirt and panties."

Which matched the rash being on her legs, forearms, and not on her trunk.

"She's allergic to something in your sleeping bag."

"It's just a thin sleeping bag, not a down-lined one or anything. I have one of those, but was afraid she'd burn up in this heat," the woman rambled, thought a moment, and then got an *aha!* look on her face. "I treated all our bags with bug spray to repel mosquitoes and such. You hear about all these diseases and viruses and I wanted to try to prevent everything I could." She winced. "I sprayed it heavy."

Trace nodded. "I'm going to give her some liquid diphenhydramine. I think that will help. If we don't see any improvement fairly quickly, then I can administer some steroids intramuscularly, but I'd rather not do that if possible."

"So, we'll need to stay here for a while?" the little girl asked. "'Cause I'm tired." She yawned to emphasize her point.

Trace laughed. "Tell you what, once your rash calms down a little, which I believe it will with the medication,

I'll let you and your mom take my cot because we can't put you back in your tent, and I'm going to want to be close in case you have further problems."

"You don't have to do that," the girl's mother assured him, looking embarrassed. "We don't want to be a bother."

"It's not a bother. I wasn't planning to sleep other than catnaps, anyway."

While overseas, in war-torn countries, there had been way too many nights he'd not slept more than in short snatches, while keeping on alert for danger to him and his patients.

Besides, he and Chrissie hadn't been planning to sleep. Far, far from it.

CHAPTER SIX

"I'M GLAD SHE's feeling better this morning," Trace told Linda Darlington as Chloe ran around the medical tent meowing happily as she pretended to be a cat.

"Me, too," the woman agreed, laughing softly as she watched her daughter. "Too bad I don't have her energy or resilience, because I sure didn't sleep enough last night to prepare me for today's activities."

The woman hadn't slept more than a few hours at most. Probably about the same as Trace. Because he'd given them his cot, he'd stretched out in a chair and caught a few hours of zees during the early morning hours. But, unlike the tired mother, he felt refreshed, excited to face the day.

Hopefully, Chrissie was the same. He'd insisted she return to her tent and rest. She was going to need it.

He had plans for her.

Plans he'd dreamed about during the short bit of shut-eye he'd gotten. Dreams in which it hadn't mattered where they were. He'd ravished Chrissie.

The way he'd wanted to ravish her last night.

The way he would have ravished her had they not been interrupted.

Would she feel the same about him, about them, this morning? Or would she have second thoughts in the light of day?

"Youth is wasted on the young," the mother continued,

interrupting his meanderings. "What about you? Do you have children?"

Trace shook his head. His life wasn't conducive to having children. It never would be. "Kids aren't my thing."

"Too bad. You're really good with Chloe. She told me this morning that you were her new boyfriend."

Trace laughed. "She only likes me because I made the itching stop."

"Perhaps," the woman said, smiling. "But I think it was more than that. You're all she's talked about since she woke up. That, and how she misses Freckles, her cat."

"Yeah, well, I'd see to it that she spends the night with Freckles and not in your tent tonight," Trace offered, glancing up to see Chrissie enter the tent, two plastic cups of steaming coffee in her hands.

"How's Chloe this morning?" she asked Linda at the same time as she handed one of the cups to Trace.

"All better." The woman beamed. "I was just telling Dr. Stevens how much we appreciate him. You, too. Y'all were great with Chloe last night. Thank you."

"No problem. Dr. Stevens here did all the work."

"What work? The wash-down and diphenhydramine you gave her did the trick." Trace glanced down at the coffee and noticed it was exactly the right color. Strong and black. Just the way he liked it. Did she recall that from before? "Thanks for this."

"You're welcome. You should probably go to the food tent before it gets busy. Ms. Perez is there, foot propped up, and is handing out napkins to people as they trickle their way through line. She's all smiles, despite the fact her ankle looks as if it was mauled."

He grinned. "I didn't think she'd leave."

"I'm glad she didn't. She was absolutely glowing as she greeted folks. She's a burst of sunshine first thing this morning."

"A morning person, like my Chloe, eh?" Linda said, motioning for the little girl to join them. "Speaking of breakfast, I'm going to take this one and head that way, too. Her dad and sister are headed that way. Thank you both, again."

"You're welcome. I'm glad to see she's back to normal."

The little girl meowed, then smiled.

Trace scratched his head. "Almost normal—I think her medicine transformed her into a cat."

Loving his comment, the little girl meowed a bunch more, making them all laugh.

"Come on, kitty. Let's go find you something to eat," her mother said, taking her hand. "Thanks, again."

"Cute kid. Makes me think of…" Chrissie's voice trailed off and rather than finish she took another sip of her coffee.

"Of?" he prompted, curious about her family. Did she have nieces and nephews? Cousins? He really knew nothing about her other than that she was a CVICU nurse who worked in Chattanooga. Did she come from a big family? A little family?

But rather than elaborate, she smiled and asked, "Were you able to get any sleep?"

"Some."

"But not much?"

"More than enough. Do I look that bad this morning?"

She ran her gaze over him and Trace fought the urge to straighten his shoulders and suck in his non-existent gut.

He was wearing what he'd put on after his shower the night before: a clean CCPO T-shirt and a pair of khaki cargo shorts. Although he'd shaved the previous night, he didn't need to run his hand over his jaw to know he'd find a light growth of stubble there.

"Not that bad," she finally said, lifting her gaze to his, mischief dancing in the green depths. "But I've seen you better."

The corners of his mouth tugged upward. If she had

regrets about what she'd said the night before, she wasn't showing them. Instead, she was outright flirting with him and he wanted to puff out his chest like a prized rooster.

"Maybe later we can talk about you seeing me better again."

She smiled a little smile that spoke volumes. "Who needs to talk?"

Oh, Chrissie, he thought as his body responded to her flirty grin and comment.

"Who indeed?"

Talking certainly wasn't what was on his mind while he took in the petite blonde woman in her mid-thigh-length shorts and CCPO medical staff T-shirt that fit her curves just right.

The rest of the medical crew had joined them in the tent and two of the members were rolling up the sides to the tent so they could see out, while another had flipped on a large commercial-grade fan to circulate air through the tent.

Outside, the event campgrounds were coming to life as volunteers and participants made their way toward the main tents. Everything would officially kick off for the day at seven. Once things got rolling, so would minor injuries.

"Do you want to come with me to grab a bite?" he asked, despite the fact that she'd already been to the food tent.

She shook her head and held out her coffee cup. "I've eaten and this will hold me over until later. I'm going to go man my triage station. I'll see you when you get back."

"Definitely," he promised. She'd be seeing him as much as he could arrange this weekend.

Beyond that, who knew? Maybe he'd suggest spending as much time together as possible before he headed back overseas.

Flirting with Trace was fun. And easier than it should be, Chrissie thought later that afternoon.

Had someone told her just twenty-four hours ago that she'd be catching Trace's eye and winking at him, she'd have told them they were certifiable. But she and Trace had some serious sparks flying back and forth between them.

Sparks that were bubbly and exciting and made her feel gloriously feminine.

Not just feminine…sexy.

Sexy.

Something she'd not felt in far too long.

Her days and nights were filled with being a good nurse and a great mother. She was content with her life. Better than content. She was happy and felt blessed.

But Savannah was right. There had been something missing. That feeling one got when an attractive man looked at you and his want was so palpable that desire itself caressed you.

That feeling one got when in the new bud of a relationship, when everything was exciting and new.

Only none of this was new. She wasn't in the bud of a relationship with Trace. Whatever happened this weekend was it. They both knew that.

So, why did she still feel so giddy?

She wasn't the kind of woman to have random affairs. Or to have affairs, period.

She was giddy. Giggly giddy, even.

And not just because Trace couldn't seem to go more than a few minutes without stealing a glance her way or finding some reason to come talk to her in between the fairly steady stream of patients who came to the tent.

"He's a good man."

Chrissie blinked up at Alexis. Somehow the doctor still managed to look exotically glamorous in her dark shorts and CCPO medical staff T-shirt. How was that even possible? "Pardon?"

"Trace. He's a good man."

"You know him well?" she couldn't keep from asking despite the fact Trace had already said he hadn't slept with the woman. Was she seeking confirmation of what he'd told her?

No, she believed him. As he'd said, he had no reason to lie to her and he hadn't made any false promises.

"Not as well as I'd have once liked, as I suspect you know."

Chrissie couldn't prevent her blush.

"I'll admit that when I heard he was going to be here, I'd hoped to kindle a spark. The moment I saw the way he looked at you I knew that wasn't going to happen." She didn't bother to hide her disappointment. "So, despite a momentary surge of jealousy, I find myself happy for him, because he really is a good guy."

With the woman's blunt honesty, it was difficult not to like her.

"How does he look at me?"

Sliding into the chair across from the triage table, Alexis laughed.

"Like he wants to gobble you up and lick the crumbs from his fingers." She air-kissed her fingertips with great show. "The way I wished he looked at me."

There went the heat in Chrissie's cheeks again.

"So, are you going to tell me about you two?"

More heated cheeks.

"I like him, if that's what you mean."

Alexis rolled her dark, heavily fringed eyes. "Tell me something I don't know."

Although she owed Alexis no explanation, she found herself wanting to talk to the woman. Probably because Alexis had worked with Trace outside this sheltered tented event world and knew a side of him that Chrissie had never seen.

"We met four years ago at this event," she said. "I haven't

seen or heard from him since. If anything, he's only gotten sexier with age, and I'm not blind."

"Neither is he. I've never known him to be so taken with someone."

"He didn't date when y'all worked together?"

"Oh, he dated, but I never saw him look at any of them, or me, the way he looks at you."

"That's…" she searched for the right word "…nice."

Alexis laughed again. "Nice? Honey, nice has nothing to do with it. Hot. Now, there's a better description. You're a lucky girl."

"You've no idea," she said, thinking of Joss. Which gave her a huge twinge of guilt. Alexis was telling her what a great man Joss's father was. How could she justify not telling him about their son?

Because memories of her own father snatching her away from her mother caused her insides to clam up with fear?

Trace wasn't her father. She knew that. But…

"You're right," the woman admitted. "I don't have any idea. Trace and I went out a few times, but I was more interested than he was. Like I said, you're a lucky girl."

Alexis confirmed what Trace had said. He hadn't slept with the beauty-queen doctor. She hadn't doubted him, but hearing the confirmation made her like Alexis all the more. Made her that much more giddy about Trace's interest.

"So tell me about you until the next patient comes in for me to see. Or we can send them Trace's way and continue with our girl talk," Alexis suggested with a wide smile that flashed her toothpaste-ad teeth again.

Pushing aside the nagging guilt her heart felt over not telling Trace about Joss, and giving in to her brain's reminder that just that morning she'd heard him say he didn't want children, Chrissie smiled and began telling Alexis about Chattanooga, her much-loved job at the hospital, her mother, and her friend Savannah.

She was surprised by how much she liked Alexis and that she could easily see herself becoming good friends with the forthright woman had they lived closer.

What in the world were Chrissie and Alexis laughing so hard at? Trace wondered as he made a quick note on the patient he'd just finished examining. The event wasn't keeping extensive medical records, but they were documenting each encounter and what was done.

Actually, to see the two women having a friendly conversation at all surprised Trace. So much for Chrissie's jealousy from yesterday.

Not that she'd had any reason to be jealous. He liked Alexis well enough. She was an intelligent, beautiful woman, but there just hadn't been any chemistry.

Chemistry wasn't a problem with Chrissie.

They had so much chemistry they could add new elements to the periodic table.

Another outburst of laughter had him sliding the paper he'd scribbled a few notes on into a manila file that would later be scanned into and stored on a computer.

Leaving his work area, he headed over to Triage. "You two are having way too much fun."

"Jealous?" Alexis asked, but not in a way he took as flirtatious, more as if she was teasing him because she'd figured out Chrissie majorly got to him.

"Absolutely. What does a man have to do to join in?"

"Just pull up a chair," Chrissie assured him, gesturing to an empty chair at a nearby table.

Trace didn't hesitate. He grabbed the chair and moved it to where the two women sat. "Now, tell me what's so funny, because I need something to make me laugh after that last blistered foot I treated."

Chrissie grimaced. "She looked like she was miserable when she hobbled in here. Is she going to be all right?"

"Yeah, but she's not going to be on her feet much for a few days. She's going to hang out on the sidelines in a chair and encourage the other participants."

"That's good," Chrissie said, her gaze locked with his and dancing with delight.

He smiled. He couldn't not smile. Which felt so damned good. Not so long ago he couldn't have brought a smile to his face had someone offered him the world.

Not since the hospital explosion in Yemen when friends had died because he'd not been able to save them.

Not since holding children ravished with starvation and disease while they died and promising himself he'd do all he could to save the next child, to bring medical care, food, supplies, into places where no sane person would venture.

Had he really deep down laughed since Kerry died?

Maybe he'd forgotten how to laugh.

Odd that a look from Chrissie could achieve that, could reach deep inside and bring forth a balm of peace and happiness.

"Well, as much as I enjoy watching the show, I'm going to leave you two alone for a bit and go grab a bottled water while we're in a lull. You want anything?" Alexis asked, cutting into his thoughts as she stood.

His gaze shifted. "I'm good. I've still got half a bottle from the last time one of the volunteers came by with drinks."

"Tsk. Tsk," Alexis scolded. "Make sure you hydrate well. Can't have you getting heatstroke on us." She turned her attention to Chrissie. "Lovely talking with you. Have fun and we'll catch up later."

"Thanks. I will." Chrissie smiled at the retreating woman. "I like her."

"I noticed. What did she mean by have fun?"

Chrissie shrugged. "You'd have to ask her."

"Despite the fact I'm convinced you know exactly what she meant?"

"Well, not exactly."

"But close?"

"Possibly."

Trace laughed. "Well, whatever she meant, I appreciate her giving us privacy. How's your day so far?"

"Not as busy as I recall us being four years ago," she admitted. "But steady for the most part."

"Not being as busy is a good thing. Hopefully it means people are taking precautions to prevent heat issues and injuries."

"I'm not complaining that we're not swamped," Chrissie assured him. "I want things to go well for the participants and volunteers. But I'm used to being busy. The gaps between patients can get tedious."

"Bite your tongue before you jinx us," he scolded.

"What? Afraid we'll have more late-night interruptions?"

"Alexis is 'manning the tent tonight,'" he reminded her. "George, one of the paramedics, volunteered to stay with her."

"I bet he did. She's a beautiful woman."

"So are you."

Her lashes lowered. "I wasn't fishing for a compliment."

"I didn't think you were, but you are a beautiful woman."

"Beauty is in the eye of the beholder."

"My eyes behold your beauty quite proficiently. As a matter of fact, I'd say they were experts at beholding your beauty."

She snorted. "I'd rather be appreciated for my brains."

"Seriously?"

She nodded.

"What is it about your brain you would like me to appreciate most? Your medulla oblongata? Your cerebellum?

Your sulcus? A little gray matter, maybe?" he teased, loving the light shining over the darkness that seemed perpetually to permeate his inner being.

She wrinkled her nose at him. "I was thinking more along the lines of my brilliant conversation skills, my amazingly humorous wit, my—"

"Propensity for the truth?"

She laughed. "Exactly."

"You have all that and more. Brains and beauty."

"And you, Dr. Stevens, have the gift of the gab."

"Not really."

"No?" She arched a brow at him. "Because so far you've done a good job of talking me up."

"Is that what I'm doing?"

"Aren't you?"

He grinned. "I'm glad you changed your mind, Chrissie."

Red stained her cheeks and she glanced around the tent to make sure no one else could hear.

"Shh, I'd rather not advertise."

"No one knows what we're talking about, and if they did, so what? We're two consenting adults."

"True, but I'd just as soon not broadcast our personal business to the entire medical crew."

"I'll forewarn you that Bud and Agnes will take one look at us and know."

"You think?"

He nodded. "They knew we were involved four years ago. It won't be difficult to figure out that we've rekindled the fire."

She studied him. "Does that bother you?"

"I wasn't the one worried about someone overhearing our conversation," he reminded her, reaching out to brush his finger across her cheek as if he were wiping away a speck. He hadn't been. He'd just wanted to touch her, to feel her soft skin beneath his fingertip, to reassure himself that she was real.

"True, but…"

"It doesn't bother me if they know, Chrissie. They figured out long ago that I'm no saint."

After all, Kerry had died on his watch.

"I'm not so sure about that. So far, every time I've seen Agnes, she's sung your praises."

Taking a deep breath, he shrugged. "I pay her to do that."

"Sure you do."

A hobbling group of women made their way into the tent and Trace stood from the chair and went to meet them.

"Right this way, ladies. We'll get you triaged and taken care of."

CHAPTER SEVEN

UNFORTUNATELY ONE OF the male volunteers had spotted a wasp nest and taken it upon himself to knock it down.

Instead, the wasps had knocked him down and attempted to take several others along the way. In the end, three different people had gotten stung. Ethan Meadows, the man who'd stirred up the wasps to begin with, had sustained a significant number of stings and had several areas of fairly extensive swelling.

Chrissie had ice packs on the sting patients and Trace was keeping a close check on Ethan due to the number of sting sites he had.

The rest of the afternoon passed quickly and they had a rush of sore feet and minor musculoskeletal issues right before time for the children's Olympic-style games started up.

Chrissie had learned that this was the first year they'd added the children's events. Bud and Agnes had made a decision to make the event more family friendly as CCPO was for children and they were hoping this would be a success.

Both of the event founders had been in and out of the tent, checking on the volunteers, and specifically, she got the impression they were checking on Trace.

As if they were worried about him.

A few hours later, the crew took turns sneaking off to the food tent to grab something to eat.

When Chrissie got ready to go, she did a quick visual search for Trace.

"One step ahead of you," he said from close behind her. "Let's grab something and get a quick nap afterward."

"A nap?" She eyed him suspiciously. "It would be suffocating in my tent right now. Plus, I have a roomie."

He waggled his brows. "Then you should go to my tent."

"Do you have a tent?"

He looked upward. "Do I have a tent? Now, what kind of a question is that to ask a man?"

"A realistic one."

He laughed. "Yes, I have a tent, Chrissie. It's near some trees so it does have a little shade, but still, it's probably near as hot as yours. Is that a problem?"

"No." She shook her head. "Not a problem."

"Good answer."

Chrissie wouldn't let herself question whether or not it was. She'd made her mind up that she was going to enjoy this weekend with Trace all she could. For this one weekend she'd be a normal, healthy, twenty-eight-year-old female with a sex drive, not responsible single-mom Chattanooga Chrissie.

Although thoughts of Joss, of telling Trace about Joss, kept sneaking in and Chrissie would guiltily shove them aside. She couldn't tell Trace about Joss. He didn't want to know. He was a good man, would feel responsible. He didn't want children or to be tied down.

What if he did and Joss had to go through the hell Chrissie had? What if Trace took him overseas to some God-forsaken place and she never saw her son again?

Shaking her irrational fears from her mind, Chrissie went to get into the line to collect food.

"We're not eating here," Trace informed her.

Biting her lip, she stared at him. "We're not?"

"Nope. Wait here."

He walked to where a woman greeted him with a huge smile, nodded, then reached behind the counter where she was working.

She brought up a backpack and handed it to Trace. She said something to him, but Chrissie couldn't make out her words. He laughed, nodded, then thanked the woman.

Trace grabbed a couple of bottled waters from a volunteer manning a large iced container of drinks, then took Chrissie's hand and led her down a path away from the food station.

"You up for an adventure?"

"In your hot tent?" she guessed, by far not opposed to the idea. She was quite in favor of getting hot and sweaty with Trace. But she was pretty sure they were headed in the opposite direction from Trace's tent. From everyone's tents.

"Nah." He shook his head. "I'm saving my tent for later."

His answer piqued her curiosity. He wasn't going to haul her to his tent first chance he got? Go figure. She'd admitted she wanted him and he was going to drag out the moment in torturous ways. If she didn't know better she might think it was because he didn't want her as much as she wanted him. She did know better. His desire was in his eyes every time their gazes locked.

Still, she was curious as to what he had up his sleeve. "Okay, take me on an adventure."

Truth was, every second with Trace was an adventure. Had been every second she'd ever been in his presence.

When he led her to a gas-powered, four-wheel-drive all-terrain vehicle, reached into his cargo-shorts pocket and pulled out a key, Chrissie couldn't hide her surprise.

"What are you doing?"

He grinned. "What does it look like I'm doing?"

"Where are we going?"

"I told you. On an adventure." He opened the backpack the food-station woman had given him and dropped the bottled waters into it. "You mind wearing that? I would, but I'd rather have you pressed against me without a bag with our lunch in between us. Plus, I don't think you'd be nearly as comfortable."

"Not a problem." She slid the straps over her shoulders, letting the bag hang against her back. It wasn't super heavy, despite being stuffed full.

He handed her a helmet that had been hanging from one of the handle bars. "I know it's hot, but I want to make sure I keep you safe while we're on our adventure. Helmet on. Can't have us being the ones needing use of the medical station."

Staring at the machine nervously, she took the helmet. "I've never ridden on one of these. I'm not sure I'm going to like it."

If her nerves at the mere thought of just climbing onto the four-wheeled machine were any indication, she was pretty sure she wouldn't.

"Sure you will. You're an adventurous kind of girl."

Ha, that was a joke and a half. Unless working and spending every other spare moment with her son qualified as adventurous. Although she loved the unknowns of her nursing job and Joss was full of life and kept her hopping, she didn't think many would qualify work and motherhood as making her an "adventurous' kind of girl.

"Not that adventurous."

In reality, she supposed many would consider her boring, but she didn't feel that way with Trace, nor was he looking at her as if he found her boring.

"Except with you," she added. "You bring out my adventurous spirit."

Putting on his helmet, he grinned. "Works for me."

"What?" she asked, sliding the helmet on and fiddling with the strap until she had it snapped into place and snug beneath her chin.

Too bad they didn't make full-body helmets. She'd feel safer.

"You only being adventurous with me." He checked her helmet, then climbed onto the ATV and patted the seat behind him. "Hop aboard my chariot."

She snickered, not budging from where she stood, staring at the machine. "Some chariot."

"Don't judge a chariot by its ugly green color. It'll get us where we're going."

"Which is?"

He just grinned and patted the seat again. "I'm more of a show kind of guy than a tell kind of guy."

"Yeah, I remember that about you, but it's a vague memory. I may need a reminder soon."

He laughed, but didn't even try to steal a kiss, which he easily could have. Although there were vehicles and several motor homes around the area, she didn't see a single person. Maybe she should steal a kiss. Maybe that would distract him from wanting to go anywhere on the four-wheeler.

But part of her wanted to know what he had planned.

A strong enough part that she took a deep breath and steeled herself for whatever the "adventure" brought her way.

Hoping she didn't make a fool of herself by being terrified of riding on the four-wheeler, because, seriously, she wasn't feeling brave at all, Chrissie climbed on behind him.

"Wrap your arms around me and hang on," he advised when she settled onto the vehicle.

Advice Chrissie had no problem taking. She slid her arms around his waist and locked her fingers together. Her body was pressed snugly against his as he turned a switch and the vehicle roared to life between her legs. Oh, my.

"Hang on," he told her again, and then they were off.

Chrissie closed her eyes and said a little prayer that

she didn't cut off Trace's air supply by clinging onto him too tightly.

"You okay?" he called over the engine noise.

"Fine," she said, loosening her grip a fraction and forcing her eyelids apart to stare through the helmet's clear visor.

Okay, this wasn't so bad. Actually, the wind whipping at her body felt good. Not as good as the man she pressed up against, but not bad.

At first, Trace kept the vehicle fairly slow, as they were still in the outskirts of the event area, but soon, they'd left behind the tents and the few people they'd encountered and were making their way through a lightly wooded area.

When they drove free of the woods and came into a grassy field, Trace called over the roar of the engine, "You ready?"

She knew what he meant. He'd been so cautious through the event area, through the woods, that instinctively she'd relaxed. Trace wouldn't do anything stupid. He'd keep her safe.

"Yes!"

She was. Ready for whatever he wanted.

The intensity between them for the past twenty-four hours-plus, on top of having her body firmly pressed against his, had her oh, so ready. Add in the vibration of the vehicle and, yeah, she was ready.

More than ready.

Unable to resist, she splayed her hands across his belly, loving the flat planes beneath her fingertips. She fanned them upward, pressed herself tighter against him, flattening her breasts into his back, and almost groaned at the pleasure.

But before she could do more, he gunned the gas and they took off across the field in a smooth motion that spoke of an easy familiarity with riding ATVs, and maybe being acclimatized to having women try to seduce him.

Which, she supposed, was what she was doing.

Because she wanted him.

Pressing her helmet against his shoulder, she held on tight as she adjusted to the increased speed. Within seconds, she lifted her head and let the wind whip against the exposed parts of her body.

Okay, this was one adventure she could seriously get used to.

Only she wasn't sure she'd feel nearly as comfortable, nearly as safe, with anyone other than Trace.

What was it about the man that made her feel safe?

Funny, she hadn't thought about him making her feel safe four years ago, but he had.

Safe to be herself.

Safe to express herself.

Safe to tell him what she wanted, show him what she wanted.

Safe to feel all the delicious things he did to her body and to give right back.

That was the difference between Trace and any other man she'd ever met. With Trace, she hadn't felt self-conscious or nervous, she'd just felt…alive.

Adventurous!

Just as she did this very moment.

Laughter bubbled out from between her lips.

She wasn't sure how long they rode, but soon they came to another wooded area, and Trace significantly slowed their pace as they made their way through the trees.

Within a few minutes they came to a stream and just when Chrissie braced herself for the splash sure to come as he drove right through the foot or so of moving water, he brought the ATV to a stop and killed the engine.

"Out of gas?" she teased as he undid his chin strap, and

pulled the helmet from his head. He hung it on the handlebar by the strap, then climbed off the four-wheeler, and reached for her hand.

"I hope not. That would be a long walk back."

She let him help her off the ATV and undo her chin strap, pulling the helmet from her head.

Figuring her hair was a mess from the helmet, heat, and sweat, she ran her fingers through it while he hung up the helmet.

"Don't. You look beautiful."

"You sure you had your visor pulled down? I think you may have gotten bugs in your eyes during our ride."

He laughed. "Not hardly."

Removing a rolled-up blanket that had been strapped to the back of the ATV, Trace spread it out a few feet from the stream.

"This is beautiful," she told him, looking around. It really was. The area wasn't heavily wooded, but enough so that it made her feel as if she were in some private enchanted forest, especially with the few sprigs of purple flowers that grew around the grassy area where he had spread the blanket. "Are we going to be in trouble for being here?"

He shook his head.

"You're sure?"

"Yep. I know the owner."

Something in the way he answered had her asking, "Bud?"

He shook his head again. "No, my father."

His father? She glanced around the gorgeous scenery again, taking in the gurgling stream, the green trees, the thick, grassy areas, the blue sky peeking in around the leaves.

"It's a beautiful piece of property."

"Yeah, he bought it several years back with plans to

modernize it into an upscale suburb and golf course, but hasn't done so yet."

"Why not?"

"Mostly, because Bud and Agnes need the section they use for the event. Still, there's several hundred more acres beyond what the event uses, so I guess he could develop and not affect the event."

Sunshine danced on the water and where it hit the ground beneath the leaf cover above.

"It would be a shame for this to be destroyed to make a subdivision," she mused.

"I agree. Can I have the bag, please?"

She removed the backpack and handed it to him.

"Have a seat and I'll serve you lunch."

"A picnic?" she asked, sitting down near him on the blanket.

He grinned. "Yes."

He pulled out two plastic-wrapped sandwiches, a couple bags of baby carrots, fruit, and the two bottled waters. "If you're a good girl and eat all your food, I have dessert for you."

She just bet he did and he looked pretty scrumptious. "Oh, really?"

Nodding, he reached back into the bag and removed a small bottle of hand sanitizer. Holding out the bottle, he squirted a generous dollop into her hand then another into his own.

"Thank you for doing this, but are you sure it's okay for us to be away from the medical station this long? I'll admit I'm feeling a little guilty."

He smiled a smile that said he understood and didn't judge her anxiety. "Alexis has my number and instructions to call if it gets busy. We could be back in twenty minutes tops."

Interesting.

"Alexis, huh? Was she in on this?"

"Not really. I just asked if she minded holding the fort down while I stole you away for a while. I think she approved."

"I like her more and more."

"She's okay," he conceded, not sounding overly concerned one way or the other as he dug around in the backpack.

"For a beautiful cardiologist who volunteers to help raise awareness and funds for children with cancer."

"Well, yeah, at least she has that going for her." His tone was teasing. He pulled out a zipper-closed plastic bag that had napkins, et cetera, in it. "Hungry?"

"Starved."

Something in the way she answered must have keyed him into what she was feeling because he paused from digging more items out of the backpack, and he glanced at her. "Yeah?"

She nodded.

He scratched his head. "What am I doing?"

She shrugged. "I don't know. What are you doing?"

"Not what I want to be doing."

She fought the urge to lick her lips because they definitely felt dry. "Which is?"

"Touching you."

No more suppressing her tongue after that comment. She moistened her lips.

"Well." She stared straight into his eyes. "Today is your lucky day because if you act now, you can touch me."

He arched a brow. "If I act later?"

"You can touch me, then, too."

Trace touched.

Just a light brush of his fingertip over her cheek that he continued down her throat, toying at her T-shirt collar.

But, oh, what a touch.

Despite the September heat, goose bumps prickled her skin and caused his to do the same.

She was looking at him. He could feel her gaze hot on his face, but his stayed in tune with the trail his finger was blazing; he was mesmerized by what his touch was doing to her flesh.

More than just his finger, because now he brushed his hand down her arm, light, feathery, surreal as the sun dappled on the ground around them, giving a magical feel as the wind blew, gently swaying the tree limbs above them and kissing their skin with the breeze.

Lower down her arm he moved until he touched her hand. He traced each finger, noting her short, clean nails. She wore no jewelry other than a pair of small diamond stud earrings, something he'd noticed four years ago, as well. He'd bet anything the earrings were the same ones she'd had on then, that she wore them continuously. Had they been a gift from someone? A family member or a former man in her life?

He laced their hands and lifted hers to press a kiss there.

"You know this isn't necessary, right?" Her voice was low in her throat, almost husky as their eyes met. "You don't have to seduce me or convince me to say yes. I'm yours for the taking."

He groaned. "I'm going to take you."

"Then get on with it."

He laughed at the full pout of her lips, but he'd be lying if he didn't admit, at least to himself, that her urgency thrilled him.

"What's your rush?" He slipped his hand beneath her T-shirt hem and lifted upward. With her help, he pulled the shirt over her head, revealing her peach-colored bra and creamy skin beneath.

He sucked in a breath at what he'd uncovered, then resumed his exploration by rubbing his hands over her bare shoulders, down her sides.

Rather than answer his question with words, Chrissie reached behind her, undid her bra, then slipped free of the material.

"There," she said, guiding his hand to cover her breast. "That's better."

She was right. That was better.

But not good enough.

He lowered and took her nipple into his mouth and sucked on the pebbled flesh. He'd already been hard. He'd been hard from the moment he'd touched her cheek, had been fighting an erection the entire ride over to his favorite spot along Horse Shoe Creek. Now, he was painfully so, but refused to rush this.

It had been four years since he'd kissed her, touched her, been inside her.

Four years too long.

He didn't want it to be over before he got started. Once inside her, he didn't think he was going to last long.

At least, not nearly long enough.

All night wouldn't be nearly long enough.

He planned to give her as much pleasure as he could before giving in to the hedonistic need within him that just wanted to thrust deep inside her and possess her with all his might, to claim her body with his in the most elemental way.

Just the thought had him groaning against her full breast. He really liked the added roundness to her bosom, her hips, the new hourglass curves of her body.

Her fingers were in his hair now, threading through the locks and pulling him closer. She moaned and her arms slightly buckled beneath her as she arched toward him.

"Lie back," he ordered, gently pushing her against the blanket. There was a thick bed of grass and moss beneath them to serve as a cushion, but he wouldn't put his weight on her, not until he was ready to take her, just in case. He wanted her comfortable so nothing would distract from what he was doing.

"I'm going to take off your shorts, Chrissie."

Eyes closed, she nodded, but as his fingers slid beneath her waistband she slightly sat up and stopped him by grasping his head and pulling his mouth to hers.

She kissed him.

Not a gentle kiss, but a kiss full of hot need.

A kiss that demanded his very being.

A kiss that gave her complete control of him.

"Chrissie," he breathed the second their lips parted.

He helped her when she pulled off his shirt. He helped her when she undid his shorts and freed him to her greedy touch.

He almost lost it.

"Take your shorts off," he ordered as he slid out of his own, grabbing a condom from his pocket before he was too far gone to care. He almost already was.

He heard her gasp and winced. Hell. How could he have forgotten the jagged scar along his left lower abdomen?

"What happened?"

"Long story." He didn't want to talk about what had happened in Shiara right now. Not ever really.

She ran her finger over the puckered skin, but Trace was having no more of it. He didn't want her pity or whatever that was in her eyes. He wanted the passion from before she'd seen his damaged flesh. The passion that was still there and that he was determined to hold onto.

He ripped open the condom, had the prophylactic on in record speed, and rolled on top of her. "You're sure?"

Rolling her eyes at his question, she lifted her hips to where he nudged against her. "Please."

Making sure to support his weight, Trace pushed into her. Slow and steady at first, then faster, until he couldn't think, couldn't breathe, couldn't do anything but feel as the amazing heat between their bodies built, then combusted.

She cried out in release before he did, but just barely as he toppled over right behind, then collapsed.

"I forgot," she whispered against his throat, her arms wrapped tightly around him as she held him close. "I forgot how amazing sex was with you."

He propped himself up on his elbows and stared down at her, at the awe and joy in her sated eyes. Something shifted in his chest. He didn't know how to label it, just that she moved him in powerful ways.

"I didn't," he admitted, kissing the tip of her nose. "I've thought about you, this, a million times."

CHAPTER EIGHT

STILL TRYING TO catch her breath, Chrissie stretched to where she could kiss Trace.

Thank goodness she'd decided to take full advantage of him being close and wanting her.

The man was amazing. Simply and purely amazing.

He still felt amazing and full between her legs, almost to the point that she'd question whether or not he'd orgasmed. Almost.

She squeezed her inner thighs around him, eliciting a manly growl.

"Unless you're prepared for round two, I'd advise you not do that again, because, lady, you make me feel like Superman."

Although she was sweaty and breathy from round one, Chrissie gave him a look that hopefully left no doubt in his mind of what she wanted. She planned to take advantage of every second with him. With a saucy smile, she squeezed her thighs again and liked the light that instantly lit in his hot gaze.

Later, much later, she would question him on what had happened to his beautiful body.

The following morning, Chrissie stood on her tiptoes to the side of the main stage and listened to the farewell program with a heavy heart.

She had slept in Trace's tent with him the night before. They'd had to be quiet, to keep their movements and reactions under control, but they had made love. Twice.

She was a little sore today, but not so much that she didn't wonder if they'd get the opportunity to make love again, before she headed back to Chattanooga that afternoon.

Back to Joss. Trace's son.

She sucked in a breath and reminded herself the same thing she'd reminded herself of over and over during their night together. She wasn't going to go there.

Currently, Agnes was on the main stage giving a final speech and congratulations to all the participants and volunteers on the fabulous job they'd done. Between the previously obtained participant sponsors and the multiple weekend events, they'd raised seven figures to further their cause and Agnes couldn't be prouder.

Having worked the night before, Alexis had headed out that morning after exchanging numbers with Chrissie and promising that they would get together again at some point in the future.

Who knew if they really would, but it was a nice sentiment.

All that was left after Agnes's talk was the final farewell from Bud. Then the participants would head out. The remaining volunteers would pack up leftover supplies. Rented and donated equipment companies had already started arriving to collect their items. Perishables would be donated and anything they could use for the next event would be boxed up and labeled in plastic bins.

Trace and Chrissie planned to help break down the medical station, so they would get to spend a little more time together. But every second seemed like sand falling faster and faster through an hourglass that would separate them forever.

Because despite how wonderful the past twenty-four hours had been, no matter how wonderfully sweet and tender Trace had been that last time he'd made love to her just before dawn, she didn't fool herself that it was anything more than exactly what they'd agreed to.

A no-strings weekend affair.

In just a few hours, they'd say goodbye. She'd go home. He'd leave for parts unknown again or whatever it was he planned to do with the rest of his life.

The end.

She didn't regret their weekend.

Far from it.

Despite the nagging ache in her chest, she was grateful she'd been given the opportunity to get to know Trace better, that this time they'd talked during those long hours about things besides, "Oh, that feels so good!" Not what had happened to him to cause the scar, as he'd brushed off her questions each time she'd asked, but they had talked about a lot of things. She was grateful that if Joss ever asked about his father she could smile and tell him about a man she knew cared about others and made a difference in the world.

A man she wished Joss could know firsthand.

Not going there, she repeated over and over in her head. They'd agreed to a no-strings-attached weekend. He'd said he didn't want children four years ago and he'd repeated the sentiment to Chloe's mother. To tell him would be selfish.

Would be risky, the fear that lurked within her added.

"What are you thinking?"

She cut her gaze to the man occupying her thoughts and went for the truth. Mostly.

"That you and I will be saying goodbye in a few hours."

His expression tightened, then he seemed to make a quick decision. "We don't have to."

Her heart skipped a beat. What was he saying?

"You could stay in Atlanta tonight," he suggested, excitement glittering to life in his eyes. "I could take you somewhere nice for dinner and we could spend the evening together." His gaze searched hers. "The night."

Oh, how he tempted her.

But she'd only made arrangements with Savannah to keep Joss until this evening. Plus, she missed her little boy.

She needed to get back to Chattanooga, to her life there.

She looked into Trace's face and saw so much of her son there. Same eyes, same straight nose, same strong chin. Same stubborn determination.

What would he think if he knew they'd had a son together?

That they had a beautiful three-year-old little boy who was the spitting image of him? Would he want to know Joss? Would he care? Or would he take off for parts unknown without batting an eyelash?

What if he took Joss from her? Her father had never wanted her and he had still tried to take her. Not that Trace was anything like her father, but once upon a time her mother had believed in her father, too.

Panic filled Chrissie and she shook her head.

"No, we can't spend the night together?" he asked, misinterpreting her head shake.

She wasn't staying, wasn't going to call Savannah to beg for one more night. Her friend would say yes, but…

"I need to go home, Trace."

His disappointment was palpable. "Are you scheduled to work tomorrow?"

"Not until Tuesday, but—"

"But you need to go home to do laundry and wash your hair?"

His tone was so sarcastic and unlike anything she'd heard come from his mouth that she was a little taken aback.

"I didn't say that, but I do need to go home."

His gaze was steely. "Why?"

"I have things I have to do, Trace. A life there that I've been away from all weekend."

"A life that can't wait one more day?"

She closed her eyes. She wanted to stay with him, wanted to let him bring her body over the top time and time again, but then she'd be faced with leaving tomorrow. Then, she'd be faced with explaining to Savannah why she needed another night, not that her friend wouldn't be understanding. Savannah would probably be the opposite and encourage her to go for it.

But every second she spent with Trace made her question more and more how he'd react if she told him about Joss.

Every smile, every touch, every laugh they shared made her crave to see him with their son, to hear and see the two of them interact, laugh, play.

Every time she considered telling Trace she battled guilt and the terror she'd faced as a child at the hands of her father.

She couldn't spend more time with Trace. She just couldn't.

"No, it can't." She braced herself for whatever his reaction might be, but when he spoke he sounded like his normal self again.

"We would have had a great time, Chrissie. I won't lie and say I'm not disappointed."

Sighing in relief, she reached for his hand. "We have had a great time. That I need to go home now doesn't change that."

Glancing at her, he considered what she said, then grinned. "You're right. We have had a great time. Thank you."

They finished listening to the event farewell then made their way back over to the medical station. They worked side by side, chatted, made a few jokes with the other volunteers who'd stayed to help, but the last few grains of sand quickly fell and soon it was time for Chrissie to go.

She didn't want to. She wanted to stay, to spend every single second that he'd give her for however long that might be. Silly. She'd already had more than she'd ever dreamed she would just in getting to see him again, to make love to him again.

She'd also learned so many things about him during the hours they'd lain in his sleeping bag talking.

He was an only child. He'd gone to private schools his whole life, including college, and medical school. His father had wanted him in the family business, but Trace had wanted to be a doctor, so he had become one. Bud and Agnes really were his godparents and he considered them the major influences on who he was. His mother had a good heart, but was a social butterfly who lived in the shadows of his father and was content there. Trace never had been. Both his parents were in good health and his grandparents had died of old age.

All things that were important to know about her son's father's family.

More guilt hit her.

Before this weekend, she'd never really considered tracking Trace down to tell him about Joss. Not more than in brief little snatches.

By the time she'd realized she was pregnant almost three months had gone by since she'd seen him. He hadn't contacted her. Not once. She'd had no reason to think he'd have wanted to know about their son. Quite the opposite, really.

She still didn't.

Just because they shared a dynamic chemistry didn't mean a thing except that they were highly sexually compatible.

That they most definitely were.

Ugh. She had to stop with this internal battle. There were compelling reasons why she wasn't going to tell Trace.

Chrissie said goodbye to the volunteers she'd met. Trace got hung up talking to one of them who was considering signing on with Doctors Around the World, and while they talked Chrissie went to track down Agnes and Bud to say her goodbyes. She found Agnes supervising the equipment-rental company breaking down the food service area.

"You headed out?" Agnes asked when she spotted Chrissie coming toward her.

"I am. I packed my things up into my car this morning and we just finished packing the supplies in the medical station."

Agnes stopped what she'd been doing, wiped her hands down the side of her shirt. "Hope we'll see you again next year."

Next year.

Would Trace be there or would he still be off in another country doing good for those in need?

She and Joss needed him.

The thought was silly, but it ran through her mind, causing her to wince.

No, she and Joss did not need him. She took great care of her little family.

"I'm not sure where I'll be next year, but maybe." She gave an answer because Agnes waited for one.

"Trace know you're about to leave?"

"He was helping the crew load up the heavy stuff, then got caught up talking about Doctors Around the World when I headed this way. I'll find him and say goodbye before I leave."

Although it would be better to just go.

"You two going to see each other again?"

She fought grimacing at Agnes's question. "No."

Disappointment marred Agnes's face and she gave a

little shake of her head. "I hate to hear that. You're good for that boy."

Trace was hardly a boy, but Chrissie wasn't going to point that out.

"He was good for me, too."

The weekend had been good for her. As hard as the thought of saying goodbye to Trace was, she was glad she'd come to the event, glad she'd volunteered and been a part of something so wonderful to help others, glad she'd run into Trace and put the bitterness she held toward him to rest.

Hopefully for good.

Hopefully she'd go home and love their little boy and only think of Trace with fond memories of the man who'd given her life's most precious gift. Her son.

He'd been honest with her. He wanted nothing more than what they'd already shared. Well, that and one more night of hot, steamy sex in the comfort of a bed.

Funny, but she had a difficult time imagining anything being better than what they'd already shared on a blanket dappled in sunshine and a sleeping bag in the shadows.

Yeah, it was time to go because she was becoming an emotional mess.

She looked at Agnes and the woman saw right through her.

"You need to tell him."

Knowing what she was about to do, she shook her head. "It's better this way."

Agnes wasn't buying it. "Better for who?"

"Both of us."

"Are you married?"

"What?" she asked at Agnes's unexpected question.

"I'm just trying to imagine what reason there could be for you to walk away from Trace."

What about the facts that he'd be leaving to go over-seas, that he didn't want a committed relationship, that he didn't want children? What about Chrissie's baggage that dogged her with the fear of him grabbing Joss and running, even when she logically knew Trace would never do such a thing?

What about the fact that Trace could so easily break her heart?

"I know you don't understand, Agnes, and for that I'm sorry, but I had no expectations and neither did Trace."

The older woman shook her head. "Young people these days."

Yeah, she supposed to Agnes it did seem that she probably did sleep around without another thought, but, even with as much as she liked Agnes, she didn't know the woman well enough to explain to her that wasn't the case.

Even if she did, that would raise too many other questions. Like why had she slept with Trace so quickly four years ago? Why had she set aside common sense and had sex with him repeatedly this weekend?

Because Trace was different.

He always had been.

What that difference was she couldn't allow herself to label, especially not while Agnes studied her with an expression that wavered from disappointed to sympathetic.

Yeah, if she allowed herself to really care about Trace she'd need sympathy, because she'd be facing even bigger heartache than she had the last time they'd said goodbye.

Good thing she'd gone into this knowing all they had was the weekend because falling for Trace would have been easy.

Which was why she hugged Agnes and said goodbye.

Goodbye to Agnes, to Atlanta, and to Trace.

"What do you mean she left?" Trace frowned at the woman he'd loved and admired his whole life.

Agnes had marched into the empty shell of the medical tent where he'd been talking to one of the volunteers and insisted upon speaking to him. He was grateful she'd waited until they'd left the medical tent to announce her news in private.

"You heard me," Agnes countered, her hands going onto her hips as she gave him a motherly stare-down. "Apparently, you didn't say or do the right things, because she told me bye and apparently already had her car packed, because she left."

Yeah, he'd helped her carry her things to her car that morning after they'd broken her tent down.

"I said and did the right things," Trace argued. He'd been upfront with her that time spent with him was only for the weekend.

It didn't matter that she'd just left without saying goodbye.

Not really.

She'd probably done them both a big favor, because he'd have tried to convince her to spend the night with him again.

She'd already said no so trying to persuade her further would have been pathetic on his part.

He wasn't a pathetic or desperate kind of guy.

At least, he never had been in the past.

These last four years hadn't presented him with much opportunity to date or have relationships with women. Sure, there had been a few female volunteers, but for the most part he'd been celibate and hadn't had any interest in dating.

Or in sex.

He'd blamed his lack of interest on the situations he'd been in. On the stress and the extreme conditions of the areas where he'd been working.

Maybe it had been more than that.

Maybe it had been memories of a certain woman.

"Well," Agnes interrupted his thoughts. "What are you going to do about her leaving?"

He blinked at his godmother and almost smiled at her feigned, or not so feigned, outrage. "Not one thing."

He wasn't. Although he wanted one more night, he could see the plus sides to her having left. Saying goodbye to Chrissie wouldn't have been easy. Odd, as he didn't recall having problems telling her goodbye four years ago. Then again, he'd been leaving that week for parts unknown so he'd been saying goodbye to pretty much everyone.

He'd be doing that again within a few weeks.

Agnes frowned. "You're not going to go after her?"

"She left without saying goodbye," he reminded her, shoving his hands into his cargo-shorts pockets and fiddling with his keys. "A woman doesn't do that if she wants a man to come after her."

"Sure, she does."

Maybe in some cases, but not theirs. He shook his head. "That's not the kind of relationship we have."

Agnes harrumphed. "Well, sex every four years doesn't seem to be a very normal kind of relationship, if you ask me."

Trace winced, but stood his ground. "I didn't."

He was not talking sex with Agnes. Nope. He wasn't going to do it no matter how well meant her intentions were.

"Don't give me that look or that attitude," she warned in her most motherly tone. More motherly than his own mother's usual tone for sure.

"I know you like her," Agnes continued, not backing down.

"I never said I didn't," he reminded her, knowing that to resist was futile. Agnes had always been able to read him and it wasn't as if he and Chrissie had tried to hide their attraction to each other. At least, not after she'd gotten past her initial hang-up.

"Then why would you let her walk away?" Agnes's question echoed what was running through his mind.

Crossing his arms, he considered the woman he'd adored all his life, then shrugged. "She was avoiding having to say goodbye. I understand that."

On some levels, he really did.

"Well, I'm glad you do, because I sure don't," Agnes huffed. "I think you should go after her and see what happens."

Trace laughed. What would be the point?

"I already know what would happen."

Agnes's salt-and-pepper brow arched. "What's that?"

"We'd say goodbye."

"You seem so sure." Her disappointment was palpable.

Trace let out a long breath. "Whether today, tomorrow, or next week, we'd have to say goodbye. I'm leaving and will be gone for months on end. Perhaps years. This way is best."

Chrissie was still telling herself that leaving was the best thing for her and Trace when she was at Savannah's house that evening. The farther away she got from Atlanta, the more unsure she became.

Part of her knew she'd done the right thing.

A goodbye between her and Trace would have been messy. Just look at how messy their talking about it during the farewell had been.

But she did hate that she hadn't got to touch him one last time. That she hadn't gotten to feel his lips against hers one last time as they shared a goodbye kiss. That there'd been no additional time for talking, for asking him about what had happened to him.

But then she'd think of Joss and the panicky, got-to-escape, how-could-I-not-have-told-him? feelings would take over again and she'd heavy-foot the gas pedal. She'd gotten home in record time.

"There you go again," Savannah accused, eyeing her from across the living room where she held her baby, nursing her. "Something happened this weekend."

Chrissie looked at her friend with an obviously guilty expression because her friend's eyes widened.

"Something did happen!" Savannah exclaimed, louder than she should have as Amelia stopped nursing and whimpered. Savannah quickly settled her daughter and whispered, "Tell me."

Chrissie looked down at the sleeping little boy curled in her arms. Joss had been so excited when she'd gotten there, had given her a welcome home card he and his "Auntie" Savannah had made. Savannah had insisted they stay for dinner, during which her husband Charlie had been called into the hospital and had to leave. When they'd finished eating, while Savannah had recounted Joss's adventures over the weekend, Joss had climbed into Chrissie's lap and dozed off almost immediately. She hadn't minded. She loved these moments of holding him close, of snuggling his little body, and feeling his heart next to hers.

Something she'd denied Trace from ever knowing by not telling him about his son. Guilt stung her eyes and she sniffled.

She was not going to cry. She wasn't. No way.

"Tell me," Savannah insisted a little louder when Chrissie still hesitated.

"I…" What did she say to Savannah? How did she begin to explain to her best friend that she'd had a repeat of the weekend that had given her Joss?

Well, hopefully, not a full repeat as they'd used protection every time, and surely odds wouldn't be on her getting pregnant twice while protected?

Her head spun for a brief moment. The thought of being

pregnant with Trace's baby again didn't repel the way it should have. Maybe it was because Joss was curled in her arms and she'd missed him so much. Maybe it was because Savannah was nursing Amelia and had never looked happier than she did these days.

Maybe it was something more.

"He was there," she confessed.

"He?" Eyes wide, Savannah dropped her gaze to Joss. "The guy from before?"

Face on fire, Chrissie nodded.

"You had sex with him again!"

"Shh!" Chrissie winced and fought the urge to cover Joss's ears. As irrational as it was, she didn't want her son to hear this conversation. Not that he was aware of anything going on around him. He was out for the count.

"You slept with Joss's dad?" Savannah stage-whispered.

Knowing she'd eventually tell Savannah everything, Chrissie nodded. She really needed to talk, to let out some of the strong emotions flowing through her. Maybe Savannah could make sense of them. Chrissie sure couldn't.

"I did and it was great. Better than I remembered."

Savannah smiled. "That's wonderful."

Chrissie could see the matchmaking wheels spinning in her best friend's head.

"It was wonderful, but *was* is the key word. It was just a fling. Just like before."

Savannah frowned. "What do you mean?"

"We agreed to have a no-strings-attached affair for the weekend and that's what we had. End of story."

"No, not end of story, because you have strings."

"No, I don't," Chrissie denied. Yeah, she had feelings for Trace. How could she not, but those weren't strings. They were…tiny threads of nothingness.

"Hello, you are holding the biggest string there is."

She shook her head. "Joss isn't a string between Trace and me."

"Trace? That's his name?"

Chrissie nodded. Hearing her best friend say Trace's name for the first time felt good in an odd sort of way. As if it somehow made him more real. As if she hadn't imagined this past weekend and the man who had rocked her world.

Of course she hadn't. Proof really did lie in her arms.

"He doesn't know about Joss." Why she blurted that particular tidbit out Chrissie wasn't sure. But she did blurt it out. She also had fire burning her face.

Savannah's thin brows veed. "Why didn't you tell him?"

Wishing she could fan her face, she shrugged. "Probably for the same reasons you didn't tell Charlie you were pregnant those first few months."

Chrissie's comment had Savannah relenting a little, but only a little.

"Chrissie, you need to tell him. He is Joss's father. I know I didn't tell Charlie to begin with, but I should have. The longer I waited, the more difficult admitting the truth became."

Savannah had found out she was pregnant on the very day Charlie had told her he had taken a job two hours away and was moving. Without her. It had taken a while for Savannah and Charlie to work out their differences, but now Chrissie's friend had her happily-ever-after.

Chrissie winced. "We were only supposed to be an affair. He doesn't want to be burdened with a kid."

Her friend fixed her with a glare. "Is that how you feel about Joss?"

"Of course not!" She tightened her hold around her sleeping son. "Joss is my whole world."

Savannah gave her another sharp look as if to say, *Exactly.*

"Fine, I see your point, but you don't understand. He works with Doctors Around the World and he's leaving soon."

"Then you really should have told him while you were in Atlanta."

In between their sneaky kisses or perhaps by the stream? Or maybe right before she'd left Atlanta.

See you later, Trace. And, oh, by the way, we have a three-year-old son you know nothing about.

Wrong. She shouldn't have told him anything. He was leaving. He didn't want kids. She'd done him a favor.

"Does this have to do with your father and what happened when you were young?"

"No," she denied. "Maybe." She realized the tears she wasn't going to shed had made their way down her cheeks. "Possibly. I don't know, Savannah. I wanted to tell him, but he told me four years ago that he planned never to marry or have children. He still feels that way. Still, I thought about telling him of Joss but never could say the words. He wouldn't really take Joss away from me. At least, I don't believe he would. But my mom never would have left me with my dad if she'd thought he would kidnap me either."

Not that Chrissie had realized at first what her dad had done. He'd told her they were going on a special vacation together and she'd always craved her father's attention, so she'd been a happy little girl. It was only days later, when he still hadn't let her call her mother, would get angry that she wanted to, had slapped her when she'd started crying for her mother, that she'd started questioning their vacation that wasn't much more than sleeping in different cars, cars she'd later learned he'd stolen along their way, and long hours on the road.

"Most men aren't like your father, Chrissie." Savannah shuddered and kissed the top of Amelia's head. "Thank God."

"Trace lives a very different life from most men, Savannah. He's with DAW and goes into dangerous places. He is a good man, would feel obligated. Not knowing is better for him."

Only, if the roles were reversed, she'd want to know. She'd want to be a part of Joss's life. Would Trace?

"I don't have his number or any way of getting in touch with him," she said as much for her benefit as for Savannah's.

She didn't have Trace's number. There had been no need for number exchanges at the event. Not before and not this time. To have exchanged numbers would have implied a future they didn't share.

Only, she did have Alexis's cell-phone number and she knew the beautiful Atlanta cardiologist had Trace's number.

"Chrissie, I can see how much you are struggling with this. Which tells me what I need to know. You have to tell him."

Feeling overwhelmed with emotion and fatigue, she shook her head. Too much had happened in Atlanta. She needed to think, to figure out exactly what she wanted to say to Trace, to be sure of whatever decisions she made because those decisions forever impacted her son.

And Trace.

CHAPTER NINE

CHRISSIE DIDN'T KNOW what she wanted.

She didn't want the traditional happily-ever-after. She didn't fool herself that she'd ever have that and, honestly, she wasn't in a rush to search for it. She was content to raise Joss and after he left to forge his own life, then she'd worry about her personal life, or lack thereof.

Overall, she was pretty happy with her life as it was.

At least, she had been.

Before her weekend in Atlanta with Trace.

Now, there was a restlessness that moved through her.

A week had gone by.

He'd probably already left Atlanta for some deprived part of the world where he was selflessly helping others.

She couldn't berate him for that.

What he was doing was admirable, heroic even.

He didn't know he was missing the precious youth of his son.

Because he didn't know he had a son.

Because she hadn't told him. What kind of horribly selfish person was she?

One who had been kidnapped by her father, an inner voice defended.

Somehow the defense kept falling flat and never resolving Chrissie's growing guilt.

"Why are you crying, Mommy?"

Chrissie blinked at Joss. She'd spread a blanket in their backyard to read a nursing magazine while he played in his sandbox with a shovel, pail, and myriad toy cars and trucks. Apparently, he'd noticed his mother's tears.

Which was more than she could say for herself.

She hadn't realized she was crying. Again. She'd cried way too often over the past week.

Over guilt, she told herself, not because she was missing Trace, not because of the ache in her chest at the thought of never seeing him again.

"Are you sad?" he asked, wiping his gritty fingers across her cheek to clear her tears.

"A little," she answered him, bending to press a kiss to the top of his blond head. "Mommy was thinking about a friend."

Who wasn't really a friend at all, but a lover.

An amazing lover whom she missed.

She missed Trace. Which made no sense. She'd known she wouldn't see him beyond the event weekend. But she missed him.

Not because of his out-of-this-world bedroom skills, but because of his quick smile and wit, the way his eyes lit up when they met hers, the intelligent conversations they'd shared.

Okay, so she missed his bedroom skills, too.

"We could go see your friend," Joss offered with his three-year-old's logic. "Then you wouldn't be sad no more."

She smiled at him. "*Any* more, and you're right."

If only she believed that, but seeing Trace again, if that was even a possibility, might destroy everything she knew and loved. Was she willing to risk it?

Was it fair to Joss, to Trace, if she wasn't?

Wasn't that the real cloud hanging over her the past week? The knowledge that whatever she decided would have such a terrible impact on the person she loved most in the world, on herself, on Trace?

Chrissie loved her job in the CVICU most days. She'd operated as the charge nurse on the unit for a couple of years and really liked the team of nurses and doctors she worked with. They were a good crew.

Especially now that her bestie was back working on an as-needed basis. Like today.

"I'm so glad you're here," she told Savannah. "I know you miss Amelia, but you made my life better by coming in."

Savannah grinned. "The timing was perfect as Charlie was off work today so he could be at home with Amelia. It'll give them some good bonding time together. I'll just have to sneak away a couple of times to pump milk, but other than that I'm happy to be back in the land of adulthood."

Staying home with Joss hadn't been an option. Chrissie had worked like crazy during her pregnancy, saving and putting back as much as she could to cover the expenses of a baby. Fortunately, she'd always been frugal and had bought her little house not long after she'd graduated from nursing school. It was down the road from her mother and, although nothing fancy, she loved her two-bed, one-bath home in its quiet little neighborhood. All of which had made welcoming Joss into her life much easier. Her mother adored her grandson. Her mother had helped her tremendously as she'd made the transition from single woman to single mom, offering to babysit and a shoulder to cry on.

She'd not needed the shoulder, but had welcomed her mother's help with Joss while she'd been at work because she'd hated leaving him. Knowing he was with her mother had at least lightened that guilt. Maybe it was a guilt all working moms felt—the need to be at work and to do a good job there and the need to be with their child and to be a good mom.

Regardless, she was grateful for her mother, and pleased that Savannah had been able to spend the first months of her daughter's life with Amelia.

"We're pretty booked up. I've got a room and you're assigned to two," she told her friend, then let the nurse who'd stayed over to cover until Savannah could get there give her report.

In the meanwhile, Chrissie went to check her patient. A young man in his twenties who'd had a valve replacement the day before.

The boy was still on the ventilator and asleep when Chrissie went in to check him. His father sat in a chair next to the bed and opened his eyes when she entered the room.

"Hi," she greeted the tired-looking man.

The man nodded acknowledgment, but turned his attention immediately to the pale young man lying in the bed with multiple tubes and wires attached to his body. "How is he?"

Chrissie scanned over the telemetry. "Still holding his own." She smiled at the man empathetically. "He should start stirring some soon."

"I hope so. I miss seeing this kid's smile. He's my whole world."

"I understand. I have a three-year-old son. He's my whole world, too."

The man continued, obviously needing to talk. "He has to be okay."

"Dr. Flowers expects him to recover fully," she reminded him.

"I pray so." The man raked his fingers through his salt-and-pepper hair. "We've only connected a few years ago. Now, I can't imagine my life without him."

"Oh?" Chrissie gazed at the man, who was leaning forward, staring at the rise and fall of the young man's bandaged chest.

He sighed, his gaze flickering to hers for a brief moment. "His mother and I weren't married. She got ill a few years back and told him about me. After she passed, he looked me up." Wincing, he shook off a memory. "I was a jerk to begin with. I didn't believe he was mine."

At Chrissie's grimace, the man elaborated.

"How could I have known? His mother and I only dated for a short while and then I never saw her again. I never even thought about her until he showed up in my life almost twenty years later. If only she'd told me."

Chrissie's chest tightened to where she could barely breathe. "What would you have done?"

Startled at her question, the man met her gaze. "I'm not sure, but I do know my son would have known who I was, not just my name, and that in some shape, form, or fashion, I'd have been a father to him. She should have told me. For her not to have, and to have deprived me of knowing my kid, was selfish." Red heightened his cheeks, contrasting with his otherwise pale face. "It's probably wrong to be angry at the dead, but I struggle with it every day."

With her insides shaking, Chrissie finished checking her patient.

When she left the room, she was sweating.

Yet icy cold inside.

If only she'd told me. For her not to have...was selfish.

Was that a sentiment Trace would someday feel? That she'd been selfish to deprive him of Joss?

It was how she'd feel if she were the one missing their son's life.

She glanced around the CVICU. For a morning that had started a bit chaotic due to being short-handed, now everything was, for the moment, calm and smooth, thanks to Savannah coming in and covering their short-staffed situation.

With clammy hands, she pulled out her phone, then went into an empty patient room and pulled the sliding glass door closed.

She had to call Alexis, then Trace. Now. She couldn't wait another minute, couldn't second-guess herself or let the past, or her baggage, interfere with doing what she knew she had to do.

Trace had gotten his next assignment with DAW. He'd start out in Africa again for at least six months. Unfortunately, he wouldn't be leaving for almost three weeks and that had him restless. He was ready to get back to work.

He'd met Bud and Agnes for lunch at a downtown Atlanta restaurant to spend some time with them prior to leaving. A week had passed since the fund-raiser event and he'd not seen them since. Bud always took Agnes on a mini-vacation the week after the event and they'd just gotten home the day before.

He enjoyed listening to the details of their cruise. Years ago, he'd met them on a regular basis for lunch and realized as he sat across from them how much he missed doing so.

"Have you talked to Chrissie?"

Agnes's question caught him off guard.

"We made no plans to stay in touch. You know that."

The older woman looked at her husband and shook her head. "Young people these days are so blind to what's right in front of them."

Bud smiled indulgently at his wife. "What's that, honey?"

"Don't tell me you didn't see what I saw at the event, because I know better."

Bud patted her hand. "Agnes, if the boy says he doesn't want to stay in touch with the girl then he doesn't want to stay in touch with her."

"No, that's not what that means, Bud. It means he's not smart enough to go after her."

"Agnes, I leave in a couple of weeks," he reminded her. "Even if I wanted to go after Chrissie, what would be the point?"

An *aha!* look brightened her face. "Do you want to?"

Good ol' Agnes. She didn't beat around the bush.

"No, Agnes, I don't want to pursue a woman." Which might not be a hundred percent the truth because he had thought about Chrissie a lot over the past week.

But he always came back to the same conclusion. She'd left without saying goodbye for a reason. Because she'd known, like him, that they had no future together.

He couldn't justify interfering in her life when he'd be on another continent. What were they supposed to do? Teleconference stay in touch? He wouldn't do that to her.

"See, I told you there was more between them than met the eye," Agnes spoke up, nudging her husband, and sending Trace an I-told-you-so look.

"Oh, there was plenty that met the eye," Bud countered. "But whatever was between them was exactly like the boy said, between him and the girl."

Agnes just shook her head at her husband.

His cell phone rang and Trace was grateful for the escape from the current conversation.

"Sorry." He pulled out the phone and answered.

"Trace?" a familiar female voice asked. "This is Chrissie."

His heart pounded, but a repeated "Hello," was all he said due to the curious stares he was receiving from the couple across the restaurant table.

"Is this a bad time?" she asked, her voice almost sounding as if she hoped he said it was.

"Could've been worse."

"Oh." She paused a moment. "I…maybe I could call back at a more convenient time."

"There's no need," he assured, mouthing "sorry" to Bud and Agnes. "What can I do for you?"

"I… I want to see you."

His heart leapt, but he kept his expression neutral under Agnes's eagle eyes. Not that she knew who he was talking to, but somehow she'd always had a way of figuring things out.

"What's changed?" he asked. After all, she'd left without saying goodbye to him.

"I'd rather not say over the phone."

"You're in Atlanta?" He was going for nonchalant, partly because of Agnes's hawk eyes and partly because he didn't want to sound overly eager to Chrissie.

Regardless of his efforts, Agnes was looking more and more interested in his conversation. He'd really rather not have to explain his phone call and have her asking questions he probably wouldn't be able to answer.

"No, I'm in Chattanooga, but…"

"You expect me to drive there?"

"Would you?" She sounded hopeful. "That would definitely be easier given the circumstances."

What circumstances? Part of Trace wanted to agree, but the curious stares of the couple across the table from him had him holding his guns.

"I'm a busy man." He was coming off as a jerk. Then again, he hadn't been the one to drive away without so much as a *see ya*. A little anger and bitterness was to be expected, surely?

"I know," she admitted, sounding remorseful and making him feel every bit the prize jerk he was being.

"I wasn't sure if you were still in the States," she continued. "Are you?"

"I'm in Atlanta still."

"Oh. That's good."

"Why are you calling?" he asked, because she was definitely stalling by talking in circles.

"I had a baby."

No longer caring that Agnes and Bud were listening in
on every word he said, Trace frowned at her blurted-out
shocker.

"That's impossible. It's only been a week."

If he'd thought about his response, he'd have known that
was not what she meant but her comment had caught him
so off guard he hadn't been thinking. Maybe he hadn't been
breathing either because he felt light-headed.

"Not now," she clarified, her voice shaky. "I… I had a
baby before coming to Atlanta this time, Trace."

Chrissie had a baby. She'd been curvier than before, but
he'd just figured she'd put on a few pounds. Definitely, he'd
never suspected she'd given birth. He didn't recall any noticeable stretch marks on her belly, but then, not all women
got many stretch marks. Plus, he'd been so paranoid about
his own scars that he might not have noticed.

Or so caught up in his physical need that he might not
have noticed because he'd wanted her something fierce.
They'd taken things slower in his tent, but they'd been in
the dark and had needed to feel their way.

Chrissie had a baby.

Chrissie was a mother.

His brain reeled at the implications.

"That's why you just left? Because you have a baby?"

Agnes's eyes were saucers now and Bud was likely going
to have bruises from how she was elbowing him.

"Yes." Chrissie sounded flustered.

"I don't understand why that meant you couldn't say
goodbye to me."

"You and I have a baby, Trace." She enunciated each
word with great clarity. "A three-year-old son."

She kept talking, but her language might as well have

been foreign because Trace couldn't make out her words, just bits and pieces of sounds that echoed through his mind.

You and I have a baby. A three-year-old son.

He was her baby's father?

He was a father?

She was lying.

They didn't have a son.

He didn't have a child.

Only it *was* possible…

CHAPTER TEN

CHRISSIE HAD WORKED five twelve-hour shifts straight and was exhausted when she picked Joss up from her mother's that evening. Still, she put on a happy face for him, fed him, then gave him his bath.

Three bedtime stories and lots of giggles later she put him to bed, then went to shower.

When her phone rang, she figured it was Savannah to check on her after her mini-meltdown at work that day. Calling Trace and blurting out the truth wasn't exactly what she'd planned, at least, not over the phone. She could hardly believe that she'd let a patient get to her that intensely. She'd call Savannah back when she got out of the shower.

Letting the hot water sluice over her body and wash away the day's grime, she wished she could as easily wash away the stress. If only it were that easy.

A downpour wouldn't wash away her day's stresses. Not today. Stress she'd caused herself by calling Trace. Why had she called him?

Because a pitiful man sitting over his unconscious son's body had gotten to her as she'd listened to his story. Bits and pieces of that story had resonated a little too close. Had reinforced what had been eating at her from the moment she'd laid eyes on Trace again.

She had to tell him about Joss. Not to was wrong. She hadn't needed to hear the man's words to know that. But maybe she'd needed to hear them to make her get beyond the past and act.

Because she was scared. And selfish.

When she got out of the shower, the number showing on the cell phone wasn't Savannah's.

It was the number she'd programmed into her phone after Alexis had given it to her. The number she had called earlier that day because she'd gotten so emotionally tangled up that the need to call him had about done her in.

Trace's number.

He'd called.

Her phone vibrated in her hand and played a series of musical notes.

Correction. He was calling. Trace was calling.

With shaky fingers, she slid her fingertip across the phone screen to answer the call. "Hello."

"Chrissie."

"Trace." Their one word responses couldn't go on, so she added, "Good to hear from you."

"Is it?"

She winced. Not quite sure how to take his comment, she opted to ignore it. It was good to hear from him compared to not hearing from him, but she didn't really know what to say.

"Why are you calling, Trace?"

"You thought I wouldn't after the bombshell you dropped?"

Heat crawled up Chrissie's neck.

"You got off the phone with me rather abruptly. I wasn't sure what to expect." Ha. He'd essentially hung up on her, leaving her a bumbling mess that Savannah had found crying in the empty patient room she'd called him from.

Ugh. How she hated the tangled mess she found herself in. Stupid conscience. Stupid her for going to Atlanta. Stupid. Stupid. Stupid.

Everything had been just fine until she'd seen Trace again. She'd been happy, content with her life with Joss. Then she'd had to go and mess everything up by going back to the place where it all started.

The moment she'd seen Trace she should have left.

Only part of her acknowledged she'd gone to Atlanta with the hopes of possibly seeing him again.

Which meant what exactly?

She'd brought this mess tumbling down upon herself for sure.

"I needed to process what you said."

That she could understand. She hadn't meant to tell him over the phone. She'd meant to set up a time they could meet, talk, that she could tell him about Joss, show him a picture, let him decide how he wanted to proceed with becoming a part of Joss's life.

If he wanted to be a part of Joss's life.

"Have you?" she whispered, her voice twisting up in her throat.

His sigh was palpable across the phone. "As much as I can."

Chrissie shifted the phone to her opposite hand and pulled a baggy T-shirt over her wet head, thinking that might help her feel less uncomfortable talking to him. Getting dressed sure couldn't hurt, because standing wrapped only in a towel was doing nothing for her nerves.

His silence wasn't, either.

"And?" she finally asked, pulling on a pair of panties, and carrying her towel back to the bathroom and hanging it over the side of the tub.

She wasn't sure she wanted to know what Trace had concluded, but was ready to prepare for whatever the near future was about to bring, because obviously she'd reached a point where she was no longer able to deal with her guilty conscience.

"I want to meet him."

She wasn't sure if the noise that escaped her was a sigh in relief or a whimper of despair. Maybe a deformed bit of both.

She went into her living room, sat on her sofa, and hugged her knees up to her. "When?"

"Now."

"Now?"

"You heard me."

"I... He's asleep." Not that that made any sense, but it was what she said. Her head was being bombarded with so many thoughts that nothing made sense. Maybe it never would again.

"Maybe asleep is better."

"You're in Atlanta."

"I'm not."

He wasn't in Atlanta. Her breath came in rapid little breaths she had to consciously stop by inhaling a deep, slow one.

"You're here." It wasn't a question. Trace was there. In Tennessee. In Chattanooga.

"Parked at a gas station. I want to come to your house."

Trace was here! She gripped her phone tighter.

"I just got out of the shower. I'm not even dressed." Panties and an oversized T-shirt didn't count. Not where Trace was concerned. "I wasn't expecting company."

"I'm not coming to see you, Chrissie," he reminded her. "I want to see the boy."

The boy? Probably because of her already raw nerves, but his calling Joss "the boy" irritated.

"His name is Joss," she reminded him with enough force to make her point. "I told you that."

"Joss," he said. "I want to see Joss."

"I..." She took a deep breath. "Okay, fine. Give me fifteen minutes and I'll let you in. Be quiet, though, because he really is asleep."

She gave him the address, then hung up and pulled on a pair of sweats, put her bra back on beneath her shirt so she didn't feel so exposed, and was combing through her damp hair when she heard his car in her driveway.

Five minutes. Ugh. Of course he'd come straight there, even though she'd asked for fifteen minutes. Maybe he'd sit and wait the extra ten minutes she'd asked for—minutes in which she'd planned to do a quick run-through clean of her house.

No such luck.

Within seconds, he was knocking on her front door.

Her heart skipped a couple of beats and her head spun.

Trace was at her house. Knew about Joss. Was about to see their son for the first time.

A wave of intense protectiveness swept over her, making her question every move she'd made that had led up to this moment. Making her wonder if she should snatch up her son and run.

Good grief. Where had that thought come from? She was not like her father. She'd never do that.

Only, hadn't she already kept their son away from Trace?

Remorse and guilt flooded her as she opened her front door and saw the pale, almost ill-looking man standing on her porch.

What had she done?

Sorrow lit in Chrissie's eyes, but at the moment Trace didn't care.

She'd called him with some trumped-up story about having had his son.

How was that even possible?

He knew how, but that he could have fathered a son and

not known for years just seemed unfathomable. That she would have kept that from him was unfathomable.

He still wasn't sure he believed her.

And if the truth was that he had fathered her son?

Well, she'd be a wealthy lady because his parents would be thrilled to hand her over whatever she wanted in exchange for her precious offspring.

Not that he'd let them.

Not that he thought Chrissie the gold-digger type anyway.

Then again, maybe he'd been overseas too long.

His head hurt. His neck and shoulder muscles ached with the tension that had struck him from the moment she'd uttered her life-shattering revelation.

He didn't know what he'd do if she'd told the truth. What he'd say. At the moment, he just wanted to get past the woman in the doorway and to the child she was claiming was his.

He'd look at the boy and know, wouldn't he?

Surely a father would look at his child and inherently know "that's mine."

"I asked for fifteen minutes," Chrissie said, crossing her arms across her chest. She'd been telling the truth about just getting out of the shower. Her hair was damp, her skin still had that just-washed glow, and the scent of her shampoo permeated his senses despite his state of mind.

Yeah, she'd asked for fifteen minutes, but he'd not been able to wait. Funny, but for four years he hadn't known the kid existed, and now that he did he hadn't been able to delay another ten minutes.

She shouldn't have asked him to. Not after having already made him wait so long to see what she claimed belonged to him.

"Where is he?"

"Asleep. I told you—"

"I want to see him." He was being blunt, was being rude, even, with his brusqueness, but if Chrissie had given birth to his son and not told him, then he hated to consider the ramifications.

She didn't move out of the doorway, just stared at him with a mixture of fear, uncertainty, and protectiveness.

"What are you planning to do?"

Good question and not one he knew the answer to. Just that he needed to see the child and he hadn't been able to wait.

"I won't let you hurt him, Trace."

Trace clenched his fingers into his palms. "Seriously? You think I drove all this way to hurt a kid? Just what kind of opinion do you have of me, Chrissie?"

Remorse softened her expression a little.

"The kind that meant you kept my son from me for four years?"

His voice rose in pitch and she shushed him, making his insides bristle further.

"Please don't wake him. He doesn't know about you. He wouldn't understand if he woke and you were here."

"He normally sleeps through when you have male company?" Yeah, he was being a sarcastic jerk, but he wasn't in a forgiving mood.

"Not that it's any of your business, but I don't have male company."

"Right."

She held her stance. "The only guy in my life is Joss and he's three years old and asleep in his bed. There's not been anyone else, not since you."

His gaze narrowed. "Since four years ago?"

"If you mean, have I gone on dates, then yes, Trace, I have gone on a few. If you mean, have I had sex with anyone besides you in the past four years, then the answer is no, I haven't."

He found that difficult to believe. She was a sensual woman, so responsive and passionate. But he didn't want to think about that, or whether or not she'd been with anyone other than him. At the moment, his priorities lay elsewhere.

"Your sleeping habits over the past four years really aren't my business." Yet the thought that she'd not been with anyone since him did please him, as crazy as that was. Then again, at the moment, everything, every thought, felt crazy. "Where is his room?"

Chrissie's lower lip disappeared between her teeth at his question. She stepped aside, allowing him to enter the house.

"I'll show you."

Taking note of the photos on the walls of a healthy, blond-haired little boy who had no issues smiling for a camera, Trace followed Chrissie to the short hallway and into a room lit only by a superhero nightlight.

A curled-up little body lay in a plastic car bed with a mattress in the center. The bed sat low to the floor and Trace knelt beside it, focusing through the low light on the tow-headed child.

The sleeping boy faced where Trace knelt and he could make out his features. Trace sensed Chrissie beside him, could sense her nervousness, but didn't look her way. What did she think he was going to do? Grab the kid and run?

Long lashes fanned across the boy's cheeks and he had a full lower lip that made him think of Chrissie's pouty mouth.

Was the boy his?

Trace's blood felt like acid as it moved through him. Shouldn't he know? Shouldn't he be able to immediately tell?

He reached out to touch him and Chrissie moved to stop him. He cut his gaze toward her and his look must have said everything, because she backed away without a word.

Trace touched Joss.

His son?

Hadn't he known when he'd seen the eyes staring back at him from the photos on Chrissie's walls?

Hard emotions slammed into him.

He was touching his son.

Joss was his.

He gently cupped the boy's head in his palm in a caress and trembled at the enormity of the moment.

This was his son. He was touching a living, breathing human child he'd helped make.

Next to him, Chrissie made a noise and he realized she was crying. Louder than she should be if they were not to wake the boy. He gave her a look that said to stop, but that only made things worse as she broke into a full-out sob.

The little boy shifted in his sleep, moving against Trace's hand.

With one last stroke of his fingertips across the soft blond hair, Trace stood, grabbed Chrissie's wrist, and pulled her from the room.

"Were you trying to wake him?" he accused when they got back to the living room.

She shook her head.

"If he'd awakened and I was there with you crying it would have traumatized him. Is that what you were hoping for? To make him not trust me from the beginning?"

"No," she denied, looking horrified at his accusation. "Of course not. How could you think that?"

"How could I think otherwise? I have a son who doesn't know me from a stranger because you kept him from me."

She winced at his accusation. "I didn't know where you were."

"Did you look?"

Guilt written all over her face, she closed her eyes. "No."

"Then don't tell me you didn't know where I was. I

wouldn't have been that difficult to track down. You knew I lived in Atlanta…that I'd been at the CCPO event. All you had to do was ask Agnes and she'd have gotten word to me."

"I can't change the past, Trace. I thought you wouldn't want to know."

"Why would you think that?"

"You're the one who told me you didn't want a relationship, didn't want children, *ever*. I was a weekend fling. Someone you'd had a good time with and nothing more. We weren't dating, or an item, or involved in any way. I wasn't supposed to get pregnant."

She was right.

"Did you get pregnant on purpose?"

Her chin jutted forward. "You know I didn't."

"Why did you suddenly decide to tell me?"

"It wasn't suddenly." She wiped at the tears still running down her cheeks. "I'd been thinking about it since first seeing you in the medical tent again."

Right. That was why she'd not bothered to tell him while they'd been in Atlanta.

"I'm staying here," he announced, surprising both him and her with his decision.

Her eyes were wide. "Here as in my house?"

He nodded.

"I don't think—"

"That's right. You don't think. Nor do you get to have a say in this. You have kept my son from me for four years."

She collapsed onto the sofa as if her legs would no longer hold her. Her head drooped low, the tears starting again full force.

"I am going to get to know my son the best I can in what time I have left before I leave and you're going to help me do it so it causes him as little stress as possible."

"How am I supposed to do that?" she asked, looking up at him through her red-rimmed eyes.

"By making me a welcomed houseguest, by being friendly to me so he doesn't pick up on any negative feelings, by telling him the truth."

"You want me to tell him that you're his father?" She sounded horrified.

"You think it better to lie to him and tell him I'm some random guy you've decided to let move in?"

"There's not room in my house for you, Trace."

He glanced around the living room. "This is a mansion compared to some of the hellholes where I've worked over the past four years. I'll be fine."

Not that he thought for one second she was concerned about his comfort. She didn't want him there. Too bad. He wanted every second possible with his son, to get to know the boy and for his son to get to know him. He'd figure the rest out later. For now that was the only game plan he had.

"But—"

"I'm staying and we're not lying about who I am."

"But—" she repeated.

"You'll tell him tomorrow when he wakes up that I am his father."

"But—"

"I don't have time for games, Chrissie. I'll be leaving for Africa soon. In a couple of weeks."

"Oh."

"Yeah, oh. He'll stay with me while you go to work." Which just occurred to him. "Do you work tomorrow?"

Staying with the boy on day one would be awkward, but he'd figure it out.

"No, I'm off for the next four days."

"That's good. That will give him time to get used to me before he stays with me." And then Trace would have to leave soon thereafter. How long would it be before he'd be back in the States? Six months? A year? Maybe longer?

"He's not staying alone with you."

"He is." Trace cut his gaze to Chrissie's watery-eyed one. Under other circumstances he could feel badly for her, would have wanted to comfort her.

These weren't other circumstances.

CHAPTER ELEVEN

SEEING TRACE'S PAIN and frustration hurt.

She couldn't argue with him. Not when in many ways he was right.

She had kept their son away from him, something that no matter how she tried to make up for, she'd never be able to. In some ways she was no better than her father.

She could remind him that he'd said he didn't want children, but she'd never presented him with the option of wanting Joss.

"Fine. Stay here." She gestured to the sofa. "I'll grab a pillow and a blanket."

He shook his head. "I don't need them. You do."

Was he kidding? Her brow lifted. "I'm sleeping on the sofa?"

He nodded. "If Joss wakes up in the middle of the night, it might scare him to find a strange man on the sofa. Which means I can't stay on the sofa. Unless you've got another bedroom where you can put me, I'm taking your room where I can lock the door to prevent him from finding me unexpectedly."

He was putting her on the sofa and taking her bed.

"I haven't changed my sheets this week."

He didn't look impressed. "I've survived worse than dirty sheets."

She'd done this. She'd set this wheel into motion. No,

she hadn't really expected him to show up at her house and announce he was staying, but it wasn't as if she'd expected to tell him they'd had a child and him to say, *That's nice* and never to hear from him again.

Or maybe she had.

Maybe she'd simply been appeasing her conscience and had hoped he'd stay away so she could go on with the way things had been before seeing him again.

"What am I supposed to tell my mother?"

For the briefest of moments, she thought she'd reached him. But after that flash of indecision, his expression steeled again.

"The truth."

The truth?

Her mother had never pushed too hard for her to spill the details of how she'd ended up pregnant. She'd always been a good daughter, had rarely bucked her mother's wishes. She had probably guessed that her daughter had gotten pregnant while at the CCPO event four years ago. When she'd burst into tears when asked about Joss's father, her mother had accepted her answer that he was no longer in the picture and getting help from him wasn't an option. She'd never asked since.

How would she react to him now living in her house? To his just showing up out of the blue?

Well, maybe, not so out of the blue. Her family knew she'd been in Atlanta for CCPO again a week ago.

Heaviness tugged at her shoulders.

"How long do you plan to stay?"

He shrugged. "Until I have to leave."

How would that affect Joss? For Trace to come waltzing in, play the role of daddy for a few weeks, then disappear again?

"You can't just come into Joss's life, then walk away as if he doesn't exist. He wouldn't understand that."

He crossed his arms and stared at her as if she were a pesky fly. "Not once have I said anything about walking away from my son as if he doesn't exist."

She crossed her arms, too, and did her best to stare him down the way he was her. And not to react to his *my son* because those words scared her a little. He hadn't said "our son."

She swallowed the lump forming in her throat. "You plan to stay in Chattanooga?"

Because she wouldn't acknowledge that he might mean something other than his staying here.

She wouldn't let him take Joss to Africa. She wasn't sure she could stop him forever, but for the moment she was Joss's legal guardian and had final say.

"You know that isn't the case. I'm booked on a flight a couple of weeks from now. In the meantime, I'm going to get to know my son. He's going to get to know me and you are going to facilitate that so it goes as smoothly as possible given the unfortunate circumstances."

His tone brooked no argument, nor did his retreating back as he stepped outside.

Heart racing, she ran to the front door, watched him walk around to the front seat of an expensive-looking SUV. He grabbed an overnight bag from the front floorboard, then headed back her way.

"Miss me?" he quipped, looking way more relaxed and comfortable than he should considering he was invading her home as an unwanted houseguest and as a man who had just met his son for the first time a few minutes ago.

"You wish," she countered, glaring at him.

Not acknowledging her quip, he stepped around her, headed toward the hallway, then paused. "You need anything out of here before I crash?"

He was really going to sleep in her room, in her bed,

and let her take the sofa? Sure, his reasons made sense, but still…

"Yes." She pushed past him and went into her room, grabbed one of the pillows off her full-sized bed, then glanced around the room. The room was about twelve by twelve and dominated by the queen-sized bed. There was a stack of books on her night stand, a mix of hers and Joss's. Some clean clothes were draped over a wicker chair that had been her grandmother's, waiting on her to hang them in her closet. At least she'd semi-made her bed that morning.

Then again, what did it matter? She hadn't invited him. He wasn't her guest. If her house was a total wreck, tough.

On that note, she turned, expecting to see him standing behind her, but he wasn't. He'd stopped by Joss's room, probably to stare at their son.

She took a deep breath, pulled a blanket out of a plastic bin from under her bed.

This time when she turned to leave her room, seeing Trace standing in her bedroom doorway caused her heart to stop.

Or pretty darn close.

Who would have thought Trace would be in her house, standing in her bedroom doorway?

Never in her wildest dreams had she thought that would ever happen.

Because for all her fear over his meeting Joss, for all her nervousness at what the future held, the man was breathtaking.

Which didn't sit well because she needed all her wits about her, not to get distracted by his soulful eyes, broad shoulders, and overflowing charisma. Not that he'd shown much charm since arriving at her house.

Determined to protect her heart, she narrowed her gaze at him. "The bathroom is down the hallway. Stay out of my drawers."

He laughed and it was a dry, harsh sound. "No worries, Chrissie."

She wasn't sure they were talking about the same drawers, but what did it matter? He'd made his point loud and clear.

He was there because of their son. Not her.

Trace had slept very little and was wide awake as the first streams of morning light came through Chrissie's unshaded windows.

Part of him felt like a jerk for taking her room. Another truly believed he should be behind locked doors in case Joss woke prior to him and Chrissie. He didn't want to scare the kid.

The kid.

His kid.

He hadn't really questioned Chrissie. Logic said he should get a paternity test. Not to would just be foolish on his part. But when he'd knelt beside the bed staring at the peacefully sleeping boy in the dimly lit room, he'd not been thinking, *What if?* He'd been thinking, *That's mine.*

Because he wanted the boy to be his.

He'd not planned to have children, so how much he wanted Joss to be his didn't make logical sense.

How could he so desperately want what Chrissie had told him to be true?

He believed her.

All night he'd battled between anger, a sense of betrayal, uncertainty, and awe that he'd fathered a child.

Restless, he pushed the sheet back and got up.

Going to the living room, panic hit him when he saw the empty sofa. Had she taken off in the middle of the night?

Turning, he went to Joss's room, pushed open the door and stopped short at what he saw.

Chrissie's small frame was curled on the car bed with

her son's little body pressed up against hers. The little boy's hand rested on his mother's.

Morning light lit the room, and with him lying next to Chrissie it was easy to see his resemblance to his mother.

Same blond hair, same beautiful porcelain skin.

He sat down in a rocking chair, careful to keep the chair from squeaking, and watched the sleeping mother and child.

His child.

His and Chrissie's child.

As angry as he was at her for not telling him about Joss, he couldn't imagine anyone that he'd rather have as a mother of his child. Certainly, Chrissie had haunted him while he'd been overseas.

While she'd been raising their child.

While he'd been lying in a hospital recovering, she'd been here, with their son. And he hadn't known.

Another surge of betrayal burst through him that she hadn't told him. How could she have not told him?

If not before, how could she have driven away a week ago without saying a word? Without telling him that she'd given birth to his son?

Every moment they'd spent together had been a deception.

Every breath, every touch, every look, every smile, every laugh—all had been lies.

Because she'd known he had a son and she hadn't told him.

Which brought him back to why she'd told him yesterday.

He knew very little about her, other than that she'd volunteered at CCPO as a nurse, drove him crazy sexually, and lived in Chattanooga.

From what he'd seen of her home, it wasn't fancy or very big, but was clean and well-cared-for. As he'd told her the night before, he'd lived in worse overseas.

Much worse.

Because Chrissie's home was filled with love.

Whatever her reasons in telling him about Joss, she loved their son.

It oozed from the picture-filled walls.

It oozed from the way Chrissie held him even in sleep.

Not that she was asleep, because his gaze suddenly collided with her green one. She studied him and he returned the favor.

She didn't move, just lay there watching him. Her hair was tousled from sleep and he had an immediate flashback to a week ago when he'd awakened next to her. That morning they'd stared into each other's eyes in a very different way.

There had been no hurt, no anger.

He felt both at the moment. Betrayed.

How could she have kept their son from him?

Even if he could understand her not telling him four years ago, why hadn't she told him a week ago?

How could she have had sex with him, spent that much time with him, all the while knowing what she'd done?

What kind of person did that?

Taking care to be quiet, he got up and left the room.

Mainly because the longer he sat, the more upset he got. He paced across to stare at a photo of a baby Joss with a toothy grin.

He sensed Chrissie behind him before he heard her.

Still, he didn't turn, just stared at the photo.

He'd missed so much. "You should have told me."

"We went through this last night. How was I supposed to know you'd want to know?"

He spun to look at her. She still wore her sweats and baggy T-shirt. Her hair went in several different directions. She was beautiful, but all he could think was how much she'd stolen from him.

"He's my son," he reminded her, liking how the words sounded on his tongue. "Why wouldn't I want to know?"

"Not every man does."

"Yeah, well, I'm not every man."

She raked her fingers through her hair. "No, you aren't."

"What's that supposed to mean?"

She flinched. "Can we not do this today?"

"What?"

"I don't want to argue with you, Trace."

"Yeah, well, you should have thought about that before you kept my son from me."

"You know, Trace, that goes two ways?"

"I didn't keep our son from you."

"No, you didn't, but guess what? You didn't come looking for me, either."

"There's a big difference. I didn't know you were pregnant, Chrissie."

Her chin shot up defiantly. "You didn't ask."

"Seriously?" He rounded on her. "A man is supposed to have to ask a woman to find out that she's pregnant?"

She closed her eyes. "Okay, you're right. That didn't make sense. Not really. I—"

"Not at all," he interrupted. "You should have told me and you know it."

"Mommy?"

Both Trace's and Chrissie's heads spun toward the little boy standing in the doorway. He wore superhero pajamas and his fair hair was a little tousled, but his eyes were what got to Trace. He had inherited the Stevens eyes. He'd noticed it in the photos, but in person Joss's eyes were mirror reflections of his own. Of his father's.

"Hey, baby," Chrissie greeted, going over and scooping him into her arms and kissing the top of his head.

The little boy patted her cheek, staring back at Trace with suspicion through eyes identical to his own.

His knees went weak and he reached out to steady himself. Joss was his.

His son who looked at him and saw a stranger.

A stranger who had been arguing with his mother.

Trace took a deep breath.

Today was going to be difficult because he wanted to take the boy and hug him, to have him hug him back, to have his little hands against his cheek the way he was touching Chrissie.

It wasn't going to happen.

Not without patience.

Trace had learned a lot about patience during his time overseas, but this might be the hardest thing he'd ever done. Plus, he only had limited time before he'd be gone.

A very limited time.

"Joss," Chrissie said in a soft tone. "This is Mommy's friend."

At her introduction, Trace's jaw worked. Had she thought he was kidding when he said she'd tell the truth?

He'd lost enough time with Joss.

He wouldn't lose more, nor would he have his kid thinking he was just one of Mommy's friends.

Chrissie felt Joss's fingers tangle into her hair, while he continued to stare at Trace. The finger tangling was something he frequently did when overly tired or nervous.

She'd never had any non-related man to their house, so how tightly her son's legs dug into her waist didn't surprise her. He definitely had his reservations about waking up to her arguing with a stranger.

A stranger who desperately didn't want to be a stranger.

Trace's restraint showed in every sinew of his body, which probably didn't reassure Joss.

Her stomach twisted much tighter than Joss's fingers in her hair.

Trace wanted her to tell Joss that he was his father.

She had to tell him, but how did one tell a child that he was looking at a father he didn't know he had?

"Chrissie." Trace stressed her name.

She walked over closer to Trace, causing Joss to cling tighter. No doubt her own nerves were affecting his comfort level, too, but there was nothing she could do about that. No way were her nerves going to settle.

"Joss…" she did her best to keep her voice calm, reassuring, but her insides felt completely the opposite "…Trace is a very special person who is going to stay with us for a while. Can you say hello?"

Her son made a grunting sound and turned his head away from Trace, burying his face against her chest.

Trace's expression was taut, his normally tan skin pale, his eyes watery and desperate for recognition.

Her heart ached with misery for him. She couldn't imagine seeing her child for the first time and him rejecting her when all she wanted to do was love him.

The look in Trace's eyes said he did want to love their son and how she handled the next few minutes would make a major impact on how Joss responded to Trace.

"Joss, do you remember our stories about daddies?" She leaned back, trying to maneuver Joss to where she could see his face, but he burrowed down farther against her chest. "Well, Trace is your daddy. Isn't that wonderful?"

That got Joss's attention and he mumbled something against her chest that she couldn't make out.

"What was that, baby?"

But whatever Joss had said was lost and he apparently wasn't repeating. Just as well because she thought he had said he didn't want a daddy.

She glanced up at Trace and gave a weak smile, then tried again. "Joss, do you think you could show Trace…

um…your daddy your trains? He really likes trains and I bet he'd love to see yours."

"You have trains?" Trace tried, his voice overly eager. "Your mom is right. I love trains."

"Do you like Thomas?" Joss mumbled, still not looking up from his hunkered-against-her position.

Trace looked at her for help.

"Joss, if you'll go show Trace…um…your daddy, your trains, I'll cook us some breakfast. I can make those smiley-face pancakes you like." She tried to keep her voice normal, level, not as if she'd just introduced her son to his father.

But Joss wasn't having any of it.

Trains weren't going to distract him from the fact that there was a strange man in their house and his mommy was full of over-the-top tension.

"Do your trains make noise?" Trace asked, not giving up. "Can you tell your daddy what your trains say?"

With a shy glance toward Trace, then a return to burying his face into her neck, Joss shook his head. He wasn't an overly shy child, typically, but no doubt the surprise of an unexpected houseguest and the fact they'd been arguing hadn't set the right tone. Trace should have gotten a hotel, let her talk to Joss and ease him into the idea of having a daddy.

Or maybe she should have just told Joss about his dad from the beginning. Or vice versa.

"Can I show him your trains?" she asked, hoping to help break the ice, but Joss shook his head.

"Pancakes."

"Okay," she agreed with her son's one-word response, then glanced at Trace. "Trace, why don't you help me cook breakfast? Joss can help, too. He's a really great helper."

CHAPTER TWELVE

CHRISSIE WASN'T SURE what was running through Joss's head, but he'd not let her out of his sight all day. He didn't have the opportunity to meet many strangers, but she'd not realized quite how clingy he was. Maybe it was that he'd met Trace in such an unusual way within their home and their raised voices had possibly awakened him. Regardless, her son had been superclingy and had wanted to be held more than he had since he'd first learned to walk.

Not that she didn't normally love the opportunity to hold her usually energetic three-year-old fireball, but Joss's clinginess was over exaggerated and breaking her heart for Trace.

They'd stayed in, played trains, watched one of Joss's favorite cartoon movies, and then gone for a walk around her neighborhood, while pushing him in his stroller. She'd made them grilled cheese sandwiches and cut fresh fruit for their lunch. To her surprise Trace had cleaned the kitchen while she'd colored with Joss. When he'd joined them, Joss had given him a suspicious look, but had shared a crayon and one of his books.

She'd tried to sneak away to start a load of laundry, a never-ending job, but Joss followed her into the tiny room off the kitchen where the washer and dryer were located and stayed with her until she'd finished.

She'd cooked dinner, given Joss a bath, read a half-dozen stories, and eventually he'd gone to sleep.

Trace had been right there all day, but Joss hadn't warmed to him despite his great efforts.

It bothered Chrissie a great deal.

Partly because Joss had never responded to anyone in such a guarded way. But mostly, because she knew her son treating his father as a stranger was her fault.

Because she hadn't included him in Joss's life.

She could make a thousand excuses, some of them valid, some of them less so. No excuse changed the truth. It was her fault Joss didn't know and love Trace.

She couldn't make her son warm up to his father, but she could do her best to make sure he didn't pick up on bad vibes from her.

Easier said than done.

She'd fought vibes all day.

Nervous vibes.

Scared-about-her-future vibes.

Attracted-to-a-man-she-was-pretty-sure-hated-her vibes.

How could he not?

She couldn't blame him. Wouldn't she hate someone who had kept such a precious miracle from her?

But how could she have known Trace would want to know Joss?

Duh. That one was easy. She could have known if she'd told him, given him the opportunity to make the choice of whether or not he wanted to be a part of their son's life.

She hadn't.

"I don't know how you get anything done," Trace said when they got back into the living room after Joss was settled in.

"Some days are easier than others," she admitted.

"I'm sorry he was standoffish. He'll get used to you and warm up."

"I know," Trace said, but the emotion in his voice gave truth to how affected he'd been. "It's not as if I expected him to start calling me Daddy today."

But the crackle in his voice said he had hoped for it.

What had she done? she wondered, her heart doing a little crackling of its own. How could she ever make up for depriving Trace of the first years of their son's life?

"I'm going to go for a run," he announced.

Surprised by his sudden announcement and disappearance out of her front door, Chrissie stared at the now empty room with a heavy heart.

A heavy heart because she was confused by the emotions battling for dominance within her. Especially the great sense of loss she felt that Trace was no longer in her home.

She did a few of the chores she usually did on her days off work, then showered. When a sweaty Trace came back into the house, she was sitting on the sofa, feet tucked beneath her, reading a book.

That she felt relieved he'd returned made no sense. Of course he'd returned. His SUV was parked in her driveway. Had she thought he'd keep running all the way to Atlanta?

"You okay if I shower now?" His gaze didn't quite meet hers.

"That's fine."

He paused before heading out of the living room. "I'll grab my bag out of your bedroom and take the sofa tonight."

More guilt hit her.

"I don't mind sleeping with Joss again," she offered.

He shook his head. "Nah, I think it would be best if you get back to your normal routine as much as possible."

Maybe he was right.

He turned to go and the need to say something more burned inside her.

"I'm sorry, Trace."

If not for the slightest pause in his step she'd have thought he didn't hear her. But his steps had paused, then resumed without his acknowledging her apology.

Chrissie let out a long sigh.

What a mess she'd made.

Three days had passed since Trace's arrival and Chrissie would return to work the following morning. They'd decided to go to the aquarium on her last day off before she pulled another five twelve-hour shifts in a row.

Although Trace had been with them almost non-stop over the past three days, Joss hadn't warmed to him.

Typically, Joss was a people person and a natural-born charmer, like his father, but with Trace he was standoffish and almost cruel in how he refused to interact.

For the most part, Trace remained patient and just kept trying, but his frustration was palpable.

Maybe that was what Joss sensed that kept him from interacting with or freely smiling at Trace.

"I'm excited to see the penguins, Joss," Trace said as he attempted to get Joss out of his car seat. To no avail. Joss stubbornly insisted upon Chrissie unbuckling him and holding his hand as he jumped from the car onto the hot pavement.

Once on the pavement, he ignored Trace's outstretched hand and kept a death grip on Chrissie's.

Trace's look her way was full of pure disgust.

This was her fault, his eyes said. She'd done this.

Guilt filled her. She deserved his scorn.

Then again, who would have thought Joss would react so negatively? Because her son's reaction to his father was beyond anything she could have imagined from her sweet little boy.

Joss intentionally tried to exclude Trace more often than

not. Just as he was currently doing, ignoring Trace and tugging on her hand.

"Can I get in the water?"

Ahead of them there was a small artsy-looking fountain just below a warped rainbow-shaped bridge walkway where several children were splashing.

"Maybe after we see the penguins," she told him with a gentle tone. "Your daddy is excited to see them. Do you think he'll like the manta rays, too?"

Joss loved the aquarium and especially the exhibit where visitors could reach into the water and "pet" manta rays that passed by. She'd bought them an annual pass earlier in the year and, though they'd been several times, his fascination with the aquatic life had never waned.

Until today.

"I don't want to see the manta rays." Joss's lower lip hung low. "I want to play in the water."

Good grief. Trace probably thought Joss was a spoiled brat. Hopefully he'd take into account that the child had just had his entire world turned upside down with meeting his father.

Still, she didn't want to encourage his behavior.

"After we go inside to show your daddy the penguins," she repeated with what she hoped was the right combination of gentleness and sternness. "If you be good."

Joss's gaze, so similar to Trace's, took on a steely stubbornness. "He can go by himself. We don't want him here."

Trace winced.

Chrissie let out a frustrated sigh. "Of course we want your daddy here. We want to show him the penguins and let him pet the manta rays."

Joss gave her a look that said she could verbalize whatever she wanted, but he wasn't buying it.

Trace didn't look as if he was either.

Then again, as much as Trace was trying, maybe he was

trying too hard, and scowling too much when he failed. Maybe that was why Joss wouldn't relax.

Or maybe her smart little three-year-old was still picking up on his mother's nervousness.

Trace bought his ticket, then they waited in line to enter the aquarium. Within a few minutes they were riding the long escalator up to the top.

"Do you think the otters will be playing today?" she asked Joss, hoping to distract him out of his sour mood.

The little boy's eyes lit with interest, but then he seemed to recall that he wasn't happy with his mother or life in general.

Frustrated with Joss's behavior but afraid she'd just make things worse by scolding him, plus knowing it couldn't be easy on him to have unexpectedly had Trace move in with them three days ago, Chrissie turned to Trace. She'd caused this tension. It was up to her to break the ice.

"These cute little otters live at the top of the aquarium. Sometimes when we visit, they are sleeping and sometimes they are playing." She injected as much perkiness as she could muster. "We like when they are playing, don't we, Joss?"

Joss didn't answer.

Chrissie kept right on talking as if all were wonderful. Not that she felt wonderful. Not that Trace looked as if he was having a good time. Certainly, Joss seemed determined not to enjoy himself.

Fine. She could do this. She'd dealt with worse situations. At least, she thought she had, even if she couldn't think of any.

The otters were playing and that went a long way to lightening Joss's mood. When one swam near the thick glass wall that allowed seeing his underwater antics, Joss's eyes grew big.

"Look," he exclaimed, pointing excitedly.

"I think he likes you," Chrissie praised when the otter seemed to be checking Joss out as much as the little boy was checking out him.

"He probably recognizes me from when I came before."

"Maybe so." She turned to Trace. "Cute, huh?"

His gaze met hers and something flickered that put an entirely different nervous energy in her belly.

"Adorable," he said, bending to Joss's level to eye the otter next to their son.

After watching the otters for a while longer, they slowly made their way through the different exhibits.

They hung out in the butterfly area for a while. A large monarch landed on Trace's finger.

"Look," Trace breathed in an excited whisper, as if he was afraid if he made too much noise the butterfly would take flight.

"It's beautiful," Chrissie said.

The butterfly seemed to have taken up residence on Trace's finger, not minding one bit when Trace knelt and offered the butterfly to Joss.

The boy regarded the butterfly with longing. "Do you think he'll fly off if I hold him?"

"Only one way to find out." Trace gently transferred the butterfly to Joss's stretched-out finger.

Chrissie held her breath during the transfer, praying the butterfly cooperated, and amazingly it did, resting on Joss's finger while he did his best to keep his hand still.

A proud Joss looked up at her and grinned. "Take my picture."

Heart melting, Chrissie got out her cell phone and snapped a couple of shots of Joss holding the butterfly. Trace stood to the side watching.

"Step in behind Joss so I can get your picture with him and the butterfly," she suggested, elated when Trace complied. A little dazed, too, at the thought she was about to take a photo of her son with his father.

With shaky hands, she snapped several pictures of a smiling Joss holding a butterfly and a smiling Trace standing behind him with his hand on Joss's shoulder. No matter what happened, she'd treasure the photos and believed someday Joss would, too.

Sharing his butterfly must have won Trace more than a few brownie points because Joss lost his scowl for the rest of the morning. He still wouldn't hold Trace's hand but at least he was showing some of his normal enthusiasm for the trip and had become talkative, telling Trace about the different exhibits.

"I don't see the alligator," Trace said, scratching his head and pretending not to see the alligator that was beneath the water in a river exhibit.

"Right there." Joss pointed against the glass in the direction the alligator rested.

Trace bent down to Joss's level. "Where?"

"Right there." Joss tapped the thick clear wall separating the viewing area from the exhibit. "You have to see him. He's huge."

"Now I see him. Thank you," he told the little boy as he looked in the right direction. "I'd hate to have missed seeing him."

"He has big teeth," Joss pointed out, even though you couldn't see much as the alligator's mouth was closed.

"The better to eat me with," Trace teased, chomping his teeth.

"Trace," Savannah laughed.

"What? I'm just pointing that out. Just in case."

"Just in case what?"

His expression suggested that maybe he thought she might push him in—not that she could. The glass wall was too high for that.

Not that she'd thought of doing such a thing, anyway.

At least not now that both of her guys were finally smiling.

They continued their trek through the aquarium, going down one floor at a time, petted the manta rays, which Joss loved, then finished up their tour at the souvenir shop.

"Can I have a toy, Mommy, please?"

"Not today, Joss. We bought the stuffed penguin the last time we were here and I told you we wouldn't get anything the next time we came."

"But I need a manta ray."

Yeah, her sweet little angel was on a roll.

"Not today."

"Why not?"

The question had come from Trace and had both Chrissie and Joss looking his way.

Chrissie didn't want to argue with him, especially not in front of Joss. She forced a smile. "Because Joss toy the last time he came and we don't get ys every time. He knows that."

She didn't want Joss to grow up spoiled and unappreciative of life's blessings. She tried to find a balance and for the most part felt she succeeded. Her son knew they didn't get new souvenirs at every visit.

Trace bent to Joss's level. "If you want the manta ray, I'll buy it for you. An otter, too, if you want it."

Joss's eyes immediately went to hers. If she'd already told him no on something, she didn't allow others to then do it for him. At three, he already knew this, although he wasn't beyond trying on occasion with his grandmother.

Trying to choose her words carefully, Chrissie started to explain to Trace that she'd already said no and that was the end of it. Because she had final say. Because she was the parent.

But so was Trace.

That was when the full ramifications of Trace being in their lives hit her.

She no longer had final say over decisions where Joss was concerned. She no longer got to decide what was good for him and what was bad for him and how much was just right. At least, not by herself she didn't get to decide those things.

If he wanted to buy Joss the entire store, he had just as much right to do that as she had to say no.

What if she and Trace fundamentally disagreed on even the most basic of things when it came to child rearing?

What if they never agreed and one always said no and the other always said yes? What if Joss grew to hate her because she was the parent who tried to create boundaries and Trace showered him with gifts?

What if Joss treated her the way he treated Trace?

Her skin began to shrink around her body, squeezing her insides to where she felt as if she were about to cave in on herself. To where every breath was a struggle.

Her gaze met Trace's and she tried to speak, but nothing came out. Nothing.

Panic rising in her throat, she glanced around the shop, her mind racing, her feet itching, her knees weak.

"No—just no." With that, she grabbed Joss's hand and walked over to a shark book display and fought the paralysis taking hold of her body.

Because she wanted to run, with Joss, and never turn back.

But she wasn't like her father. No matter how strong that urge inside her was, she knew she wasn't.

Not quite understanding what had just happened, Trace watched Chrissie practically freeze next to a book display.

His gaze dropped down to where Chrissie clinched Joss's little hand in a death grip.

Obviously confused, Joss kept turning to look at him expectantly, waiting for him to respond.

Because he was the adult here. Not that he had any clue what had just happened.

He wanted to give Joss things, for Joss to have something physical that he'd given him. A stuffed manta ray was as good a place to start as any.

"I'll get the manta ray and meet you two out front," he offered.

"Fine," Chrissie agreed, keeping her back to him.

Too bad, because he'd really like to see what was in those expressive eyes of hers right now.

Joss was looking at him though. And not in a good way. His little face squished up, his eyes watered, then he shook his head. "I don't need a manta ray."

His tone sounded almost identical to what Chrissie's had earlier, only with a big heap of sadness.

Good grief. More was going on here than whether or not a stuffed toy was going to be bought. Way more. Not that Trace understood what was running through Chrissie's head, but something sure was.

"I'd like to buy you one, but if you want to wait until next time, we can."

The tears welling in his eyes threatened to spill down his cheeks. "Can we go home?"

All kinds of heartstrings were pulling in dozens of directions as he looked into his son's sorrowful eyes.

"Yes, we can."

Only Joss had to go to the bathroom. When Chrissie started to take him into the women's room, which was what he guessed she usually did rather than let Joss go into a bathroom alone, Trace had to speak up.

"I'll take him with me into the men's room."

Fear lit her eyes. Real, no-holds-barred fear. Which confused Trace every bit as much as her behavior over his buying the kid a stuffed manta ray.

"It's really no bother," she protested. "It's what we usually do."

"Chrissie, it's ridiculous for him to go into the ladies' room when I'm right here and can take him to the men's room."

"But…"

He watched the very real struggle on her face, watched the physical effort she had to exert for her to let go of the boy's hand.

"Okay. I'll be waiting." She glanced around, through the glass. "There. On that bench. I'll be waiting right there. Don't take too long. Please."

Trace really wanted to question her on the stress in her voice. It was only a trip to the bathroom. Was it a trust thing? Did she think he wouldn't keep an eye on their son? That he'd scold him if he had an accident? That he'd forget to make him wash his hands? What?

Although Chrissie's saying no had robbed him of the chance of giving his son a present, Joss's need for the bathroom had given him the gift of holding Joss's hand without the boy pulling away, whether that was out of courtesy or out of knowledge that they were in a public place and he needed to be holding an adult's hand. Either way, Trace was grateful for the tiny hand clasped inside his.

Trace stayed right with Joss, talked to him, and was proud of the way the three-year-old, who was in such a hurry to get back to his mother, managed himself in the bathroom, including automatically wanting to wash his hands afterward. Chrissie had taught their son well.

When they exited the bathroom, Joss spotted Chrissie immediately, even prior to Trace doing so.

"There she is!" he called, sounding relieved she was

there. Had he thought she was leaving them despite her saying she'd be waiting?

Then again, the relief on Chrissie's face at spotting them had Trace pausing. What the…?

Joss pulled on Trace's hand, wanting to dash toward where Chrissie sat on a bench close to where the water was that Joss had wanted to get into earlier.

"Slow down, son," Trace told him, falling back into step with his son. "We're headed that way."

But Joss kept on tugging, setting as fast a pace as possible to his mother.

When they joined her, Chrissie looked up, her gaze searching them both, as if looking for battle scars.

She glanced toward the water. "Do you still want to play in the water?"

But rather than answer immediately, Joss studied her face, trying to gauge her expression on what she wanted him to say, as if he wasn't quite sure how to take her odd behavior in the aquarium shop.

Which irked Trace. Was she emotionally manipulating their son because he'd spoken up to buy the boy something she'd said no to? Did the fact Joss had lightened up to him a little bother her and she wanted to add the tension back?

He hadn't thought she was trying to prevent Joss from warming to him, but maybe she was.

"I'd like to play in the water," Chrissie added, smiling at her son, albeit a little weakly. "And I bet your daddy would like to play in the water, too."

Okay, so maybe he was being paranoid. Or letting his frustration over her having rushed out of the souvenir shop mess with his head. Or maybe everything these days was messing with his head.

Joss and his reluctance to have much to do with him. Chrissie and his mixed-up feelings for her. Physically, he wanted her and ached for her. Emotionally, he'd never felt more betrayed.

Joss glanced up at Trace with big, uncertain eyes. "Would you?"

Oh, heaven of heavens.

"I would."

More than anything in the world he'd like to play in the water with this little boy.

And his mother.

Chrissie left the bench and went to the pool of water. She sat on the edge, obviously not caring that her shorts were likely to have damp spots when she stood. She slipped her sandals off and put her feet into the water.

"That's cold," she said, wrapping her arms around her chest and pretending to shiver despite the hot sun.

Relaxing, Joss laughed and joined her, quickly stripping off his own shoes.

"Brr…" he said as he stepped into the water and wrapped his little arms around himself. "It is cold."

"Unless you're a penguin," Chrissie added, sending a tiny splash her son's way. "And then it's just right."

"I'm a penguin," Joss said, a big smile on his face, as if all was perfect in his world and always had been. "A big ole penguin looking for a fish to eat."

He made a chomping motion.

Finally relaxing, too, Chrissie laughed.

Trace watched in amazement at how quickly Joss had gone from pouty to remorseful to carefree as he pranced around in the water that came up to the edge of his shorts. Each exaggerated step he took splashed water all around him, but not nearly so much as when he smacked the water with his little hands and burst into giggles.

"Daddy," Chrissie called, sending a spray of water in Trace's direction. "You afraid this penguin is going to mistake you for a big juicy fish?"

Joss made a chomping noise toward Trace, seeming okay that Chrissie had included him in their fun.

"Nah, we penguins can tell other penguins apart from big juicy fish quite easily." He kicked off his shoes, stepped into the water, and made a chomping noise that was a decent imitation of the sounds Joss was making.

"Mommy is a big juicy fish," Joss declared, heading her way, and giggling when Trace did the same. "We're going to get you, fishy-fishy."

"Are you a hungry penguin?" she teased when Trace got close.

"Very hungry." He made another chomping sound and Joss squealed, half in delight and half in possible concern.

"Don't really eat her. She's my mommy."

"Good point," Trace agreed, his eyes still locked with Chrissie's, trying to read what had triggered her mood change.

If it hadn't been an intentional attempt to keep emotional distance between him and Joss, and he had to admit to himself that, up to that point, she'd gone above and beyond in trying to get Joss to warm to him, then what?

Whatever it had been, she seemed determined to keep a smile on her face now.

Or on Joss's at any rate, because their son burst into excited squeals when Chrissie splashed Trace with water again.

"That does it. You're mine, fishy-fishy," he warned, calling her by the same name as Joss had used.

"Nope, she's mine," Joss corrected, splashing over to where Chrissie was and pretending to gobble her up. "Mmm... She tastes good."

At which Trace's mind took off in a completely non-innocent way as his gaze met hers.

"Yeah, she does."

Chrissie's eyes darkened. His gut tightened.

Without a doubt, he knew he should have kept that thought to himself because the last thing he needed was to complicate things further by becoming involved physically with Chrissie again.

CHAPTER THIRTEEN

"TODAY WAS A better day," Chrissie mused that evening as she and Trace slipped out of Joss's bedroom.

They'd bathed him, read to him, and put him to bed quite some time ago. Joss had been a bit wound up and it had taken a good thirty minutes to get him settled. She'd tried to let Trace read to him, but Joss had insisted she read his stories. Even so, Joss hadn't been opposed to Trace being in the room, listening to the stories. Instead of the resentment from the previous nights, he'd instead cast his gaze at his father during the "good' parts, as if gauging Trace's reaction.

Eventually he'd dozed off to sleep.

Trace didn't respond to her comment until they were in the living room. His question felt more like an attack.

"Why didn't you let him have a manta ray?"

"What?" she asked, sitting on the far end of the sofa. His question caught her off guard. Mainly, because the rest of their day had been fairly good, considering. Joss hadn't been so standoffish and Chrissie had managed not to break down at the thought that Trace had just as much say in the raising of their son as she did, that he had just as much right to their son as she did.

Even now the thought just felt wrong.

"You heard me," Trace pointed out, taking the other end of the sofa. "What was the big deal about him getting a stuffed animal? He should be able to have a keepsake from the first time he went to the aquarium with me."

When he put it that way…

"Sorry." She really was. About so many things. Like her irrational fear that Trace might have taken off with Joss when she'd left them alone. "I wasn't thinking about it being the first time he went with you when I said no. I don't want him spoiled and had told him the last time we were there that if he got something that day, that he wouldn't be able to the next time he came."

Trace crossed his arms and stared at her from the other end of the sofa. His scowl didn't relent. "Okay, so you were going for consistency in your parenting. I understand that. But maybe you'd like to explain what was such a big deal about me taking him to the bathroom?"

"No, I wouldn't like to explain that." Because how petty did it sound that she'd panicked at the thought that she no longer had final say over her son, but now shared that responsibility with Trace? That she'd been afraid he might take off with their son if she left them alone? Trace had given her no reason to think he'd do that, so pretty petty.

The deepening furrow of his brows warned he wasn't going to let her answer ride.

A damn burst inside her and emotions came gushing forward full-force.

"You're not the only one dealing with a lot of new, mixed emotions, you know," she blurted out, surprising both her and Trace with her intensity. "I wasn't expecting you to come here and demand to stay at my house and interrupt our lives."

His brow lifted. "You thought I'd stay away after your phone call?"

"I didn't know what to think. You were the one who said you didn't want children. Four years ago and less than two weeks ago. Plus, you're leaving the country again soon. When I called I thought you might already have gone."

"And yet you called."

He made it sound like a dirty thing that she had done. Did he wish he could go back to not knowing Joss existed?

"You don't have to be here. Just go back to Atlanta or wherever it is you'd rather be. There's nothing Joss and I need from you."

"No, you've done a really good job convincing my son that he doesn't need a father."

"Of course I have. I want him to grow up happy and healthy and if he bemoaned the fact that he didn't have a father it might affect his mental and emotional health." Didn't she know firsthand how growing up without a father felt? "I'd never knowingly let that happen."

"But you would have allowed him to grow up without a father had our paths not crossed again at CCPO?"

"Probably," she admitted, hating that it was true, but acknowledging it all the same. "I'd convinced myself I was doing you a favor in not telling you."

"Because?"

"Because I thought you were living the high life in Atlanta…that you didn't want to be tied down by a relationship and kids." She tossed his former claim back at him.

"And what is it you want, Chrissie? What is it you hope to gain from having told me about Joss?"

He had money and was probably implying that was why she'd told him. If so, he was wrong.

"There isn't a thing you have that I want," she declared with a tilt of her chin.

Her angry spark had his brow arching.

"Isn't there?"

She shook her head.

"We both know that if I touched you, you'd go up in smoke."

No, she didn't know that. Well, maybe she did, but she wasn't admitting to a thing.

"If you think I haven't noticed how you watch me, you're wrong."

Okay, so maybe she watched him. A lot.

"You're a man living in my house uninvited. Of course I watch you. Trying to make sure you don't steal the silverware."

"Ha," he snorted. "Real funny."

"Despite your claims of wealth, I know nothing about you, Trace. Nothing. So don't you go making fun of me trying to protect my son and myself."

He considered her answer a moment, then said, "You know all you've asked to find out."

"Fine. Since you keep bringing him up, tell me about your father."

"I don't talk about my dad."

Yeah, neither did she, but still, she tossed her hands up in frustration. "Exactly my point. You say one thing and do another. Just as I asked you to tell me what happened to your side and you didn't."

The struggle on his face was real. "What is it you want to know about my father?"

"Why don't you get along with him?" She could tell that her question wasn't one he'd been expecting or that he wanted to answer. The struggle intensified.

"Because he's a wealthy businessman who thinks he can control everyone and everything if he waves around enough money."

"Can he?"

"What?"

"Control everyone and everything with money?"

Trace shrugged. "Just about."

"But not you?"

"No."

A lot of things began to click in her mind. "He's why you went overseas?"

"No," he immediately denied.

But she knew the real reason was probably yes.

They sat in silence a moment.

"What are your intentions, Trace?"

"Regarding you? I have no intentions. I don't do relationships or marriage."

"Not in regards to me." Why would he think she was even asking that? Because of his off-the-wall comment in the wading pool? "In regards to Joss. What are you going to do?"

"I'm going to stay with him tomorrow to watch him while you go to work."

She fought grimacing. "I don't think that's a good idea. My mother is planning to watch him. She said she'd come here about ten—that way you could still spend time with Joss, but she'd be here to help."

She had called her mother and told her only the basics. When she'd begun asking questions, Chrissie had promised she'd call her at break the following day and fill her in.

"I do think it's a good idea. He and I need time to bond."

Which came back to that shared power over their son. There she went thinking she got final say, rather than sharing the responsibility with Trace. Guilt and remorse were powerful motivators, but she still couldn't agree with him.

"Do you think you're ready to be alone with Joss all day? There's a lot to taking care of him, Trace."

"I've been with him for four days, Chrissie. I won't claim to have your vast experience with parenting, but I'm a grown man, lived in war-torn countries, and a medical doctor. I think I'll survive a day alone with my three-year-old son. I don't need your mother to babysit us both."

His barb regarding her having excluded him from gaining parenting experience wasn't lost.

She grabbed a sofa pillow and hugged it to her. "Yeah, it's not you I was worried about."

His gaze narrowed. "You think I'd hurt my son?"

"Not intentionally."

"Which means what?

"That I think you want him to like you so much that it blinds you to being able to think logically around him like a real parent."

She regretted her word choice the moment it left her mouth, but couldn't take the "real" back no matter how much she wished she could.

His face darkened to an angry red. "I'd say it's normal for a father to want his son to like him, to be his friend."

"It's not your job to be his friend, Trace. You're a parent, not a bestie."

"I'm not sure I even know what you mean by that."

"Which just proves my point."

"You'll have to excuse me. I've only been a parent for four days. Nature didn't notify me of my pending parenthood four years ago and neither did my son's mother."

He got up and went to the front door. "I'm going for a run, but I will be back and I will watch my son tomorrow. Leave me written instructions on anything you think is vital I know that a 'real' father would know about their son."

With those sharp emotional digs, he stormed out of the front door and was gone.

Ha. It would serve him right if she locked him out of the house.

Not that she would, but the thought made her feel a little better.

But not much.

With sleeping on Chrissie's sofa, not waking up as she moved around the house in preparation for leaving for work was impossible.

Trace had always been a light sleeper, but, since his time overseas, he often felt he slept with one eye open and one ear on guard.

Not one for pretense, he sat up and was stretching when Chrissie entered the room.

Her gaze immediately went to his bare chest and a rosy blush stained her cheeks.

"Um…" she muttered, stopping in her tracks and not seeming to know what to say.

Trace glanced down at his bare chest. "Something wrong?"

"You shouldn't sleep half naked."

He laughed. "I'm wearing shorts, Chrissie."

Her gaze went back to his chest, then jerked away. "Whatever."

"Does my lack of shirt bother you?"

"Yes."

"Why?"

"You know why," she snapped.

Excitement rushed through him. "You like what you see?"

"You know you're a beautiful man. You don't need forced compliments from me."

Only maybe he did because her words pleased him more than they should have.

"My scar doesn't bother you? You mentioned it yesterday. Some women would find it ugly."

Her gaze dropped to where his shorts rode low, revealing the edge of his puckered skin. The pink to her cheeks turned ashen and he wondered what she thought.

"How I find you doesn't matter, Trace. What matters is that you take care of our son today. My mom will be here not too long after Joss wakes."

He sighed. She was right.

"You have my cell-phone number," she reminded him,

determined to be all business. "I've written down my mother's number and my friend Savannah's number in case you need anything before Mom gets here. I left the paper on the kitchen countertop. If you can't reach me, call either of them."

"It's ridiculous for you to have your mother come here. I've got this."

"But she will be here. Promise you'll call if you need anything," she insisted.

"If I run into problems, I'll call." He stood, noting that her gaze followed the descent of the blanket as it dropped to the floor, then her eyes traced back up to meet his.

How his body could respond to her when he was so aggravated at her lack of confidence in him, he wasn't sure, but, same as always, his body responded.

"Um…that's good," she muttered, dragging her gaze away.

Trace stepped from the sofa, yawning, then raking his fingers through his hair. "Yeah, but Joss and I are going to have a good day, despite having your mom looking over my shoulder, so I won't be calling."

He was still telling himself that an hour later when Joss refused to eat. He'd awakened earlier than Chrissie had thought he would as it was still almost an hour before her mother would arrive. After a while of cajoling him, answering Chrissie's second text asking how things were going, Trace decided Joss would eat when hunger hit him.

But when the boy started crying for his mother and Trace couldn't get him to stop, he realized he was going to have to get them out of the house so he could distract him from Chrissie's absence. Either that or have her mother walk into the house with Joss upset. Then Chrissie really wouldn't trust him with their son.

"Joss, before you woke up this morning, I was researching some of the things we could do. I'd like to go to the train station to ride in a train. Would you like that?"

Joss didn't look overly excited. "I like trains."

Not that liking trains improved his flat-tire attitude much. Every movement seemed to be a chore. Joss complained of his stomach hurting and still refused to eat.

Trace let out a big sigh and went in search of the bag Chrissie had brought with them each time they'd left the house. A bag from which she'd magically pulled out anything Joss had needed when they'd been away from her home.

He searched through the bag, checking contents, doing his best to figure out what might be missing from what Chrissie packed. He grabbed a couple of juice boxes from the fridge, and filled a plastic container of dry cereal. He shouldn't need more than that as he'd buy his and Joss's lunch at The Chattanooga Choo-Choo hotel where the train would leave from.

He'd buy anything else he might have forgotten.

He'd gone the night before and bought a car seat so he and Joss wouldn't be trapped at the house all day. No doubt, Chrissie wouldn't want him going anywhere with their son as she hadn't mentioned leaving a seat for him to use and surely she knew he wouldn't have taken his son out without a seat. Joss's safety and well-being was everything. On that, he and Chrissie agreed.

Unfortunately, Joss seemed back into his uncooperative state and sat down in the gravel, saying he wanted his mommy, while Trace figured out how to securely fasten the car seat into the back seat of his SUV.

"Your mommy is at work, but she will be home this evening." Patience, he reminded himself. He had to be patient. Joss would grow to love him, too. Would eventually accept him as his father. Maybe not before he had to leave, though. "You and I are going to go ride a train and have some boy fun."

"I don't want to have boy fun," his son whined. "I want Mommy."

Yeah, Trace didn't blame him. Given the option of hanging with Chrissie or himself, he'd choose Chrissie, too.

"Mommy is at work," he repeated. "You and I are going on an adventure. It'll be great," Trace assured him. Definitely more fun than them staying home and him trying to figure out what to do all day long with Chrissie's mother casting a critical eye. What had she even told her mother about him? Had she been honest and admitted that Trace hadn't known about Joss or was he the villain in her eyes? "Your mom will be home tonight when she gets off work."

In the meantime, he wanted to bond with Joss and believed their being alone was the best way of achieving that. He'd shoot Chrissie's mother a text once they reached the Choo-Choo.

"My stomach hurts," Joss complained.

Trace sighed. Today would get better, just as it had at the aquarium. He and Joss would have a good time. Once he got Joss to the trains, he'd get excited about their trip. This would be a good day.

"I brought you some juice and cereal. I'll give it to you once I get you fastened into your car seat."

Was Joss allowed to eat while in his car seat? Surely. He was three years old and fed himself his meals and snacks.

Trace battled getting the car-seat strap properly fitted through the appropriate part of the car seat. Joss watched him conquer the car seat, but didn't look nearly as impressed as Trace felt he should.

He picked Joss up and put him in the seat, letting Joss help him fasten the seat's buckle into place.

"Great job," he praised, hoping for a smile.

Looking quite miserable, Joss asked, "Can I have my juice?"

Counting to ten, Trace dug into the bag and pulled out one of the juice boxes. "Here ya go, pal."

Joss took the juice box, staring at it expectantly, then back up at Trace. Did Chrissie open the boxes? He hadn't noticed her doing so, but Joss was waiting for him to do something and putting the straw in seemed the most likely.

"Can I get that for you?" he asked, not wanting to offend if he was misreading his son.

Joss nodded, then shook his head. "I'm not thirsty now."

Trace wasn't going to argue. He took the box and put it back into the insulated side pocket of the bag. "Fine. You can have it later."

He wanted to take the top off his car, but decided he'd save that for another day. A day when Joss was showing a little more excitement regarding riding with him. Today, the boy looked two steps away from crying.

He probably was.

He'd asked for Chrissie more than a dozen times and had looked devastated when he'd realized she had gone to work and left him alone with Trace.

He'd even asked about going to his nanna's and had looked disappointed when Trace had said they'd be spending the day together and would see his nanna later that afternoon.

Apparently, despite the gains made the previous day, Trace still wasn't worthy of spending the day alone with.

Maybe that was to be expected. He was still essentially a stranger and Joss wasn't used to staying with him. No problem. They were going to have a great first father-son day. They had to start somewhere and that somewhere was today.

Only Joss didn't seem as eager to get things going.

Nor did he want to walk when Trace got him out of the car at the hotel where he'd buy the tickets for their train ride.

"Fine, I'll carry you." After all, that was what Chrissie had done when the boy had clung to her. He'd enjoy a little Joss clinging to him.

Not that Joss planned to give him the opportunity.

"I don't want you to carry me. I want to go home."

"We're going to ride the train, then we'll get some lunch, then, if you still want to go home—" and he hoped the boy wasn't in a rush by that time "—then we'll go home."

Looking on the verge of crying, Joss let his lower lip droop. "My belly hurts."

Lord, help me, Trace prayed. *Help me do and say the right things to make this child trust me and care for me.*

"That's what happens when you don't eat," Trace reminded him gently. "Would you like some of your juice and cereal now while I buy our tickets? You'll feel better after you eat something."

Joss looked hesitant, but nodded. Trace dug out a juice box and container of dry cereal and handed them to his son.

Joss stared up at him in confusion.

Oh, yeah, he needed to pop the straw into the juice box. He did so, then handed it back to his son.

Joss frowned, handed him the container of cereal back, then took the juice container with both hands.

After he'd taken a drink, he handed the juice box back to Trace.

"Thank you," the boy said, wiping the back of his hand across his mouth.

Trace took the drink box. Which left the bag draped over Trace's shoulder and the juice box and cereal in his hands. He dropped the cereal back into the bag, held onto the juice, then reached for Joss.

He'd text Chrissie's mother in a few, after they got the tickets.

"You want me to carry you?" he offered, hoping his eagerness didn't come through to the point of scaring Joss.

Joss's lower lip disappeared between his teeth and he shook his head.

Trace would have been better off carrying the boy though, because Joss moved at the slowest speed Trace had ever seen him move. He kept a hold on Joss's hand and tried not to say too much when Joss wriggled.

Tried to focus on the fact that, although Joss wouldn't let him carry him, the boy was holding his hand, something he wouldn't do just a few days ago.

Besides, they still had a good thirty minutes to explore the trains before theirs took off so what did it matter if they took a little longer getting their tickets?

Things went downhill fast once they were actually on the train and moving, though.

Joss began to cry, repeatedly asking for Chrissie. No doubt the other passengers wondered if he was some pervert having kidnapped Joss as he refused to be consoled.

"Joss, we'll go see your mommy when we're through with the train ride."

Joss's tears didn't let up and his little body shook with his distress.

Trace shouldn't have been surprised when the juice Joss had drunk came back up, splattering over the hem of Trace's T-shirt, soaking his shorts, and running down his legs and splattering onto Joss's T-shirt and shorts as well.

Good grief. He hadn't realized Joss had drunk that much of the juice.

Joss's little face looked horrified at what he'd done,

almost fearful of how Trace was going to react as his gaze lifted.

Protectiveness surged through him, making him want to hug the boy to him and reassure him.

"It's okay, buddy. You threw up because you got so upset crying. Try to calm down. I'll get you and this mess cleaned up. No big deal." He had the package of wipes in the bag, plus he'd seen a change of clothes in the bag when he'd rummaged through it that morning.

Joss sucked in a sobbing breath, the tears still flowing.

"Shh, it's okay to be okay," Trace repeated, gently touching his son's face in hopes of comforting him.

His skin felt on fire and a cold, cold fear gripped Trace.

One that the last time he recalled feeling was when a bomb had gone off and he'd awakened from a nightmare where coworkers and innocent people had senselessly died and many more, including himself, had been injured.

Joss grabbed hold of his right lower abdomen and cried out as if in intense pain.

Please let me be wrong. Please.

He didn't want his son ill. He didn't want to explain to Chrissie how he'd misread everything their son had done that morning and ignored that Joss had appendicitis.

Dear God, please don't let someone else he loved die on his watch.

"You thought I wouldn't stop by the hospital when you're finally not with him so we can talk?" Savannah gave Chrissie a *duh* look.

Chrissie blinked at her best friend. She'd clocked out and gone on break after her friend had shown up in the CVICU. They'd gone down to the hospital cafeteria. It was early, but Chrissie had grabbed a yogurt as she'd take this as her break. Thank goodness the unit was slow that morning so she could escape for a little while with Savannah.

Or maybe not so good as her friend's expression warned she wanted every minute detail of the previous four days. She'd already called her mother, who was running a little late as Chrissie had caught her on her way out of her house, and given her the five-minute study-guide version.

"Um...no, I didn't think you'd show up at work today. Would serve you right if I had you clock in and work the rest of the day," she half teased. Part of her would like to beg her friend to cover the rest of her shift so Chrissie could leave and check on Trace and Joss. They were fine, of course. She was just being an overprotective mom. Besides, her mother would be with them soon. "Does Charlie have Amelia?"

Savannah nodded. "He's watching her while I go to the grocery store and run errands. He says I need to be sure to take 'me' time."

See—Savannah trusted Charlie with Amelia. A dad watching their child was perfectly normal. So why had Chrissie's gut been cramping all morning?

"Confronting me at work falls under the category of 'me' time?"

Savannah shrugged. "Better than me showing up at your house with him there and wanting to know all the juicy details."

"Agreed. Then again, if you wanted to pop by unexpectedly and check on him and Joss after you leave here, that would be fine by me."

Not that she didn't think they'd be fine. They would be. So why was she so nervous?

"You have to give him credit for being willing to watch Joss. Not all men would have volunteered for that so soon. That he wants to be an active part of Joss's life is a good thing."

"Joss isn't used to him, though."

"Joss is going to have to spend time with him to get

used to him, Chrissie. Maybe it's better if you aren't there to run interference so they can get to know each other on their own terms. I hope your mom gives them some space."

"He's leaving the country in a matter of days." Chrissie frowned. "Besides, whose side are you on?"

Savannah's brow rose. "Is this a matter of choosing sides? You should want Joss to be close to his dad."

A dart of guilt pierced her. "He'll be leaving again soon," she repeated. "But, you're right. They need to spend as much time together as possible. I do want that, but…"

She did.

"But you're scared and feel your relationship with your son is threatened by his very presence?"

"If I agreed, that would make me a terrible person and mother, wouldn't it?"

"Or maybe it just means you're human with normal fears and worries?"

Chrissie's head felt heavy and she let her chin fall toward her chest. "He hates me."

"Trace?"

She nodded, wishing she hadn't eaten the yogurt as it felt thick and putrid in her stomach.

"He told you that?"

"No, but I see it in how he looks at me sometimes." How he'd teased her that morning flashed through her mind and her cheeks flushed. That hadn't been hate, but the chemistry between them didn't make anything better. If anything it just added to the confusion.

"That blush tells me that's not the only way he looks at you."

"We have always had phenomenal chemistry," she admitted, not for the first time.

"You're sleeping with him?" Savannah sounded hopeful.

Chrissie shook her head. "He's not so much as kissed me since showing up at my house."

"But you want him to do much more than that?"

She sighed. "It's no secret I find him attractive." Remembering how he'd looked stretching that morning without his shirt made her think she was way underplaying how Trace affected her. She'd not been able to look at him because looking made her want.

"Then why aren't you kissing him?"

Chrissie met her friend's gaze. "What?"

"You said he hadn't so much as kissed you. What about you? Have you kissed him?"

"No, of course not."

Savannah's gaze was piercing. "My question is why not?"

"Everything is so complicated. Sex would just make it more so."

"How?"

"I'd think that was obvious."

"Well, it's not. How would sex make things more complicated? If you ask me, sex might make things better."

"That's because the man you have sex with loves you," she pointed out.

"Trace doesn't love you?"

"No," she answered, but clamped her mouth shut before her next thought came rolling off her tongue, because it couldn't be true.

She didn't wish Trace loved her.

To wish that would make her have to question why she'd wish for such a silly thing. Especially when she knew he hated her for what she'd done. And that he was leaving. Last time four years had passed before he'd returned to the States.

She was saved from Savannah probing deeper by her cell phone going off. Something was probably going on in the CVICU where they needed her to return to the floor. She grabbed her phone, readying to head back to the unit.

"Hey, Mom, how are things there?" she said instead when it was her mother's voice she heard.

"They aren't here."

Chrissie's heart shriveled up in her chest. "What do you mean?"

"Joss isn't here. Trace isn't here. There's not a car here. He's taken him, Chrissie. He's taken Joss!"

Her mother's panic matched her own.

Trace had taken Joss. She'd only left him alone with their son for a few hours and he'd done the unthinkable. He'd taken Joss.

All the blood in Chrissie's body migrated to pound in her temples.

What did she do? Call the police and report that her son had been kidnapped?

No. First thing she needed to do was call Trace. To see if there was a perfectly logical explanation for why he and Joss weren't at the house, why he hadn't let her know they were leaving.

"I've got to go, Mom. I'm going to call Trace to see why they aren't there."

At her comment, Savannah's eyes widened.

"I'll let you know what I find out," Chrissie promised her mother, hanging up the phone, then meeting her friend's eyes. "He's not there. He and Joss are gone. Oh, God. They're not there."

Her insides were crumbling and Savannah moved to put her arm around her shoulder as Chrissie's hand shook. Tears blinded her as she went to type in Trace's number.

But before she could get the first number punched in, her phone rang again.

"Trace! Where are you?" she demanded when she saw who the caller was.

"He's going to be okay."

His first words didn't reassure her. Nor did the loud whine of the siren coming over the phone.

"What's wrong with Joss? Where are you? Why aren't you at the house? My mom just called to say no one was at the house. What have you done?" Chrissie's legs went weak and she grabbed hold of the table to keep from falling from her chair as she demanded, "I knew I shouldn't have left him with you. What did you let happen to my baby?"

CHAPTER FOURTEEN

TRACE WINCED AT Chrissie's question. Not that he didn't deserve her accusation and so much more.

How could he have been so blind to what was happening? He was a doctor and he'd missed all the signs. Had ignored what his son had told him because he'd thought Joss just didn't want to go with him.

Then again, Kerry had died on his watch too. If he'd been paying closer attention, maybe he'd have noticed she was slipping, maybe her doctors could have bought her more time before the cancer stole her last breath.

With Joss's not feeling well and lack of cooperation, texting Chrissie's mom had completely slipped Trace's mind. Which meant Chrissie had likely been in a panic before he'd said the first word. What he had to tell her wasn't going to help matters.

"We're on our way to your hospital by ambulance. We think Joss has appendicitis." We being him and the paramedics who'd been waiting where the train had made an emergency stop. "I wanted to spend time with him and took him to ride the trains. We were going to ride, have lunch, and then be home long before you got off work. But things didn't go as planned and Joss got sick," he rushed out. "We should be there in—" he glanced at the paramedic monitoring Joss "—four minutes max."

Once Trace had realized what was going on, his brain

had finally kicked into gear and he'd called 911 as he'd stripped Joss's dirty T-shirt and shorts off him. He hadn't bothered to redress him, not with his temperature spiked so high.

A couple on the train with their older boys had moved up and offered to help clean up, as had the conductor, who'd radioed the engineer to alert him as to what was happening in one of his passenger cars. Trace hadn't cared about the mess. All he'd cared about was the little boy who'd been sobbing in pain, asking over and over for his mother as the train had rushed forward to where Joss could be transferred to an ambulance.

While Trace held his hand, the paramedics had started an intravenous line and given Joss something to ease his discomfort as they rushed him toward the emergency room.

Chrissie chewed his ear some more and Trace let her for a moment, knowing he deserved her wrath. Then, he cut the call short so he could focus on his son, whose hand he still held.

"Mommy," Joss mumbled in his sedated state.

"I called her, buddy. She'll be waiting for you in the emergency room."

She was.

The moment the back of the ambulance opened, Chrissie came rushing out of the hospital.

"Oh, God," she moaned, her gaze assessing Joss on the stretcher as the paramedics unloaded him from the ambulance. "Joss, Mommy's here," she told him, rushing alongside the stretcher as they wheeled Joss into the hospital.

Trace kept up with the stretcher as well.

"Mommy's here," she told Joss over and over until the emergency-room nurse hugged Chrissie, pulling her back from the stretcher. "No," she protested.

"They need to do imaging. You can't be in the room. I'm sorry."

Trace wanted to argue, wanted to say he and Chrissie could go in with their son, but he knew to do so would slow down everything.

"Come on, Chrissie. Let them do their job so Joss can get the best care as quickly as possible."

Never had Trace felt a bigger failure than when Chrissie turned to him.

"Don't you tell me what to do when it comes to my son," she hissed at him. "I never should have left him with you. Never."

Chrissie felt Trace's flinch all the way to her core, but she couldn't retract her words. Just as she couldn't retract the things she'd said to him when he'd called her.

Seemed she was always saying something she wished she could take back when it came to Trace.

But the sound of the siren, knowing her baby was hurt, the sight of Joss's little body lying on that stretcher, had undone her.

She liked to think of herself as an empathetic, compassionate nurse, but never had she experienced anything to prepare her for the pain and fear of seeing her child like that.

She'd lashed out at Trace.

Maybe because she'd already been in a panic, thinking Trace had taken her son, just as her father had run with her.

He hadn't. He'd wanted to take Joss for a train ride. He'd wanted to give their son a fun day and had had no intentions of kidnapping him.

But Chrissie couldn't erase the devastation she'd felt at her mother's words that no one was at her house and she'd taken all her emotions out on Trace.

That had been an hour ago. Or a day ago. Or a week ago. Time had no meaning to Chrissie and with the way each second dragged by she'd believe years had passed since her son had been taken for emergency surgery for a ruptured appendix.

She, Trace, her mother, and Savannah had been left in a surgery waiting area where the walls kept closing in around Chrissie. She had cried so many tears on Savannah's shoulder that no doubt Charlie would think his wife had been caught in a downpour by the time she finally made it home.

Her poor mother was almost as big a mess as she was that she hadn't gotten to Chrissie's house earlier, that somehow this was all her fault for having run late.

Her mother had avoided Trace, other than to glare at him as if he were the devil, but Savannah had introduced herself, had hugged him, too, trying to ease his distress.

But not Chrissie.

Chrissie couldn't bring herself to even look at him.

Because looking at him hurt.

Hurt because Joss looked like him.

Hurt because she'd verbally attacked him.

Hurt because she wanted so much more than what they had.

Hurt because he'd allowed this to happen to their son.

Logically, she knew he hadn't *allowed* Joss to get sick, that appendicitis could just as easily have happened while he'd been in her care, while he'd been in Trace and her mother's care at her house. But it hadn't. It had happened while he'd been in Trace's care away from their house when Trace shouldn't have taken him anywhere.

How long had Joss's belly hurt? Had he been trying to be brave in front of his father? Had he cried and Trace ignored him? Had the pain and rupture hit suddenly?

How much longer was this surgery going to take?

She prayed and prayed. Over and over. *Please, please, please, let Joss be okay.*

When she and Trace were called to a consult room, Chrissie could barely walk, but she refused his offered hand.

She couldn't touch him, couldn't feel, could only focus on Joss.

"How is he?" she asked the nurse showing them to the room.

"I'm sorry. I honestly don't know any news on your son. I was buzzed and asked to put you in the consult room for Dr. Rodriguez."

If something bad had happened, the nurse would know, right?

Then again, why wouldn't they have told a patient's family straight away that all was okay so they could quit worrying?

"Joss needs a blood transfusion," the doctor said immediately upon entering the consult room. "He has a rare blood type and we, unfortunately, have had a run on that type today. I need to type and cross you both for a match."

"I'm B positive," Chrissie said, knowing her type from having donated at multiple blood drives over the years.

"It's me," Trace said, fighting the guilt inside him that he'd allowed this to happen to his son, that even now his blood was delaying his son's care. "I'm O Rh negative."

He was a much sought-after donor as any blood type could receive his blood, but when it came to him receiving blood his options were limited to only someone who was an exact match. Something that had been problematic and almost cost him his life in Yemen after his injuries. Apparently, he'd passed that along to his son.

"Take whatever you need from me," he offered. He'd give every drop to save his son. Anything to help Joss. Anything to wipe the agony from Chrissie's face.

Seeing her pain, hearing her sobs, as they'd waited on news of their son had torn his insides to bits. Had brought memories of Kerry and when she'd passed to the forefront of his mind. Memories of Bud and Agnes mourning their daughter. Memories of Trace's own heart breaking at the loss of the first girl he'd loved. Guilt that he'd been there when she'd passed, and that he'd felt a failure ever since, that he should have been able to do something to save her.

Wasn't that why he'd become a doctor? So he could save people? Yet no matter how many he saved, there were so many more he couldn't.

He'd not even been able to spend a day alone with his son without something happening to him.

His gaze cut to Chrissie's red-rimmed eyes, her swollen face, and emotion swamped him. If Joss didn't pull through, she would never forgive him.

If Joss didn't pull through, Trace would never forgive himself.

Once Joss was in recovery, the hospital staff allowed Chrissie and Trace back to see him.

Trace felt the curious stares. No wonder. Chrissie worked here. Anyone who knew her knew she was a single mom, yet here he was, claiming to be Joss's father, giving blood.

Claiming to be Joss's father.

He *was* his father.

He hadn't needed a DNA test. Joss's eyes had been enough to convince him. If he had needed more proof, Joss's blood type would have been all he'd have needed.

"Joss, baby, Mommy is here," Chrissie cooed over and over in a soft voice as she held Joss's hand and waited for him to fully wake up.

His lashes fluttered.

"Mommy's here," she repeated.

"Mommy?" Joss said, his voice hoarse and weak. "My belly hurts."

Trace's insides wrenched. How many times had Joss said that earlier in the day? Too many. He'd been so determined to prove that he could take care of his son by himself and all he'd done was prove the complete opposite. He'd been wrong to take Joss to the train station, to go around Chrissie's wishes. So very wrong.

"Yes, baby. You had surgery on your belly. It's going to hurt for a while, but then it'll be all better," she promised.

Joss's eyes closed back.

"How's he doing?" Dr. Rodriguez asked, coming into the recovery area. "My partner did his operation, but he's caught me up on the details."

"Still trying to wake up," Chrissie told him. "But you just missed him opening his eyes."

"Poor thing," the surgeon commiserated. "He's going to hurt when he wakes up."

"Yeah, he said his belly was hurting when he opened his eyes a minute ago," Chrissie empathized, stroking her fingertip over Joss's hand.

"Tough little guy—he had to be in a lot of pain prior to the rupture."

Yeah, he had been but his obtuse father had thought he just didn't want to spend the day with him and had been determined he was going to anyway.

Trace shook his head. How could he have been so stupid? So blind? So selfish?

His son could have died because of him.

Joss would have been better off if Chrissie hadn't told Trace.

He was leaving in less than two weeks. He shouldn't have come to Chattanooga. He would go back overseas where he could help others rather than interfere where he wasn't wanted or needed.

"Where's my daddy?"

At Joss's question, Chrissie looked behind her to where Trace had been standing. The recovery room bay was now empty except for the nurse standing ten or so feet away at a computer where she was charting.

"Your daddy was here just a few minutes ago, baby," she assured a droopy-eyed Joss. "He's been very worried about you."

She wasn't sure where Trace had stepped away to, but was sure he'd be back soon.

Only he wasn't.

Not that evening. Not that night. Not the next morning. Not the next evening or night.

Not the following day when Joss was released to go home.

Chrissie had called his cell phone, but it had repeatedly gone straight to voicemail. She'd left a dozen messages, but hadn't heard back from him.

Not once.

A week ago, Joss had never met his father.

Now, he kept asking about where he was, obviously missed him, and Chrissie didn't know what to tell him.

Was Trace coming back or had he left for good?

In just over a week, he'd be gone to Africa.

Anger built inside her that he'd just left without saying goodbye, without anything.

Joss had been home for two days, was doing great, and Chrissie had difficulty focusing on anything other than that Trace had come into their lives, made an impression on Joss, then just left without even telling him goodbye.

Yes, she'd been angry with him over taking Joss without her knowledge or permission, had lashed out at him, but to just disappear without saying goodbye to their son? How could he do that?

Had he already gone back overseas?

How dared he? How dared he come into her house and give them a glimpse of how things could have been had their situation been different, then just leave without a word?

How dared he think she'd just let him walk away without a backward glance?

Because she wouldn't.

Not without giving him a piece of her mind.

Which was just as well as she'd already given him a piece of her heart.

Trace's mother lifted her wineglass to her lips and took a more than generous sip. "How is it best for a child not to know his grandparents?"

Trace grimaced. He'd hated telling his parents about Joss for fear they'd contact Chrissie, but he'd not wanted to put Bud and Agnes in the awkward position of knowing his parents had a grandchild they knew nothing about. They'd looked pretty pleased right up until he'd asked them to stay away from Chrissie and Joss.

"It just is," he finally said, taking a sip of his drink. He didn't expect his parents to understand, just prayed they'd respect his wishes.

"Do you really think we're such horrible parents, Trace? After all, we raised you and I've always believed you turned out okay."

"You thought wrong," he corrected his mother.

"Hogwash," Agnes spoke up from across the table from Trace. "You're seriously going back overseas because Joss had a bout of appendicitis?"

"I was already scheduled to go back overseas, and he didn't just have a bout of appendicitis. He almost died."

"Because of something that was completely beyond your control," Agnes told him.

"I should have known something more was going on with him."

Just as he should have known something more was going on with Kerry the day she died.

"Really? Because a three-year-old conveys what's going on inside him that well?" Agnes challenged.

Trace let out a long sigh. Agnes and Bud loved him. As much as he didn't agree with them on most accounts, his parents loved him, too. He wasn't going to win this battle.

"All I'm asking is that you don't interfere in Chrissie and Joss's life. Nothing beyond that, especially not these accolades of why I'm not at fault that Joss almost died. I know what I did."

What he'd done was be so caught up in what *he* wanted, in wanting to *make* his son love him and want to spend time with him, that he'd almost let him die.

Chrissie had been right not to trust him with Joss's care.

Bud and Agnes shouldn't have trusted him to sit with Kerry that day.

Agnes's phone rang and, glancing at the number, she excused herself and left the table to take the call.

"Trace, I think you're making a mistake stepping away from your son," his father said from the head of the table.

"It's my mistake to make." The mistake had been going to Chrissie's and meeting Joss in the first place.

"That boy is the heir to my fortune," Trace's father spoke up as if that was the perfect argument.

"Chrissie doesn't want your fortune. She just wants Joss and he's better off with her."

"Son, I try to stay out of matters that aren't really my business, but I agree with your dad on this," Bud interjected. "You need to be a part of the boy's life."

"That isn't an option." His being a part of Joss's life had almost cost Joss's life. "I'm leaving and won't be back in the States for at least six months."

"Staying is an option. You just have to choose not to go." This came from Trace's father again.

Trace's mother took another sip of her wine. "We want you to stay. We've always wanted you to stay. You know that."

Trace wondered why he'd put himself through this torture. Why had he agreed to dinner with his parents and Bud and Agnes?

Because other than the two people he'd left behind in Chattanooga, these four were the most important people in his life.

Because they loved him.

Just as he loved them.

Only…only he'd shut them out since Kerry had died. All of them to some degree. But mostly his parents.

Because Kerry dying had hurt and no matter how much money his father threw at him afterward, nothing could bring her back. After a while he'd started feeling suffocated by everyone's attempts to make his life better and he'd left for medical school, so no one else would die on his watch, and then he'd opted to join DAW.

Because he'd needed space between him and those he loved. Why? Had he been afraid to feel?

Was he still afraid to feel?

"Trace?" Agnes said, coming back into the room, her expression grim. "That was Chrissie. Joss needs you in Chattanooga."

"What?" He rose from the table, Agnes's worried expression immediately putting him on alert.

"Joss needs you. Now. Apparently he has some rare blood type and…" Agnes's voice trailed off.

That Agnes wouldn't meet his eyes escalated Trace's fear.

He'd been in touch with Joss's doctor every day. The man had his cell number and instructions to call if there were any changes. Joss had been doing well, had been home for a couple of days. What had happened?

He should call Chrissie. If Joss needed him, his blood, he had to go.

Trace's father stood. "I'll have the helicopter here in fifteen minutes and arrange for a car to meet you in Chattanooga."

"I… Yes, that would be best." He needed to get there as quickly as possible.

Not that they'd let him donate again this quickly. In which case…

"Actually—" he turned to his father, who shared his rare blood type "—can you go with me?"

His dad gave him a startled look. "Me? You want me to go?"

"I may need you there. Joss may need you."

"Then let's go."

Chrissie's phone buzzed.

"He's on his way."

"Wow." She hadn't been sure Agnes could pull off getting Trace to come back to Chattanooga to talk, but Agnes had assured her he would. When she'd called Trace's godmother she'd just been going after an address and to make sure Trace was still in Atlanta.

"His dad is with him," Agnes continued.

"His dad? Why is Trace's dad coming with him?"

"Long story." Agnes gave a little laugh. "Trace may have misunderstood something I said and thought Joss needed another blood transfusion."

"What?" Then why Trace was headed to Chattanooga clicked. "Agnes, when you said you'd make sure he came back, I didn't realize you were going to deceive him." Chrissie's heart sank. "I don't feel good about that. I've deceived him too much already."

"I didn't say Joss needed a blood transfusion. Besides, that boy's pride didn't need to get in his way."

That boy was a handsome grown man who Chrissie was angry at and yet…

"Oh, Agnes, he's coming because he's worried about Joss."

Which meant he wasn't coming for her, but for their son.

Which was okay.

If she had to choose, wasn't that what she'd pick? For Trace to be concerned about his son? For him to be there if Joss needed him? Obviously if he was on his way, he would be there for Joss.

Trace was on his way!

"You have to let him know Joss isn't in any danger. He's recovering wonderfully." She didn't want Trace worrying. She could only imagine the horror he must be experiencing.

"He'll be at your house any moment and you can tell him then."

"Any moment?" She'd thought she'd have a couple of hours to mentally prepare what she wanted to say.

"They took his dad's helicopter."

"His dad has a helicopter?"

Agnes laughed. "Oh, honey, you really have no clue, do you?"

Chrissie tried not to be insulted but wasn't sure she succeeded. "What am I supposed to say to him?"

"Now, that's something only you know. I'd guess a good place to start would be why you called me to get his information."

"If he's worried that Joss needs a blood transfusion, wouldn't he go to the hospital instead of here?"

Agnes laughed again. "You underestimate me. The car meeting them in Chattanooga knows where to bring them."

Them. As in Trace and his father.

"Agnes, Trace and I can't talk with his father with us."

"I know that, but you also need someone to watch Joss."

"Trace's dad is going to watch Joss? Isn't he like some kind of uptight businessman?"

"That's how some see him."

"But not you?"

"Not ever. He's a good man who is excited at the prospect of meeting his grandson."

"I just got Joss to bed, Agnes. He's still recovering."

"Fine. I'll call and let Randolph know he's to leave with the car."

Chrissie responded to Agnes, said goodbye to the woman, but couldn't have repeated what she'd said. Her mind was racing.

Trace was going to be there any moment.

What was she going to say to him?

The truth? That she and Joss had missed him? That they wanted him in their lives? That she was sorry for the things she'd said, done? That she knew Joss's appendicitis wasn't his fault?

That she'd attacked him because of her own inner beast that had worried he'd kidnapped their son?

He hadn't. He'd only wanted to love Joss, to get their son to open up to him and love him back.

Would he think her crazy? Selfish, perhaps, if they kept him from leaving to serve the world's poor, sick and injured?

Maybe she was selfish but she didn't want him to go back overseas. She wanted him here. With her. With Joss.

A car pulled in her drive and she went to the front door, not wanting Trace to knock in case it woke Joss. They needed to talk without their son overhearing.

She watched him get out of an expensive-looking black sedan, lean back down to say something to whomever still sat in the backseat. His father, she supposed. Looking confused, Trace closed the car door and headed toward the house. When the car pulled away, he paused, frowned, then met her gaze.

What if he was angry Agnes had sent him on false pretenses? How much did it even cost to have a helicopter bring you?

"Chrissie," he said, stepping onto the porch.

"Joss is fine," she blurted out.

Looking a bit dazed, he flexed his jaw. "That's what my father told me right before we pulled into your driveway."

She nodded. "Agnes said she was going to call him."

"You lied to her?"

"No," she quickly denied. "I called for your address, to make sure you hadn't left yet. Nothing more. She said she'd have you come to me. I assumed she'd talk you into it."

"He doesn't need to be dragged around so soon after his surgery."

"He's doing great. Played almost normal today."

He glanced past her into the house. "Where is he?"

"Asleep. He was tired, so I bathed him and put him to bed about twenty minutes ago."

"Can I see him?"

"Of course." The night he'd shown up at her house, insisting to see Joss, flashed through her mind. "He's missed you, Trace. So much."

His eyes cut to her. "Don't say that."

"Why?"

His jaw clenched. "Because it's not true."

"It is true. He's asked about you repeatedly. He wants to know where you are."

Trace took a deep breath. "What'd you tell him?"

"That you had to go home to Atlanta."

Trace nodded. He had had to go to Atlanta. Or so he'd told himself. Mainly, he'd had to get away because he'd felt such guilt over Joss. Like such a failure to his son.

"I've missed you, too."

Chrissie's words cut into his thoughts.

"Why?"

She gave a trembling smile. "Why not?"

It wasn't much of an answer, but she stepped aside and motioned for him to enter her house. He did so before she changed her mind. Before he changed his mind and took off after his father's hired car.

"You can go to his room if you want."

Her voice was wobbly and Trace found himself turning to look at her instead.

"I leave next week."

She nodded as if she understood, but he wasn't sure she did. Still, he needed to see Joss, to reassure himself that he was okay. Since Agnes's dramatic implication, he'd had a sick feeling in his stomach and he needed to see Joss to convince himself that he really was okay.

His nightlight illuminating his precious face, Joss slept on his car bed, snuggled up in his covers, and looking at peace with the world.

Just seeing him wasn't enough.

Trace went to the bed, sat on the edge, and touched Joss's face, brushing his finger over his soft cheek.

The little boy's eyes opened and Trace felt guilt for waking him.

"Daddy?"

His heart squeezed.

"I'm here, Joss." He touched Joss's fingers, then held his hand in his.

"Where did you go?"

"Atlanta."

"That's where Mommy said you went." Joss yawned, scooted up in the bed. "Can I go to Atlanta with you, too?"

Trace's heart swelled to the point he thought it might explode. But then he recalled that he'd almost let this child, his son, die.

That he'd been the last person with Kerry before she'd gotten so sick and died.

That he was leaving and would be gone for months.

"I'd never take you away from your mommy, Joss. She would miss you."

"We could bring her, too." Another big yawn, then he settled back onto his pillow. "She'd like Atlanta."

Trace wasn't so sure about that.

"I'm sorry I got sick."

"You couldn't help getting sick, Joss. I know that."

"You went away."

His words gutted Trace. Was that what he had thought?

"Not because you'd been sick," he assured. "Never that."

Only, was that true? Or had memories of Kerry and guilt played into his having left?

"I'm better now," Joss told him with heavy eyes. "Lots better."

He started to respond, but realized Joss's eyes had closed and he'd dozed back off. Quietly, Trace stood, turned to leave Joss's room and noticed Chrissie, crying, in the doorway.

She waited until they were both back in the living room, then said, "I want you in his life, Trace. He wants you in his life. Whenever you're home, between your assignments, whenever it's safe for him and me to visit you, we want you in our lives."

Heart pounding, he shook his head. "It's too complicated."

Staring at him from where she stood just in front of him, she frowned. "What's too complicated? You and me?"

"I meant him. Me. Everything."

"I don't understand."

"I shouldn't have taken him away from here that day, or

even attempted to watch him on my own. You were right. I've never been good at taking care of someone."

She shook her head. "No, I was wrong. You should have been with him. You have just as much right to look after him as I do. Please forgive me for thinking otherwise. What happened wasn't your fault."

He shook his head. "Thank you for taking care of him, Chrissie."

She sucked in a deep breath and stared up at him. "You're leaving aren't you?"

She made it sound as if that were something horrible. He knew better. "I can't stay."

"Please don't go."

"Because of what Joss said?"

She shook her head, then took a deep breath and stepped to him, put her hand on his cheek. "Because of you and me."

"There is no 'you and me,'" he reminded her. There wasn't. Just two beautiful weekends that had been like fairy-tale blips in reality.

She flinched, then straightened her shoulders. "I don't believe you, Trace. There's been a 'you and me' from the moment I first met you four years ago and I thought you were the most attractive man I'd ever met. I wanted you then," she admitted. She took a deep breath. "I want you now."

With that, she stood on her tiptoes and kissed him.

What was she doing? Chrissie wondered for the hundredth time. She shouldn't be kissing Trace.

Yes, she should, an inner voice argued. She should be kissing him every day for the rest of her life. Not that that was what he wanted.

He must not even want her anymore because he wasn't returning her kiss.

Then he was.

Not just returning her kiss but taking control of the kiss. Kissing her hard and full and with need.

A need she welcomed because she needed him.

Between kisses, he shook his head. "I'm no good for you and Joss."

She palmed his cheeks, making him look at her. "Why would you say that?"

"Because of what happened."

"Trace, his appendix ruptured. That wasn't your fault. I'm sorry for what I said at the hospital. I was scared, and wrong, and shouldn't have said any of those nasty things because they weren't true. I know that now. You got Joss the help he needed. You got him to the hospital. You did what needed to be done and our son is in there in his bed, healthy and sleeping."

"I'm his father. It's my job to protect him. I didn't."

"Ha. I second-guess myself when it comes to raising him every single day. I do the best I can, but I know there are so many things that I just do the best I can and hope it's enough. Now I know it's not. Like when I said I didn't want him to stay alone with you. I was wrong, Trace."

"This isn't the first time this has happened, Chrissie. I let Kerry die, too."

Horror gripped her. "Bud and Agnes's daughter? I thought she died of cancer?"

Raking his fingers through his hair, Trace then massaged his temple. "I was the last person with her before she slipped into a coma. She never woke back up."

Wondering at the pain inside him, Chrissie sank onto the sofa with a plop. "What happened?"

"She was on hospice, was dying. Someone sat with her around the clock. One minute she was talking with me, the next she closed her eyes, and never woke back up. I thought she was sleeping but she was dying."

"That wasn't your fault, Trace. No more than what happened to Joss was your fault."

"He told me his belly hurt and I thought he just wanted you so I kept trying to distract him. I forced him to leave here and to go with me. I never gave credence that his belly might really hurt."

She grimaced. "You didn't know."

"I should have. You would have." He paced across the room, turned, gave her a pained look. "I'll give you money."

She felt sucker punched. "I don't want money."

"What do you want?"

Time for the truth. It wasn't going to be easy, but she had to do it. Had to say it.

"You."

He just stared at her.

"Did you hear me, Trace? I want you. In my life, my house, my bed," she continued, letting her emotions pour out of her. "I want you. All of you."

"I…" His voice trailed off. "Why?"

"Are you kidding me?" When he didn't respond she knew he was serious. "Because…" She could tell him how wonderful she thought he was, how handsome, how sexy, how smart and funny. But none of that was what came out of her mouth. "Because I've never stopped wanting you and I don't think I ever will."

His gaze searched hers. "What are you saying?"

She gulped back the big bundle of nerves threatening to choke her. "I'm in love with you, Trace."

"I don't know what to say."

Which wasn't what she wanted to hear. Her heart fell.

"You don't have to say anything." She turned away from him, not willing to let him see the big fat tears welling up in her eyes. "I just needed to tell you how I felt, that I wanted you in my and Joss's life. I was so angry at you for just leaving us. There's so much I haven't told you." She turned to face him, scared to admit what she was about to say, words she really hadn't spoken once social services and the police had finished questioning her all those years ago. "My father kidnapped me from my mother. I thought you were doing the same thing that day with Joss. That's why I couldn't hold in my emotions and hurt and fear. I'd wanted to trust you, Trace, and I'd been afraid to, and felt you'd confirmed my worst fears."

His look of horror reflected all she already knew deep in her heart about the man standing in front of her.

"I just wanted to spend the day with him, just me and him. I wanted him to have fun with me, to enjoy being with me, to need me."

He winced. "I shouldn't have taken him. You were right to lash out at me."

"You weren't stealing him from me, Trace. You were trying to forge a relationship with him that my paranoia was interfering with."

"He's yours, Chrissie. Is that what you want to hear me say? You're his mother and he needs you. I know that."

"He's yours, too, Trace. You're his father and he needs you, too. I know that now," she admitted, believing it with all her heart. "That's why I called Agnes, because I wanted to come to Atlanta to tell you how sorry I am, to beg you to forgive me for not telling you about him, for not trusting you with him, for all the mistakes I've made." She put her hands over her face, wiped at the wetness. "I'm sorry Agnes tricked you into coming here."

Trace was nothing like her father. He was the best man she'd ever met. She'd created issues where there had been none, had let fear poison her judgment. How could Trace ever forgive her?

How could Joss ever forgive her when she explained to him that his daddy had left because of her mistakes?

"I'm not."

Chrissie lifted her gaze to Trace's, waited for him to tell her how foolish she was, how he could never forgive how deceitful and mistrusting she'd been.

"I love you, Chrissie," he said instead, almost dropping her to the floor. "Thinking of you, of being with you in Atlanta is what got me through the hell I went through overseas. When I saw you again a few weeks ago, you were as sweet as I remembered. I'm sorry for what your father did to you, Chrissie. I can't even imagine the hell you and your mother must have gone through. I'd never do that to you or Joss. Never."

Chrissie's insides shook at the sincerity in his voice, at the sincerity shining in his eyes as he gazed down at her.

"He's beautiful, Chrissie. I'd say the most beautiful thing I'd ever seen, but I'd be lying." He cupped her face. "I'm looking at the most beautiful thing I've ever seen. You."

He kissed her again. This time slower, more passionately, and she kissed him back with her all, not quite believing the things he'd said.

"Am I dreaming?" she asked, wondering if she should pinch herself. "Are you really here?"

He brushed his thumb across her cheek. "If you're dreaming, I'm having the same dream."

"So what happens now?" she asked, not quite sure what everything they'd said up to that point meant.

"What do you want to happen?"

His question was a no-brainer. She didn't have to think on it even a millisecond. She knew exactly what she wanted.

"I want you to stay here, Trace, with me and Joss forever." She took a deep breath. "But I know you're committed to leaving. Soon. If the need is within you to live in some war-torn, impoverished country, we'll go with you." She met his gaze. "That is, if you want us to."

"You know I do." When he kissed her again, she had to

agree. She did know. It was there. In his kiss. In his touch. In the way he was looking at her.

"But maybe it's time I rethink going back overseas."

"A week before leaving? I don't want you to give up something you love for me."

"If I left you and Joss, I would be giving up things I love. I'm not going back with DAW."

She couldn't believe what he was saying. She wanted this man happy, to do whatever it took to make his life complete.

"I'm glad, but I was serious," she assured him. "We'll go wherever you are."

"Chattanooga isn't so far away from Atlanta, Chrissie. Maybe we could spend time in both cities. That way Joss could know both sets of his grandparents."

Happiness burst through her whole being.

"And his grand-godparents," she added, thinking of Bud and Agnes.

"They'll spoil him. They've been waiting for years for me to give them grandchildren." He gave her a serious look. "They'll insist upon more."

"More? You mean—?" Chrissie's breath caught "—you want more children? But I thought…"

"The thought terrifies me in many ways, but, yes, I want more kids. With you. Brothers and sisters for Joss."

She threw her arms around his neck and kissed his cheek. "Oh, Trace. I do love you!"

He laughed. "Good. Now about those brothers and sisters…"

EPILOGUE

"No, DON'T YOU dare pick up that box of supplies," Agnes ordered when Chrissie bent to pick up a box.

Not that Chrissie had actually done much bending.

Her body just wasn't cooperating these days. Not with her belly in the way.

Her very round, very pregnant belly.

"You sound like my husband," she accused, wanting to help more than she knew they were going to let her.

"Yeah? I hear he's an amazing man," Trace said, coming up behind her and patting her bottom, then giving her a more serious look. "How are you holding up?"

"Fine."

"You're not too tired?"

"Trace, the event hasn't even started yet."

"I just think you should have sat this year out and stayed at my parents' place with Joss."

"And encroached on his time with his Gramps and Grammie?" she asked. "I don't think so. They've been looking forward to taking him to the Atlanta Aquarium for weeks. He loves it so much! I can't believe your dad arranged a sleepover there."

Trace grinned. "I told you they'd spoil him."

But his voice was light, happy. Although she knew Trace and his father hadn't seen eye to eye most of his adult life, they'd come to a peace from the time they'd flown to

Chattanooga together, thinking they were going to save Joss's life.

Instead, they'd saved Chrissie.

Saved her from a life with part of her heart missing.

"Just as you spoil me," she accused, wrapping her arms around his neck, but unable to pull him as close as she'd like due to her belly between them.

He leaned forward, dropped a kiss on her lips, then cupped her stomach. "You're the one who has spoiled me."

"You just keep thinking that and I'll know the truth," she teased, as she often did. The truth was, they were both spoiled by the happiness they'd found together.

A happiness that came from deep within and shined outward for the whole world to see and feel its warmth.

A happiness that was love.

The kind that would last forever.

And did.

* * * * *

If you enjoyed this story, check out these other great reads from Janice Lynn

THE NURSE'S BABY SECRET
IT STARTED AT CHRISTMAS...
SIZZLING NIGHTS WITH DR OFF-LIMITS
WINTER WEDDING IN VEGAS

All available now!

REFORMING
THE PLAYBOY

BY
KARIN BAINE

MILLS
BOON

Published in Great Britain 2017
By Mills & Boon, an imprint of HarperCollins*Publishers*
1 London Bridge Street, London, SE1 9GF

© 2017 Karin Baine

ISBN: 978-0-263-92655-2

Dear Reader,

'Ice Hockey Dude', as my hero Hunter has been affectionately known throughout the writing process, has been in the planning for a very long time. Ice hockey is a relatively new sport to Belfast, and—as with the town in my book—it brought much excitement with it. Along with a host of handsome Canadian players who did indeed fall in love with local girls and are still here over a decade later. A romance novel just waiting to happen!

As with all bad boys, Hunter Torrance has taken some taming, but with the help of my fabulous editor, Laura, I've finally wrestled him into submission. Now all we need is Charlotte Michaels, the team doctor, to forgive him his sins too and learn to trust him again…

Happy reading!

Karin xx

This book is for my sisters, Heather and Jemma,
who first got me hooked on ice hockey and encouraged
my stalking of No. 28! Also for Jaime and Lucy,
the next generation of Giants fans.

Thanks must go to Andrew, because without his help
I never would've been able to write this book. Or so he
would tell you. And to Ricky so he doesn't feel left out!

It's been a rough few years for all of us and,
though I never say it, I love you all. xx

Finally, to fellow author Annie O'Neil.
You've been an angel, and although we've yet to meet
you've become such a lovely friend.

Listen to the rhythm

Books by Karin Baine

Mills & Boon Medical Romance

Paddington Children's Hospital

Falling for the Foster Mum

French Fling to Forever
A Kiss to Change Her Life
The Doctor's Forbidden Fling
The Courage to Love Her Army Doc

Visit the Author Profile page
at millsandboon.co.uk for more titles.

CHAPTER ONE

IF ALIENS HAD landed in the middle of this rural Northern Irish town and declared her their new supreme leader, Charlotte Michaels couldn't have been any more surprised than she was now.

'Hunter Torrance? *The* Hunter Torrance is the new team physiotherapist?'

Although he was standing there, casting a shadow over her, she didn't quite believe it. Didn't want to believe it. The Ballydolan Demons was *her* team, *her* responsibility, and having ice hockey's most infamous bad boy on board wasn't going to dig them out of the hole they were in.

'Yes. Deal with it, Charlie. We need him.' Gray Sinclair, the head coach, delivered the news and strode away, leaving her face-to-face with the new signing in the arena corridor. She'd been on her way to watch the team train when the pair had ambushed her and literally stopped her in her tracks.

'Hunter Torrance, the new physio. For now. I guess my future employment will be dependent on results.' The latest addition to the team held out his hand as he introduced himself but she wasn't inclined to shake it until someone convinced her this wasn't some sort of sick joke.

'Like everything around here,' she muttered. He wasn't the only one on trial. This was her first season as team doctor, and so far, with the list of injuries they had, a run of poor results and the last physiotherapist quitting on short notice, it could be her last too.

With a build more like a willow tree than the mighty oaks usually associated with the sport, she'd worked hard to be taken seriously but now they'd landed her with a side-kick who still held the UK Ice Hockey League record for most time spent in the sin bin she was worried the professionalism of the medical staff would be in jeopardy. The ex-Demons player had undermined the team's position in the league once before and she wouldn't sit back and let him do it again. In any capacity.

He smiled at her then, even as she ignored his offer of friendship. It was a slow, lazy grin, revealing the boyish dimples which had made him a pin-up for many a girl around here. Her included. If someone had told her at eighteen she'd be working alongside this one-time NHL hunk some day she would've died with happiness. Now the sight of him here was liable to make her forget she was a strong, independent career woman and not that same vulnerable teen. Something she had no time for nine years on.

He hadn't changed much in that time, at least not physically. Although this was probably the closest she'd ever been to him without the Perspex partition separating the players from the fans. He was still as handsome as ever, only now the pretty boy-band looks had morphed into the age-appropriate man-band version. Those green eyes still sparkled beneath long, sooty lashes, his dark hair was thick and wavy, if longer than she remembered, and he was dressed in a black wool coat, tailored blue shirt and jeans rather than the familiar black and red Demons kit. Damn but he'd aged well; the mature look suited him. It was a shame she could barely look at him without the abject humiliation of her past feelings for him spoiling the view.

'It's good to be back,' he said, and continued walking

towards the rink as though he was returning to an idyllic childhood home and not the scene of his past misdemeanours.

For a moment Charlotte contemplated walking back in the other direction and locking herself in a nice quiet room somewhere until he'd gone away. He'd appeared from the shadows as if he were a bad dream. Or a good one, depending on which Charlotte was having the fantasy—the young infatuated girl or the cynical woman who knew bad boys weren't exciting or glamorous, they just screwed people over.

She didn't. Instead, she followed him towards the ice. Hunter wasn't to know she'd been enamoured with him to the point of obsession the last time he'd been on Northern Irish soil but he had cost her beloved Demons the championship with his antics. Even if she hadn't been embarrassed by her teen fantasies she still wasn't convinced he was up to the job and simply didn't trust him to do it effectively.

'Why are you here?' Her forthright attitude obviously wasn't something he was used to, or expecting. She could see him tensing next to her and she didn't like it. To her, the guarded reaction meant he had something to hide. The very nature of his defensive body language said he was fighting to keep his secrets contained but she wouldn't be fobbed off easily when it came to work matters.

'No offence but you're an *ex*-player for a reason. The drinking, the fighting, the generally bad attitude…they're not qualities I look for in a co-worker either.' His last appearance here had been a coup for the Demons to have him on board when no other team would have him. A big name for a budget price. Unfortunately, even this easygoing community hadn't been enough to tame his wild ways. He'd become a liability in the end, his playing time down to single figures for his last matches, as opposed to the many minutes he'd spent in the penalty box. Eventually people had given up on him. Charlotte too, once she'd realised he wasn't the man she'd thought he was when he'd snatched success away from the team. There'd been a collective sigh of relief when he'd flown back to Canada and she couldn't say she was happy to work alongside someone prone to such unpredictability now either.

'Ah, so you witnessed that particular phase of my life? In which case I can't expect you to be performing cartwheels on my return but I can assure you I'm here to work, not to raise hell.' Something dark flitted across his features that said he was deadly serious about being here, and sent chilly fingers reaching out to grab Charlotte by the back of the neck. She wanted desperately to believe that having him here would benefit the team, not hinder it, but she needed more proof than his word.

'I don't understand. Why would you want to come back to a team that holds memories of what I imagine was a very dark time for you? Especially to work off the ice rather than on it?' She made no apology for her blunt line of questioning. It didn't make sense to her and she'd made it a rule a long time ago to question anything she deemed suspect. She'd learned to follow her gut feeling rather than blindly take people at face value. It prevented a lot of pain and time-wasting further down the road.

'Despite…everything, I like the place. I want to make this my home again. There's also the matter of laying a few personal demons to rest and proving to you, and everyone else, I'm not that same hothead I was nine years ago.' It had taken Hunter some time to answer her but when he did he held eye contact so she was inclined to believe what he was saying, even though she doubted it was the whole truth.

'I trust you have all the relevant qualifications and experience?' Although she expected his appointment was more to do with his connections here and last-minute availability than actually being the best man for the job, she couldn't stop herself from asking. She needed someone who knew what he was doing on the medical staff with her.

'All my papers are in order if you'd like to see them.' He was teasing her now, the slight curve of his mouth telling her he wasn't intimidated by her interrogation technique.

'That won't be necessary,' she said, folding her arms across her chest as a defence against the dimples. This so wasn't fair.

'Look, I'm the first one to admit I was a screw-up. Not everyone will be happy to see me back but I'm sure we're all different people now compared to who we were back then.' He leaned back against the barrier, his coat falling open for a full-length view of the apparently new and improved Hunter.

That giddy, infatuated fan who shared Charlotte's DNA insisted on taking a good, long look. Who was to say that Mr Sophistication here wouldn't someday regress back to his rebellious alter ego too?

She'd never been a fan of that particular side of him. The young girl she'd been then had enjoyed the macho displays of the defenceman body-checking his opponents into the hoardings or dropping his gloves in a challenge fight. There was something primitive in watching that, even now, and there'd been times she'd wanted someone to defend her the way he had his teammates. He'd definitely been a crowd- and a Charlotte-pleaser for a time. But those later months when he'd fought with his own coach and smashed equipment in bad temper had made for uncomfortable viewing. It had felt like watching someone unravel in public and had come as no surprise to anyone when the Demons, or any team, had refused to renew his contract. He'd slunk back to Canada in disgrace, never to be heard of again. Until today.

'Clearly Gray thinks you've changed since this was his doing and he's the man in charge, not me. Well, I mean, if I was in charge I'd be a woman, not a man...'

'Obviously.' Hunter dropped his gaze to her feet and she followed it all the way back up to her eyes. He may as well have had X-ray vision the way he'd studied her form so carefully, smiling whilst she burned everywhere his eyes had lit upon her.

No, no, no, no, no! This wouldn't do at all. Behind the scenes of an ice-hockey team was not an appropriate place to suddenly become self-aware and he certainly wasn't an appropriate male to be the cause of it. These men were out of bounds. All of them.

Hunter mightn't be a player, or one of her patients, but he was a colleague. Given their past history, albeit a one-sided affair, his presence here complicated matters even more for her. With the team languishing in the bottom half of the league her position was already a tad precarious, without him in the picture too. Especially when he kept looking at her as though he was trying to pick her up in a seedy bar.

'Well, I'm sure you'll want to meet the team...' She backed away, reminding herself this wasn't about her, Hunter or any ridiculous crush. They were both here to do a job and a team of sweaty, macho hockey players should be a good distraction from any residual teenage nonsense.

'Maybe later. I wouldn't want to disrupt training. We should probably use the time to get to know each other better so I can convince you I'm not here as some sort of punishment.'

'That's really not necessary.' Charlotte gave a shudder. She knew all she needed to know about Hunter Torrance. Probably more than most due to her teenage obsession and enough for her to want to keep a little distance between them.

'Hey, we're both on the same team, right?'

'Not by choice,' she muttered under her breath.

It was no wonder the powers that be had kept this snippet of information from her until it was too late to do anything about it. She'd been surprised they'd found a replacement physiotherapist willing to see out the last few games of the season and hadn't asked any questions, simply glad to have help getting the team back to fighting strength for the play-off qualifiers. Now she knew the good news had come with a catch.

'Well, I'll do my best not to get in your way. Actually, I wasn't even expecting you to be here today. I thought team doctors practically only made appearances on match days with the slew of outside commitments and specialist clinics you all usually have to boost your salaries. I know this is a different league from the NHL in terms of rules, technical terms, profile and especially finances. Or are you the official welcome committee?'

She knew he was deliberately being facetious as he took a little payback for the hard time she'd given him so far. His sneer earned him her narrow-eyed stare, which usually had the power to wither a man at fifty paces, but the bad boy of the tabloids took it all in his stride. What was a dirty look in the grand scheme of things when she supposed his whole past would probably be raked over again in the national press when they got wind of his return?

'Clearly, I didn't get the memo we'd have a VIP joining us otherwise I would have dusted off my pom-poms.'

Hunter opened his mouth to say something then seemed to think better of it and simply shook his head. It was probably a good idea. She wasn't in the mood for innuendo-based banter in the workplace, even if she had left the door wide open for it.

'In answer to your question, I'm here for the play-off matches. I schedule my sports and musculoskeletal clinics around my time here so I don't miss anything.' It wasn't easy but she used her personal leave to make sure she was here for the most important dates on the hockey calendar.

'I'm sure there aren't many who have such commitment.'

He seemed impressed that she took her role here seriously but that only made her blood boil a fraction more. If he'd ever been as dedicated as she was to the game he would understand the sacrifices she made. Experience had taught her Hunter wasn't the team player the Demons needed.

'This is my team. I want to see them win and I'll do what I can to help realise that dream, but we do have our work cut out for us at the minute. Carter has a meniscus tear, Jensen has bursitis, Dempsey a groin strain, and Anderson, our star player, needs a serious attitude adjustment.' She listed those battling injury who were already causing concern for the upcoming matches. He needed to understand the workload was substantial and this job wasn't simply a position with a title.

'I'm sure we can manage between us. After all, that's what I'm here for. Not to make your life more difficult or to cause trouble. Those days are long gone. What do you say we start over with a clean slate and work together to get this team back on its feet?' He held out his hand in truce, asking that she forgive whatever sins he might've committed in her eyes.

Perhaps she was overstepping the mark here when she wasn't in any position of authority but she'd thought someone should have the Demons' best interests at heart when Gray's judgement seemed clouded by sentiment, or sympathy, or something that had no business in his team decisions. Still, the deed was done now and as a professional she knew better than to let her personal feelings get in the way of doing her job.

'Fine.' She hesitantly reached out towards him and shook on the new partnership. Her hand tingled where Hunter's gripped it so confidently and it wasn't simply because of the sheer size and power of him, making her fingers seem doll-like compared to his. There was also the moment of fantasy and reality colliding in that touch. Hunter Torrance was *actually* in her life now.

She inhaled the fresh, citrus scent of his aftershave so deeply she made herself dizzy. An entirely primal reaction that probably would've happened whether she'd known who he was or not.

For most single women he'd be the perfect package. If tall, dark, handsome and Canadian did it for you. Which it did. Why else would she be sniffing him as if he were made of chocolate and she wanted a taste? He was wrong for her on so many levels so she'd simply have to resist licking his face.

She'd done her best to fit in here as one of the crew, and making doe eyes at the new recruit wasn't very professional, it was asking for trouble. And it had definitely found her in the shape of a six-foot-four, two-hundred-pound ex-hockey-player.

Okay, so she still had stats memorised, it didn't mean anything other than she'd once been a girl with way too much time on her hands. An unhappy girl from a suddenly broken home who'd sat in her room like some fairy-tale princess in a tower, waiting for her knight in shining armour to come and rescue her. Except her hockey-playing knight had turned out to be an immature mess who had stolen the chance of that championship title from her beloved Demons and fuelled the theory all men had the ability to inflict mortal wounds to the heart. Not so much galloping off into the sunset as a life sentence distrusting anyone who dared come too close.

She knew her hostility towards him would seem uncalled for, petty even. That didn't stop her from hoping his past might catch up with him and send him back to the land of snow and ice. He'd shown he wasn't a man to be relied on when his team needed him. Surely she wouldn't be the only one to hold a grudge?

In his short time here he'd insulted and fought with many, had damaged the reputation of the club and generally been a pain in the backside to all those around him. Not everyone would be glad to see him return and she was kind of hoping those with a legitimate reason to give him a hard time would, to save her blushes and her position on staff.

Gray, the coward, had apparently left it to her to break the news to the others. It had taken all of her inner strength *not* to protest, *You were on that team he decimated, you should know better than anyone why I think he's a liability.*

She hadn't because she did her best to keep her passion for the game and her job separate. There was no fair reason he shouldn't be here if he had all the relevant experience needed for this job.

'Guys? Can we have a quick word?'

The team trooped off the ice and lined up, waiting for the news. Charlotte swallowed hard. There was definitely no going back now.

'We just wanted to tell you there's a new addition to the medical staff. Hunter Torrance will be your new physiotherapist for the rest of the season.' She didn't sugar-coat it. They could come to their own conclusions about what this meant. Her only job had been to relay the message and she'd done that as quickly and as bluntly as she could so this was over soon and she could go home to lick her wounds.

'What?'

'*The* Hunter Torrance?'

'You're kidding!'

There was a stand-off moment as they stood looking blankly at each other, no one knowing what to do with that information, including Hunter. He was frozen beside her, probably trying to decide on the fight-or-flight method of defence. She knew which one she'd prefer and would happily book him a one-way ticket back to Canada.

The first stick hit the ground with a heavy thud, then

another, and another, until he'd received a round of applause hockey-style.

Floret, the captain, stepped forward and shook Hunter's hand first. 'Good to have you on board.'

Charlotte figured the move was because he was a fellow countryman but he was soon followed by the rest of the multinational squad.

'You're a legend, man.'

'Dude, I'm sure you have stories to tell.'

Charlotte rolled her eyes as they surrounded their new physio as if he was some sort of rock star. The last thing she needed was the players taking their cue from him that bad behaviour would ultimately be rewarded.

At least Hunter had the good grace to look slightly embarrassed by the positive attention. In her opinion he didn't deserve it and by the way his cheeks had reddened and he was trying to back away from the crowd she guessed he didn't think so either. Too bad. They were both stuck in this hell now.

'They're all yours,' she muttered as she walked away unnoticed and left him at the mercy of his adoring fan club. After all, he'd insisted he could handle them and she was done for the afternoon. With the play-off matches looming, which could see them knocked out of the Final Four Weekend in Nottingham, they'd soon find out if the ex-rebel had turned over that new leaf and could justify his new place with the team.

The fan in her wanted him to work some magic and help get them match fit to fight their rivals for that place in the finals but she was a cynic at heart. She'd rather not take the chance of getting her hopes up, only to be disappointed at the last moment.

Hunter hadn't come to ruffle any more feathers. He had enough old enemies without making new ones and he certainly hadn't intended on upsetting the resident doctor. Gray had called in too many favours for him, none of which he deserved, to screw this up now. His old teammate was the one person who knew what he'd been through and had been willing to give him a chance. One he was grabbing with both hands.

Those selfish, heady days were far behind him now. There was only one reason he was back in this County Antrim town and that was for his son.

Hunter Torrance, the responsible father. It was the punchline to a very sick joke. A disgraced hockey player who'd barely been able to take care of himself now found he was the sole parent to an eight-year-old boy who'd just lost his mother in a car crash. He'd only had a few months to get used to the idea of being a father and to grieve for the relationship he could have had with Sara, the ex-girlfriend who'd hid the huge secret from him. Perhaps if he'd been in the right head space back then, able to love her, they could've been the family he'd always dreamed of having. Instead, he'd walked away from her, consumed by his own self-pity, and returned to Edmonton.

For as unreliable as the old Hunter had been, the new one was as determined for his son to have the stable upbringing he'd never had. So he'd given up everything he'd worked hard to rebuild back home to do it. Now all he had to do was convince Sara's parents, Alfie's grandparents, and everyone else here he was up to the job.

He'd expected an initial backlash over his appointment here from the players and fans but not from the rest of the medical staff. This doctor probably knew nothing of him beyond his reputation yet it seemed enough to warrant her displeasure at the prospect of having to work alongside him. Not that he could blame her. The back-slapping welcome he'd received had come as a surprise to him too. Tales of his hockey days were probably a novelty to young, up-and-coming players still caught up in the thrill of the game.

For those who'd been personally affected by his behaviour, himself included, he'd prefer to confine his exploits to the past, and he'd told them so. After he'd confirmed or denied several of the urban legends attributed to his name and number.

'Is it true you spent longer in the penalty box than on the rink for the last month of your career?'

'Yes.' He wasn't proud of it. He hadn't been trying to play the villain or even defend his own players. The issues from his childhood that he'd tried to suppress had finally come to the surface in an explosion of misdirected rage. Years of therapy had taught him that but it wasn't information he was willing to share, or a time of his life he was keen to revisit. He was a different man now. Hopefully one more at peace with his past and himself.

'Did you really punch a linesman and knock out his teeth?'

Hunter sighed. He'd long since apologised to the unfortunate man whose offside decision he'd so violently opposed. 'One tooth, but I'm afraid to say I did.'

He didn't want any impressionable young talent to think his past behaviour was an advertisement for anything other than career suicide. 'It cost me my place on the team, my life here, everything.'

By that stage he'd been completely out of control, drinking too much, lashing out and acting out the role of a child in pain seeking the attention of a family that didn't want him. Ironically it was that behaviour that had made Sara turn her back on him and deny him a chance of a family of his own.

'I imagine tales of my debauchery have been greatly exaggerated in my absence. It's probably best you don't believe everything you've heard about me and form your own opinion. Which mightn't be any more favourable when you see the new programme I've devised for you…'

Whilst a new, intensive regime wouldn't endear him to his new buddies, it was his way of proving he was serious about his job here. He hadn't moved halfway across the world to be one of the guys; he was here to make a difference to the team and secure a future for him and Alfie. Gray had clued him in on the challenges he was up against and it was possibly the reason he'd secured the job against the odds—no one else was willing to take on the responsibility of a struggling team at such short notice. Hunter had done his homework and he knew exactly what he was up against but he'd been training for this ever since he'd hit rock bottom and had decided he wanted his life back in whatever capacity was available to him. After years of therapy and retraining he certainly wasn't going to be put off by the thought of some hard graft.

If only Charlotte had stuck around she would've seen the adoration had been short-lived. He'd come prepared with notes and ideas on strengthening and stability exercises for the guys. As a player he knew how much stress the joints and muscles went through. The mechanics of the game and the repetitive actions left the body vulnerable to injury and even a slight strain could easily become a nagging injury, refusing to heal. It was his job to prevent more serious problems further down the line as well as treat them. Regardless of her departure, he'd forged ahead in implementing his new exercise regime, strapped up those who'd needed a bit of extra muscle support and massaged any problem areas in preparation for these next important games.

He'd gone on to treat Colton's groin strain with a myofascial release of the muscles involved, manipulating the connective tissue with a sustained, gentle pressure to help regain function again.

Murray's torn meniscus, caused by the trauma of the

knee joint being forcefully twisted, thankfully wasn't severe enough to warrant surgery. Hunter worked to strengthen the muscle surrounding the knee and add to the stability of the joint. The excess swelling and pain were treated with anti-inflammatory medication.

He was sorry Charlotte hadn't been here to witness his switch back into business mode. His commitment should make her job a little easier too. After all, the medical team was supposed to work together to get the most from the players. It wasn't an in-house competition to decide who deserved their place here over the other.

The noise of the crowd and the smell of the crisp, clean ice took Hunter back to his own game nights, and gave him the same adrenaline rush it always had. His first match tonight wasn't so much about that final score for him but about his personal performance. He wanted to make a good impression and shoot down all the naysayers who still believed he was a liability in any capacity here.

He filed down the players' tunnel with the rest of the game crew. It was odd being part of the team without being *part* of the team. He was almost anonymous, standing here in the shadows. The way he preferred it. It was circumstance that had dragged him back into the outer edges of the spotlight.

He ventured out far enough to glance around the arena, trying to pick out those present who'd brought this sudden and dramatic change to his way of life.

'Are you looking for someone?' Charlotte appeared beside him.

'Er…no one in particular.' The seats he'd arranged for Alfie and his grandparents were still empty but he wasn't going to share that information with anyone. He'd learned the hard way to keep details of his personal life out of the public domain and he wasn't about to jeopardise his chances of getting custody of his son for anybody. Even if it might take that look of disgust off her face.

The intense reaction he was able to draw from her with minimal goading fascinated him and he didn't know why, beyond wondering what he'd done to deserve it. She wasn't his usual type, at least not the old Hunter who'd enjoyed the company of more…appearance-obsessed ladies who'd revelled in their sexuality. Sara hadn't been bold or brash but she'd certainly given her feminine attributes a boost with beauty treatments and figure-hugging outfits.

Charlotte was a natural beauty, shining brightly through her attempts to disguise it. Even wearing her game crew red fleece and with her chestnut-brown hair swept to one side in a messy braid, she was as pretty as a picture. He wouldn't deny it but neither would he act on it even if she didn't treat him as if he was the devil incarnate. They were co-workers and all women were off limits for the foreseeable future. For once he had to think about someone other than himself and Alfie's well-being came before hockey or his love life.

'Well, if you can drag yourself away from whatever has caught your interest, the game is being played in *that* direction.' She nodded towards the ice, obviously mistaking his keenness to see his son for something more lascivious.

Given his reputation, it wasn't a huge stretch of the imagination that she should jump to that conclusion but he did wonder if she would ever give him the benefit of the doubt when it came to questioning his commitment to the job. Especially since he had no intention of correcting her or making her aware of Alfie's existence. They weren't close enough for him to share such personal information and as first impressions went he didn't think they were going to be best buds any time soon.

Still, he did take a certain pleasure in her *tut* and the roll of her eyes before she stomped away in temper. It was good that she took her work seriously but she really needed to loosen up. He wasn't the enemy, even if it was fun playing the part now and again.

Hunter's smile died on his lips as he wrenched his gaze away from his colleague's denim-clad derriere and back to the crowd. Sara's parents were in their seats, watching him with disapproval etched across their faces. Whilst he'd been busy with Charlotte he'd missed their arrival and had fallen at the first hurdle by ignoring his son in favour of a woman. It had taken a while simply to get them to tell Alfie he was his father and this was the first time he'd been allowed to see him outside their home.

They didn't want Alfie's parentage to be public knowledge any more than he did until things were settled a bit more. Their caution was understandable when he'd already left their daughter in the lurch and probably ruined her life. Unfortunately he couldn't do anything to make amends for their loss but he could try to be the parent Alfie needed him to be.

He gave a wave, his eyes now only for his son, and the swell of love that rose in his chest for the excited little boy waving back put everything into perspective once more. It didn't matter what anyone else thought of him as long as his son loved him, trusted him enough to be with him.

The O'Reillys weren't against the idea of him having custody as long as it was in the best interests of their grandson. All he had to do was make sure he was match fit for the parenting game and leave the old Hunter back on the ice. Along with any wayward thoughts towards his fiery new colleague.

CHAPTER TWO

THE ATMOSPHERE AROUND the arena was electric, everyone buoyed up for the game against the Coleraine Cobras and the chance of getting one step closer to the play-off finals. The Demons were the underdogs at present and to secure their place they needed to come out on top after playing one home and one away match to the Cobras, who were sitting at the top of the league table. It was a tall order but Charlotte kept faith along with all the other fans.

She could hardly believe she was now part of the action instead of a mere spectator sitting in the stands with everyone else. It was a privilege to be on the ground floor of the establishment but she'd also worked damned hard to get here. There was no way she would let everything she'd achieved slip through her fingers for the sake of one man's ego. Whatever, or whoever, had brought him back to town needed to take a back seat for the team's sake.

She'd had to swallow her pride and come out to stand alongside Hunter in the tunnel because that's where she needed to be—on site and focused on the players. It didn't stop her unobtrusively watching him as the lights dimmed and the crowd was whipped into a frenzy with roving spotlights and blaring sirens hailing the arrival of the home team.

Each time the lights fell on his face for a split second

she could see his eyes trained on the ice waiting, watching for that puck to drop. As intense as he'd always been.

A shiver danced its way along her spine as she recalled those past games when she'd found it difficult to watch anything other than him on the ice. It wouldn't do to regress to that sort of infatuation again and for once she should follow his example and get her head in the game. Although he perhaps wasn't as single-minded about tonight as he'd led her to believe. She'd caught sight of him waving to someone in the crowd. Someone who'd made him smile. Not that she was jealous. She pitied him really that he couldn't be alone in his own company for five minutes without the need to hook up with a woman.

The single life suited her and she believed she was stronger without a partner to fret over. Between her and the apparently lovestruck Hunter she knew she'd be the one giving her all to the team without distractions. Not everyone would put the Demons first in their life the way she did, but it was concerning he had other priorities already. They didn't need any more drama behind the scenes and if he really was serious about being part of the squad he ought to be focusing somewhere other than the contents of his trousers. It gave credence to the notion he was only back here for Hunter Torrance's benefit, not the Demons'. She doubted he'd be willing to put in the overtime or go the extra mile the way she did if he had other pursuits outside working hours.

The first two periods of play were relatively uneventful, with both sides playing it safe and focusing on defence, so there were high hopes and expectations for the third period. Especially when the Demons had several near misses, with more attempts on goal than their opponents.

'Come on, guys.' Hunter's booming voice and the thump of his hands clapping as he willed the Demons to score didn't make it easy for Charlotte to concentrate on what was going on inside the rink instead of the decoration around it.

'You must miss this.' She hadn't meant to say it aloud when they'd seen the rest of the game out in virtual silence but he was so involved, animated on behalf of the team, it occurred to her how hard it probably was to no longer be part of the action. He'd skated on this very ice, played for this very team, and seen out the last days of his career here. She'd only been a fan so her position was akin to a lottery win in some aspects while his could be seen as a demotion, standing on the sidelines now.

The roar of outrage from around the arena after a high stick incident against one of their players drowned out her observation.

'What's that?' Hunter didn't take his eyes off the play but leaned down so he could hear her better.

She swallowed. This wasn't supposed to be a *thing*, it was simply her mouth opening before she'd realised. Now he was standing so close to her she could almost feel the rasp of his stubble against her cheek.

'I…er…was just saying you must miss this.' It sounded so feeble the second time around it really wasn't worth repeating.

Of course he missed it. Hockey had been his career, his life at one time. It had been a stupid thing to say, right up there with the people who asked her if she missed her mother. Duh. Generally not unless someone brought her up and made Charlotte realise how incomplete her life was without her in it. Now she'd done the same thing to him.

'Sorry. I should be following the game too, not chatting.'

For the first time since face-off he focused his full attention on her, his eyes bright and his smile wide. Enough to make her stop breathing.

'I do miss it. However, as has been pointed out to me, I'm probably more of a hindrance than an asset to the team these days.' His mischief-making brought the heat to her cheeks, and everywhere else.

To all intents and purposes he was the team's new signing, doing his best to fit in, and she'd acted the superior know-it-all, making life difficult for him. She didn't know this man yet she'd made preconceived judgements and behaved accordingly when he'd been nothing but friendly in the face of her childishness. For someone who was all about equal rights in the workplace she knew she wouldn't have been so forgiving if a colleague had been so awful to her for no apparent reason. A little teasing in return wasn't something she should complain about.

For a second she thought about apologising. The truth was, he *was* an asset. He'd treated all those on the injury list the way any experienced physiotherapist would have. She'd checked. It was her, letting her personal embarrassment over an old crush get in the way of a harmonious working relationship.

In the end she kept her mouth shut because she didn't trust herself not to blab about her past devotion for him when she was looking into those eyes that had once stared at her from her bedroom wall. Worse, she might go the other way and insult him again so he didn't realise she was having inappropriate thoughts about him.

She had to block him out of her sight and focus back on the game, something she'd never had any trouble doing before. Usually it was more a case of not losing herself in the match and making sure she was watching the players for signs of injury. Sometimes separating Dr Michaels from fan-girl Charlie took a great deal of effort.

The dizzying pace of the players covering the ice was as heart-pumping as it got for her. The hard-hitting alpha males and the danger of the sport had always been like catnip to a girl whose life had become so troubled and lonely. That was probably why she'd been instantly drawn to Hunter the first time she'd attended a game. Everything about him had said danger and excitement.

It still did.

The hairs prickled on the back of her neck and she knew Hunter was close again before he even spoke.

'Is there something wrong with Anderson I should know about?'

The object of his concern was already on her radar, a bit more sluggish than usual, which was worrying when he was their star player.

'He has missed a few training sessions lately, which would account for him being more breathless than usual. His fitness needs working on. I'll put a word in with Gray, if he hasn't already picked up on it himself.' She doubted she'd have to point anything out. Anderson was popping up on everyone's radar lately with his diva attitude. As top goal scorer they'd let his stroppy behaviour slide but now it was affecting his performance someone was going to have to take him to task.

'Hmm. It looks more serious than that to me.'

Anderson had been making rookie mistakes all night, getting caught offside and hooking the opposition with his stick in full view of the ref.

'I assure you he'll get a full physical after the game and if I find any areas for referral I will let you know.' This was her jurisdiction and it didn't matter who the new physio was, she was still the medical lead.

They watched Anderson shoulder-charge everyone out of his path. With the giant chip perched there these days it wasn't difficult to do.

'And if the problem's mental, not physical?' Hunter crossed his arms, his shirt tightening and vacuum-packing his biceps in white cotton.

'Well, it would also be down to me to make that judgement call.'

Not you. Back off.

He smirked and shook his head. Charlotte tried to ignore it but he was so far under her skin he'd burrowed right into her bones.

'What?' she finally snapped, the thought of her past infatuation sneering at her too much to take.

'I get it. You're the sheriff in this here town and I'm merely your deputy.' He tipped his imaginary Stetson and she conceded a small smile. Well, it was better than swooning after that image and a Southern drawl double whammy.

'And don't you forget it.'

They locked eyes for a second too long, the laughter giving way to something more...serious. She looked away first and let the background game noise fill in the gaps in conversation. Just when it seemed as if they were starting to bond, stupid chemistry, or stupid rejuvenated teenage hormones, tried to turn it into something she didn't want, or need, in her life.

Before she was tempted to take another peek at him, a face was mashed into the Perspex in front of her, the violent thud shaking the very ground beneath her feet. The distorted features of a Cobra player slid down the glass, making her wince. She was always conflicted when it came to such territorial displays of male aggression. As a fan, it was a barbaric form of entertainment, watching your team dominate the other. As a medical professional, she understood the physical ramifications of such an impact and as the on-site doctor she'd be called on to treat any injuries caused to the opposition too. That was why she was standing here with her first-aid bag by her feet, for those players who couldn't shake it off and get back on their feet.

The shrill peep of the ref's whistle pierced the air.

'What was that for?' Charlotte demanded to know, along with most of the crowd rising from their seats as Anderson was reprimanded.

Hunter flinched. 'He checked him from behind. That's gonna cost him time in the penalty box.'

'Oh. I didn't see that,' she said, cowed by her own mistake. She knew it was an illegal move because it carried a risk of serious injury but she couldn't tell him she'd missed it because she'd been busy gawping at him.

'I'm guessing he hoped everyone else had missed it too. Now what's he doing? He messed up. He should own it and do the time.' Hunter threw his hands up in despair as Anderson remonstrated with virtually everyone in authority as he made his way to the penalty box.

His gestures imitated that of a clearly frustrated Gray too as he yelled at his star player from the bench. The coach was a disturbing shade of purple as he fought to control his temper and she made a mental note to check his blood pressure.

Anderson's penalty left the Demons short-handed for the dying minutes of the game and Charlotte held her breath with every other fan desperate to keep the dream alive. There were so many bodies in the goal crease as they fought for a victory it was difficult to make out who had possession. Until the klaxon sounded and the red light behind the net flashed, signalling a goal.

The Demons had defied the odds and claimed a win, sending the crowd into a furore, but Anderson's mood didn't improve when the game was over and he left the ice. He stripped off his kit and threw it piece by piece down the tunnel in temper as he clunked past Hunter and Charlotte, unleashing a string of expletives directed at no one in particular.

Despite his public celebration with the team on the ice after their narrow win, Gray's demeanour changed too when he approached them. 'I don't know what the hell is wrong with Anderson but he needs sorting out before the next game. You two are supposed to be the experts around here. Find out what's eating him and fix it, or don't expect to be signing new contracts any time soon.'

'Gray—' Hunter tried to put a hand on his shoulder in an apparent attempt to calm him down but he shrugged it off.

'I pulled a lot of strings to get you here, Hunter, and I expect a lot in return. I don't care if you talk to him as an ex-pro, sports physician or a fellow maniac, it's your job to get him match fit and right now he's following in your footsteps to career suicide.'

She could almost hear Hunter's heart fall into his shiny shoes with a thud as his so-called ally cut him down with a few cruel words. The hand of friendship fell slowly to his side, the pain of rejection chiselled into his furrowed forehead. Her previous disparaging comments aside, she kind of felt sorry for him. His past misdemeanours were always going to be thrown back in his face regardless of his subsequent achievements and acts of repentance.

'There's really no need for that, Gray.' She put herself in Hunter's position for the first time and thought how it might feel to have someone cast up the naivety of her youth. Horrendous. Soul-destroying. Unfair.

She'd spent a lifetime distancing herself from that person and if he was to be believed, so had Hunter. Switching careers from hockey pro to qualified sports therapist wasn't something that would've happened on a whim. It would've taken years of dedication and determination. All of which was being cast aside as if it was nothing because someone was in a bad mood. Or because someone was deflecting the shame of their own past.

Gray held his hand up to stop her. 'It goes for you too, Charlie. Fair or not, I need results. I'm sure you can come up with a diagnosis and treatment plan between the two of you. After all, that's what you're here for.' With that, he spun on his heel and powered towards the changing room.

She lifted an abandoned puck from the ground and

tossed it in her hand, tempted to lob it in his general direction. Two could let temper get the better of them.

Hunter caught it in mid-air. 'You don't want to do anything you might live to regret, Charlotte.' That serious face said he was speaking from painful experience. One he'd never be allowed to forget.

She let her aggression subside with a sigh, partly due to his voice of reason and perhaps because he'd used her name for the first time. Everyone here called her Charlie, in keeping with her efforts to remain one of the guys. Her full name, in that accent, made her feel positively girly. Even in her game night layers of fleece and comfort.

'He'd no right to say any of those things. At least, not the personal stuff. I guess he's kind of right about the reason we're here. He just didn't have to be so rude about it,' she huffed on his behalf, since he seemed determined not to rise to it. Not so long ago she imagined he wouldn't have thought twice about charging down there after him and duking it out.

Perhaps he had changed. Perhaps he did deserve to have someone give him the benefit of the doubt. Then again, if his one friend here couldn't let go of the past and fully trust him, why should she?

Hunter shrugged, those broad shoulders refusing to carry any more baggage upon them. 'He's right. He did call in a lot of favours for me. I owe him big time.' Either he had really matured or he was putting on an award-winning performance to dupe her into thinking he had. Especially when she was the one chomping at the bit to retaliate.

She had to remind herself he didn't owe her anything personally; there was nothing to be gained in convincing her he was anyone but himself, except to prove his commitment to the job.

'So what do we do?' Stitches and concussion she could

deal with. A burly hockey player with his finger on the self-destruct button was out of her comfort zone.

'I wouldn't want to step on your toes…' He held up his hands in mock surrender to her self-appointed superiority.

'Okay, okay. If I have to tackle an irate man twice my size, I could use the backup.'

And because Gray had said so.

'We can't do anything until we've seen to everyone else. We're going to have our work cut out for us back there, after that last scrum especially.'

'Then what? The chances Anderson is waiting patiently back there for counselling, treatment or another rollicking are slim to none.'

They had no clue what was ailing him and from her experience thus far, hockey players were stubborn about admitting any weakness. There was definitely more of an 'I can tough it out' attitude to injury than she was used to from other athletes. It made her job that much more difficult when those niggling pains turned into something more serious left untreated.

If it was some sort of chronic or traumatic acute injury sometimes it could mean the end of a career. In which case, Anderson would be even less inclined to admit there was a problem. Male pride could be a terrible affliction if left unchecked.

'You heard Gray. *We* have to find him.'

She let out her breath in a huff, which may or may not have had to do with his continual glances into the crowd.

'Unless the Demons have taken to tracking their players, how on earth are we going to do that?' By the time they finished up here he could be anywhere. It would be dark, and she would be more than a bit cheesed off with the whole drama. Especially when she was expected to do it with Mr Torrance and that brought him much too close for comfort.

'If I know my hockey players, and the heart of any

Northern Irish town, there's only one place Anderson will be sitting his time out. Let's hit the pub.'

If she didn't love her job so much she would've left him to it but these were still her players, her patients, her team, and she wasn't afraid of dropping the gloves herself to fight. It wasn't only the Demons' honour at stake here.

Not only was Gray frothing at the mouth despite the result but Hunter was struggling to find those feel-good endorphins too. It was his son's first match, the first time he'd seen his father's team in action, if not playing himself, and he hadn't been able to share it with him.

'Sorry I couldn't sit with you tonight, bud.' He managed to catch Alfie and his grandparents before they disappeared out of the arena and into the night.

'That's okay. Maybe we can come again?' He glanced up at his guardians with the same hope Hunter was still clinging to.

'We're coming to the end of the season now but perhaps I could bring Alfie for a tour behind the scenes some time?' It was a big ask, he knew, but if he was to win over his son he had to start fighting for time alone with him.

Alfie's face lit up but his grandmother shut down the notion of any unauthorised trips with a stern 'We'll see'.

The light began to dim again before flaring back to life. 'Maybe Dad could come back with us for supper?'

It was the first time Alfie had called him Dad and it choked Hunter up that he was even starting to think of him in that role. It killed him to have to let him down.

'It's getting late and I still have some work to do here. Another night, bud.' He knelt down and Alfie rushed towards him, hugged him so tightly it brought tears to his eyes. He didn't care he could barely breathe because he'd never been as happy as he was in this second. This was the beginning of the family he'd never had and the pieces were finally slotting into place.

'Come on, Alfie. It's bedtime.'

Although Hunter was thankful for the opportunities afforded him to get to know his son, he was looking forward to the days when there wouldn't be a time limit set on their relationship.

He slowly and reluctantly peeled Alfie from around his neck. 'I'll see you again soon. You be good.'

The kiss he dropped on his son's head inadequately expressed the love he felt for this child he'd been without for too long but it was all he had to give for now.

Someday they'd be watching the games and eating popcorn together before going home to their own house. Until then they'd have to snatch whatever time was granted by those who thought they knew what was best.

''Night, Dad.'

''Night, son.' He waved the trio off, watching them safely across the road until he was too misty-eyed to make them out.

He sucked in a deep breath of the cool night air to fortify his aching heart and blinked away his sentimentality. It was time to focus on the positives. Alfie was happy and safe and he had a job to do. He'd prefer to keep it that way.

It was close to midnight before they were able to leave the arena. His, or Anderson's, personal problems had to wait until the players who actually hung around after the game were properly cooled down. Ice baths and stretches were equally as important as the warm-up to keep the muscles in prime condition. He knew Charlotte had a few nicks and grazes to treat on both teams but nothing serious or unusual for men in close contact with sharp blades every day of the week. He came to knock on her door just as she was lecturing her last patient.

'Remember: RICE. Rest, ice, compression—'

'And elevation. I got it, Doc,' a weary Evenshaw replied as she strapped up his ankle.

Hunter gave him a hand down off the bed and watched him limp away. 'I hope that's nothing serious.'

'A slight sprain,' she said as she packed away the dressings and other bits and bobs she'd used to patch players together again.

Now she'd ditched her zip-up outer layer he could see she was wearing a white round-neck T-shirt. It wasn't a particularly remarkable piece of clothing, forgettable, if it wasn't for the fact she'd unwittingly exposed her toned midriff as she'd yawned and stretched.

He coughed away the sudden surge of awareness heading south of the border. It had been a long time since he'd had the pleasure of seeing a female body who wasn't a patient, otherwise he wouldn't be responding like a virgin seeing a naked woman for the first time.

'I hope you're not too tired to go Anderson-hunting?' Although it might be better if she was. Regardless of Gray's insistence and the prospect this could somehow improve working relations between him and Charlotte, he was beginning to have doubts this was a good idea.

He kept losing focus when he was around her, not concentrating on the game or the arrival of his VIPs but watching spots of colour rise in her cheeks as he baited her. There'd also been that moment when she'd stood up for him against Gray. That had been unexpected. From both sides.

Clearly he and his one and only friend still had unresolved issues. Although Hunter knew Gray had said those things in the heat of the moment, there was truth behind them. He'd let him down in the past and though the words had hurt, he'd deserved them and Gray had needed to say them. He just hoped now he'd got it off his chest they could move on again. He wouldn't dwell on it when he knew how much more pain could be caused by letting a grudge fester out of control. It had already ended one career and he didn't think he had it in him to start over again if this didn't work out.

No, it was Charlotte's attitude that had been most surprising when she'd been the most outspoken about his reputation so far. Perhaps they were starting to make progress after all and she was no longer seeing him as the Ballydolan Demon come to life. Whatever it was, it had felt good to have someone on his side after all this time. Someone whose opinion of him appeared to be turning and she wasn't afraid of saying it out loud.

'Of course I'm not too tired,' she snapped.

'Of course you're not,' he replied. For a woman who appeared so delicate on the outside she wasn't afraid of much. He got the impression she'd trawl the whole of Ireland even if she was dead on her feet if it meant sticking two fingers up at the doubters.

'Where do we start?' Charlotte was back at his side, refusing to let him forget her.

'Wherever's within walking distance.' He set off at a brisk pace, determined to get this over with and get back to his bachelor pad as soon as possible. Minus company.

'How do you know he hasn't just gone home or taken a six pack off into the woods?' Charlotte was almost running to catch up with him as she struggled back into that hideous jacket but he didn't slow down for her. With any luck she'd get fed up and go home.

That was as likely as Anderson being tucked up in bed.

'I know we Canadians are a hardy lot but we're not stupid. That would mean having to go into the bar to buy booze and take it away. Dark woods might appeal to a brooding romantic hero but he's a hockey player, he needs to blow off steam fast.'

'He could have gone home like any other disgruntled

employee after a hard day at work,' she grumbled under her breath, but she didn't know hockey players the way he did.

It was much easier to understand Anderson's state of mind when you'd been there yourself. If he was anything close to following the same pattern he himself had, not only would he be somewhere, getting drunk quickly, he'd be spoiling for a fight to unleash some more of that aggression they'd witnessed earlier.

'It's possible but if we're thinking logically, there are about six bars on the route back towards his house.' He'd asked around for details, not that there were many forthcoming. Although he knew where Anderson resided there was little information about his personal life. It wasn't because the players were reluctant to share with him—in that respect they seemed quite open to him, probably because of his hockey background. No, it seemed no one knew much about Anderson outside the team or alcohol-fuelled nights out. That in itself was dangerous. Hunter understood only too well how isolating it could be out here with no family around to catch you when you fell and pull you up by the scruff of the neck. Perhaps if he'd had someone do that for him he might've salvaged something of his sports career.

'I don't know why they need so many pubs in such a small space anyway,' she bristled, every inch the reluctant partygoer, and he was beginning to wonder why she was so against the idea of calling in at the local establishments when it was the obvious place to start their search.

Maybe she was teetotal, although that seemed as far-fetched out here as leprechauns and their crock of gold.

'So you have somewhere to go when you get kicked out of the last one?' Well, that's how he'd treated the place when he'd done his fair share of drinking and brawling here. Strangely, it had only seemed to ingratiate him more with the locals. Until he'd taken it too far, of course, and cost them the championship.

There was a very unladylike grunt behind him but he refrained from continuing the argument. Anderson was close by, he'd put money on it. The sound of the *craic* coming from behind the doors and the draw of the liquor would be too much to resist.

They started their bar crawl at The Ballydolan Inn, the first dingy building no bigger than one of the nearby cottages at the bottom of the hill. Once they made their way past the smokers outside they were hit with a wall of noise as the doors swung open. The deafening roar soon died down to a curious silence as the locals eyed them suspiciously. If this had been a Western his trigger finger would be itching, waiting for someone to make their move.

Voices rumbled low but Hunter caught the mutterings about 'that hockey player'.

He scoured the interior, imagining an angry, drunk, Canadian forward would stand out in this crowd of regulars. When he saw nothing but curious Irish eyes staring back, he was ready to leave too. He wasn't up for another round of twenty questions about his personal life after leaving this place under a dark cloud and turned to chivvy his companion back out onto the street. 'Let's try the next one.'

They received much the same welcome there at The Hillside Tavern.

'Isn't that the big hockey fella who went nuts a few years back?'

'Aye.'

'Thought he'd be dead by now.'

'Used to play hockey. No longer *nuts*. Definitely not dead but very much older and wiser.'

Hunter tackled the rumours head on as they flew around him.

There was much more back-slapping after that, propelling them both towards the bar.

'Glad to hear it.'

'Sure you'll have a wee drink for old times' sake.'

It wasn't long before a space was cleared at the bar for them.

'Your local drinking establishment?' Charlotte mocked with a raised eyebrow, finding difficulty imagining him partying in here during his time with the Demons. In her head he'd been living it up in the clubs in Belfast or exclusive house parties for the rich and famous. If she'd known he was only down the street she might have socialised a bit more herself.

'Once upon a time. It hasn't changed much.'

'I doubt it's changed at all in the last century.' It still had the dark wood interior she remembered, permeated with the smell of the peat fire and sweat.

'I suppose we should really find out if there's more than one hockey player they've been doling out booze to tonight.' She was beginning to see how easy it would be to fall into the drinking culture here. Honestly, there wasn't much else to do at night. When the game had first come here over a decade ago it had been a godsend to the young inhabitants like her, giving them somewhere fun and exciting to go without getting into trouble.

He shook hands with the landlord. 'Sorry, not tonight, Michael, I'm still on the clock. Have you seen one of ours in here? Anderson?'

'There was a big, blond fella who talks like you in here earlier but he was a bit worse for wear. He made a nuisance of himself, to be honest. Spilt a few drinks, broke a few glasses. I had to chuck him out. Sorry, if I'd known he was with you—'

'I'm sure he'll not be too far away. How long ago was this?'

'A good hour ago, I'd say.'

'Thanks.' Hunter grabbed her hand and bolted out the door with a renewed sense of urgency. The electric touch of his strong fingers clasping hers sent her pulse racing as they stole back out into the night.

He let go of her long after they had an excuse to be holding hands.

She absent-mindedly rubbed the palm of her hand where his had crossed it, mourning the loss of his touch already.

'Do you really think we're going to catch up with him?' She was a little on edge, spending so much time with Hunter. Every minute together altered her perception of the man she'd loved and hated in equal measure without ever knowing him beyond his public image. It was unsettling to find out he was as normal as anyone else. She'd moved past her crush a long time ago but she was worried it might take her somewhere more dangerous than a shallow physical attraction if she wasn't careful.

'Oh, aye.' His attempt at the local accent couldn't fail to make her laugh and she was rewarded with a toothy grin.

She'd always thought him attractive—that was a no-brainer. What teenage girl wouldn't have had her head turned by a handsome sportsman from a distant land? Finding out Hunter hadn't the hero she'd imagined him to be had been the biggest betrayal of all. Her mistake had been compounded by watching him fall apart before her eyes in those last matches until he'd convinced her there wasn't actually anything more than good looks and bad attitude there.

His short time back in the country was already beginning to change that opinion when he was doing whatever was asked for him to aid the team. That eye-opener spurred her on over the crest of the hill towards the old brick building with the faded green 'Kelly's' sign.

She was saved from further personal revelations as a rather large, unkempt figure came barrelling out of the pub door to land at their feet on the pavement. It didn't take a genius to work out what the cheer from inside and the sight of a burly barman dusting off his hands at the door meant.

'Anderson?' Hunter hunched down and brushed the dirty, bloody mop of hair out of the face of the unfortunate who'd been swiftly tossed from the premises.

'That's me,' he said with a slur. 'Gus Anderson. Man of the match. The crowd go wild.'

He was cheering now, swaying from side to side and pumping his fist in the air.

'Someone's got a high opinion of himself.' Charlotte was having second thoughts about helping if he really was this deluded. He'd almost cost them the match, the play-offs and their very jobs tonight.

'He's wasted. He doesn't know what he's saying.' Hunter struggled to get him onto his feet and although he didn't ask her to, Charlotte felt compelled to help.

She ducked under one arm of their patient, bolstering his left side. He weighed a ton, even though she knew Hunter was probably shouldering most of the weight.

'Er...now what? How are we supposed to fix *this*?'

'We can take him back to my place.' Hunter was already a bit breathless bench-pressing the man mountain so she hoped he lived somewhere close before all three of them ended up in a ditch by the side of the road.

They half dragged, half carried their wayward charge until they came to a cottage down the lane past Kelly's.

'This is your house?' The pretty chocolate-box cottage and garden didn't seem very *him*.

'Here, hold him until I get the door open.' He deposited most of Anderson's bulk around her shoulders and stopped her asking any of the questions flooding her head as she fought to stop her body being concertinaed into the ground.

Are you renting? Did you inherit? Does your girlfriend live here with you?

In hindsight she suspected that was the very reason he'd

been so ungentlemanly in the first place. Whatever the secret, he wanted to keep it to himself. Thankfully, once he opened the door and found the light switch, he shared the burden with her until they were able to dump Anderson into a nearby chair.

'We'll need to get him cleaned and sobered up.' Gray would be expecting results and now under the glare of the living-room light she could see Anderson was a bit battered and bruised.

'Let's see if we can get him up to the bathroom.' Hunter steered them towards a narrow staircase and they somehow managed to manoeuvre him into the shower cubicle, still fully clothed.

A grinning Hunter switched on the water and closed the bathroom door on Anderson's shrieks as he underwent some sobering cold-water therapy. He backed out of the room, bumping into Charlotte in the cramped hallway. She stumbled back, tripping over the upturned edge of the faded hallway carpet. There was that helpless moment when she felt herself overbalance and tip over the edge of the staircase. All she could do was brace herself for the hard, painful landing she knew was coming.

Hunter shot out an arm around her waist, catching her before she fell off that top step and pulling her roughly against his chest, knocking the breath out of her.

'Sorry. I thought we should get out while he's cooling off. I didn't mean to nearly break your neck in the process.'

Her adrenaline was pumping as much from the near miss as being pressed against his hard body.

'You're forgiven.' She aimed for a friendly smile to hide the fact he'd unnerved her by being so close but her heart was pounding so hard she could no longer hear anything but the rush of blood in her ears.

For an instant their eyes locked, this intimate moment between the two of them frozen in time. His eyes darkened as they lit on her smiling lips and the conspiratorial jovial-ity seemed to fade. He was watching her with such hunger, such focus there was no denying what it was he wanted, what he wanted to do to her. Just as before, she felt herself submit helplessly to gravity, only this time it was pulling her ever closer to his lips.

'Hey, you guys are too cruel. What, are you like SAS trainers or something?' Anderson yanked the door open and exploded the fantasy.

Hunter wrenched away from her so quickly he'd prob-ably left friction burns in the carpet.

Charlotte was more appalled by her own behaviour. They'd almost kissed. Totally inappropriate with a work colleague, especially when there was every chance he was involved with someone else. So they hadn't actually made lip contact but she was pretty sure the intention had been there on both sides and that was bad news all around. Clearly she hadn't yet reached her lifetime's worth of hu-miliation where this man was concerned.

'I'll get some coffee on the go.' Hunter took the stairs two at a time in his obvious haste to get away.

She waited until she heard him banging about in the kitchen before she dared follow. At least Anderson, who'd ditched his sodden clothes for a bath towel, made for a dis-traction from the sudden atmosphere in the house.

She reached for her trusty first-aid bag, which she'd been carrying all night, predicting it would end in some sort of medical emergency, and pulled out an alcohol wipe to cleanse the deepest scratch on his face.

'Ouch!' He drew in a quick breath as if she'd poured salt into an open wound.

'Seriously?' She'd barely touched him and, with the stench of alcohol emanating through his very pores, she'd imagined he was probably numb from the scalp down.

'It stings, man.'

'Sorry. I'll be as gentle as I can.' Perhaps she'd been a tad more abrasive than she should have when she was angry at herself for the incident at the top of the stairs. She should know better than to let her personal feelings leak into her professional manner. Although Anderson was the reason she'd been thrown together with Hunter tonight, it wasn't his fault she'd thrown herself *at* him.

'What happened back there anyway?' She tried to turn her thoughts back to her patient's current predicament, not her own, but it was easier said than done when she could still imagine Hunter's arms wrapped around her.

'At a rough guess I'd say a disagreement with some Cobra fans. Am I right? That's where the opposition hang out when they're in town.' Hunter handed him a mug of black coffee and offered her one without any indication this was in any way awkward for him after what had just occurred.

She declined. A nightcap of any description here wasn't going to happen. Once she had her big, brave soldier patched up she was packing up and running back to the safety of her own house, where she could analyse the reasons behind that almost-kiss.

Her patient took a sip of the strong-smelling brew and winced. 'Just some friendly rivalry.'

'Hmm. Well, it looks like one of your new friends took serious offence to something you either said or did. That cut on your cheek is going to need stitching.'

He was fortunate it wasn't closer to his eye but she'd lecture him tomorrow when he would remember it. It was too bad she wouldn't forget the events of tonight as easily because she knew they were going to change everything between her and Hunter at work. If she wasn't careful things were going to get even more complicated than they already were.

CHAPTER THREE

CHARLOTTE WENT TO wash up and proceeded to suture the deep cut. Hunter knew it was saving them all a hospital trip but the longer she spent in his house, the antsier he was becoming. They'd had one close call already. Only an irate Canadian water rat had pulled the brakes on that near-kiss that had come from nowhere and yet had seemed so natural. That was a direct contravention of his new dad regulations. He hadn't figured romance into his future plans at all.

As Charlotte tended to her patient, whose massive frame was wedged into the floral old-lady furniture, it struck Hunter how odd the set-up here must've appeared to her. At the time of renting the place he'd thought only of being close to Alfie. The owner had been keen to sell if he decided to stay permanently since this had been his late mother's house. One day Hunter imagined he and Alfie would put their own stamp on the décor. Until then he'd have to put up with the crocheted blankets and rocking chairs.

'All finished.' Charlotte had done a neat job, even in these unusual circumstances. Not that he was surprised when he'd seen and heard exactly how passionate she was about her work. The Demons were lucky to have her, yet Anderson hadn't even bothered to thank her.

He had an inkling they were all in for a very long night.

In the old days Hunter's first reaction to dealing with the stresses of the evening would've been to head straight to the bar. Whilst he was sorely tempted, it wouldn't solve any of their problems, so he served himself a shot of caffeine and took his position in the therapist chair.

'Do you want to talk about what happened tonight?' It would be easier than having him tear up the house in another rage-filled rampage.

Anderson eyed Charlotte sideways through his mop of wet, straggly blond hair.

'Surely you're not suddenly shy now? Charlotte's seen all of your antics tonight, don't forget.' Regardless of their personal faux pas, he didn't think she'd walk out if they were about to make a breakthrough here. As far as he'd seen, she always put her job first and wouldn't be sidelined when it came to the players' treatment on anyone's account.

'Anything you say in front of us is strictly confidential. We just want to help, Gus.' She took a seat next to Hunter on the couch, confirming that she wasn't going anywhere.

Anderson sighed. 'These Irish chicks…it's like they bewitch you or something.'

He was shaking his head but there was a ghost of a smile in there somewhere behind all that hair. It was a start, an opening to what was going on beyond the Hulkish façade. Hunter would've agreed except he didn't want his captivating companion beside him knowing that's exactly what she was doing to him. That was the only explanation of why he was veering so dangerously off track from common sense.

If there was one thing guaranteed to make a man want to smash stuff in a testosterone-fuelled rage it was woman trouble. Make that two things. Parents who wished you'd never been born had the same effect.

The big guy was on his feet, pacing. Hunter scanned the room for valuable antiques he should probably remove before he was charged for breakages but he was sure he could afford to lose the ugly owl ornament on the mantelpiece made from seashells and the tears of frightened children.

'This place was only supposed to be a stopgap, some-where I could make a name for myself and move on.'

The opposite of Hunter's career slide into oblivion here. It had been the beginning of the end for him when he'd been shipped out here but a young, up-and-coming star like Anderson had a future in the UK league, maybe even the NHL, if he didn't screw it up too.

'Unless there's something you're not telling us, the only one putting that in jeopardy is you. Trust me, that temper is gonna get you attention for all the wrong reasons. Whatever you've got going on, deal with it now before your name is one no team wants attached to them.' It was true for him almost a decade later, even with a change of career. If it wasn't for Gray throwing him a lifeline he'd be stacking shelves in the local supermarket.

Gus flopped back into the chair and Hunter waited qui-etly so he didn't spook his unpredictable companion. Char-lotte seemed to be of the same thinking as she remained quiet too. Neither of them would benefit from him kick-ing off again. Instead of forcing the issue, they let silence dominate.

He'd learned a lot from his own counselling sessions where the onus had been on him to fill the gaps in con-versation. In the end the uncomfortable lack of interaction had forced him to verbalise the feelings he'd been avoiding since seeking out his birth family, and confront the crush-ing damage their rejection had caused to his self-esteem and self-worth.

It had taken him years to tackle the subject and under-stand he wasn't the one who'd done anything wrong. By which time it had been too late and he'd lost everything and everyone else. If he could prevent the same thing hap-pening to his friend here, he would.

Whether there was a physical or emotional issue behind his behaviour, he needed to ask for help, instead of hiding behind the villain mask and pushing everyone away. He might've processed what had happened to him in his past, apportioned blame to the right people now and finally moved on, but that didn't mean there wasn't lingering frustration at having blown his hockey career along the way.

'Maggie's pregnant.' Anderson finally punctuated the silence with his shoulder-slumping admission.

Charlotte let out a long breath beside him. So it wasn't a serious injury he was battling but it was potentially a mess. At least he was opening up. It was progress; the first step towards salvaging the man and the player.

'And Maggie is?' Hunter wasn't assuming anything. She could be a fan, a one-night stand or a married woman for all the anguish this situation was apparently causing.

'We've been seeing each other for a few months. I mean, I like her. I really like her but I'm not ready for this.'

'Okay. This isn't the end of the world. I mean, I know it's a big shock but it happens to people every day and they live through it.' Charlotte attempted to reassure him and Hunter could almost see her mind ticking over, trying to figure out how they could help him come to terms with impending fatherhood.

He resisted a lecture on contraception when it wasn't going to make any difference now but he might suggest to Charlotte that they provide some literature on the subject to try and prevent more unwanted pregnancies or STDs among the players in the future. Although it did make him a feel a bit of a hypocrite when he'd made the same mistake at this guy's age. The only difference between him and Anderson was he hadn't known about Sara's pregnancy.

Perhaps that had been for the best. He hadn't been in the right frame of mind to be a father to Alfie then, or a supportive partner to Sara. By all accounts, they'd had a happier life without him and it had taken reaching rock bottom alone for him to finally get the help he'd needed to be the best dad he could be for Alfie.

'How does Maggie feel about it?' Of course it was Charlotte who remembered there was someone else's feelings in the equation here.

Gus looked at her as though it was the first time he'd even considered the effect it would have on his probably equally young girlfriend. The arrogance of youth.

'She's scared about how her parents are going to react to the news. I'm sure a hockey player wouldn't be their first choice for their daughter's baby daddy.'

'I hear ya.' Even without the drinking, fighting and generally acting like a jerk, he suspected Sara's parents would always have disapproved of him. Everyone, including him, had known he wasn't good enough. Sara and Alfie should have had a stable, reliable guy with a steady job to support them. He was doing his best to be that man for Alfie now. That's why the idea of getting together with anyone, even Charlotte, was dangerous.

He didn't miss Charlotte's raised eyebrows as he sympathised but he wasn't ready to share his own surprise baby story with anyone just yet. 'Do you have any family of your own here, Gus?'

He shook his head. 'We keep in touch from time to time but I haven't seen them for a while.'

It was too easy to distance yourself from family when living abroad, even if they did care about you, and they were the very people who could save a person from total despair. Unfortunately his hadn't.

'I would really make the effort to talk to your parents about this. You and Maggie both need the support. As someone who was effectively stranded here without any sort of emotional backup I would advise making the most of it so you don't end up making the catastrophic decisions I did.' So he'd shared a little personal info but it would be worth it to stop someone else making those same mistakes and throwing away the chance of a happy family.

Charlotte shifted in the seat next to him but he couldn't bear to look at her and see any hint of pity there. This wasn't supposed to be a group therapy session, he genuinely just wanted to help and the best way to do that was by showing some solidarity.

Anderson frowned. 'I really couldn't deal with their disappointment on top of everything else.'

'I know it's going to be a difficult conversation to have but, trust me, you don't want to go through this alone. Right now you're reacting on an emotional level. You need that grounding. Someone to give you a kick up the backside to start thinking clearly. If I'd had parents who'd given a damn, who I could've turned to for help when I needed it, I might never have left here in the first place.' Even now it was hard not to be bitter about the hand he'd been dealt: two sets of parents who'd happily sat back and watched him self-destruct. The only person who'd been there for him had been Sara but he'd been in too much pain to even let her get close emotionally.

'Hunter's right. This is too big to keep to yourself. If you're still on good terms with your mum and dad, swallow your pride and at least pick up the phone to talk to them if you can't visit in person. Make the most of having them in your life because you'll miss them when they're gone.' Charlotte was leaning forward in her seat, her arms wrapped around her waist, and he recognised that self-protecting gesture of someone who'd experienced that same isolation and loneliness, even if her experience of family sounded vastly different from his.

'You've both lost your parents?' The roles were reversed as Anderson took over the role of therapist.

'Mine aren't dead. They just wish I was. Neither my adoptive nor birth parents are in my life. Their choice, not mine.' There was no point dancing around the facts but it did make for an awkward silence as the blunt statement made an impact and he wondered if he had overshared after all.

'I...er...did lose my mum a few years ago. My dad, much like Hunter's family, has decided he'd rather not be part of my life.'

Hunter wanted to lean over and give her a hug but she probably wouldn't appreciate the public display of solidarity. Feckless parents were the worst. Which was why he worried so much about getting it right himself. His actions now would affect Alfie for the rest of his life and that was a huge responsibility, one not to be taken lightly or disregarded without a second thought.

'Listen, this isn't about us or our absent parents but you can see for yourself that the decisions you make as a parent from here on in will have long, far-reaching consequences.'

'No pressure, then,' Anderson grumbled, his immaturity stubbornly shining through despite the pep talk.

'Which is why you don't want to be hasty, acting out without giving thought to the consequences of your actions.'

Where had Charlotte been when he'd needed to hear that straight talking? If he'd had someone like her on his team during those dark times, things could've been so very different. Maybe, just maybe he wouldn't have treated Sara and everyone else here with such reckless abandon.

'I don't want to spend the rest of my days here changing diapers. I want to go places.'

'The two aren't mutually exclusive, you know. There are plenty of dads on the team whose families are quite happy to move wherever the opportunities arise. Have you had a talk about the future, or what either of you want?' It seemed hypocritical to be dishing out advice on relationships when he'd never had a successful one of any kind himself but Hunter believed his failure made him the best person for the job. He'd been that idiot incapable of dealing with his emotions and was still dealing with the repercussions. A living example of what not to do.

At least Anderson had the grace to look ashamed. 'No. I guess I didn't take the news very well when she first told me and she isn't replying to any of my messages.'

Hunter groaned at the idiocy as history repeated itself. He might not have known Sara was pregnant but it was that same lack of communication that had killed their chances of being a family. That and his descent into the red mist that had consumed him and was now beckoning Anderson to the dark side.

Had he really been this self-absorbed when Sara had been making decisions about her future and that of their baby? Probably, and it was too late to apologise. He knew now the reason behind his own meltdown but it didn't excuse his behaviour and he took full responsibility for those he'd hurt. He bore many regrets but that one hurt the most.

Thankfully it wasn't too late for Gus and Maggie.

'Here's an idea, why don't you go and see her in person, prove you're taking this seriously and stop acting like a spoilt brat?' Insulting him was a risky move but there was no time for tiptoeing around him any more.

The slight nod in agreement enabled Hunter to speak freely without worrying he might lose a couple of teeth for his trouble.

'Do you love her?'

'Yes.' There was no hesitation, which gave some hope for the parents-to-be.

'Good. That's the foundation you need to start from. Concentrate on that for now. Find out if she feels the same and work together on taking that next step. A little word from the wise, you might want to quit the temper tantrums on ice too. You don't want her to think she has two babies to deal with and getting fired isn't going to help you, Maggie or the baby. Been there, lost my shirt and the girl. Don't recommend it.'

'You're right. I need to step up and be there for her.' He made to get out of the chair and it dawned on Hunter he meant now, wearing only a towel and still slightly slurring his words. Not the best impression to give if he wanted Maggie to forgive him and understand he was taking the matter seriously.

Hunter was quicker getting to his feet. He put a hand on Anderson's shoulder and firmly guided him back into his seat.

'It's late. She's probably asleep. I have a spare room you can stay the night in. Go see her tomorrow after you've sobered up.'

'I can probably give you some coaching in effective grovelling techniques before you see her, if it'll help?' Charlotte added her weight behind the campaign to get him back into Maggie's good books. They were turning out to be quite a team after all.

'It can't hurt. Thanks for all your help, guys.' Anderson threw his arms around Hunter, catching him around the waist in an awkward man hug.

'No problem. Just remember, we're your family too.' He took the hit so Charlotte wouldn't have to, hoping Gus would go to bed before he entered the 'I love you' stage of drunkenness.

Hunter knew he was in for a long sleepless night himself. Not only was he going to have to make frequent checks on his intoxicated patient but he had a lot of thinking to do about his own life. He couldn't very well preach the importance of communication one minute and pretend there hadn't been a shift between him and Charlotte the next.

If he followed his own advice and admitted he liked her, that there was a powerful attraction pulling them towards each other, then they'd have to discuss their next step too.

The problem was if he let her into his life he was going to have to be honest about Alfie. Her reaction to that bombshell would determine what happened next.

Just as he'd told his fellow new dad, the time for playing games was over. They both had some growing up to do. These days a kiss meant much more than a kiss when it could potentially put the custody of his son at risk.

'Right, well, it's getting late. I should probably go home.' Charlotte waited until Hunter had safely ensconced his new lodger in the spare room before she made her excuses to leave.

There was no reason to hang around any longer than was necessary now her professional obligations had been fulfilled for the night and they appeared to be making progress with Gus. The biggest breakthrough for her, though, had been the sensitivity with which Hunter had handled everything. He'd given so much of himself tonight in the effort to get through to their teammate he'd really touched her heart. So much so she'd thought it a good idea to kiss him. Thank goodness for Anderson's intervention, which had averted the looming disaster.

If they had given in to whatever attraction had flickered in the moment there was no limit to the amount of damage it could have done, crossing the line of all her boundaries. She didn't want an atmosphere at work other than a professional one and didn't need any more complications that could impact on the team. It was a moment of madness she couldn't let happen again for her sake and everyone else's. That feeling of being out of control wasn't something she wanted to get used to.

'I'll walk you back to the arena so you can get your car.' Hunter was already holding the front door open for her, keen for her to hit the road.

'That's really not necessary. I'm a big girl. I can look after myself.' She'd been doing it for years and she couldn't afford to look any weaker than she already had tonight after almost kissing him.

He leaned against the door, arms folded. 'I know you can but do I really seem the sort of guy that'll stand here and watch a woman walk off into the darkness alone?'

No, he didn't. He was the perfect gentleman.

She didn't know when exactly she'd realised that after the low expectations she'd had about him. Probably around the time she'd been closing her eyes and waiting for him to kiss her.

He'd surprised her tonight with his level head and calm handling of the situation. Whilst that could only mean good things for his position with the Demons, it brought more concerns for her on a personal level. She was beginning to understand who he was beyond that hot-headed hunk who'd caught her eye and broken her teen heart. More so now he'd shared those deeply personal circumstances and given an insight as to what had been going on behind the scenes in the midst of his public meltdown.

She stepped out into the darkness and Hunter pulled the door shut behind them.

'What about Anderson? We shouldn't really leave him—' She tried one last time to put some distance between them so she had some space to put her feelings back in order. It didn't matter if Hunter Torrance was still a loose cannon or he'd turned out to be the nicest guy in the world, he had to remain off limits.

If only she could get her treacherous pounding heart to remember that every time he was near.

'He's snoring the house down already. I'm sure he won't miss me for ten minutes,' her escort insisted as he followed her down the path.

Even if she hadn't heard his heavy footsteps in the darkness, the hairs standing on the back of her neck alerted her to his presence as he caught up with her. She was doomed now to be at the mercy of her attraction whenever he was near. Not the best conditions to be working under. Together.

'I…er…think I have an apology to make. I judged you unfairly. If I'd known about your family situation… anyway, I shouldn't have been so horrible to you.' Although this being nice to each other didn't seem to be doing her any favours either. If anything, it was creating more problems for her.

'Don't worry about it. I'm used to it.'

That only increased her self-loathing for falling into line with all the other people who'd given him a hard time without just cause. She'd been there as that abandoned child and could easily have gone off the rails too. Perhaps having that one parent who'd loved her had been enough to save her from a complete breakdown when everything had gone wrong in her life. At least her mother had been there as a shoulder to cry on when she'd deemed herself unlovable, and had insisted it wasn't true. Hunter hadn't had anyone to allay his fears, only enforce them. With that little knowledge of his upbringing, it was amazing he'd ever been able to find his way back from the darkness, not that he'd ever succumbed to it.

'I know how much it hurts to be cast aside as if you're nothing. You should be proud of where you got to on your own.' She knew she was, whether her father cared or not.

'I am and ditto. If you don't mind me saying so, your dad sounds as much of a tool as mine.'

That made her laugh out loud, even though it was a sad state of affairs for them both. 'Yes, well, I try not to think about him too often.'

'Me either. Not any more. I'm all about the future these days and trying to leave the past behind.' They were walking into the car park now so she was able to see the determined set of his jaw under the arena lights. It was only natural she should wonder what, or who, that future should include.

They reached her vehicle and she found herself reluctant to end their chat, regardless of her subconscious urging her to jump in the car and hightail it out of there.

'That's definitely the healthier way to live, instead of letting old mistakes haunt you.' She'd been guilty of that on so many levels and she wasn't sure she'd ever really be free of her old ghosts. She had a growing admiration for Hunter, and his strength, if he'd truly been able to break free from his.

'Who would ever have imagined Hunter Torrance would become the spokesperson for common sense?' There was that self-deprecating smile, which almost had her sliding down the driver's door in hormonal appreciation. That mixture of handsome male and genuine good guy was too much for a girl to handle. It was usually one or the other and she didn't know how to defend against that kind of superpower combo.

'I think it did Anderson a world of good to hear it tonight. Hopefully it'll help him think clearly about his next step.' She appreciated the fact Hunter had shared those painful personal details in the hope their troubled friend would take something useful away from it. Not many would have, probably not even her unless he'd taken the lead first. It showed a real connection to the team on a personal level, which she'd doubted would ever happen.

'We made a good tag team tonight.'

'We did, didn't we?' She was smiling, proud of their joint achievement, as she made the mistake of looking up into his eyes. Her breath caught in her throat. In the aftermath of that last encounter she'd hoped she'd imagined that hunger but there it was again, flaring back to life and throwing her equilibrium into a death spiral.

'Perfect.' Hunter was focused on her soft lips tilted up towards him, beckoning him to find some comfort there after opening up old wounds. They'd both been hurt, they were both survivors and he was drawn to her more than ever before.

In that moment he was totally consumed by the need to kiss her and seal that connection once and for all. He watched her eyes close in anticipation and acceptance of his intention. There was no interruption this time, no one to prevent him from doing what came naturally.

It seemed to take for ever to close those few inches between them, as if he was moving in slow motion and preserving the memory of this first kiss for all time.

That soft cushion of her lips against his was a relief; a pleasure he'd been denying himself for some time, but soon even that wasn't enough. He wanted more, he wanted to taste her, to lose himself in her, and that's when he knew he was in trouble. If they'd stood here until daybreak, the kissing lasting until morning dew glistened in their hair, it would've ended too soon. There was a red flag waving somewhere in the distance, making sure he didn't stray too far into deep waters. That future he was so determined to get right for him and his boy didn't include anyone else in the picture.

He broke away and swivelled around to glance back in the direction of his house. 'I should probably get back to my house guest.'

Kissing Charlotte had given him that same rush of testosterone that accounted for every minute of his time in the penalty box. It was that feeling of doing what he needed to do in that moment, of being true to the man he was, and stuff the rules. He'd worked hard to regain his self-control and this set a dangerous precedent. Especially when he couldn't bring himself to regret a second of it. His whole future here was based on his repentance for similar rash decisions.

He was sure Charlotte was as confused as he was about

what was happening. Regardless of her initial hurry to get away, she'd been into that kiss as much as he had. A woman like her didn't need a complication like him messing up her orderly life but there was no denying the chemistry. They'd tried doing that and it had landed them here, making out in the middle of the car park, but anything more than this would be bad news for both of them.

She nodded, probably coming to the same conclusion.

He only got a few steps away before she called after him. 'Hunter? You don't have a girlfriend, do you?'

'No, I don't have a girlfriend, Charlotte.'

'I…er…saw you waving to someone in the stands tonight. I thought maybe—'

'I'm not with anyone. I'm not in the habit of cheating.' There was an edge to his tone but it felt like a step backwards to be accused of two-timing already.

'Right. A friend, then?'

'Goodnight, Charlotte.'

It was all he was giving her for tonight. So far he wasn't doing a very good job of resisting temptation and prioritising his son over his love life. In his defence, he hadn't planned any of this but that didn't mean he was sorry, or that he would follow it up.

Alfie was his personal business. Tonight's journey to find Anderson had been a matter of professional survival. At first. Somewhere in between those chats Charlotte had created a whole new section of his life to worry about.

She was smart, funny, beautiful, not afraid to show her emotions and up until tonight he'd been darned sure she'd hated his guts. He'd never expected her to be responsive to his advances unless it came in the form of a fist to his face. Although the impact had been pretty much the same.

Charlotte wasn't like other women he'd known. She didn't care for the man who'd played in the NHL or spent longer in the penalty box than the entire national team. Now she'd taken the time to get to know him, or as much as he'd allow, it was certainly an ego boost to find someone who liked him without the fame or notoriety. However, there was the worry that one kiss had just blown apart all the careful planning of his new life when all he could think about as he walked away was recapturing the moment.

Indeed, it was probably a small blessing he'd been lumbered with the Demons' resident troublemaker for the night or they might never have left his place. The next few hours on vomit watch would give him the space to think about what he'd done and what he was going to do about it, if anything.

He wasn't ready to share Alfie with her. It was too early to say, *Oh, yeah, here's my kid. I'm trying to get custody. I'm sure you'll make a great stand-in mom.* That wasn't fair to anyone on the back of one kiss. Neither did he want to jeopardise his chances of getting custody by flaunting a new relationship in front of the grieving O'Reillys or upsetting Alfie. He was going to have to tread very carefully now he was no longer free to behave however it suited him. Everything he did had consequences for those around him—he'd learned that the hard way and he wasn't about to make the same mistakes over again.

CHAPTER FOUR

CHARLOTTE WAS AT the rink bright and early and long before any training was due to start, with her own skates slung over her shoulder. She hadn't cut it as a hockey player herself but she could skate. The lessons had been her weekly escape from the rows and the tears of her unhappy home life.

The first skate of the day on unsullied ice always helped her unwind and unclutter her mind and she needed that more than ever this morning. There was so much to process and a lot more she needed to work through with Hunter. Despite pulling rank yesterday, they'd worked better in a partnership to get to the bottom of Anderson's diva fever and there was still a long way to go to get him back on top form. A child was supposed to be a lifelong commitment, not a problem that could, or should, be *fixed* overnight. He would need sustained support as he came to terms with the big changes in his life.

Then, of course, there was also the whole kissing Hunter thing. She was trying to work out if it had been a one-off, caused by working too closely outside office hours, or if the fire would still burn inside them both in the cold light of day. Hence the early start and restless legs. There were all sorts of implications in getting involved with a co-worker and there were risks involved she wasn't yet sure she wanted to take, no matter how tender his touch or how much she wanted more.

Unfortunately, as she made her way towards the ice it seemed she wasn't the only one to arrive early. Shouts echoed around the arena along with the sound of blades cutting through her fresh ice. She stashed her skates away until she could manage some alone time here again. This wasn't the start to the day she'd anticipated, especially as she realised the two men who'd gatecrashed her quiet morning were the same ones who'd kept her up late last night. Hunter and Anderson were so focused on their drills they didn't appear to notice they had a spectator.

Even the sight of the man with whom she'd been in a passionate clinch only hours ago gave her system a jolt to rival her early shot of caffeine. A shiver danced a merry jig along her spine at the memory of his hands there whilst his lips had caressed hers. He was a man of many fine skills.

Although he was no longer a professional player he'd certainly maintained his fitness level and she was sure he had the body to show for it. Damn it if she couldn't stop thinking about that image as her eyes followed him powering along the full length of the rink.

It took a lot of self-discipline to stay in that great a shape, even if his past antics had caused her to question it. He was still that mesmerising figure she'd never been able to take her eyes off during a game.

Hunter dropped his stick to the ice and rounded up the pucks littered around him. One by one he and his partner whacked them into the back of the net with such ferocity Charlotte was convinced they'd lodge in the advertising hoardings. It wasn't until he was skating back towards the centre that he caught sight of her on the sideline.

'Hey. I didn't see you come in.' He seemed pleased to see her if the bone-melting grin was any indication.

It was a sign that he might have seen last night as more

than a spur-of-the-moment mistake and while that felt good, it meant she might have to make some decisions on what it was she wanted to happen next. She'd sworn she wouldn't cross that line with him, only to find herself entwined with him moments later. A physical attraction was one thing but working alongside him, getting to know him, took any further shenanigans into the realms of a relationship. That was something she didn't jump into easily when too-vivid visions of her parents' messy divorce made her wary of getting in too deep with anyone, never mind a man known for his unreliability in the past. Still, she was a woman who knew how to protect her heart. She just didn't let anyone in.

'Slaying some demons, are we?' She tipped her head towards his training partner, who was more focused than he'd been when she'd seen him last time. He'd barely been able to walk then, never mind balance the weight of his bulk on two sharp blades.

'One or two. What about you? Are you up for an early morning session?'

It was an entirely innocent remark. If he'd meant to conjure up a picture of the two of them lolling around in bed on a lazy Sunday morning he would've said it with a wink and an intention to make her blush.

'I'm, uh, just here to get a few things from the office.' Skating was something she did for herself and not something she was ready to share with him. It was her private pleasure, and no longer a team pursuit. After witnessing Hunter's drills, she wasn't sure he'd understand that distinction.

Anderson acknowledged her with a nod. 'I think I'll hit the showers. I have a lot to do today.'

Left alone with Hunter in his old Demons shirt she wasn't prepared for the memories it brought back of him at his best, including last night when he'd had her in his arms. It was too early in the morning to be dealing with raging hormones, too scary to start examining what the hell was happening and definitely too public to find out what came next.

'That's one way to get Anderson to work out his frustrations but I don't want him to think brute strength is the answer to all his problems.' It might work in hockey but he was going to need to adopt a gentler, more methodical approach to his personal life.

He cocked his head to one side, a smirk playing across his lips. 'Are you calling me a brute?'

Charlotte gulped. *Brute* conjured up all sorts of primitive connotations she certainly didn't need to associate with him when she was already having trouble controlling herself around him.

'With the penalty minutes you've clocked up over the years, some might say *brute* was appropriate.'

'Ouch.'

It was a low blow but she'd do whatever it took to put an end to this apparent flirting. She couldn't cope with it. Wobbly knees would destroy the illusion she was confident about what she was doing here and turn her into Bambi on ice instead.

'I see Anderson's almost human today.' She changed the subject, using Anderson as a buffer for this unresolved sexual tension between them. He was the poster child for bad judgement and rash decisions. She was probably one more Hunter clinch away from an epic breakdown of equipment-smashing proportions and she didn't even know it.

Once she'd pulled the brakes on the hot and meaningful exchanged glances, Hunter followed suit and put a bit more space between them.

'I think we've made some progress. He has some work to do but it was his decision to get started early and make up some ground today. I do know he's serious about getting back on track with the club.'

'Gray will be happy.'

'That might be overstating it but at least there's a chance he'll think again about getting people fired.'

'That's a win all round, then. It's good to start the day on a high. I'll check in with Anderson later and see how he's getting on. I need to take a look at those stitches again anyway.' It wasn't that she didn't trust Hunter's word but she wanted to see, and speak to, Anderson herself to gauge his mood. She wanted to be optimistic about his future as well as her own but she was also a realist. That sort of behaviour wasn't often cured overnight and she, along with Gray, would still be watching him with a careful eye.

'Be my guest.'

'Right, I have a few things to sort out for Nottingham so I should go.' She was already making her way towards the exit and away from trouble.

'You're being hopeful. We still have an away match to win before we get there.'

'I like to be organised.' It wasn't that she was overly optimistic about their chances. A hockey fan through and through, she'd booked her flights for the Final Four Weekend long before Hunter had come on the scene. She would be there no matter who made it to the finals and if the Demons were there it would be all the sweeter.

The doctor didn't usually travel with the team but she'd be happy to combine work with pleasure. Except now it would mean she and Hunter would be spending more time together in close proximity. If they carried on from where they'd left off last night there was a danger it would all burn out of control and she knew better than to let her heart overrule her head.

He didn't try to stop her leaving, for which she was grateful. One more romantic recall into his arms and she knew they'd be melting the very ground they were standing on. She'd used up her quota of bravado in walking away and she would make sure she left enough time for Mr Torrance to have packed up his kit before she ventured out of the office again and risked another pulse-racing encounter. He was just too much excitement for this sleepy town and always had been.

She grabbed what she needed from the filing cabinet and was ready to leave when the sound of running water coming from somewhere nearby alerted her to the fact she wasn't alone.

'Anderson, is that you?' she called out before she entered the changing room, as she always did so anyone who wished to preserve their modesty could do so. Not that they were usually shy about parading in the buff. She was sure they'd done it on purpose in those early days just to get her flustered but she was used to it now. Men's naked bodies were part of the fixtures around here.

The shower shut off and she hoped to goodness he covered up before he came out to speak to her. A serious conversation about his state of mind would go more smoothly if she wasn't worried about a lapse in eye contact.

'I…uh…just wanted to see you…er…to make sure you were all right after last night.'

'Do you make a habit of dropping in on the players when they're in the showers?' A bemused Hunter, not Anderson, padded out barefoot and double-towelled, with one around his waist and another in his hand, drying his hair.

Holy six pack!

She was sure her mouth was dropping open and closed like a sea creature stranded on the shore, fighting for survival. Eventually she forced herself to speak before he felt it his duty to come and give her mouth to mouth.

'I don't get my kicks spying on naked hockey players, thank you very much.' Only ex-hockey players.

'Oh, yes, we're much too *brutish* for you, aren't we?' He tossed the hair-drying towel aside and she was finding difficulty coming up with an argument, or even why she wanted one as he walked towards her.

'If we're talking sexy Canadian stereotypes I'm more a Gilbert Blythe kind of girl,' she lied, wanting to focus on someone the opposite of the muscle-bound hunk advancing on her. It would be dangerous to admit to the attraction here, alone in a small room with Hunter naked except for a scrap of white fabric.

'I'll start calling you Carrots, then, shall I?' He had every right to look pleased with himself when he'd just scored extra hottie points.

'You know *Anne of Green Gables*?' Now she came to think of it, he did resemble her other teenage fantasy boyfriend with his dark wavy hair and that accent that made every *Sorry* impossible to forgive.

'Read it, and watched the mini-series as an essential part of getting inside the female psyche at an early age. I even wore a flat cap for a while.' He smiled bashfully at the memory and Charlotte couldn't help but sigh out loud.

'Yes, well, we're all older, wiser and much more cynical these days.'

'Perhaps, but there's always room for a little romance, don't you think?' He was doing it again, staring at her with such naked lust it took her breath away.

She was doing her best to remain strong and avoid falling too quickly under his spell again but her mouth was dry with want. A droplet of water fell from the ends of his tousled hair and she watched it with the thirst of a traveller lost in the desert, searching for that life-giving oasis. It splashed onto his shoulder and trickled over the muscular planes of his chest, its journey gaining momentum over the smooth skin, unimpeded until it reached that trail of dark hair from navel to...

Oh. He'd caught her staring.

'Do you shave?' It was the first thing that popped into

her head so she said it to divert her thoughts from where they were headed. Except she hadn't given any thought to where her gaze was lingering.

His taut belly moved with his laughter. 'No. Do you?'

She frowned, not quite understanding his meaning. Did he think she had a hairy chest? Then the penny dropped and she wished the ground would too.

'I didn't mean… I was talking about your chest. I wasn't staring at your…'

She so was.

He cleared his throat, clearly as embarrassed as she was by her staring. She would've imagined someone with his history would've been used to it and that lack of arrogance only added to his appeal for her. There was nothing more off-putting than a man who was fully aware of his looks and used them to his advantage.

'About last night—'

'I'll leave you to get dressed. I only came in to get a few things.' She could tell he was gearing up to give her the brush-off. If he'd wanted anything more they wouldn't be standing here, making small talk, while he was dressed in nothing but a towel. Until this second she hadn't realised it was her who didn't want this to be over already.

'Wait.' He grabbed hold of her arm, pulled her back so they were almost nose to nose, his hot breath mingling with hers. His freshly soaped skin was warm and wet against hers, reminding her he was *au naturel* below that towel.

'What are we doing, Hunter?' This was her chance to reclaim control. If she truly wanted to prevent this from happening she should've been pushing him away, not welcoming his touch as though she'd been waiting for it all her life.

'Probably something really, really stupid.' At least Hunter was acknowledging that he was also powerless against this attraction as he took her in his arms.

Any fight left her at that first contact and she surrendered to the next. There was something more urgent in his kiss this time, matching her need to make up for lost time. As if the pressure of fighting these feelings had finally been too much and had exploded in a frenzy of body parts desperate to connect.

His tongue courted hers and with his two hands planted firmly on her backside, he pulled her closer, leaving her in no doubt about how much he wanted her. He was as hard for her as she was wet for him, their mutual appreciation reaching critical levels.

Her carefully layered shirt and sweater combo, chosen to keep her body temperature regulated for skating purposes, now seemed excessive for this increasingly hot interlude. Arousal coursed through her veins, reaching her every nerve ending until she was nothing but a mass of erogenous zones.

He was the only man capable of making her act this recklessly but she wasn't so far gone she was prepared to lose her inhibitions in public. It definitely wouldn't aid her career if the team doctor was to be discovered getting passionate with the half-naked physio in the locker room.

'This is a mistake. Someone could walk in at any time. You were right. This is a stupid idea.'

'Charlotte, wait!' Hunter could only watch as she bolted from the building. It would only cause more of a scene if he ran after her, his towel at half-mast around his waist.

He did, however, dress as quickly, and as cautiously, as he could without causing serious injury to himself as he waited for the after-effects of their unexpected, extremely hot tryst to wear off.

So much for careful planning and taking things slowly. Apparently his impulsive side hadn't left him altogether, although he would deny any man not to respond as primitively as he had to the hungry way she'd stared at his body.

Her emotions were as easy to read now as they had been that first day they'd met and she'd made no attempt to disguise her contempt for him.

After Sara and the years he'd missed of Alfie's life he preferred knowing where he stood. No good came of secrets and that went for him too. He'd deliberated telling her about Alfie's existence when he'd been unsure last night had been anything other than a moment of weakness. Given this morning's events and the persistent frequency of the tightness in his jeans, the chemistry with Charlotte was rapidly invading all areas of his life.

He might be wary of inviting someone to share his most personal, private secrets but if her hasty exit was anything to go by, so was Charlotte. It was important she knew they were braving this strange new land together.

She didn't seem the type to engage in passionate embraces on a whim; she wasn't one of the puck bunnies who'd kill to be in that position with a player in the locker room. If she was he would've heard about it by now. Players weren't known for their discretion on such matters. Then again, until recently he hadn't been the settling-down type whose only goal was a steady cheque to pay a mortgage. People weren't always who they appeared to be but he trusted his instincts. She was the first woman he'd had time for since finding out about his son and that had to mean something, something he was keen to explore.

He chased her down to the car park and called after her. 'Can we at least talk about this?'

Apparently not as her little silver hatchback screeched away from the arena.

For someone who spent most of her spare time at the arena, Charlotte did a good job of eluding Hunter until the night of their away match and even then she'd driven rather than taken a seat on the team bus. Something that hadn't gone unnoticed by the others, who'd wondered what had caused her to forsake her free ride when she normally insisted on travelling, despite the away team providing their own medical support. Hunter had simply kept his head down and muttered something about her having other errands to run. It wasn't as if he could put his hands up and say it was his fault she wanted to be on her own. That he'd made her act as irresponsibly as he once had and now she regretted it.

He felt the need to apologise the minute he cast his eyes on her, even though they hadn't done anything wrong. Under the fluorescent lights of a jam-packed concourse probably wasn't the ideal spot to confront what had happened but she hadn't left him much option when she kept dodging him.

'Charlotte, you have to talk to me at some point. I'm sorry if I made you uncomfortable but we still have to work together.' There wasn't much hope for more than that since a couple of kisses had sent her scurrying into the shadows.

They were jostled by the stampeding crowds keen to get their pre-game snacks and drinks from the nearby concession stands. Hunter took her by the elbow and gently led her to a corner where there was considerably less footfall and noise going on around them.

'Did anyone see us? In the changing room, I mean.' The events had clearly been at the forefront of her mind when she launched into her fears immediately, rather than continuing to dance around the subject.

'No. Our secret's safe.' He only managed a half-smile at the thought of being someone's dirty little secret. For her sake he wanted to laugh it off, pretend the matter wasn't of any great significance so they could move on past it. In reality, though, he would rather be someone Charlotte was proud to be seen with regardless of what people thought. Not being reminded that he was still the man no one wished to be associated with.

'Good.' A delicate blush stained her skin but it was difficult to tell if it was through embarrassment or heat at the memory. He knew which one would be easier for him to stomach.

'Charlotte—'

'Hunter—'

They stumbled over each other attempting to address the chasm that had opened up between them after their latest indiscretion. In ordinary circumstances making out should have spelled the beginning of a relationship, not the end of one. It might be wishful thinking on his part but he was holding onto the small hope it was circumstance alone that had caused Charlotte's sudden retreat from him.

'I'm sorry if I put you in a compromising position at work but, for the record, we haven't done anything wrong.' They'd only done what had come naturally, albeit at the wrong time and in the wrong place.

She glanced around, obviously still skittish about getting caught even when the passers-by were more interested in getting to their seats before the puck dropped than two people freaked out by their attraction to one another. 'I know... It's just... I wasn't expecting this.'

He understood her fears, he had reservations himself, but for altogether different reasons. Whilst she might be concerned she'd be nothing more than a notch on his bedpost, he feared the opposite.

'Neither was I. We can take things at whatever pace you want.' One thing was for sure, it was impossible to walk away and pretend nothing was happening.

She studied him closely, as if she was trying to work out if he was spinning her a line or he was being genuine. That hurt more than she could ever have imagined.

'It's not only what nearly happened, or could happen between us that I'm worried about. I don't know you, not really.' This was a very different woman from the one who'd been in his arms not long ago, a cautious Charlotte who probably didn't make a habit of the sort of behaviour he'd been famous for.

He couldn't blame her. They'd taken a risk of being spotted, of being ridiculed or, worse, sacked on the spot. Sara's parents would've had a field day with the news and then he'd have had to explain to his son why he'd screwed up their future together for a woman he'd just met. Only he knew he wouldn't have put either his or Charlotte's livelihoods at risk for something trivial and it was frustrating he couldn't get that point across.

'Now, how can we rectify that if you won't be in the same room as me? Hmm?' He tilted his head to one side and gave her his best hound dog impression so she'd stop seeing him as some sort of threat.

That earned him a soft, sweet laugh. 'So you found the flaw in my total avoidance ploy, huh?'

Hunter sucked a breath in through his teeth. 'Not the most practical tactic when we do play for the same team.'

'Always thinking about the long game and not the interim strategy, that's me.' The skin at the corners of her eyes creased with laughter, a most welcome sight after an anxious few days of silence.

'Sometimes it does you good to act on impulse and not worry about what happens further down the line.'

'And how did that work out for you?'

He'd been talking about letting their attraction win out over common sense but Charlotte's raised eyebrow suggested another nod back at his hockey days.

'I said sometimes. Not as a lifestyle choice. Sometimes the most spontaneous moments can bring the greatest pleasure.' He lowered his voice so his next words were for her ears only. 'I have many regrets, Charlotte, but kissing you will never be one of them.'

If it wasn't for the constant stream of people nudging past he would be tempted to do it again.

He was running the risk of scaring her off again by being so blatant about his desires but it was going to take at least one of them being honest if there was a chance of repeating the experience.

'Hunter... I...'

He watched her gulp and swallow, struggling to form a reply, and waited patiently for the verdict on his gamble.

The klaxon sounded from deep inside the arena, signalling the end of the pre-game warm-up and penetrating their bubble. The teams would be making their way off the ice after their drills and stretches to prepare for the game behind the scenes. Where he and Charlotte should be.

'We really need to hustle our backsides down there before Gray starts on the warpath.' She turned away from him, timing, as ever, against them.

Hunter mused over whether or not to force this conversation to its conclusion so he would know once and for all where he stood with her. She was driving him crazy. Since it had taken this long to pin her down he figured it wouldn't help matters to put her job in jeopardy again by making her tardy.

'We wouldn't want that but, believe me, I'm still keen on that getting to know each other idea.'

Charlotte almost fell down the steps at Hunter's insistence they pick up where they'd left off. Especially when his hand was at her back, escorting her towards the changing rooms and heating her skin with the warmth of his touch. She'd been stupid to think a few days and some distance from him would put any lustful thoughts out of her head. One glimpse of him, a promise of more of the same and her willpower had dissolved.

It had been all too tempting to ignore her duty to the players and the team in favour of spending time with him again. The very reason she'd beaten herself up over the last time they'd lost track of where, and who, they were. When she was with him nothing else seemed to matter and that was dangerous when she was putting her job at risk for a man she barely knew beyond how good his lips felt on hers. She didn't know where they went from here and she certainly didn't want to have to commit to anything if it left her position on the team vulnerable, so she was glad she'd been buzzed out of her reverie in the nick of time.

They were lucky that Gray hadn't missed them either and they were able to merge back into the team preparations as if nothing had happened. On the outside at least. Her insides were having difficulty catching up with her logical brain, still fluttering and unsettled by being so close to Hunter.

At least being squashed in behind the bench as a stowaway on the away side meant they were most definitely in a crowd and close enough to the action to keep their minds where they were supposed to be—on the ice.

'Anderson seems to have recovered form. Good job, you two.' There was a brief nod from Gray as the player stretched his legs, skating rings around the opposition in the opening minutes of the game.

He didn't ask what was behind the transformation, more concerned with results than the journey, and neither Charlotte nor Hunter volunteered the information. She knew from her subsequent conversations with him that he and Maggie were trying to work things out and that in itself had improved his mood and his play, but Anderson's private life was exactly that and unless he chose to share the details of his recent troubles, they would remain confidential.

She and Hunter exchanged smiles over the pat on the back from their leader before he went back to discussing tactics with the rest of his men. Their joint effort with Anderson certainly appeared to have yielded favourable results and she could see Hunter stood a little taller with the recognition. She couldn't help but wonder how long it had been since someone had actually congratulated him on a job well done.

For a long time he'd probably endured nothing but negativity and scepticism over his work ethic and she was as guilty as everyone else who'd refused to give him a break. So wrapped up in her own thoughts and feelings about how she'd been affected by his presence here, she'd given virtually no thought to the positive addition he'd *actually* been to the team. Perhaps it was self-preservation. She didn't need any more reason to like him when he was already sidestepping around those work-colleague boundaries.

The volume levels of the crowd rose around her at a skirmish out by the Demons' goal as they went all out to defend. It was hard to see what was going on through the throng of bodies vying for prominence. Suddenly there was a cry for the medic. As the crowd parted and anxious players called for help, it became obvious there was something seriously wrong. One body remained prone on the ice, the area around him rapidly turning scarlet with blood. It was Colton, the Demons' winger.

Hunter swore, grabbed a towel and had vaulted over the bench before she'd even taken her first step onto the rink. Two Demons players arrived either side of her and escorted her quickly over to the scene so she didn't slip on the ice.

'Ambulance. Now!' she shouted to the Cobras' medical staff, who were making their way over too. The amount of blood spurting from Colton's leg told of the severity of the injury and this was no time for territory marking.

'It's an artery.' Hunter dropped to his knees and held the towel to the deep gash across the thigh, probably caused by the blade of someone's skate in the melee.

'Keep applying the pressure. Colton? We need to try and elevate this leg.' In such circumstances there was al-

ways a chance of a patient bleeding to death as the blood
was pumping so quickly from the heart and a cut artery
was a time-critical wound. Everything she and Hunter did
now to stem the flow of blood could determine whether or
not he survived.

'Charlotte?' Hunter directed her attention to the once-
white towel, which was now a bright red, infused with
their patient's blood. It would only take losing two pints
of blood before he went into shock. There was no more
time to waste.

'Give me your belt.' She didn't even wait for a response
and simply helped herself. Despite the adrenaline pumping in her own veins and the struggle to keep her breathing regulated in the midst of the drama, her fingers worked
nimbly to unbuckle his belt.

She tugged him roughly towards her and whipped the
strip of leather from around his waist. All the time he kept
pressure on the wound without blinking an eye at her, as
if having bossy women strip him was an everyday occur-
rence. Or he knew exactly what she was doing. The belt
made a perfect tourniquet around the thigh and she pulled
it just tight enough to hopefully slow the bleeding but not
cut off total supply to the limb.

'Nicely done, Doctor.' Hunter offered his support with
a smile and a wink. He was the one grounding source for
her in the midst of the drama. It was a comfort knowing
that she wasn't in this alone.

'You too, Mr Torrance. Now let's get you to hospital,
Colton.'

It was only as they rushed off the ice towards the waiting ambulance that the uneasy silence around the arena
became noticeable. Everyone had been waiting with bated
breath to see the fate of the injured player. It didn't matter
what side he was on when there was a life at stake. She was
glad she hadn't felt that weight of expectation on her shoul-

ders as she'd worked and that had been down to Hunter's assistance. It wasn't that she couldn't treat this sort of injury solo—after all, that was the nature of her job here. No, it was simply…reassuring for someone to have her back.

She relayed all the relevant information to the paramedics so they could radio ahead to the hospital and prep for surgery. With Hunter still taking charge of wound pressure, they both climbed into the vehicle alongside their patient.

'We need oxygen, double cannula and get fluids started.' She was talking to herself as much as anyone else in the vicinity so she had all bases covered.

The back of an ambulance made for a small workspace and she couldn't help but brush against Hunter with every bump in the road as she inserted the cannulas into Colton's hands.

'Sorry,' she said as they went around a corner and she was forced to brace herself against Hunter's frame to steady herself. It was more important to get the IV and much-needed pain relief up and running than continue her ill-conceived avoid-body-contact-with-Hunter plan.

'No problem.'

She didn't take her eyes off her patient but she could feel the warmth of Hunter's slow grin on her back. It made her shiver all the same.

'Will I make it back for the final period, Doc?' The pale Colton was trying to sit up and displaying that hockey-player spirit that demanded to see the game out, no matter what. On this occasion she was definitely going to have to disappoint him.

'I'm afraid not. You're going to have to go straight into Theatre to have that artery stitched.' She wasn't even sure if they'd finish the match after that scare.

'Even Gray should understand you missing the rest of the game. I don't think he'll be docking your wages this once.' Hunter attempted to soften the blow and she appreciated it. It probably aided Colton's compliance to have a kindred spirit on board, someone who knew from personal experience how it felt to be left on the sidelines.

'But I'll be okay to play in the finals?' The pleading eyes were begging for reassurance but Charlotte didn't have it in her to lie, even to a seriously injured man.

'Don't worry about that for now. First things first. We need to get you into Theatre. We're almost at the hospital now.' They'd done as much as they could for Colton but her mind would be much more at ease when she knew the surgeon was doing his bit to save his life too.

'I'll phone Gray as soon as we arrive and let him know you're keen to get back ASAP.' Hunter wasn't making him any promises other than to relay a progress report but he was providing that extra reassurance she was beginning to realise she could count on. Even though they both knew Colton was probably finished for the season, there was no need to give him more reason to worry before he went into surgery.

It wasn't until they'd handed over their patient into the hands of the hospital staff that Charlotte was able to take time for some deep fortifying breaths. She could only watch, her stomach in knots, as he was stretchered away down the corridor at high speed, her part in ensuring his survival over for now.

'Wow. That was a rush.'

It seemed she wasn't the only one coming down from the adrenaline high as Hunter let out an unsteady breath next to her.

'Not one I'm in a hurry to experience again, thanks.' Now she had time and space to think about events, the enormity of the undertaking was beginning to hit home.

A chill penetrated her bones and set her knees trembling. She practically fell into one of the chairs lining the corridor.

'Your first life-or-death emergency?' Hunter landed in

the seat next to her with a heavy thud and she could see he wasn't unaffected by the drama either. It was a comfort to see her reaction was totally normal.

She nodded. Her eyes were already beginning to well up as emotion built inside her and she didn't trust herself to talk without her voice cracking. They'd very nearly lost one of their own tonight and the responsibility of keeping him alive had rested heavily on her shoulders. It was the nature of the path she'd chosen but her work in sports therapy tended more towards joint and muscle problems than life-threatening crises. Tonight had been a sobering reminder of the serious commitment she'd made to her career and the team.

'Mine too.' He reached across and squeezed her hand. It was the closest she'd get to the hug she needed right now.

She swallowed the unprofessional tears away since she was the one who'd actually trained for this and focused on the fact Colton was alive.

'You certainly seemed to know what you were doing back there.' As she recalled, he'd applied pressure to the wound area before she'd even told him to.

'Well, I do have some training in the field. I was at medical school briefly before I decided to toss it all in for hockey.'

Her eyes widened at that new information. 'Ah. So the physiotherapy didn't totally come out of left field? You could easily have been Dr Hunter Torrance?'

'Medicine was definitely something I was interested in pursuing. Actually, I'm not sure which career was more about rebelling against my parents.'

'Your relationship with them was that strained?'

He nodded solemnly. 'I was adopted and always made very aware of the fact. Told I should be grateful they'd taken me on. At eighteen I decided to find my birth parents, only to be rejected again. They didn't want me any more then than when I was born. Becoming a doctor would've stuck it to those who thought I would never amount to anything but the idea of being a hockey player…well, it was glamorous and exciting and something I knew they'd envy. Until I screwed it all up, of course.'

It was her turn to squeeze back. 'Don't be so hard on yourself. We've all had our struggles. Yours just happened to be very public.'

Her heart broke for his younger self who'd so obviously been hurting and searching for acceptance. She was able to see that explosive behaviour in a different light now she knew it had been more than bad temper at play and forgave him every wrong he'd done in her eyes. Not only had he been dealing with that loneliness and isolation of his personal circumstances but he'd been demonised by the press and disappointed fans. Even when he'd shown up, full of remorse, she'd clung onto her own grudge and dismissed his claims. It only added to the injustice done to him and to the guilt she was feeling as a result.

If she imagined her trials and tribulations with her parents playing out in arenas around the country she doubted she would have recovered as effectively as he had. When he'd turned up professing to have changed his life she'd assumed sports medicine was second best, the closest he could get to the ice without playing again. That the Demons' medical staff was the consolation prize when it had been the jackpot to her. To find out he had that calling to help others ingrained in him after all challenged her preconceived ideas about his character and stripped away some of those fears about getting involved with him.

She was fast running out of excuses to avoid her feelings, leaving only the outright terror at the thought of putting her heart on the line again. What if she gave it away only to find it cast aside like an unwanted toy when something, someone better came along? She hadn't been enough for her father to stick around and she didn't want to put herself in the position again of letting someone else have so much control over her emotions or her life.

The only certainty she had with Hunter tonight was there would be no escape from these growing feelings for him until they knew for sure Colton had pulled through.

CHAPTER FIVE

HUNTER WASN'T USED to being the one receiving pats on the back or hand squeezes and he couldn't decide if the squirming in his seat was because he was uneasy over it or *too* comfortable with it. It seemed as though he was finally finding his feet as part of the team. More than that, he and Charlotte had formed their own partnership. Not so long ago professional courtesy would've been all he'd wanted from her but they'd gone way beyond that point. He wouldn't have shared details of his personal life with the same woman who'd turned her nose up at him when they'd first met. There had definitely been a shift in their dynamic and it wasn't only down to the random bouts of kissing.

'You didn't do so badly under the spotlight tonight. Actually, you were kind of amazing out there.' The way she'd handled the situation so calmly and efficiently had shown everyone this was so much more than a job to her. She was dedicated to the team but also a medical professional whom any man could trust with his life. Maybe even with the knowledge of his son.

'We're good together.' Her coy smile suggested she was thinking about more than their time in the cramped confines of the ambulance.

'That we are, and if I recall there was a promise made about getting to know each other a little better.' It was as important to him to be upfront and honest about what this was as it was for her. A relationship for him now was always going to include someone else and he was done with secrets.

'Well, we've made a start. I had no idea about your time in medical school.'

'That makes it your turn for the Q and A. Let's start with an easy one. Why the Demons? What made you join the team?' He wanted to know everything that made her tick so he could work out what it was that kept putting obstacles in their path. Even if he ignored the comings and goings of the staff and patients flooding through the emergency department and stole another kiss from her, he knew she'd be running again by tomorrow.

'I've been into hockey since the arena opened.'

'A real fan, then?' He knew she enjoyed hockey nights, he'd seen it, but he hadn't realised her love of the game had come before her role on the team.

'You could say that,' she muttered under her breath, but he could see no reason why she'd be embarrassed by it.

At a time when most young girls would've been more interested in fashion and make-up, she'd committed her time to a sport that wasn't for the faint-hearted. It explained so much about her character.

'That must've been around the time I played here?' He did the mental calculations. The chances were he'd seen her in passing at one time or another.

'Yeah.' Her embarrassment continued to flare a crimson contrast to her porcelain skin, the same flushed look she had every time he kissed her.

'It's kinda hot, knowing you're a *real* hockey fan.' He wanted to reach out and tilt her chin up to look at him and make that connection again but he didn't. An invisible barrier had been hastily erected since their last moment of weakness but he thought he could break it down again with a hit of honesty. Hockey had been his life and it was a new experience having someone who understood that commitment and passion.

He'd screwed up his own career but his love of the game had never diminished. That was why he'd jumped at the chance Gray had given him to work here. He could've come over, set up his own practice and eventually built up a client list, but as the Demons' physio he got a chance to recapture that passion. Now he could do that with Charlotte too if she would only let him.

'I'm a Demon through and through.' She sighed as if it was a bad thing when he'd seen her loyalty as a positive. It gave them more common ground other than this mutual attraction they were having difficulty with.

'Good. I'm sure Gray's glad he'll never have to worry about losing you to a rival team.'

'You don't understand,' she said, her downcast gaze giving him sudden reason for concern. He wasn't used to her being so cagey with him. Usually she was very vocal with her opinion.

'So why don't you tell me what it is that's bothering you?' He wanted to understand so they could move past whatever was causing this stumbling block between them. If she couldn't share this obviously personal problem with him, it was going to be very difficult to confide in her about his son. Trust was a two-way street for him.

She took a deep breath, refilling her lungs and doing nothing to allay his worries that there was a serious problem here. 'I'll admit I wasn't the *kindest* person to you on meeting for the first time but I, uh, might've held a bit of a grudge against you.'

'Oh?' It didn't come as any great surprise but he was interested to know the reasons behind it.

'Well…you kinda ruined my life.'

They were the words Hunter had always expected to hear from someone but they still hit hard. He didn't know what he'd done to Charlotte to deserve them but he wasn't in any doubt that he did. After all, ruining people's lives was what he'd done best before he'd turned his own around.

He was staring at her as if she'd gone stark raving mad. Maybe she finally had. It would explain why she was about to spill her biggest, most humiliating secret but it was now or never. She couldn't avoid this any more when he was opening up to her and showing he was just as human and flawed as she was. Perhaps after this confession, whatever the outcome, she'd finally be able to move on from that chapter of her life. As long as he kept the story to himself and saved her from prolonged mortification.

She gulped in another breath and prepared to unload her greatest shame. In the middle of a busy hospital, waiting for news on the fate of one of their players for goodness' sake. She was beginning to think she should've told the whole sorry story from the outset and saved herself a whole heap of trouble. After this bombshell he wouldn't be so keen to get up close and personal with her.

'It might sound dramatic but teenage girls are, and when the one thing they love falls apart their whole world collapses. You have to realise ice hockey coming here was a big deal. When they built the arena, drafted in all of these handsome Canadians and Americans to play in that first team, it was like a hurricane sweeping in through our town. It was dangerous and exciting and turned everything upside down. I needed something to cling to while my home life was in freefall. In the lead-up to their divorce my parents were constantly fighting and hockey became my escape.'

'Did I do something to hurt you? It was a difficult period for me. I wronged a lot of people and I'm doing my best to make it up.' There was genuine confusion creasing his brow into a frown but how could she clear this up without coming across as the pathetic, sad case she'd been?

'We only met in passing at fan events, signings and such.

Nothing you'd remember.' Why should she, a gangly wall-flower, have stuck out in his mind when there'd been so many confident, beautiful women tugging at his jersey?

'Sorry,' he said, the need to apologise for his past so deeply ingrained he wouldn't even know what he was saying it for.

Charlotte ached for the young boy who, like her, had probably grown up taking his parents' disinterest to heart, believing he'd been at fault. It put a different perspective on the rebellious player he'd been, whose misdemeanours now seemed so obviously a cry for help from someone suffering tremendous pain. His return here, facing up to those he'd hurt, had taken a lot of courage and she hadn't given him enough credit for it.

'It's not your fault. Really. I invested a lot in the team. Some might say too much. When you got tossed out of the championship match and we lost, I took it personally. A decade later and I guess I still couldn't shake off that disappointment when we were first introduced. I was afraid you might let us down again.' That wasn't half the story behind her initial resistance but it was the least humiliating half.

'It's understandable. I was a mixed-up kid and I let a lot of people down during that time. All I can do is apologise and hope you'll forgive me.' With that lopsided smile, that resignation as he accepted any blame that could be apportioned to him, it was impossible not to forgive him anything.

'I'll hold my hands up and say you're not the person I feared you were. I've seen what you've done for the team already, how you've handled Anderson and, of course, tonight when we fought to save Colton. There's no question of your commitment.'

'But there's obviously something else going on I don't know about when you keep running out on me.' He took her other hand, forced her to turn around in her seat to face him. Close enough for him to see through any lies.

She swallowed hard. This was where things got tricky. 'You were a big name in a small pond when you came here the first time. Exotic. Irresistible to a vulnerable teenage girl whose life seemed like it was falling apart. I might've developed a bit of a crush.'

That was putting it mildly but even that admission managed to raise his eyebrows and widen his grin.

He rested his hand on his heart. 'I'm flattered.'

'Don't get carried away. I *had* a crush. Past tense. There's no need to get all big-headed about it.' His ego didn't need to know adult Charlotte was beginning to develop more mature feelings on the subject. He'd probably worked that out for himself by now anyway.

'We never met or went on a date?'

'No. I just invested a lot of faith in you and let myself get carried away. I was genuinely devastated when you got thrown out of that game and we lost the championship.' With hindsight she was able to see that her lonely teen self had been dealing with so many intense emotions at the time she'd probably transferred some of that onto his shoulders, believing that he'd failed her too.

It was a relief knowing he didn't think she had a screw loose, that he was on her side, but that didn't make the situation any easier for her to come to terms with.

'Do you see now why I gave you such a hard time in the beginning?'

'I do. All I can do is say sorry. Again.'

'I guess seeing you back here awakened all of those old feelings. It didn't help that I'd got it into my head you were hiding the real reason for your return. As I said, my issues.'

The colour slowly drained from his face. He edged back in his seat, regaining his personal space, and it was then she realised then she'd touched a nerve, that she might be on the verge of unravelling the truth behind his sudden reappearance. She instantly regretted this whole honesty thing. Whatever he was hiding, she had a feeling she wasn't going to like it.

Hunter was so overwhelmed with the information, so conflicted about how he should react, he was beginning to wish he'd waited until they were off the premises for the emotional edition of show and tell. If at all.

The line of this conversation deserved a dark, quiet corner somewhere with a stiff drink for both of them.

He hadn't suspected there was a history of anything other than his damaged reputation and it was almost worse, knowing the truth. It wasn't only the possibility of him failing her that had made her wary, it was the fact he already had. There was nothing he could do to rectify that except be honest about who he was now. He couldn't go on letting her think it was solely her paranoia keeping them from making any sort of commitment to each other.

That brought him right back to the subject he'd been avoiding. Alfie.

'I haven't told you the real reason I came back.'

She flinched, preparing herself for the worst and making him feel as though he was about to throw away that game all over again.

'I knew it.'

He could already see the barricades shutting down around her. Usually she had no problem telling him what she thought of him.

That defensive stance she'd taken instead might've been a better course of action for him than lashing out or self-medicating with alcohol. It could've saved his hockey career. Then again, it wasn't good to keep things bottled inside and isolate yourself, letting everything build up until some day it exploded and caused chaos, or slowly killed you from the inside out. He didn't want either for Charlotte, only for her to be happy.

'It's nothing bad. At least, I don't think so.'

Any earlier playfulness had vanished, any hint of a smile now evened out to a harsh thin line across her lips, and Hunter knew he should've found the courage to tell her about Alfie earlier. It didn't matter whether she minded if he was a father or not now, the damage had been done with the omission.

'I have a son, Alfie. I came back for him.'

He waited for a response but she said nothing.

'I didn't know he existed until a few months ago. My ex, Sara, was pregnant when I went back to Canada and didn't tell me. We all know what a mess I was back then so I can't blame her for not wanting me around. She died in a road accident last year and her parents got in touch. They thought Alfie should have one parent in his life at least. Although they aren't keen for me to have custody until they're one hundred percent sure it's best for him. Hence the move back to Northern Ireland and the need for a steady job.'

'I'm sorry to hear about Sara. I'm sure it all came as a great shock to you.' The news he had a son had all but rendered her mute so she could only imagine how floored he'd been on finding out. It took any sort of relationship between them to a different level, one she wasn't sure she was ready for. Although Hunter hadn't been given a choice in the matter either by the sound of it.

He would have had every right to be angry about being denied the opportunity of that father role all this time only to have the responsibility dropped on him without a moment's notice. It showed the true strength of his character that he was trying to do the best thing for his son and put him first.

Discovering this new side of him had its pros and cons. It

made her warm to him even more when the circumstances had just become even more complex.

'This was supposed to be a chance for me to make amends with all the people I hurt.'

'You seem to be doing pretty well with that as far as I can see.'

'I'm sorry I didn't tell you this up front but let's face it, we didn't exactly hit it off at the start. I understand why now, of course, but at the time there didn't seem the need to get involved in each other's personal lives.' He held his hands up but she knew that first day must have been akin to walking into the lions' den for him, with the lioness fiercely defending her territory.

'I understand.' She really did. If he'd announced he'd come back for his illegitimate son she probably would've imagined it was some sort of ploy to gain sympathy during those first days when she'd still believed the very worst about him. Actually spending time with him had taught her he was the new man he'd proclaimed to be after all.

'It's still early days for me and Alfie. I'm struggling to bond with him as it is without bringing someone else into his life. It was never my intention to get involved with anyone whilst I'm working towards gaining custody, and his trust. Despite the ridiculous urban myths, I'm not some sort of Lothario who'll welcome a string of *aunties* into his life.'

'No?'

'No. I'm deadly serious about all of my responsibilities these days.' He held eye contact with her until she saw the sincerity of his words reflected there.

She gave a tiny shiver, realising the significance of his decision to tell her about Alfie if he didn't invite just anyone into his son's life.

'It's my eternal shame Sara decided it was better to raise Alfie alone in secret than have his reckless, volatile father in his life. A decision I'm sure was very difficult for her to make and I don't want to hurt anyone to that extent again.'

'So, what's the problem between you and Alfie now? Is he having trouble coming to terms with having you in his life?' Charlotte understood that his ex had been trying to protect her son from the kind of questionable parenting she'd been subjected to but the very idea Hunter was considering other people's feelings already made him a better father than hers had ever been.

'Quite the opposite. I think I'm a bit of a novelty given he's never had a father figure in his life before. Not something I'm proud of and I desperately want to make up for lost time but I am a bit out of my depth. It's not helped by his overprotective grandparents who daren't let him out of their sight.'

'Okay, so he likes you, he wants to spend time with you… Surely they wouldn't mind if the two of you spent the afternoon together? Maybe somewhere local so they don't worry too much?' It wasn't fair that he should still be made to keep something of a distance when he genuinely wanted to be part of his child's life. She would've been devastated to find out her father had been kept from spending time with her. Unfortunately the opposite had been true for her. Her father had wanted to forget she'd ever been born so he could pretend he was still young, free and single.

'This is all new to me too. I'm not sure what kids' activities are age-appropriate for an eight-year-old. I don't have any experience of adventure playgrounds or family days out. At that age I was already practically living at the skating rink.'

'Can Alfie skate?' That sense of escape on the ice was something they definitely shared. As the son of a hockey player she would've imagined Alfie would've had that desire tenfold too.

'I don't think so. I don't know for sure. Sara wasn't into hockey and I doubt I did anything to persuade her otherwise.'

'Why don't you bring him to the rink? If he can't skate, I'm sure you could teach him. What eight-year-old boy wouldn't want to do that with his dad?' She put forward the suggestion with a shrug. It was all she'd ever wanted to do, with or without adult supervision.

'You're right. I'd have done anything to have had someone take me by the hand and lead me around the rink, showing some sort of affection, or even interest. Like all those other childhood skills, I taught myself how to do it because my parents hadn't had the time to spare. You know, I think they regretted my adoption because I got in the way of their self-indulgent lifestyle. They probably hadn't meant for me to be much more than a cute accessory, when I'd been a living, breathing little boy in desperate need of a loving home. That's why it's so important to me to get this right for Alfie.'

'I get it. We have neglectful fathers in common. Mine seemed to think divorcing my mum meant ending his relationship with me too. He threw nineteen years of marriage and family away for a fling with someone half his age. The one person I thought would always be there to protect me was the same person who broke my heart, and my mum's. I guess I was too much of a reminder of his failure as a so-called family man but he just walked away, leaving me confused about what I'd done wrong and why we weren't enough to make him happy. That betrayal of trust is hard to get past.'

'It is. I don't think I ever truly gave myself to Sara because I was always waiting for that final kick in the teeth. I needed to hold part of me back. Just in case.'

She nodded. 'I understand. I didn't even date until university because I was so cynical about the idea of love after the divorce. I missed out on those silly things young girls do at that age. There was no snogging in the back row of the cinema or hanging out in the local park in the dark for me because I didn't want to get close to anyone again. I couldn't go through that trauma a second time.' She shrugged. So much time had passed it shouldn't really hurt as much as it still did.

'See, this is why I want to be the best parent I can be for my son. I don't want to be the cause of him suffering that same uncertainty and fear. We need time together but just the two of us in the middle of that arena seems a bit intense. There's no distractions, you know, unlike the cinema or something. Maybe I should take him there instead then there's no pressure to talk. I don't even know if we've got anything in common other than our DNA.'

'You need to talk, to get to know each other the way we are.' She nudged his elbow to stop him fretting even more than he had been about the situation.

'It will help you bond much quicker than sitting in silence in a dark cinema. Listen, if it would help I could pop by and say hello, see how you're getting on. If all else fails we can break out a DVD at your place or something.'

Hunter was trying to do the right thing. All he needed was a little push in the right direction and if it meant one family could be saved some heartache she was happy to help. He deserved to have someone fighting in his corner and it might salve her conscience a fraction about her initial treatment of him.

'I'd really appreciate that, Charlotte. Exactly when did you get so good at dishing out advice to new fathers? Did you take a parenting class or something?'

She snorted at that. 'Definitely not. It's come from years of experience in how not to raise a child.'

'I'm sorry you had to go through it to be able to help

me now but I am grateful to have a wingman for my first dad date with my son.'

'I'll pass on your thanks to the man who made it all possible if I ever see him again.' It was highly unlikely. Last she'd heard he'd started a new family and the last thing he'd want would be his adult daughter turning up and spoiling the doting dad illusion.

'So, as far as keeping secrets are concerned, am I forgiven?'

'You're forgiven.' How could he not be when he'd welcomed her into that sacred circle of trust?

This should've been the moment she'd wished him good luck and backed away. He and Alfie were a package deal and accepting that meant leaning towards the kind of commitment she'd always tried to avoid. She preferred her life uncomplicated but now there was a child involved it would change everything. She couldn't imagine the range of emotion he must've gone through on finding out he had an eight-year-old son he'd been denied all knowledge of but he'd accepted the role without blame or recriminations and had shown a maturity he'd been lacking during his last days here. Family hadn't worked out well for her in the past and this had bad idea written all over it. Except his determination to make a better life for his son made him the noble, loving sort of man she wanted to be around more.

All she could do was try and keep whatever emotional detachment she could from Hunter and Hunter junior and let them make that connection without becoming a part of it.

It was a long night waiting for news on Colton. Not to mention uncomfortable. Hunter had stretched his legs, making several trips to the vending machine for something calling itself coffee, and Charlotte had made several attempts to garner some information, to no avail. In the end the only way they were able to make themselves in any way comfortable was to lean their bodies against each other.

On a personal level they had taken baby steps forward but it would be inappropriate to take advantage of that when they were technically still on the clock and waiting for an update on their friend. That didn't mean it wasn't killing him, having her resting her head on his shoulder and not be able to pull her closer.

His cell buzzed in his pocket and he had to read the text from Gray twice before the contents sank in. He gave Charlotte a gentle shake.

'Hmm?' The sleepy response and the nuzzling further into his neck made a direct call to the side of him that had a tendency to forget the need for discretion.

'I've had a message from Gray. Look. We won.'

'What?' She blinked at the screen.

'They finished the match. We're in the finals.' He couldn't quite believe it himself. The pride in the men who'd played out the game and won despite the awful circumstances swelled so deeply inside him he was fit to bust.

Charlotte stared at him then back at the screen and suddenly launched herself at him. Her arms wound around his neck in a tight hug.

'We're in the finals,' she said, and he couldn't help but laugh with sheer relief. It was the best news they'd heard all night.

'Dr Michaels? Sorry to keep you waiting but I just wanted to let you know Mr Colton is out of Theatre. The surgery went as well as we hoped for. We had to open up the thigh in order to operate so there is a significant wound that will be at risk of infection but he's out of immediate danger. We'll be keeping a close eye on him over the next forty-eight hours.' The surgeon who'd met them on admittance delivered another helping of good news with that same relieved grin he was sure they were all sporting.

'Can we see him?' Charlotte was wide awake now, on her feet, and would probably be in the room, checking on him, if she knew which ward he was on.

'He's sleeping now. I don't want to disturb him and it might be best if you change before you do see him.' There was a nod towards their crumpled attire and Hunter saw Charlotte tense next to him but it wasn't something she should take offence at.

'Of course. It wouldn't do much to aid his recovery to see us covered in his blood. Would it, Charlotte?'

He saw the penny drop as she gazed first at his crimson-stained shirt then her own. They'd scrubbed their hands clean since their arrival in the building but the evidence of the evening's battle for Colton's survival was in the very fabric of their clothes.

'No. It wouldn't be very nice to be reminded. We'll come back in the morning to see how he is. Thank you for everything you've done tonight.' She shook hands with the man in green scrubs first and Hunter did the same.

'I think you two played a huge part here too. Now go get some rest.'

Hunter waited until the surgeon was out of sight before he took Charlotte's hand and marched her out of the building.

'What are you doing? Where are we going?' She was digging her heels in as they rounded the corner but they both needed to blow off some steam after the night they'd had.

'We need to celebrate. Do you really think the rest of the team aren't out partying now they know Colton's okay and they've bagged a place in the finals? We'll be lucky if they've recovered from their hangovers in time for the trip to Nottingham.'

'Look at the state of us.'

'It's getting dark. No one will see.' It was that time just

before complete darkness moved in when everything was a muted shade of grey. The perfect camouflage for them to venture out in public without someone thinking they were two criminals escaping the scene of a brutal crime.

'Yeah, outdoors.' She didn't sound convinced but she followed him nonetheless.

That small sign of trust was a bigger prize to him than tonight's win over the Cobras. Now he was under pressure to produce something to deserve it. In the middle of nowhere. The gas station he'd set his sights on at the end of the road might not appear to be the ideal venue for first-class entertaining but he was determined to make this night memorable for the right reasons. He wanted to do something for her after she'd been there for him tonight, listening and advising on how to connect with his son.

'Wait here. I'll only be a few minutes.'

'What are you up to, Hunter?'

'Shopping,' he said vaguely, before leaving her on the other side of the automatic door. In truth he had no idea himself what he was doing but he'd improvise. They deserved some down time and a little fun following the stresses of the day. He for one wasn't ready to go home alone and attempt sleep when he knew his mind would be running over the alternative outcomes of their medical intervention and what could have happened out there on the ice.

Distraction filled two carrier bags and he hoped there was enough there to persuade his companion to remain in his company for a while longer.

'We all need to go through those silly teenage rites of passage and although there's no back row for us to mess around in, I'm sure I saw a forest park somewhere nearby.' He began his march again, thankful that the spring weather was being kind for once. It was mild enough for them to sit outdoors without hypothermia claiming them and that was unusual for this place. He'd been here when the first daffodils had been poking their heads through a layer of snow at this time of year. It was positively balmy here in comparison.

'Surely you're not being serious?' Her laugh rang through the darkness like musical wind chimes, bringing life to the still night.

He could just about make out the dull edges of the nearby picnic tables against the linear forms of the trees in the background.

'Always. Which is exactly why we both need a time out from being adults. I thought we could combine dinner, celebrating our win and Colton's recovery and pretend we're still teenagers all at the same time,' he said as he deposited his purchases on the wooden bench.

'In a picnic? Here? At this time of the night?' She wasn't more than a dark smudge now in the fading light but she did take her place at the table, waiting to see what he had planned. He had her engaged in something other than hockey or painful childhood memories at least.

'Never let it be said Hunter Torrance doesn't know how to party.' He unpacked a plaid travel rug he'd picked up at the cash register and laid it out.

'I don't think that was ever in doubt, was it?'

'Well, I've never done it *sober*. This was the closest I could get to alcohol.' He produced two small bottles of non-alcoholic sparkling white grape juice.

'I'm sure if I could see it I'd be impressed all the same.'

'Aha!' He rummaged in the bottom of the bag for the two glass candle holders and set one at either end of the bench before lighting them with the small box of matches he'd purchased too.

Charlotte sniffed the air. 'That smells very, uh, sweet.'

'Vanilla ice-cream, I think it said on the box.'

They flickered to life and cast a small pool of light over

the scene. Charlotte's smiling face was revealed in the glow of the small flames and made all this effort worth it.

'It's making me hungry.'

'Good. Now, I'm afraid they didn't have a fine dining section because you know I would totally have shopped there. You'll just have to make do with chicken salad sandwiches and if you're good I might even let you have a cookie.'

There were many *oohs* and *aahs* as he laid out their makeshift dinner, both pretending this was some kind of grandiose feast. It could have been a three-course gourmet dinner as they wolfed it down with the same gusto.

'Do you woo all the ladies in your life with moonlit picnics in the park?' Charlotte surprised him with the question just as he was taking a mouthful of not-champagne fizz. Tears sprang to his eyes as he gulped it down the wrong way.

'I can honestly say this is another first. There have been no other picnics and very few ladies since Sara.' He couldn't even remember the last time he'd been this relaxed. These past years he'd been working his backside off, trying to rectify the mistakes he'd made, with no time for frivolity. Cutting loose with Charlotte showed him it didn't have to have negative connotations. The only thing that would make this perfect would be if Alfie was here too. It was all so easy when he was with Charlotte and he wished his rapport with his son could evolve as naturally too.

'Well, thank you. You've made me feel very special tonight.' She couldn't believe he had done this for her and had tried not to get too carried away with the romance if it was simply part of his usual seduction technique.

He'd come halfway across the world, given up his life there to come and be a proper father to Alfie, and she knew his son was his priority. Not that she would expect him to put someone he'd just met above that but they did seem to keep gravitating back towards one another.

'That's because you are. Didn't I say I'd share my cookies with you? I don't do that with just anyone.' He grinned and offered her the packet of chocolate-chip heaven.

She snacked on the crumbly biscuit and watched with fascination as he tidied the rubbish into the bin and laid the rug down on a patch of grass with the candles either side. 'Have I just sold my soul for a cookie? Is this where you sacrifice me to appease the hockey gods?'

'We could do that or, you know, just chill with some star-gazing.' He made himself as comfortable as he could, trying to fit his large frame onto half of the small rug, with his knees bent and his hands behind his head.

She had nothing to lose by joining him. Except perhaps all feeling in her backside when she tried to get up off the cold ground again.

'This is what you did as a teenager? I imagined something more rock and roll.'

'It might've involved a beer or two I'd sneaked out of the house but, yeah, I liked to lie in the quiet and just look at the stars. I used to imagine what was out there in the universe waiting for me, prayed there was more to life than the one I had.'

'You and me both.' Although she'd chosen hockey games as her fantasy landscape.

'Those three bright stars in a row are Orion's belt and that right there is the Big Dipper.' He pointed up at the constellation of seven stars.

'I think we call that The Plough over here but I've never taken much interest, to be honest.' There'd been nothing there to capture her imagination until tonight when Hunter had been so transfixed and the most relaxed she'd seen him to date. He looked just like the naïve kid they'd probably both been before real life had crept in and made them so jaded.

'I'm a bit of a nerd about it, I guess. I could bore you with the names of all those stars if I had a mind to but we're supposed to be having fun.'

'I *am* having fun. I didn't know you were into astronomy. I'm finding out so much about you tonight.' She knew every time she looked up at the sky from now on she'd always think of him and this night together. This gesture to recapture the childhood ripped from her was something she'd never forget.

He turned his head to look at her. 'Isn't that what you wanted?'

They were lying so close together she could see the twinkle in his eye. He hadn't planned this, she was pretty sure, but it had done the job. Hunter had told her everything she needed to know in order for her to let him into her heart. It didn't make it any less scary about taking that chance on him.

She reached across him so her face was only millimetres from his, her chest brushing against his, and watched his throat bob as he swallowed. As quick as a flash she grabbed the cookie from his hand and stole back to her own side of the blanket.

'This is what I wanted,' she said, and took a bite of her ill-gotten gains. It would do him good to be kept on his toes now she'd laid herself bare emotionally.

'Yeah? Are you sure that's all you have a craving for?' He rolled over and pinned her to the ground with one arm either side of her body and began kissing his way along her neck. It was so damn hot the much-sought-after cookie slid from her hand into the grass, now totally forgotten.

'Uh…maybe not.' She threaded her fingers through his hair as every blast of hot breath on her skin sent her into raptures. It was true. Ever since that first kiss she'd craved more of this, more of him, and tonight had taught her that life was so fragile you just had to grab the good times where you could.

'Good,' he murmured as he closed his mouth around hers and sealed her fate. She was lost to him now, whatever the consequences.

They ignored the first drops of rain as they fell, so wrapped up in each other they didn't care. Even when the candles fizzled out and Charlotte could feel the dampness on Hunter's skin she was reluctant to break away from him again. She was content where she was with his body pressed against hers and passion keeping them both warm. Unfortunately it couldn't keep them dry when the heavens opened and doused the flames.

She let out a shriek as they scrambled to their feet, the rain so heavy it was dripping off the ends of their noses and their clothes were sticking to their skin. It would've been romantic if not for the sudden drop in temperature and the very real possibility of pneumonia. They snatched up their waterlogged belongings and headed straight for shelter in the wooden hut where the forest route map was displayed.

'I'll phone for a taxi back to the arena so you can get your car.' Hunter wrapped her in the blanket, which was slightly less sodden than her clothes, and pulled out his phone.

Charlotte chattered her thanks through her teeth. As much as she didn't want this night to end, she needed a hot shower and a warm pair of pyjamas to get her body temperature back out of the danger zone. Sharing a bed naked with Hunter would undoubtedly have the same effect but sleeping with him wasn't going to make things any less complicated.

'I'd say that was a successful first date, wouldn't you?' Hunter tucked his phone back in his pocket and huddled in beside her.

'Is that what it was?'

'We're together outside of work commitments… Good food, great company… I'd call that a date.' He nodded his head, pretending that he'd planned the whole thing all along. If that had been the case he might've added an umbrella or a hot-water bottle to his purchases.

'You're a smooth operator, Mr Torrance, I'll give you that.' It had been her best first date ever.

A car approached from the main road and dazzled them in the headlights. Their ride back to reality.

'So, my place or yours?' Hunter leaned in and made her very tempted to carry on the impulsive nature of the evening but she was a woman who didn't give any part of herself so easily.

'It's a first date, isn't it? I'm afraid I'm just not that kind of girl.' She dropped a kiss on his cheek and walked nonchalantly towards the taxi, hoping their next dates would live up to the high standard of this one.

CHAPTER SIX

HUNTER WONDERED IF Charlotte might've had second thoughts about getting involved with a father and son when there was no sign of her at the rink. Now she'd had time to think about the implications of his tangled personal life there was a possibility she'd back out of the offer to support him today. They'd had fun in the park together but she hadn't signed on for a third party. Neither had he.

The strong connection he'd made with Charlotte hadn't figured in his plans when he'd moved out here but he couldn't imagine not having her in his life now. He didn't want anything to affect his relationship with Alfie but she was good for him and surely his happiness would filter through to his son too? A dad who'd found someone he enjoyed spending time with and could really talk with had to be better for him than a man still locked in his own world of guilt and regret.

His day was made with the sight of her walking in and giving him a tentative wave, as if she didn't really know if this was a good idea either. Hunter waved back, careful not to let go of Alfie as he took his first wobbly steps on the ice. This was an exercise in trust and if he let him fall it would be difficult to get him to have faith in him again.

He'd had to get Sara's parents to agree to this unsupervised afternoon out with Alfie and it did feel a little as though he was betraying their trust by inviting Charlotte along too. They hadn't been thrilled about the prospect of their grandson pulling on his first skates and Charlotte had been right about treading softly, not rushing things, when his relationship with the O'Reillys was still fragile, to say the least, but her presence meant a lot to him.

He tried to convince himself that this *chance* meeting wasn't deceiving anyone. It was more about having a friendly face around, someone to help fill the long silences with his son when he couldn't quite find the words himself. After their impromptu picnic in the park he was also happy to see her on a more personal level. He wanted that chance to reconnect and maybe even advance their relationship a little further too.

'I've got you. Don't worry.' He grabbed Alfie's arm to steady him as he began to lose his balance. One heavy fall could be all it took for him to lose interest in the idea of skating altogether and he wanted this to be the one thing he could do for his son that no one else could.

Alfie was still getting his bearings, clinging onto the barrier with one hand and Hunter with the other, as he tottered around the rink.

'Hi. I just thought I'd call in and let you know I've been up to the hospital to see Colton. He's doing well, all things considered, though he's not happy about missing Nottingham.' Charlotte skated out to meet them halfway around.

'That's good. I'll try and get up to see him myself at some point.' For some reason he felt as skittish as a boy on his first date. He was glad to hear his teammate was on the mend but he couldn't get past the worry over this meeting to truly relax. He'd spent more hours lying awake fretting over this than he'd ever had before a big game.

There weren't many women he imagined would've been willing to take on a hockey reject and his grieving son with such understanding. He was almost afraid to think his luck might be changing for the better since moving back here. Now he'd made amends for his past misdeeds perhaps karma had decided to give him a break after all.

'Hi!' Alfie too greeted her, giving Hunter the opening for an introduction.

To his credit, the boy wasn't shy about meeting new people, not even with the man who'd turned up after eight years, claiming to be his father.

'Alfie, this is Charlotte. She's the doctor for the Demons. Charlotte, this is Alfie, my son.' It still choked him up to say it out loud and held such significance the words deserved a choir of angels and light splitting the heavens to accompany them.

There was pride in being able to claim this beautiful boy as his own. The best thing he'd ever accomplished in his life was being his father, albeit a recent surprise. It also made him question his parents' behaviour more than ever. By blood, or through adoption, being a parent was a privilege, not a right, and those who'd professed to be his guardians had taken it for granted, abused that position.

After being declined the role and the chance of being there for Alfie's milestones, he couldn't imagine treating a child with the disdain he'd been subjected to. He hated all of those involved, or not, in his upbringing yet there was still a morsel of sympathy to be found in the situation. They'd never experienced the love and special bond between parent and child, and never would. More than that, they'd never know their grandson. He'd let them all know about Alfie's existence because there had been too many secrets to date but their selfishness would never let them accept another child into their lives. It was better for Alfie, and him, that it remain that way. He was just so afraid of making the same mistakes he was literally tongue-tied around him.

'Cool. Hi, Charlotte.' Alfie reached out to shake her hand and Hunter was pleasantly surprised that Sara and her parents had raised such a well-mannered young man.

It made life easier for him and gave him more reason to be proud, even though he didn't deserve any credit for how he'd turned out. All he could do was continue to raise him in a manner of which Sara would've approved.

'Well, hello, Alfie.' Charlotte too appeared completely bowled over by his charm, which boded well for the afternoon ahead.

Hunter didn't know what he would've done if Alfie had blanked her or taken umbrage to her being here with them because he was sure as hell glad to have her here.

Unfortunately, Alfie's gesture left him off balance since he'd let go of the barrier. His blades slid from underneath him and Hunter had a job keeping him upright.

'Whoa, there.' Luckily Charlotte was there too to take his other arm and help steady him.

'I'm not very good at this.' Alfie's head went down and Hunter was afraid this wasn't as much fun for him as they'd both anticipated.

'It's all about balance. If you hold your arms out straight and bend your knees a little, you shouldn't need to hold onto anything.'

'Like this?' He recognised that stubborn tilt of the chin as his son gradually let go of his hand. That independent streak had definitely made its way into the next generation.

'You're a natural. Now just push off with one foot and follow it with the other. Good lad.' Hunter thought he would literally burst with pride at how quickly his boy was learning and following in his footsteps.

'I'm doing it!' The over-exuberance at his success set Alfie off kilter again and the wobble was enough to bring Hunter and Charlotte back to catch hold of him again.

'This is your first time, right? Well, you're already doing better than I did. The first time I stepped onto the ice I ended up flat on my backside, with a bruise the size of a dinner plate.' Charlotte moved in before his confidence was too dented with one of her own painful tales.

'Well, they do say the most important thing to learn is how to fall properly. If you do feel yourself falling, bend your knees and sort of squat. Put your hands out to break your fall but make sure you clench your fingers into fists first.' He demonstrated the safest way to fall because it was a key part of the learning experience.

'Do you know something? I was able to skate by the end of that first lesson. All it takes is a bit of courage. Something I'm sure you have oodles of. Then someday you might even be able to play your dad at hockey.' She gave Hunter a wink and he almost lost his own footing. He'd been right to take her up on her offer today. If it was possible he could have both of these fantastic people in his life he would find a way to do it. As much as Alfie demanded he fulfil his responsibilities as a father, Charlotte was there to remind him he was still a man with his own wants and needs. He was able to be himself here today in their company, a whole person and not just someone playing the role he thought people wanted.

'And beat him?' Alfie's eyes were wide at the prospect, as if it was the coolest thing he'd ever heard.

'Probably.' Hunter wouldn't care. It would mean the world to him simply to be able to play hockey with his son.

'Can I try again on my own?'

'Sure.'

He happily stepped aside to let burgeoning confidence take flight, every shaky step bringing him closer to his son.

The three of them began to make their way slowly around the ice, he and Charlotte on standby to catch their student if he fell, but it wasn't long before Alfie was striking out on his own. Watching his son skate out onto centre ice could've been a scene straight out of Hunter's dreams about the future come true. A future which he was hoping Charlotte might become a part of.

He did what he always did to distract his mind and grabbed an abandoned stick left from practice and lined up an attempt on goal. There was nothing like smashing pucks into the net to prevent him from getting soppy about finding someone who really understood and accepted him, chequered history and all.

Before his stick made contact with the rubber disc, Charlotte appeared from nowhere with another hockey stick and intercepted the puck from him. She took off behind the net to slot in a wraparound goal herself.

'Easy,' she taunted, skating backwards down the ice, leaving him with his mouth hanging open and Alfie cheering.

'Where did you learn to skate like that?' He was impressed. She had proper hockey skills that went beyond the remit of the team doctor. Usually, all that was required for that position was an ability not to fall over if and when they attended casualties on the ice, and even then that was with assistance.

Just when he thought he knew everything about her, she went and surprised him again.

'I took some lessons when I was a teenager.' Things had been getting a bit too cosy for Charlotte, too much like a family day out, and she'd decided to break out a few of her moves to shake things up. She wanted Hunter and Alfie to bond but she was worried she was becoming too involved.

Goodness knew why she'd volunteered to crash this father-son bonding session. It wasn't as if she had any more experience than Hunter did in these matters. She just knew by making the effort he was a good dad and she wanted to encourage the sort of relationship she'd always dreamed of with her own father. This waver in Hunter's confidence over his parenting made him all the more human and less of that two-dimensional pin-up on her wall with no real feelings or worth.

In the space of a few days he'd become so much more to so many people. The team needed him as their physio and friend, Alfie needed him as a father and, well, she just needed him. He'd invaded all areas of her life and suddenly she couldn't imagine not having him there to talk to, to have fun with, and to kiss when the urge took her. Yet meeting Alfie today represented a commitment of sorts on both sides and that terrified the hell out of her.

Today was simply about being emotional support for Hunter. By all accounts, it was the first time anyone had stepped up for him in that way. She was keen to make a good impression on Alfie too. The fact Hunter had kept him a secret told her exactly how much he meant to him.

She'd never contemplated having a child of her own, much less someone else's. That responsibility for another's well-being wasn't something she was prepared to take on when this thing with Hunter would probably fade before it got serious anyway. He had his son, she had her career, and those were totally conflicting priorities that could never gel long term.

No, she'd let this attraction play out until it became obvious they were still a world apart. That's why it was probably best for this informal meeting with Alfie here at the rink where there was no pressure. She didn't want him confused into thinking she was going to be a potential mother figure. That would be too much, too soon, for all of them. He'd end up hating her before getting to know her if he thought she was staking a claim on his father when he'd only just found him. It was a minefield already.

With a flick of the wrist she scooped up another puck and tapped it from side to side, daring him to take it from her. Okay, she was showing off but she could see Alfie was enjoying the sparring. He'd even picked up a stick himself and she knew there was nothing father and son would love more than to face each other on the ice. Leaving her out of it.

Hunter suddenly set off down the ice towards her, and she gave an inward yelp whilst briefly thinking about making a run for it. Face on, he made an intimidating opponent, shoulders broad even without the padding of his kit, and thickly muscled thighs driving his every move. It was no wonder he'd struck fear into the opposition and love hearts into the eyes of his fans.

In this game you couldn't show any weakness, even when a powerhouse was headed straight for you. She stood her ground, hands clenched around the stick, bracing herself for the hit. At the last second before inevitable impact, he pivoted his hips and came to a slow stop, scooting ice over her skates.

'Just remember, us *brutes* have skills of our own,' he said, easily reclaiming the puck now she'd been rendered immobile.

Some men might have been miffed at getting challenged by a girl, many had in various aspects of her life when they'd underestimated her abilities. Not Hunter. That oh-so-kissable mouth was turned up at the corners as he squared up to her. Charlotte tried to come up with a smart comment to get him to back out of her personal space but he was so close, giving her that tachycardia-inducing smoulder, she could barely think straight.

'I think it's Alfie's turn to take a few shots.' She turned away from Hunter so she was no longer under his thrall. This exercise was supposed to cool things down, not turn her and the ice into a puddle with the heat they were generating.

'Sure.' Hunter adopted the goalie position, almost filling the net with his broad frame, whilst she skated back to find him a new challenger.

'I'm not sure I can...' Alfie was managing to balance with his stick resting on the ice but they all knew it would be a different story if he took a swing at a puck.

'Don't worry, I'll help you.' This was about him and his father having fun together and she wouldn't let this time end on anything but a high. She wanted him to make the memories she'd never had with her dad so he always had something to look back on fondly.

She skated behind Alfie and placed her hands either side of his waist. 'You keep your feet on the ice and I'll push. When we get close enough to the net you slide that puck in wherever you think you can get it past your dad.'

'Got it.' Alfie leaned over, knees bent and hockey stick in hand.

'We're coming for ya, Hunter!' she bellowed, getting caught up in Alfie's determination to show off his new skills.

'Bring it on.' The Demons' sexy substitute goalie grinned, urging his opponents to take their best shot.

She steered Alfie on a steady course to meet him and as soon as they reached the goal crease, he guided the puck to the tiny space uncovered to Hunter's left. Hunter stretched too late to prevent it from going in and Charlotte wasn't sure if she or Alfie cheered loudest.

In their race for a goal, no one managed to think about how they were going to stop and they collided with Hunter, all three tumbling into a heap. He took the brunt of the fall so they landed on top of him, laughing, in the back of the net.

'This is the best day ever!' Alfie took turns to hug them, the unsolicited affection taking her by surprise. She was like a rabbit in the headlights, unsure how to proceed for her own safety in case one wrong move spelled the end of life as she knew it. This was supposed to bring Hunter and his son closer, not pull her into the relationship. Yet she couldn't seem to help herself hugging him back, her heart melted by the gesture.

Hunter mouthed a *thank you* over the head of his son and she found she no longer noticed the cold seeping in through her clothes. The duo of Torrance smiles was more than enough to keep her warm. She was sure it was Hunter who'd become suddenly misty-eyed, not her, but the ball of emotion almost blocking her airway told a different story.

This was how a father was supposed to love his child and it highlighted even more what she'd missed out on all of these years. Parenting wasn't something that could be done from a distance. These two needed each other to feel complete and it was a revelation to someone who, up until now, had been content in her own company.

Family time was much more fun than she remembered.

Hunter couldn't remember his life ever being so full, or being so at ease with everything in it. It had been a busy few days and not solely because they were preparing for the play-offs. The afternoon he'd spent with Alfie had been such a success he'd been granted more access by the O'Reillys. It was all down to Charlotte. She'd had more faith in his abilities as a father than he'd had and simply having her there had helped put him at ease. That skating session had almost been like watching Alfie walk for the first time in hockey terms and as close to those missed milestones as he'd ever get. He'd be grateful to her for ever for facilitating that special day. It just wouldn't have been the same without her.

Since then he'd been able to pick his son up from school, take him out for pizza and generally do all the other things dads took for granted. As cautious as the O'Reillys were about his credentials as a reliable adult, he got the impression they were glad to have someone to share the childcare with and get some of their freedom back too.

The only downside of the whole situation was that he hadn't been able to spend as much time with Charlotte alone as he'd expected. It would be a balancing act of his time, trying to make sure neither was too freaked out by the other's presence in his life, but if Charlotte was going to be in his life she'd have to understand that Alfie came first. He was wary of letting things get too serious when he couldn't fully commit to her. Experience had taught him a very harsh lesson—a romantic relationship impacted on more than just him.

It was one thing to risk his heart again but he was a dad now. He'd hurt Sara by being so cavalier with her emotions and he wasn't about to do that to his son too. Unlike his parents, he cared about the damage he could inflict with a careless attitude towards his charge. He just hoped Charlotte was on board with his parenting approach too. Especially since he'd had to cancel their date tonight at short notice to babysit Alfie so the O'Reillys could visit a friend in hospital.

'Can we watch this one, Dad?' His companion for the evening selected a movie for them to watch together, a hugely popular animation that ordinarily would have seen him reaching for the remote control. Not tonight. He'd be content to sit on the couch with his son even if there was nothing but a blank screen in front of them.

'Anything you want, bud. Your choice.'

'Did you watch this when you were my age?' Alfie tilted his head to one side with that quizzical look Hunter had come to recognise. He'd become increasingly curious about his father's background, and whilst it was heart-warming that he had an interest in getting to know him better, Hunter didn't want him to delve too deeply. If possible, he'd prefer to avoid conversations about his family as long as possible.

'No. This wasn't out when I was a kid.'

'But you had cartoons in Canada, right?'

'Sure. Although the graphics are better these days.' And not the billion-dollar merchandise factory they were now. At least, he'd never had any expensive movie franchise toys but that could've been entirely down to his adoptive parents' refusal to spend that kind of money on a son they barely cared existed.

On the flip side, if he and Alfie enjoyed watching this together, Santa Claus would be raiding the workshop for every related item he could find this Christmas.

'Does it snow all the time in Canada? We only get it here sometimes and then the rain washes it away.'

'It depends on the time of year. We have seasons like everyone else.'

Alfie thought for a moment and Hunter was on tenterhooks waiting to hear what would come out of his mouth next. The boy was clearly trying to process their different backgrounds and try to relate better to his father.

'Can we go someday? To Canada? Together?'

Hunter had been so consumed with getting his life set up here it had never occurred to him that Alfie might want to visit his homeland in return. It might be kind of cool to take him back, show him the sights and make some happier memories there. Some closure would be good.

'We'll have to talk to your grandparents about that but a vacation would be nice. Someday.' He wouldn't make any promises he couldn't keep but he would have the summer relatively free…

Alfie jumped up on the couch next to him, close enough for Hunter to know he was after something else. 'Maybe we could visit your mum and dad too? Do they know about me?'

They'd done it again. Somehow his parents still managed to ruin the good times without even trying.

'Yes, they know about you, Alfie, but I'm afraid I'm not really in contact with them any more. I'm sure we wouldn't find the time to see them anyway with all the cool things there are to do out there. You know Canada's the home of the Stanley Cup, the championship trophy for the winner of the NHL play-offs? I'd really love to take you to a hockey game over there if I could.' It was difficult to be diplomatic and avoid hurting Alfie's feelings at the same time. He could rage about his parents and what terrible people they were but there was no point in them being a black cloud in his son's life too.

'Oh. Okay.'

Not even the prospect of an NHL game was able to lift his spirits again and Hunter knew the kid just wanted to get to know his family. It was better for him in the end to keep his distance but he knew that heart-sinking realisation that wishing for something simply wasn't enough to make to happen.

'Don't worry. You've got me and your grandparents here to love you and we're not going anywhere.' He wrapped an arm around his son and gave him a reassuring hug. It was important in these circumstances that Alfie learned to focus on the positives, who and what he did have around him. It had taken years for Hunter to do that.

'And Charlotte?' Alfie looked up at him with hope in his eyes and Hunter was afraid he was going to have to disappoint him even more.

'Well, uh…' He didn't want to lie but neither did he know what the future held for him and Charlotte or how long she would be in their lives.

The doorbell rang and saved him from having to explain his complicated love life to an eight-year-old. He jumped up and practically sprinted to the front door to avoid that conversation.

'Hi, Charlotte.'

It had been Alfie's idea to invite her along too and Hunter had worried it was asking too much of her. Her last involvement with Alfie had been as a favour to him in an effort to get to know his son. A cosy family night in might be taking things too far, too quickly. Then he saw the bag of popcorn and the huge bar of chocolate in her hands and he realised she was in this with him.

'Are you sure this is okay? I mean, this is your time together. I wouldn't have come except he was so insistent on the phone...' She was already turning back before she'd given him the chance to invite her inside and he could see the debate going on in her head about whether or not this was a good idea.

The significance of her coming here tonight wasn't lost on either of them. She wanted to be part of this tonight, part of their lives and, regardless of the long-term implications, Hunter couldn't have wished for a better addition to the evening.

He threw the door open wide. 'Come in. You're more than welcome.'

The only thing that stopped Charlotte from throwing the movie night treats at Hunter and beating a hasty retreat was the sound of Alfie laughing in the next room. He was the reason she was there, gatecrashing their father-son time again, simply because she didn't want to let him down. Hunter had been very apologetic with the last-minute change of plans and his son's plea for her to come over, and she had the impression he wasn't any more comfortable with the set-up than she was. It was natural for him to protect Alfie by keeping her at a distance—after all, she'd had the same worries about getting involved when there was a child in the picture—but she and Alfie already seemed to have formed a bond of their own. Goodness knew, she'd missed seeing both of them these past couple of days.

'Thanks. If I'd been left alone with all this junk food in the house I might have been tempted to pig out.'

'I'm sure I can find someone to help you out with that. I'll get a bowl.' He took the bag of popcorn from her, leaned in close until his cheek was touching hers and whispered, 'I'm really glad you're here.'

With those words of acceptance she was able to walk into the house knowing she'd made the right decision in the end by taking the risk.

'Hey, Alfie.' She peeked into the living room to say hello and make sure he was still on board with her being there.

'Charlotte! Guess what? My dad's going to take me to Canada and we're going to see someone called Stanley and an ice hockey match.'

She needn't have worried as Alfie launched himself at her, fit to bust with his news.

'Really? That sounds amazing.' Relations really had improved if they were thinking about taking an unsupervised holiday and she was pleased they were getting on so well.

Hunter walked in armed with the sugary treats and rolled his eyes. 'Now, Alfie, what did I say?'

'Maybe. Someday,' he muttered into his shoes.

Those same words made Charlotte's stomach sink for him. She'd heard them over and over again when she'd asked her father if they could spend time together in the early days of her parents' separation. In his case they had always meant never but she knew Hunter was different. He was trying to build his relationship with his child, not walk away from it.

He set the snacks on the coffee table as he huffed out a breath. 'Well, I guess it won't hurt to price the flights in the meantime.'

His solid confirmation as one of the good guys immediately lifted the mood in the room and by the time the credits rolled and they'd scoffed their fill, Alfie was sound asleep in her lap and she was cuddled up against Hunter. The perfect night in.

'You two really seem to be hitting it off,' she whispered, so as not to wake the sleeping boy.

'You too. I'm really glad you came. The only reason I didn't suggest it myself was because I didn't think it would match up to the evening I'd originally planned for us.' He stroked her arm with the back of his hand, raising goosebumps with every stroke.

'Oh? And what did that include?' Whatever it was, it would be hard to top this right now, but he was being so playful it was impossible to resist finding out exactly what he'd had in mind.

'Dinner, music, a little wine…' His phone buzzed on the coffee table next to the empty popcorn bowl and robbed her from finding out what the rest of that evening entailed.

'I guess that means time's up?'

He nodded, already moving away from her. 'They're home from the hospital and keen to get Alfie to bed.'

'It's a shame they won't let him spend the night when he seems so at home here.' It seemed the most obvious thing in the world to someone on the outside, looking in, but she knew Hunter wouldn't do anything to rock the boat with Alfie's grandparents. He was being more patient than she would ever have expected given his strong emotions when it came to his son. During his playing days it would've taken a lot less for him to lash out and turn any precarious situation into complete chaos. She believed he'd changed from those days and she prayed Alfie's guardians would recognise it soon too.

He simply shrugged and gave a half-smile as he rose from his seat. 'Maybe. Someday.'

From him that was an optimistic outlook on what had to be an increasingly infuriating acquiescence to their wishes.

She eased Alfie's head onto a cushion so she was free again and reached for her shoes, which she'd kicked off at Hunter's request to make herself comfortable.

'What are you doing?' he demanded with a glare, arms folded across his chest.

'Getting ready to go home.' She was under no illusion she'd be part of Alfie's bedtime routine. It wouldn't do Hunter's cause any good if she rocked up at the O'Reillys' with the two of them. They were grieving for their daughter, about to hand over custody of their grandson, and she doubted having a strange woman on the scene would instil their confidence in Hunter any further.

'Is that what you want?' He was still frowning at her and for the life of her she couldn't figure out what she'd done wrong.

'I'm not going to insist on accompanying you back with Alfie, if that's what you mean. You can rest easy on that account. I'm done gatecrashing for the night.' She really didn't want him to be under the misapprehension she was going to wedge herself into both of their lives at every given opportunity. This was a one-off. Probably.

'That's not what I meant. I just thought you might wait here until I came back.'

Charlotte sank back into her seat. It might've been a swoon if she'd been standing up, like a regency heroine who'd been propositioned by an infamous rake.

'Oh? Now, why would I do that?' She couldn't help herself. Every time he alluded to spending some alone time she wanted him to spell out in graphic detail what he imagined that would include. It was as close as they got to dirty talk with a child in the room.

Hunter leaned down and whispered in her ear. 'I think we're past the dinner stage but there's always time for music, a little wine…'

In the end it was his unspoken intentions that had her bunching the upholstery in her hands as she fought arousal from completely taking control of her body. She was still sitting there, clutching the furniture, as he scooped Alfie up and took him home.

There was no mistaking what would happen if she waited for him to come back and she had to admit the idea of spending the rest of the night with him, in bed, sounded delicious. If it wasn't for the implications tomorrow morning. Then there would be no confusion about what was going on between her and Hunter. A few kisses here and there and they could still keep up the pretence there wasn't something serious going on that could alter the course of their lives.

Yet her feet still refused to move and her heart wouldn't quit yearning for the chance to truly be with him. Even for one night. It was a risk when every step forward with him brought her closer to that family commitment she didn't want, but tonight had shown her some risks were worth taking.

Not for the first time Hunter was glad he'd found a house close to Alfie. As much as he wanted to get back to Charlotte as quickly as possible, he was still able to take his time putting his son to bed. He was sure the grandparents hadn't approved of tonight's snack choices but he reckoned he had eight years of treats to make up to his son and a little junk food was fine in moderation. After all, someday these sorts of decisions would be entirely down to him. The consolation for their disapproval was Alfie's sleepy smile as he tucked the covers around him, which said he'd enjoyed the evening every bit as Hunter had.

Alfie had treated Charlotte more as a friend than a threat, or someone trying to replace his mother, and that was all he could ask for. In turn, she'd been her warm, kind, funny self and not once had she patronised or treated him with anything other than affection.

He hadn't even known he'd wanted her there until she'd

been in front of him, but it meant everything to him that she'd wanted to spend time with them just for fun. There'd been no obligation, no plea from him to be a conversation starter this time, but she'd voluntarily pitched up to see them anyway. To him that proved she saw Alfie as more than an inconvenience or someone she was simply forced to endure. She genuinely cared. There weren't too many women who would've taken a last-minute date cancellation so well, never mind brought treats for her replacement. He was a lucky guy. One who desperately wanted to believe he could have it all.

The lights were still on in the cottage when he pulled up outside and he hoped that meant she was still inside, waiting for him. He hadn't planned any of tonight's events, they'd pretty much happened organically, but he did know he wanted to spend the rest of the night with Charlotte.

He let himself into the house to find her in the kitchen, pouring two glasses of wine. The hypnotic swing of her hips as she danced along to the radio drew him straight to her. Just like the earlier cosy family scene on the couch, it was too easy to forget this welcome-home sight was a one-off. But it was fun to play make believe every once in a while. He wrapped his arms around her waist and kissed the back of her neck.

'I found a bottle of white in your fridge. I hope that's all right?' She turned around to hand him a glass and took a sip from her own. He watched the liquid coat her lips and a sudden thirst came upon him that had nothing to do with alcohol.

'Was tonight that bad you couldn't wait for me to get back?' he teased, and took a sip before placing the glass back on the kitchen counter.

'I thought it would get the wine and music out of the way quicker so I could see what else you had planned.' She bit the inside of her cheek as she teased him right back.

He slowly and silently took the glass from her and set it down. Somewhere in the distance the saxophone sounds of nineties power ballads set the mood for seduction as he moved in. 'Nothing's planned. I thought we'd just see where the night takes us again.'

It took him straight to her parted lips to indulge in the tangy taste of wine and temptation. He inhaled the scent of her sweet perfume as he bunched her hair in his hands and deepened the kiss. She was most definitely real and his for as long as she wanted.

Over these past days she'd given him everything he could ever have asked for, joining forces to help him at work and at home, and trusting him not to let her down. That was a big deal given her past history and he wanted more than anything to prove he'd been worth the risk.

He cupped her breast through her grey sweater but the bulky fabric was too big a barrier between them for his liking. He loved her urban look, especially the tight black jeans that were showcasing her pert backside and long legs tonight, but the top layers left too much to the imagination.

'Take it off,' he demanded, his desire to see her, feel her turning his voice to a growl.

She leaned back and did as he asked, revealing a decidedly feminine silky black bra. He brushed his thumb over one nipple until it tented under the silk covering. Charlotte arched her back and primal instinct took over as he latched his mouth around the suckable point, taking fabric and all into his warm mouth. He flicked his tongue over the covered tip but it wasn't enough to satisfy either of them. He yanked the straps of her bra down her arms to free those perky nipples for his full attention. She fitted perfectly into the palms of his hands and he lapped his tongue over the soft mounds of flesh, lingering on the sensitive rosy peaks until her groans of pleasure were filling his head.

He skated his hand down her flat midriff, popped open

the button on her jeans and made her gasp as he slowly unzipped her. Beneath her silky underwear he sought her moist heat with his fingers, sliding inside her so easily his breath caught in his throat. She was ready and waiting for him, yet he wanted to do this for her, give her some of the pleasure she'd already given him.

He made small lazy circles at first, opening her up to him, exploring her, with the slow, intimate rub. Those ever-increasing circles soon picked up pace to match her desire, stimulating that little nub of nerve endings that had his body at its mercy too. When he pushed his thumb into her she clutched at his shirt and he knew she was close. Her body tensed around him and his excitement reached critical levels right along with her.

She buried her face into his chest to muffle her groans, panting as he pushed deep inside her and that final burst of climax claimed her.

He was having trouble breathing himself and rested his head against her shoulder. 'Next time, I want to hear you scream, Charlotte.'

'Next time?' she said through hiccupping breaths as she adjusted her underwear.

'The night's still young and so are we.' Every muscle in his body was trembling with restraint but he didn't want this to be the end.

He took her by the hand and led her up to his bedroom, every creaking stair beneath their feet making this feel more illicit by the second when he'd never been more certain he wanted to be with someone in his life. This wasn't some random hook-up or a habit he'd simply fallen into and hadn't had the courage to break. He was emotionally involved with Charlotte and that made this virgin territory for him. Once he gave himself to her he knew there was no taking it back. It was a step into the unknown he was willing to take.

Charlotte's heart was about to force its way out of her ribcage if this man insisted on more of the same. This much arousal couldn't be good for a person. He'd brought her to orgasm without even getting naked and she was afraid once he did she'd end up needing a resus team. Not that it was stopping her from stepping into his bedroom. She'd always longed to see the wonders of the world.

She gave a shiver once the door closed and it wasn't only because she was still only half-dressed. Caught in the undercurrent of their passion, she walked towards him, being pulled ever deeper until she was in danger of drowning. Hunter undid the top buttons of his navy piqué shirt, which was stretched so tightly across his broad chest she couldn't wait for him to take it off. She lifted the hem and ensured he stripped off in double quick time to reveal a body that deserved its own social media account.

Sleeping with Hunter was a bigger event than she could ever imagine for who he was now, not who he *had* been. This wasn't about a teen fantasy come true, this was a real desire to be together, a connection between two adults who needed to get this attraction out of their system so they could get back to who they were outside it.

Okay, so she was trying to have her cake and eat it but she had a very sweet tooth and a libido that apparently wouldn't quit around him. Except every second she spent with him claimed a bigger piece of her heart with his name on it.

She mightn't be ready to be part of a family, or want to get hurt again, but it didn't mean she was made of stone. In these few moments of peace there was no talk of work, family or the future, only the silent acceptance of attraction. Here, away from the messy reality of getting involved, it seemed possible they could be together without causing some sort of cosmic fallout to rip the universe apart.

Watching each other undress was somehow as erotic as

tearing their clothes off in haste. Perhaps it was because they never broke eye contact, the moment more significant than simply getting naked. They were stripping away the layers of their past, the outside influences they had no need for in the bedroom and concentrating on what it was they wanted here and now. Each other.

That didn't mean she couldn't see the impressive evidence of his arousal. It was difficult to miss.

She was only self-conscious about standing here stripped bare before him for a few seconds because when he started kissing her she didn't care about anything else. He guided her towards the bed and she took him with her down onto the mattress, body to body, mouth to mouth, heart to heart.

With his finger and thumb he pinched her pebbled nipple and made her gasp with delight. Now he was aware that was her weak spot, he latched on tightly, sucking her into his mouth until she was bucking against him with unbridled lust.

She reached down and gripped his erection, sliding her hand along his shaft until she made him equally as breathless.

'As much as I don't want you to stop what you're doing, we need some protection.'

It was understandable he'd be more careful after having one unplanned pregnancy but she was restless against the sheets, waiting for him to grab the condom from his nightstand.

He lowered himself between her thighs and kissed her on the mouth as he joined his body to hers. Their breath mingled with a mutual gasp of relief now the veil had fallen. There was no more pretence that this wasn't what they'd been waiting for, regardless of all the obstacles in their way.

Charlotte hitched her knees up to her waist, drew him deeper inside and lost all inhibitions in favour of revisiting that place of utter bliss he'd taken her to earlier. She was close to the edge again already when she should have been exhausted after the last time, not coiled and waiting for more.

So far Hunter had been a gentleman. If that gentleman was a sexy stud acting out all of her very grown-up fantasies at once. She wanted him hard and fast, slow and steady, every which way he would oblige.

He filled her, stretched her with every stroke, and she rode with him, watching the intensity of the moment play across his features. The way he looked deep into her eyes every time he joined his body to hers, the breathy sound of her name as he buried his head in her neck and the tender kisses he placed on her skin said this was more than sex for him too.

If that was all this had ever been about they could have ended this in the kitchen or on the stairs, but he'd taken his time to make this right. It was as perfect as she could ever have hoped, except for one tiny flaw. She didn't want it to be over.

This feeling of completion was to be cherished, not thrown away because she was afraid of being hurt again. Regardless of the lectures to herself on the contrary, she'd fallen for him, again, and she wondered if she was hurting herself more by denying them a future together if there could be one waiting.

Hunter panted close to her ear and prevented her from over-thinking when it was far more enjoyable just to feel. She clenched her inner muscles as another wave of arousal crashed over her and clung tighter to him, her groans matching his as they reached breaking point together. Her cry filled the room as he fulfilled the promise to make her scream and she surrendered her body, her heart, once and for all.

After what they'd just shared it was going to be harder than ever to maintain that emotional distance she'd been clinging to desperately since he'd appeared in her life. She'd given him everything of herself now and she was trusting him not to fail her when she was taking the greatest risk of them all. Her heart.

CHAPTER SEVEN

HUNTER FOUGHT CONSCIOUSNESS because that meant leaving the warm, comfy confines of his bed and he wasn't ready to tear himself away just yet. He was happy where he was, thank you very much, with Charlotte's naked body draped across his, her hair splayed over his chest keeping him warm since the covers had hit the floor long ago. Probably some time in the early hours of the morning when his amorous companion had given him the best early-morning wake-up call he could ever remember.

If rendering him immobile with exhaustion was her ploy to keep him here as her sex slave he wouldn't have a problem with it.

Last night had been amazing on so many different levels. He was making such great progress with Alfie he'd been afraid to push for more time in case he upset Sara's parents, but Charlotte's support had given him the courage to move things forward and it was beginning to pay off. His dream of being a proper, twenty-four-hour father to Alfie was within reaching distance. What part in that picture Charlotte was going to play he wasn't certain but their time together recently had convinced him it could be a possibility.

'I suppose we should really get up,' Charlotte mumbled into his chest, letting him know she was awake too and they had responsibilities other than their libidos.

He grunted his displeasure at the idea because talking took energy that could be better spent with one last period of play. Charlotte reached across him to turn the alarm clock around, her breasts squashing against him and re-awakening a certain part of his body.

He ran his hand over her pert backside, wondering if he could manoeuvre her into another performance of her cowgirl routine.

'I wanted to check in on Anderson today and see how things were between him and Maggie before he's shipped off to Nottingham.'

'You're thinking about another man already? You really are insatiable,' he teased. It was unsurprising she was starting the day with work at the forefront of her mind when she was so emotionally attached to the team. Her dedication was just one more thing to admire in her. Even if it did come at the cost of his comfort.

She smacked his chest. 'As much as I would love to lie here with you all day, we have jobs to do and people who need our help. You need to get up.'

'I'm nearly there,' he grumbled, knowing she was right even if his idea of how to spend these last moments alone sounded more fun.

'You can stay here if you want or meet me over at Anderson's in about an hour. I need to go home and get changed. It'll only cause a stir if I turn up in last night's clothes.'

Hunter watched with growing admiration as she walked around the room, still naked, collecting their discarded clothes from the floor. He propped himself up on his elbows to better enjoy the scenery.

'I think you missed something down here.'

His shirt, followed by his trousers, landed on his head, obscuring the view, but he could hear her tutting nearby.

'As soon as I put my mind to rest that everyone is match

fit for the play-offs, I'm all yours. In the meantime, you need to be a big boy and get yourself dressed.'

'Spoilsport.' Though he hated to agree and deny himself these remaining moments with her, he had a few last-minute tasks to do himself, including saying goodbye to his son. Which he wasn't looking forward to. Even a couple of days apart was going to be quite a wrench for him.

By the time he'd taken his blindfold off, she'd wrapped the smooth curves of her body in the bulky quilt off the bed. Playtime was over.

He was aware her job and her reputation were everything to her but that didn't mean he'd go quietly. Sleeping together marked a change in their relationship and not something they should simply walk away from without acknowledging it. She clutched her quilted modesty tighter as he crossed the room towards her.

'I had a good time last night.'

'Me too.' She watched him through lowered lashes, surprisingly coy after everything they'd done together, to each other.

He wanted to tell her that he didn't want it to be over between them, that they should make a go of this, but those past mistakes haunted him still. Sara had had to deal with the mess he'd left behind for years and he didn't want to do the same thing to Charlotte if he wasn't one hundred per cent certain this was going to work out. The only definite commitment he was able to make was to his son.

'I guess we should face the outside world, though. I'll grab a shower and meet you at Anderson's. You can let yourself out, right?' He walked out of the bedroom towards the bathroom because he was having serious thoughts about throwing her over his shoulder and carrying her back to bed, pretending there was nothing to keep them from being together.

'Right. I'll see you there, then.'

Hunter didn't want to think about how small her voice seemed as he shut the bathroom door on her because he knew whatever happened next someone was bound to get hurt.

Charlotte was almost praying Hunter wouldn't be at Anderson's house as she walked the short distance from her place to his. It wasn't that she still wanted proof he didn't have her commitment to the job, she needed a time out when she could think clearly without their naked bodies getting involved. After last night she was risking her peace of mind more than ever by continuing to be with him. This wasn't just about him now, he came with an Alfie attachment, and she was fast falling for them both.

'Good morning, Dr Michaels.' Hunter joined her on the doorstep, waiting to be permitted entry to Anderson's personal life.

'Morning, Mr Torrance.' Pretending they hadn't just spent the last twelve hours naked together was going to be tough when her insides were already dancing with glee at the sound of his voice.

'Thank goodness you're here, Doc. There's something wrong with Maggie.' Anderson opened the door so quickly they were almost sucked inside by the vacuum he'd created.

'Where is she?' Charlotte pushed past him in search of the patient.

'On the couch. We were just talking and she collapsed.' Anderson and Hunter followed her into the living room where the red-headed Maggie was slumped in her chair.

Charlotte hunched down beside her as she started to come around. 'Maggie? My name's Charlotte. I'm a doctor. Gus said you aren't feeling too well.'

'Just a little woozy.'

Charlotte checked her pulse and felt her forehead but there were no obvious signs of anything serious.

Anderson appeared at her side, clutching at Maggie's hand. 'Is she okay? Is the baby going to be all right?'

'How far gone are you, Maggie?' There was already a small bump visible under her tight tank top but she wanted confirmation.

'Coming up on three months now but I only found out a few weeks ago.'

Which coincided with Anderson's descent into madness.

'How have you been feeling generally? Any nausea? Tiredness?'

Maggie nodded. 'Morning sickness, although it seems to go on for most of the day. I can't seem to keep anything down.'

'The first trimester is generally the hardest. It should start to get better from here on.' Not that she knew, or had ever intended to find out.

Hunter appeared at her side with a glass of water. 'I hear ginger biscuits can help with that.'

She couldn't help staring at him. That definitely wasn't information generally found in anatomy textbooks.

He shrugged. 'Internet forums. You know...'

She did know. Without a doubt he'd researched every aspect of parenthood the minute he'd found out about Alfie because that's the sort of man he was now. A wonderful, caring father who wouldn't leave anything to chance.

'I'll get some today,' Anderson assured Maggie, still refusing to let go of her hand. At least they appeared to have patched up their differences and that was good news for everyone.

'Have you had your scan yet?' It would probably put their minds at rest if they could see their baby was all right and might help Anderson get used to the idea of becoming a father. Make it real.

Maggie checked her watch. 'We were just on our way

to the hospital for the appointment. We can still make it if we try.'

'You need to take it easy. Tell her, Doc.'

'Gus is right, you do need to take it easy, but I don't think there's anything serious going on. You're probably a little dehydrated. Make sure you mention everything at your appointment. You are going too, aren't you, Gus?' Charlotte would be happier if Maggie was checked over at the hospital where they could run any necessary tests to rule out anything more sinister and it would be better if Maggie had his support.

'I wouldn't miss it for the world.' He rested his hand protectively on Maggie's burgeoning bump, every inch the proud father-to-be.

Whatever had happened between the couple since Charlotte and Hunter's chat, he appeared to have grown up overnight and accepted his responsibilities. It seemed some men were capable of changing and maturing when they became family men, even if her father hadn't been one of them.

'I have to make another house call but I can give you a lift to the hospital if it would help? Trust me, you don't want to miss a minute of this pregnancy.' There was sadness in Hunter's voice and Charlotte knew all too well the reasons behind it. He'd been denied these early moments—the scans, the first kick and the anticipation of the birth. He was a good father and he deserved to have that chance all over again. That was exactly why this romance was never going to work long term. She wasn't the woman he needed to complete his family.

'That would be great, thanks. Are you okay to walk, sweetheart?' Gus was on his feet immediately, clearly keen to see his baby and get the all-clear as soon as possible.

She knew very well the difference a couple of days could make when it came to relationships when her uncomplicated singleton life now seemed a long way away.

'I'm fine.' Maggie smiled at him, the look of a woman in love that said they'd worked on those communication issues.

Hunter chivvied them all outside to his car. 'Are you coming too? I thought we could make that last house call together. We can both say goodbye before we leave for the play-offs.'

'If that's what you want…'

She knew exactly who and what he was talking about and damn if she wasn't a little choked up. It was a step further into his life, and into Alfie's, by taking her with him to say goodbye. That made this more than a casual affair. She knew he wouldn't risk hurting his son with such a move unless it really meant something and it suddenly made her want to take a step back.

Perhaps the intensity of last night had made her too carefree with her heart because now she felt as though she was standing on a trapdoor, just waiting for the drop to certain doom. She wasn't part of this family and that left even more chance she'd be the one left behind if things went wrong. As much as she wanted to be with Hunter, her self-preservation meant more.

They dropped Anderson and Maggie off at the hospital before they picked Alfie up for a spot of lunch since he was still on half-term holidays for school. If he hadn't already phoned ahead and told him they were coming, Charlotte would've backed out there and then.

She remained in the car at the O'Reillys' rather than cause any controversy by showing up on the doorstep and making any sort of claim on their grandson. In contrast, Alfie had bounced up as pleased as Punch to see her, and at any other time she would've been put at ease about joining them.

They called into the local fast-food place where the Torrance men devoured burgers the size of dinner plates before Hunter broached the subject of their trip.

'You know I have to go away for a few days?'

'With the team?' Alfie asked through a mouthful of fries.

'That's right. It's play-off season and we have to go to Nottingham for the weekend. I'll phone you every morning,' he promised, and Charlotte imagined it was as much for his own peace of mind as his son's.

Alfie paused in mid-chew and flicked a glance between Hunter and Charlotte before he swallowed. 'Is Charlotte going too?'

'Hmm-mmm.' She nodded then made a well-timed exit towards the bathroom, leaving Hunter to have that particularly delicate conversation with his son.

It was awkward on so many levels, not least because they hadn't discussed this weekend away as a couple. They'd be travelling for work purposes but it would be naïve for either of them to think things would remain strictly professional between them for the duration of the trip now. At best she was hoping they could have a what-happens-at-the-play-offs-stays-at-the-play-offs attitude to save her from getting involved any deeper and still get to enjoy the physical side. Not that they could explain that to an eight-year-old boy and she wasn't even going to attempt it. That was Hunter's call and nobody would thank her for interfering.

Unfortunately there was a queue for the one bathroom on the premises and she was forced to stand in the hallway around the corner, where she could hear the conversation she'd tried to avoid.

'She's the doctor for the team so, yes, she'll be travelling too.'

'Is she your girlfriend?'

Charlotte had to smile at the forthright Canadian side of the gene pool. Why dance around a subject you wanted a straight answer to?

'I guess… We've been spending a lot of time together. Would that be a problem?'

Alfie was worryingly silent, and Charlotte's heart was in her throat, waiting for the answer. It must be so much worse for Hunter. If his son didn't want her to be in their lives she knew he wouldn't force the issue, and where would that leave her? Time ticked by like treacle as they both waited for Alfie's verdict.

'I like her.'

'Me too.'

'Is she going to be my new mum?'

'I...er...it's too soon to be thinking about that. I don't know. Would you want her to be?'

'Well, she wouldn't be my *real* mum but she is cool.'

Charlotte's heart stuttered right along with Hunter's voice and she was unsure whether to duck back into the bathroom or leave the premises altogether. She couldn't breathe. The last thing she wanted was for Alfie to rely on her being around. The boy had only just found his father, found a stable influence, and it wasn't fair she should be included when she knew nothing of how to parent. She couldn't bear the pressure of that expectation if she and Hunter didn't work out. Didn't want to be the cause of more pain and loss for him when she knew all too well how devastating that could be to a child.

There was no way she was lining herself up to be Alfie's mum, or anyone else's, and if that was what Hunter was looking for it was definitely time to back off. She'd already let herself get too involved, permitting her heart to take over from common sense.

Hunter and Alfie were still too raw to include her as anything but a passing acquaintance in their lives, even if they couldn't see it. If she was going to risk her heart and her dignity again, she needed some chance of a happy ending too. The wicked stepmother never got hers. It usually comprised a grisly death or a lifetime of misery.

She waited until they broke apart before she re-joined

them. It would've been insensitive to interrupt them and immature to walk out without saying a word. In Alfie's eyes she didn't want to be anything more than a friend. A non-threatening, nothing-serious female friend. It was probably best if it stayed that way.

She plastered a big smile over her slowly breaking heart. 'Who wants some ice cream?'

It was her prerogative to eat her body weight in chocolate fudge ice cream to console herself when she was going to have to put a stop to this runaway affair.

'Me!' Hunter and Alfie chorused with their hands in the air.

She was honestly delighted for them that they'd built the foundation for a lovely life together. It just shouldn't include her in it.

By the time they'd polished off their desserts it was nearly curfew time for Hunter and Alfie. She'd seen him anxiously checking his watch, not wanting his allotted time with his son to end but unwilling to get on the wrong side of Alfie's gatekeepers. It was difficult for him and she wouldn't purposely make things any more complicated for either of them.

'Could you drop me home before you take Alfie back?' She ignored Hunter's startled reaction to her request, knowing full well he'd avoid a scene in front of Alfie by asking why.

In his head it probably made more sense for her to wait here or in his car until he'd dropped him off, so they could continue their quality time together. However, for her, that time had passed. If she made the decision to break up with him now before anything else happened it would be kinder in the long run. He got to keep his son and she got custody of her dignity.

They travelled the short distance back with Hunter quietly seething in the driver's seat next to her, hunched over the steering wheel, jaw clenched, forbidding a conversation he didn't want to have in front of his son.

'Thanks for lunch.' She was already unbuckling her seat belt and opening the car door before either of them had a chance to respond.

Unfortunately Hunter's quick reflexes hadn't waned since his hockey-playing days. She heard the engine being turned off and the car door open and close before she even had her house keys in her hand.

'Why the sudden rush to get away? I know I've been a bit preoccupied with Alfie but I promise I'll devote my full attention to you for the rest of the evening.' The growl in his voice and the sudden darkening in his eyes was promise enough of a good time.

Charlotte's libido insisted she abandon the moral high ground to taste the delights he was offering her. A night of passion from the man who could turn her insides to mush with innuendo alone was almost too hot to even contemplate. Every time he looked at her that way her body shivered in anticipation, but the fantasy was over.

'I would never deny you that time with your son. I know every second is precious after missing so much. That's why I'm taking a step back, Hunter. It's too much, too soon for me. I have enough to worry about with the play-offs. I'm sorry, this simply isn't going to work.'

There, she was letting him off the hook. He should be grateful she was making this easy for him, not frowning as though someone had confiscated his skates. Fatherhood had to be about more than his ego.

'I don't understand.'

He wouldn't because she wasn't going to tell him she'd overheard their heart to heart and make him feel any guiltier than he already did.

'Of course you're going to need to spend time with your son, it's only natural. What kind of person would I be if I didn't understand that? You two are making great progress and with Anderson back on track too we should probably quit while we're ahead. If you think about it, neither of us are in the right place to start anything just now.' She forced brightness into her eyes and smile to hide the shadow suddenly cast over her heart.

She was being honest in that she wouldn't deny them their time together—this was a child who needed his father, and vice versa. This situation simply highlighted the need for all the defence mechanisms she'd somehow forgotten in the chaos of getting to know them both.

It just proved how much you had to sacrifice for the greater good where kids were concerned, even when they weren't yours.

He stood there, forcing her to watch the pain and confusion burrow into his handsome features. So this was how it felt to hurt someone? How did her father or Hunter's parents ever live with themselves when her stomach was churning with self-loathing and a sudden urge to whip herself with birch branches?

'We've got the play-offs. We should concentrate on that and put this all behind us.'

'And you'll find that easy to do?'

'Yes.'

The intensity of his stare burning a hole into her soul, searching for the truth, made her breath catch on the lie. At least at the end of the season they'd be able to concentrate on their other priorities, away from each other.

'Right.'

It was a body-check to his ego but he'd get over it, over her, in no time at all. Really, they'd only known each other for a few short days. Not enough to expect him to spend the night crying wrapped in a comfy duvet, the way she'd probably spend her night. That was totally her prerogative. As was trying to be altruistic here.

'So I guess I'll see you at the airport.' She didn't hang around so she could feel any worse. This wasn't going to be a clean break when she'd be flying off soon for a weekend away with the very man she should be avoiding at all costs. There was a very strong chance she'd discover breaking up with him was the last thing she wanted to do.

CHAPTER EIGHT

ORDINARILY THE PLAY-OFFS were the high point of the season and this one should have been especially sweet for Hunter. He was back with the Demons and they'd made it to the finals. However, he seemed to have built an immunity to play-off fever. He was excited for the guys but it was no longer the most important thing in his life.

It had been harder than he'd imagined leaving Northern Ireland, leaving Alfie, even for a few days. He missed his son already. There was a hole in his chest, a void in his day and that awful sick feeling that something was missing. Not even his numerous phone calls home had helped improve his general mood.

In the end he'd had to concede it wasn't only his newly forged role of father that had him propping up the bar, staring into his drink, while the rest of the team was getting an early night.

He was missing Charlotte too. It didn't matter they'd shared the plane, the bus and the workload getting here, the emotional ties had disintegrated. Worse still, he didn't even know why it had happened or why it was bothering him so much.

He'd taken the grilling from the O'Reillys over Charlotte because naturally they'd wanted to know who she was. Regardless of the fact she'd cooled significantly towards him since their night together he'd defended his right to see her and had stood up to them when apparently having her in his, or Alfie's, life was no longer an issue. Somewhere deep down he'd believed Charlotte was worth taking the stand.

Ultimately it had been Alfie himself who'd put the argument to bed with a simple 'I like Charlotte. She's not my mum but she's Daddy's friend. And mine?' he'd added hopefully.

Hunter had nodded, only wishing Charlotte could've seen their situation in such simple terms too. He hadn't been actively searching for a mother for his son if that's what had scared her off. They'd been getting along well, so well perhaps he'd gotten too carried away with the idea of becoming a cosy threesome and she'd picked up on it. It was difficult not to let his hopes and dreams for the future shine through when he'd had everything he'd ever wanted as they'd skated around the rink hand in hand.

Charlotte would never take Sara's place in Hunter's heart because she'd given him Alfie but she did hold a much bigger part of it. Damn it if he hadn't gone and fallen for her. Now he was actually capable of loving himself and his son, it had left the door open for a wonderful woman just like her. Only her.

In trying to do right by everyone he'd messed everything up. He'd upset the O'Reillys and lost Charlotte, none of which was going to help his relationship with Alfie. This do-over had simply been a repeat of his past mistakes. Compounded this time because his son was old enough to witness his foul-ups and experience the consequences.

As he stared down at the murky depths of his pint he considered downing it and ordering some shots. A few years ago that's exactly how he would've coped with this—by blanking it all out so he didn't feel anything. Only the image of the disappointed faces of those close to him wouldn't let him flush everything he'd worked so hard for down the toilet. He'd done that once before and it had been too damned hard to get back to where he was now to go down that same dead end.

'Hunter Torrance. I'd heard you were back in town.'

He almost had the self-pity knocked out of him as a meaty palm slapped him squarely between the shoulder blades. His hand clenched in a fist in an automatic response and released again when he saw who it was. Chris Cooper, CC to his teammates, had spent a couple of seasons at the Demons before he'd moved to England to play.

Now he was assured it wasn't someone here in Nottingham wanting to settle an old score, Hunter happily shook hands and ordered his old friend a drink.

'Yeah. I'm the physio for the Demons these days.'

'I'd heard that.' CC nodded sympathetically, as many did on hearing about the career change. It didn't bother Hunter any more.

'And you? Still involved in the game?' He hadn't kept in touch with anyone, too busy trying to sort his own life out to keep track of anyone else's.

'You could say that.' CC grinned and took a mouthful of lager.

Hunter did the same, his mouth suddenly dry with that awful sensation he'd missed something big. Most of the guys he'd played alongside were retired these days and he hadn't seen any familiar names on the coach roster apart from Gray. That only left 'Management?'

'I made a few property investments along the way, made my name there after I retired and was able to buy my way back into the game. I'm part owner of the London Lasers now.' There was no boasting there, more of an I-know-I'm-a-lucky-son-of-a-gun vibe from him, but to have that sort of clout in the industry took more than a well-timed gamble.

'Impressive. So I take it you're settled in London, then? Wife? Kids?' CC had been a blow-in, just like him, so there would've been some reason for him to stick around after his playing days were over. Perhaps if Hunter had known about Alfie he wouldn't have left either.

'Married to Lenora for five years and we have two girls, Lily and Daisy.' He was beaming now, his already ruddy complexion shining with pride, and Hunter was alarmed to find he envied his marital status more than his bank balance.

Precisely when had he become the settling-down type, yearning for a wife and two point four children? Probably around the time Alfie and Charlotte had crashed into his life and turned it inside out. He'd had his days of partying and reckless behaviour. Now he found more pleasure in simply being in the company of those he loved. He didn't have to chase the good times any more when they came so easily. At least they had done until recently. He took another gulp of beer.

'What about you? Who, or what, brought you back?'

It was a simple question, an obvious one between two old friends catching up, yet Hunter took his time replying. His circumstances weren't wrapped up as succinctly as his new drinking buddy's but he was done with keeping secrets.

'I have a son, Alfie. Things didn't work out between me and his mum. As I'm sure you're aware, I...er...had a few problems back in the day.'

'Kudos to you for getting back on your feet.' CC held his glass up to toast him before a split second of panic hit. 'This is okay, isn't it? I mean, I'm not enabling your fall off the wagon here or anything?'

That was always going to be a worry for everyone who'd witnessed his overindulgence, and something he made sure to keep in check himself, but he wasn't that same hurting, out-of-control kid any more.

He clinked his glass to CC's. 'Those days are long gone. I'll be tucked up in bed after this one. I've turned into something of a bore since becoming a dad.'

'Some might call it being responsible. There's nothing like having kids to curtail the partying. So, you're settled for good in Ireland?'

'That's where Alfie is.' He'd never really considered being anywhere else.

'And you have a permanent position with the Demons? It's all set in stone?' CC was digging even deeper than Charlotte had in the beginning but Hunter had no more skeletons lurking in his closet. At least, none he was aware of.

'Well, no. Not as yet. I was drafted in on a handshake. I'd like to stay on but I'll be working on building up my own practice too once I'm settled.' That had been his original plan but reaching out to Gray had given him his lucky break and enabled him to make the move sooner than expected. It might've been a trial run but it was also a pay cheque whilst he got to know his son.

'Hmm.' CC twirled the cardboard beer mat between his fingers, his mind working overtime somewhere else.

'Hmm, what?'

'We could do with a stand-up guy like you with the Lasers. We've built up quite a medical team focused on strengthening our players. It would be good to have you on board next season.' The steely set of his jaw said this was a serious offer, not a throw-away comment over drinks.

'Are you serious? I mean, the last time we saw each other I was a bit worse for wear.' Whilst the job offer had damn near knocked him off his bar stool, he didn't want CC to be mixing him up with someone else.

'I think tossing the entire team's collection of sticks across the ice was a particular highlight but, yes, I'm serious.' He rested his elbow on the bar top and leaned in. 'Look, everyone deserves a second chance. I've been there myself. Let's just say there was a dark period in between hockey and the property empire. I know what it takes to start over and that's the kind of strength and determination I like to see on a résumé. Besides, who's in a better position to know what hockey players' bodies go through than an ex-pro?'

This had come so out of the blue Hunter couldn't process it and found himself having to break it down in simple terms to get his head around it. 'You're *actually* offering me a job? In London? Wow!'

CC nodded and his belief in Hunter's abilities on face value made it tempting to latch onto the exciting opportunity. A job in London could set him up financially for some time to come and offer so many opportunities for him and Alfie. A new city, new team might finally help him put the past behind him for good. He'd only been in the dad role for a short time and he'd already fallen back into old habits by getting involved with someone without properly thinking it through. He still had to find a way to break it to Alfie that Charlotte would no longer be in their lives and the last thing he wanted to do was let his son get hurt in the crossfire of his love life.

A new start away from the everyday reminders of his failures might be just what they needed to start healing. It wouldn't hurt to find out a bit more about it at least.

'Come see me tomorrow before the game. We can have a proper discussion in private.' CC pulled a business card from his wallet and gave it to Hunter.

CC downed his pint and shook Hunter's hand as he got up to leave. 'Oh, and good luck for the finals. You're gonna need it.' Even here and now between old teammates the competitive spirit was alive and kicking.

'We don't need luck when we've got skills, bro.' Hunter popped the sophisticated silver and black calling card into the back of his wallet along with the picture of his son.

As he'd discovered, life never panned out the way he often expected and he had to make the most of opportunities like this where he could. It wasn't every day he found people who still had faith in him. Charlotte had been the first person in a very long time to show that belief in him as a father and a medical professional and he'd lost her. Perhaps it was time to start over with a clean slate somewhere new.

The atmosphere between Charlotte and Hunter since that afternoon with Alfie felt as though someone had run the Zamboni right through it, coating the surface with fresh ice. It seemed to her they were both afraid to take the first step out and be responsible for leaving deep grooves in the calm, crisp surface.

Things had been as cool as could be since they'd boarded the plane to Nottingham. They hadn't moved on from small talk about the team injury list. It was probably for the best. If they ventured into more personal matters she might actually break and tell him she'd overheard his conversation with Alfie and panicked and she didn't want him to talk her around, tell her things would work out. She was getting in way too deep.

Hunter Torrance, her colleague as well as a single father, was more heartbreak waiting to happen. More than she was going through now. She could just about bear the broken glass stabbing pain in her chest every time she saw him, every time she imagined his lips on hers. Another afternoon spent playing happy families only to have it torn apart again would shatter what was left of her soul.

If she'd let herself get drawn any further into their developing relationship it would've meant opening her heart up for two, double the potential sense of loss when it didn't work out. It couldn't work out. Hunter was a family man now and she was a career woman. One successful season with the Demons and her client list would be a mile long at her own clinic. Her job was her baby and it wouldn't hurt anyone but her if she failed at it. Not that she had any intention of that now it would be receiving her full attention again.

'Anderson certainly seems to be back on form. He showed me the baby scan. I guess fatherhood really does change a man.' Even with the sound of the crowd ringing in her ears she couldn't bear the silence between her and Hunter as they stood and watched the game, or the noise of her own thoughts.

The Demons had five minutes left in the third and final period of play in their match with the Glasgow Braves. They were one nil down and to her amazement Anderson hadn't lost his cool once, even after a dodgy offside decision. He'd taken it on the chin and got straight back into the game without wasting a second of play. A week ago he'd probably have been in danger of being prosecuted for GBH.

'Maggie's here, supporting him, and I know they've told their folks about the baby so I guess it all worked out. It's amazing what simple communication can do for a couple.' The barbed comment said he was still miffed by the way she'd ended things.

Okay, she mightn't have handled it perfectly but she'd been in a panic. She didn't respond well when cornered and that's how she'd felt, trapped, listening to his heart to heart with his son. Over these past years she'd learned to run rather than walk away when things started to get serious and they didn't get more serious than having a kid in the picture.

'Hunter, I—' Her lame apology and explanation was cut off by a deafening cheer as Anderson scored an unassisted goal.

He didn't hear her attempt to build bridges, celebrating the equaliser with his own 'Yes!' as he punched the air.

That unexpected surge of vocal passion gave her chills beneath her fleecy jacket, pinching her nipples into little beads of need begging to experience that passion again for herself.

She would've failed to snag his interest again even if she had figured out what to say as tempers began to fray on the ice. With everything to lose in this semi-final both teams were involved in a bit of pushing and shoving, trying to reclaim possession of the puck. One of the Glasgow players received a two-minute penalty for roughing, giving the Demons a power play, an extra man on the ice, in the dying moments of the game.

Shot after shot was launched at the opposition's net with the one-player advantage, each successfully blocked by the net minder as the seconds ticked down on the scoreboard,

Ten. Nine. Eight…

The sound of sticks hitting rubber echoed around the arena as players valiantly fought for victory and fans held their breath for that last burst of emotion, be it joy or sorrow.

Time seemed to stand still, players moving in slow motion as they made their final attack. The battery of Demons launched themselves down the ice in a fearsome display of gladiatorial determination to survive the battle.

Seven. Six. Five…

The puck passed from player to player, taking the game towards the opposition. Both teams crowded into the penalty area, a scrum ensuing in the goalmouth. The Demons' captain, Floret, claimed the last shot with a mighty thwack.

Goal!

The Demons were play-off finalists.

The arena erupted and as ecstatic as Charlotte was about the win, she knew she and Hunter wouldn't have a chance to reconnect for the rest of the evening. Tonight's success and preparation for tomorrow's battle would keep them otherwise engaged. She should've been glad there was less chance she'd have to explore that idea of communication he was keen on but tomorrow officially ended the season, and with it this period of her life with Hunter. Even if they both returned next season, this break sounded the death knell of their relationship.

Instead of making her feel light and carefree, the thought of no longer being part of Hunter's or Alfie's lives left her feeling numb.

It was difficult to get the players to sit still long enough for a post-game check-up. They were still buzzing behind the scenes long after that final klaxon sounded their win.

'You need that hand seen to.' She practically had to drag Evenshaw into the room so she could treat him.

'Don't fuss. It's only a scratch,' he said, wiping the blood down his shorts.

Men, why did they have to be so damn stubborn?

Take Hunter, for example. She'd ended their relationship and yet he wouldn't stop staring at her as if he had a right to.

As the visiting side at the arena, they didn't have the luxury of the space they had at home to treat their patients. She was currently sharing the small box room with Hunter, acutely aware of his eyes on her regardless of the sweaty players swarming in and out.

With an antiseptic wipe she cleaned the blood away from her patient's palm and watched him wince despite his pro-testations anything was wrong. It was a clean slice, prob-ably from someone's blade, which thankfully wasn't too deep. She'd seen a lot worse recently. It was a sport where speed, sharp skates and rivalry definitely didn't mix well.

'You'll be pleased to know you don't need stitches.'

'See. I told you.' He attempted to get up to join the rowdy celebrations next door.

'Sit.' She pushed him back down into the chair so she could dress the wound properly.

'Yes, ma'am! I do like a woman in charge.' His toothless grin and flirty wink got him nothing except a cuff on the shoulder.

It was a joke, something she didn't take too seriously, but one look at Hunter and she was worried he might wade in and try to protect her honour.

'Ouch. Not so hard.' The unfortunate player on the massage table took the brunt of his apparent rage. Some might have said kneading muscles a tad too roughly was an improvement on smashing up equipment but Charlotte doubted his current patient would agree.

'Sorry.' Hunter returned his gaze from Charlotte back to the burly thighs of the net-minder who'd overstretched during his heroic saves.

'So...can I go now?' Her patient's impatience drew Hunter's attention once more.

'Er...yes. Try to keep that dressing dry and stay away from sharp objects.'

'Yes, ma'am.' He didn't need to be told twice and bolted towards the ruckus going on in the locker room.

'You're finished too.' Hunter gave his permission for the net-minder to go and join the celebrations too as he went to wash his hands.

Within seconds Charlotte and Hunter were alone for the first time since she'd called things off and she tried to get out as quickly as possible to avoid a scene.

'I'm looking forward to the team dinner. It's the most important meal for staff as well as players. I think we all need to replenish our energy stores with protein and slow-acting carbs. I'm starving.' It was a lie. Food was the last thing on her mind but if they were going to have to talk she wanted to keep it neutral.

'What happened to us, Charlotte?' Hunter seemed to see straight through her bluster, his calm, measured voice a contrast to her erratic rambling. It made her question who was actually having more trouble accepting the break-up.

'It doesn't matter, it's over.'

'Just tell me why and I'll walk away. I won't bother you again.'

She knew she couldn't keep lying to him because he'd torture himself about what he'd done wrong when in truth he'd only ever done right by his son.

'I overheard you and Alfie talking and I… I couldn't have him thinking that I'm going to be part of this new life you have planned together. It would only end in tears. His and mine if we'd carried on believing in the fairy-tale. I'm sorry.'

He stared at her, unblinking, probably trying to rewind back to that supposedly private conversation. 'Charlotte, he's a frightened eight-year-old boy still mourning the loss of his mother. You think I should've put him right and said we're just having a fling? I was trying to protect his feelings, to reassure him there isn't going to be any more disruption in his life. I wasn't asking you to be his replacement mother. All I wanted was for you to give us a chance. I'm trying to be careful about saying and doing the right thing so I don't hurt anyone again the way I did his mother.' Hunter's sincerity climbed along the back of her neck and stood the hairs there to attention.

'I guess it doesn't matter now.' If only they'd managed to leave emotions other than rampant lust out of the equation she might still be with him. Except she knew her feelings for him had gone way past merely the physical aspects of being together and distance was no longer a safety net for her fragile heart.

'I guess not.'

'We'll chalk it up as another one of those teenage impulses we needed to get out of our system.' She forced a smile but she felt sick to the stomach pretending that was all it had been to her, and to him. A part of her wanted him to fight for her and salvage something of what they'd had but he remained silent, unmoved by the suggestion.

There was a sharp knock on the door, calling time on their heated confessional. 'Let's go, people. The party bus is here.'

'We should really try and catch up with everyone before they leave without us.' She turned towards the door, unable to look at him any more without tears filling her eyes. It really was over.

Hunter needed to go along with Charlotte's decision to end things because it had become impossible to ignore the growing feelings he had for her. She was much more than a friend to him. Generally, his buddies were a lot hairier, missing a few teeth, and only good company over a beer or two. He didn't spend every waking moment thinking about kissing them or wanting to knock out one of their players for coming onto her.

After everything she'd told him about her past he could see why she was wary about getting too close but that chemistry between them wouldn't simply dissipate because they deemed it inconvenient. It made London seem more appealing by the second if Charlotte was never going to be part of the family he wanted for himself and Alfie. He couldn't see her day after day at work, pining for her yet knowing she didn't feel about him the way he did about her. She was right—it wasn't fair for Alfie either to watch him develop an attachment to someone who wasn't in this for the long haul. There didn't seem any point in fighting for someone who clearly didn't want them in her life.

They made their way back out the maze of corridors to find the team bus but a familiar meaty hand on his back soon stopped him in his steps.

'Good game, eh? I suppose it doesn't matter to you who wins or loses now. After today I do expect your loyalties to lie with the Lasers. Glad to have you on board, bud.' Another back-slap Hunter could've done without forced a strained smile on his face. CC wasn't to know his timing was completely off. It was no one else's fault but his own that he hadn't mentioned their conversation with Charlotte yet.

'What's he talking about?' She was staring at him, not seeing CC's departure, only his revelation.

'I've been offered a permanent position with the Lasers.'

'You're leaving?' Her brow knitted into an ever-deepening wound.

'I agreed to a meeting. That's all.'

'What about Alfie?'

'It was Alfie I was thinking about when I said I might be interested. I thought it could be a new start for both of us in London.'

'What about the team?'

'It was only meant to be a temporary position. I'm sure Gray would understand if it came down to it.'

'What about me?' Her voice was small, almost impossible to hear even in the relative quiet of the arena as the Zamboni trundled out to begin cleaning the ice. If only life was as easy to start afresh, leaving no trace of past traumas, people would be a lot happier with their lot.

'You said you didn't want to be part of us.' Yet he could see the hurt etched in her furrowed brow and her soulful brown eyes.

'So the first sign of trouble and you're running away again? I thought you were the kind of man who fought for the things that mattered? I guess that really doesn't include me.' She folded her arms across her chest as if she was protecting her heart. He knew his was breaking with every painful second he spent with her, unable to touch her or tell her how he really felt about her because there was no room for second thoughts when it came to Alfie's future.

'I'm not running from anything. You were the one who didn't want commitment, remember? I was just—'

'Keeping your options open? I said I didn't want to commit to you and Alfie because I was afraid I'd get hurt. Turned out I was right all along. There is no room for me in your life. Not really. I'll always be the one you leave behind if a better offer comes along.'

'I'm a washed-up hockey player in the back of beyond. Of course I'm going to jump at the chance of a better life for my boy. He is always going to come first.' He couldn't care less about the money or social status, that stuff had stopped being important a long time ago. The truth was, the idea of him, Alfie and Charlotte cosied up in his cottage would be bliss if it were possible. Recent events had shown him it wasn't. It was selfish of him to have believed he could have everything he wanted, someone was always going to suffer as a result.

Ten years ago this would've been much easier. That cavalier attitude to other people's feelings wouldn't have given him this stabbing pain in his gut. At times such as this he missed the old Hunter who hadn't cared about anything except making time to wallow in liquor or his own self-pity.

'Of course he is. Well, good luck in London, then.' Charlotte turned her back on him and walked away, her refusal to lose her cool and get emotional harder to watch than if she'd burst into tears. It signalled her retreat back to where she'd been when they'd first met. She'd been right in trying to protect herself from him all along. He was still making those same mistakes, hurting people he loved and walking away from the devastation.

This was the last time and it was for the right reasons. From now on he was completely devoted to Alfie. As he should've been from the start.

CHAPTER NINE

DINNER HAD BEEN an awkward affair. At least between him and Charlotte. Much like having to live under the same roof after a break-up. An impossible situation that couldn't be avoided and made for a very frosty atmosphere. It wasn't helped now they were back on the team coach on the way back to the hotel with darkness falling outside. She'd taken the aisle seat across from his rather than the empty one beside him. Close enough to prevent any questions being asked about why they were avoiding each other but also putting that significant distance between them. If there'd been no other available seats it wouldn't have come as a surprise if she'd chosen to sit on the floor rather than next to him again.

He didn't blame her. All he'd done lately was confirm both of their fears he would always be the same flaky guy he'd always been, no matter how hard he tried.

'Right, guys. Can I have your attention front and centre, please?' Gray stood at the front of the coach, clapping his hands for attention, diverting it from poker games, cellphones or the very attractive team doctor.

The bus lurched over a pothole, jogging everyone in their seats except Gray, who was undeterred from his motivational speech at the front. He simply planted his feet on either side of the aisle and gripped the headrests of the front seats. 'I know I've already said it—'

'Yeah. Probably at the last speech you gave about ten minutes ago.' The brave heckler at the back prompted a chorus of whoops and whistles.

Gray raised his hand to calm the noise back to an acceptable level. One where his voice was the only one getting airtime.

'Let's not get too cocky. As I was going to say, congratulations on tonight's win. You deserved it and I know we were all thinking of Colton out there.' He started a round of applause for the performance, which Hunter and Charlotte enthusiastically joined.

Getting to the final was a big deal. The season tended to be pretty flat if it ended before they made it to Nottingham so the fact they'd made it all this way had left most of them on a high. With any luck they'd be taking the trip back home with some silverware so they didn't have to come back down to earth too soon.

Gray motioned for silence again. 'That being said…'

There was a collective groan as they waited for the kicker.

'Tomorrow is another day, another game, and there's no time for resting on our laurels. I want you all up bright and early for drill practice.'

Another groan went up. Although Gray didn't linger on sentiment too long, pride was there in his grin. Somehow he managed to make Hunter feel a part of it all. That sense of belonging was something he'd been searching for a long time but he was afraid to embrace it. Nothing in his life had ever been secure for long and he wanted to change that for Alfie as well as himself.

Suddenly, there was a loud bang, followed by the screech of tyres as the bus jolted from side to side and the driver tried to regain control.

This wasn't good.

Gray, who was still out of his seat, was flung to the

floor but he was too far out of reach for Hunter to make a grab for him.

They seemed to gather speed, the confused shouts in the dark adding to the sense of disorientation. The coach veered off down some sort of embankment, branches clawing at the windows failing to slow them down. Glass smashed all around as gnarly limbs reached in and grabbed at the passengers inside.

He glanced over at Charlotte, who was hanging on to the armrest so hard her knuckles were white. He hated being this helpless, pinned by his seat belt as they hurtled at speed and unable to protect her. The driver was hitting the brakes and doing his best to swerve through the trees threatening their survival.

After what seemed an eternity of pinballing between obstacles in their path, there was another loud crash. Even Hunter was lifted out of his seat with the force of the impact as the vehicle hit its final resting place, wedged into a tree trunk.

For a few stunned seconds the only sound was the dying breath of the engine and the flickering headlights before they gave up the ghost and plunged them into complete darkness. He fumbled in his pocket for his cellphone to call for help but there was no signal. At least it came in handy as a torch if nothing else. Some of the others had had the same idea and fireflies of light began to appear in the shadows. He undid his seat belt and went to Charlotte first.

'Are you okay?' He shone the light in her face, forcing her to blink. She was pale but conscious and the relief was so overwhelming it was all he could do not to gather her up into his arms and hug her tight.

'I'm fine. You?'

'I'm good.' Now he knew she wasn't badly hurt.

'Can you smell smoke?'

Hunter sniffed the air and swore. There was no mistaking that acrid odour slowly filling the bus and his lungs.

'We need to see who's been hurt.' She unclipped her seat belt, her thoughts firmly on the welfare of everyone else.

'We've got to get them as far from here as possible.' From the front of the bus he could see the smoke curling out from beneath the crumpled hood and there was no time to waste.

The electrics were shot so he was forced to use brute strength to prise the doors open and let some much-needed air into the vehicle. He helped the driver stagger outside into the night first and went back to assist those who needed it.

'Gray? Can you hear me?' Charlotte was kneeling by Gray, checking his pulse. He was lying face down in the aisle, unmoving, and blocking the exit route for everyone else.

Hunter went cold at the thought of the injuries he could've sustained, tossed around like a ragdoll. Unlike everyone else, he'd been on his feet, unsecured and unprotected, as they'd bumped and smashed their way down the embankment. While Charlotte took care of Gray, he quickly checked the bus for other casualties but luckily everyone else seemed okay.

'Guys, can you make your way out of the emergency exit at the back and get as far from the bus as you can, please?' he shouted to those moving about at the back so they weren't putting themselves in more danger by waiting here if there was a chance of fire on board.

He crouched down beside Charlotte, holding his own breath and waiting desperately to hear any sound of life coming from his friend on the floor.

There was a moan as Gray came to and let Hunter breathe again.

'We have to get him out of here.'

'We really shouldn't move him until we know the extent of his injuries. He took quite a knock back there.' The doctor in Charlotte protested about the proposed evacuation and he understood why—she didn't want to exacerbate any injuries he'd already received, but they were fast running out of options.

'Charlotte, we have to move. Now.'

She followed his gaze outside, where flames were already beginning to lick at the windscreen.

'Okay, but we need to be careful.'

'On the count of three we'll roll him over onto his back. One…'

'Two…'

'Three.'

Charlotte cradled Gray's head so he wasn't jarred too much and Hunter eased him into a better position for them to help him. He was breathing at least and there was no sign of blood. That didn't mean there weren't any internal injuries but they couldn't leave him here. Charlotte was already coughing violently and Hunter's eyes were streaming from the effects of the smoke. If they left him here he'd die from smoke inhalation alone.

'You come down this end and take his feet and I'll do the heavy lifting.' It was going to be awkward trying to get him off this bus in one piece but he knew neither of them were leaving without him.

With another count of three they managed to lift him off the floor. Charlotte backed down the aisle, steering Hunter towards the door with Gray's full weight resting in his arms. His lungs burned with the effort as they stumbled their way down the couple of steps. They didn't stop even when they got outside just in case there was a fuel leak that could see them all blown sky high.

'Careful setting him down,' Charlotte reminded him as they reached the road, where the rest of the guys were. A few of them bundled their jackets together to pull together a makeshift bed so at least they weren't laying him directly on the cold, wet tarmac.

Hunter had never been as glad in his life to hear Gray groan as they set him down and he knew his stubborn friend would be okay.

'Is everyone else here?' Hunter yelled to the crowd standing at the side of the road.

'We'll do a head count.' Charlotte made sure Gray was comfortable before she was back on her feet, giving everyone a provisional check-over and singling out those she suspected needed medical treatment. 'You have some cuts on your face. There could be some glass left in there. Take a seat on that tree stump over there. Has anyone phoned for an ambulance?'

'Wait, where's Scotty?' As far as Hunter could see at first glance the team was all here but their kit man was noticeably absent.

'I thought he was behind us.' Floret confirmed he'd been on the bus but there was no sign of him in this current line-up.

'I'll go back and look for him.' He wouldn't be able to live with himself if he'd left someone behind in the wreckage.

'Hunter, you can't.' He felt Charlotte's hand on his arm but even her touch wasn't enough to deter him from doing what was right. Scotty had family too and he knew if he'd been in the same position he'd want someone looking out for him.

'I have to. I promise I'll be careful.'

'In that case, I'm coming with you.' Charlotte stubbornly strode alongside him and he knew he was wasting time fighting a losing battle.

'Scotty? Are you here?' he bellowed as they reached the clearing where the bus was barely recognisable as anything other than a cloud of smoke.

'Over there.' Charlotte pointed towards a flash of colour in the midst of the grey, a small figure sitting huddled on the ground at the back of the bus.

'Scotty? You can't stay here. The bus is on fire.' He hooked a hand under his elbow and helped him to his feet but the stunned kit man didn't seem to grasp the severity of the situation.

'Let's go.' Charlotte was there as always when he needed a hand and took Scotty's other arm so they were able to hurry him away from the scene. As they climbed the embankment towards safety there was a loud bang and the sound of smashing glass as the fire took hold and blew out what was left of the windows. It had been a close call, as his pulse rate would attest to.

'Scotty, are you all right? Talk to me.'

He heard the concern in Charlotte's voice a fraction of a second before their patient's legs went from beneath him and he collapsed, a deadweight in their arms. They had no choice but to fall to the ground with him only metres away from the road.

Charlotte felt his forehead. 'His skin is clammy.'

She took his wrist. 'His pulse is rapid and faint. I think he's going into shock.'

Hunter positioned him on the ground so his head was low and his legs were raised and supported to increase the flow of blood to his head. Charlotte loosened the collar of his shirt to make it easier for him to breathe.

The distant sound of sirens filtered through the night.

'We need to keep him warm.' Charlotte whipped her jacket from around her shoulders and tucked it in around him. 'The ambulance is on the way, Scotty. Give me a nod that you understand what's happening.'

There was a small acknowledgement.

Charlotte was working hard to keep him engaged, checking his level of response, and Hunter knew it was because there was a danger this was more than emotional shock after the accident. It could also be a life-threatening medical condition as a result of insufficient blood flow through the body, leading to a heart attack or organ damage.

'Hello?' The crunch of forest debris underfoot and sweeping torch beams dancing in the distance signalled the arrival of the emergency services, guided by a few of the players.

'We're over here!' Hunter shouted, and waved them over.

Charlotte gave the rundown of injuries, the most serious ones being Gray's and Scotty's. The paramedics ably took over, checking Scotty's vitals and wrapping him in a warm blanket. As Hunter and Charlotte got up from the damp earth, she began shivering uncontrollably. He held her close, trying to transfer some body heat.

'We should get you seen too.'

'I'll be all right. I just have to make sure the others get checked over at the hospital and I'll go back to the hotel for a bath and bed. You should probably let Alfie know we're okay in case the press gets hold of the news we've had an accident.'

'I will as soon as I know you're going to be okay.' He was a little taken aback she was thinking about Alfie when she'd been so sure she didn't want to be part of their family. That instinct to reassure him, the knowledge his welfare was the uppermost thought in her mind, said she was already invested in them both. It was a revelation that changed his own ideas about what was best for all of them. If there was a chance they could be together and work this out, he wanted to cling to it.

'I can't believe you followed me down here.'

'I wasn't just going to sit back and watch you get hurt, now, was I?' She'd put herself at risk for him and Hunter struggled with the urge to kiss her. In that moment all that mattered was that she was safe. He brushed away bits of leaves and twigs that had become tangled in her hair along the way and the movement revealed a small cut on her forehead he'd missed up until now.

'You're hurt.' He reached out and sticky blood coated his fingers.

'I banged my head on the seat in front when we hit that tree. I'll probably have an egg-shaped reminder in the morning.' She moved her hair back over her face to hide it, as if that would somehow solve the problem.

'You could have whiplash or concussion even. You know what could happen if that's left untreated. Do you have any pain? Blurred vision?' Head injuries, especially those caused by a high-impact crash, could lead to serious complications, ones he wasn't going to risk.

'Hey, who's the doctor here? I think you've a tendency to overstep your jurisdiction, Mr Torrance.' Her defences were back up as she stepped back from him and out of his hold.

Unfortunately, it was in that second her knees buckled and belied that she wasn't as indestructible as she made out. Hunter made a grab for her before she could hit the ground and scooped her up into his arms. Despite her huge personality, she weighed virtually nothing and he was reminded of how vulnerable she really was despite her insistence otherwise. He wasn't prepared to take any risks where her health was concerned.

She might claim she didn't want him in her life but that didn't mean he'd simply stop caring about her. She'd made an impression on his heart that could never be erased, even if he did move to London.

'Let's get you into the ambulance with the others.' He carried her up through the trees himself, with no intention of leaving her until he knew she was safe.

Charlotte's head was in a whirl and it wasn't entirely down to the knock she'd taken in last night's crash. Hunter's words and actions towards her simply didn't marry. One minute she was finding out he was planning a move to London with no thought for her, the next he was refusing to leave her hospital bedside, playing the role of a concerned partner. It wasn't fair when she was supposed to be getting used to not having him around. How could she remain aloof and disinterested in someone who was so clearly passionate about helping others, and about her?

He'd stayed with her until she'd been discharged in the early hours of the morning when she'd assured the medical staff she'd return if any other symptoms of concussion occurred. Gray had been kept in for observation and apparently they'd run a battery of tests on Scotty too. When she'd begged the nurses for information they'd told her he was on an IV for fluid resuscitation to raise his blood pressure again and they were looking at an ECG and bloods to determine any underlying heart problems. A bump on the head seemed minor in comparison but Hunter had insisted she get checked over too.

He'd even offered to stay with her back at the hotel—on the floor, of course—in case she needed him during the night. She hadn't accepted his offer because one night simply wasn't enough any more. She wanted for ever. For too long she'd been denying she was in love with the man because she'd known it would bring her nothing but heartache, and she'd been right. When she'd found out about the job in London the sense of betrayal, the knowledge he would happily abandon her in pursuit of his ego, had turned her into that wounded, lonely girl again.

In the end she hadn't even had breakfast with him. He'd been a complete no-show for the meal with the team, and was still missing here at training. Uneasiness settled heavily in her stomach along with the few bites of toast she'd managed. She knew where he was, he was off making great plans for his future in London without her.

Last night had proved to her how far she'd fallen for him because she'd never been as scared in her life as she'd been when he'd said he was going back to that bus. She didn't want to imagine her life without him in it if something had happened to him. It didn't matter because she hadn't fought any harder than he had to save the relationship and he'd taken that as her acceptance of his choice to leave.

If she'd only told him she was in love with him, that she wanted to spend every day with him and Alfie, he might've stayed, but she'd been too scared to take that risk and she'd lost him anyway. She didn't know whether to laugh or cry at her own stupidity, continuing to let the past overshadow the good things in her life now, and in the early hours of the morning it had been a hideous combination of both.

There was one familiar face waiting at the arena for practice but it wasn't the one she'd hoped to see.

'Gray? What on earth are you doing here?'

'The same as everyone else, I expect,' he said, coming to watch the drills out on the ice alongside her.

She rolled her eyes at him. 'You know very well what I mean. What are you doing out of hospital?'

'They sent me home so someone who actually needed a bed could have one.' He folded down one of the seats and gingerly sat down, clutching his right side.

'Hmm. Well, if they *actually* discharged you I'm sure they told you to rest.' She doubted his version of events. If nothing else, they were supposed to notify her when he was released to avoid this very situation.

'Nothing's broken, just a couple of badly bruised ribs.' He adjusted his position and sucked in a breath even with that minimal effort.

'I'm sure it's still painful though.' It didn't take a doctor to know that sitting all day in an uncomfortable chair in a cold arena wasn't going to help a rib injury.

He patted his jacket pocket. 'I've got my painkillers right here. It'll take more than a few bruised ribs for me to miss this game.'

'Well, take it as easy as you can.' Which was akin to asking a lion not to roar, but she was well aware nothing she said would persuade him to rest and aid healing.

'How are the rest of the guys? Are they fit enough to win?'

'They're a bit shaken up, battered and bruised, but there's nothing to rule them out of playing. Scotty got the all-clear too but he's doing the sensible thing and staying in bed, like he was told.'

It might be harder to keep their minds on the game after the shock of the crash. Although now Gray was here it would be a relief for them to see him and he'd certainly be a motivator to get them going. That only left one of their party MIA.

'Good.'

'Did, uh, Hunter pick you up from the hospital?' She was grasping for a rational, painless explanation for his absence. If Gray had discharged himself, as she suspected, he would've sworn any accomplice to secrecy until the deed was done.

'I phoned a cab. Where is he anyway?' He turned his head as much as his injury would allow to scour the building.

'He had to…er…take care of something. I said I would manage here until he got back.' The lie burned her tongue as well as her cheeks in the knowledge he hadn't trusted her with any such courtesy.

As it turned out, Hunter didn't make an appearance until training was over, and then without a hint of urgency in his swagger.

'You do know the season isn't over yet?' Gray arched an eyebrow at him, clearly not amused by his sudden unreliability.

Hunter shrugged off his jacket and rolled up his sleeves. 'I do know and I'm here with plenty of time to spare before the big game.'

'I hope so, for your sake.'

'Uh, Gray? I need to have a word with you. In private.' He flicked a glance at Charlotte, sufficient to justify her paranoia.

Only a few hours ago he hadn't wanted to leave her side. Now it appeared she was somehow in the way, a nuisance he couldn't wait to be rid of.

'Don't mind me. I'm only here to do a job after all.' She bristled past the two men before her anguish at her dismissal manifested in not very professional tears of self-pity.

When it came to Hunter choosing between her and, well, anything, she knew she'd lose every time.

'I do hope your personal problems aren't leaking into your career prospects again,' Gray said as they both watched Charlotte storm off.

There was no point in pretending he had the wrong idea about their relationship when she showed her emotions so clearly for everyone to see. Right now, they could both see she was royally ticked off at him.

'That's exactly what I'm trying to avoid and why I wanted to talk to you.' He inhaled a lungful of air to fortify himself. It wasn't going to be an easy conversation with any of those affected by his future plans.

Gray fixed him with a steely stare. 'You've been given a second chance here.'

'For which I'll be eternally in your debt. I don't want to mess things up with Alfie, that's why I've had to make a few tough decisions.'

'That doesn't sound good. You do know I'm recovering

from my injuries here and my team, which has just been in a road accident, is about to play in the final? Couldn't this wait?'

Hunter understood Gray's frustration. It was bad timing, like every other major event in his life. The difference was that he was taking control this time, not simply letting events carry him along.

Work got in the way of the talk he so desperately needed to have with Charlotte. Although they'd been given the all-clear last night, a lot of the guys were suffering from more aches and pains than usual as a result of the accident. The trauma and exposure had kept him up to his elbows in deep-tissue massages for most of the morning. He was running out of time to set the record straight with her but he couldn't let the team down now. This was the last time he'd have the opportunity to show Gray he'd been worth the risk. If he got the Demons fighting fit to win this final they might forgive him for trying to walk out on them. Even if Charlotte couldn't.

They kept missing each other, with players coming and going between them, and having to grab breaks where they could. Not that this conversation was ever going to be one they could squeeze in between patients.

It wasn't until near the end of the game she ventured down into the tunnel, away from the bench and a mass audience.

'About this morning…' This wasn't the time or place he'd been hoping to have this conversation, with the soundtrack of bodies slamming into the hoardings playing in the background, but he needed to explain what had happened.

'Is it a done deal?'

'Pardon?' Her need to get straight to the point always threw him. That's why it had made her reluctance to talk through the end of their relationship so hard to come to terms with.

'Is it too late?'

'For what?'

'Us.'

It took a moment for the line of her questioning to register and when it did it felt as though a weight had been lifted off his chest. That didn't mean he was happy to be left guessing exactly what it was she wanted this time.

'What are you saying, Charlotte? It was only yesterday you were telling me there was no way this could work, that you didn't want to be part of my and Alfie's lives.' He still had to be careful that she meant this—that she knew exactly what she was getting into and didn't run out on him again when it hit home.

'I was scared, Hunter, afraid to get close in case I'm not enough to keep you happy. Last night when I thought you might get hurt…it made me realise it doesn't matter how much I fight it, I'm already in love with you. I'm sorry I let my fears get in the way of what we had, what we could have if you'll still have me. I should've been prepared to take a risk, the way you did in letting me into your life with Alfie. Is there still a chance? Do you love me?' She barely took a breath and left Hunter dizzy with the rapid speed of her admissions, but there was only one thing that mattered at the end of all this. She loved him.

'Of course I love you!' When she'd been hurt last night it had become very clear to him how much she meant to him. He would've swapped places with her himself if he'd been able to and taken away even the slightest discomfort for her. He loved her and it was time to stop running away from the fact.

When she'd had doubts about being part of his family he'd snatched hold of that excuse and used it to justify a move to London. She was right, the first sign of trouble and his instinct was to run. Not any more. This time he was prepared to stay and fight.

Last night had made him see everything in a different light. She hadn't given a thought for her own safety in the chaos, following him back to the accident site to ensure his. Then there'd been her concern for Alfie, the boy she'd tried to convince herself and him she could never get close to. They were meant to be together, to be a family, if only they could face their fears instead of being overwhelmed by them.

She took a deep breath. 'That's all I needed to know... If London is where you're going to be, I'll come too. I'm sure I can set up my practice there just as easily. I'll do whatever it takes for us to make a real go of this. You and Alfie are worth the risk.' Her smile as she handed her heart to him on a plate just about broke him. He'd never imagined anyone could love him enough to give up everything for him.

'You would really do that?'

'I'll go and hand my resignation in to Gray as soon as the match is over.'

'You don't have to, Charlotte. I'm not going to London. I met with CC this morning to tell him I'm staying put. Everything I want is in Ireland and right here.' When he'd sat at that desk across from his prospective new boss and the life he'd laid out before him it had all seemed so cold and impersonal without Charlotte in it. He'd almost had the perfect family he'd always wanted and had been close to throwing it all away. He'd been willing to crawl to the ends of the earth to retrieve that final missing piece of the puzzle. Charlotte had simply got there first. 'Perhaps I was keeping you at a bit of a distance because I was worried I'd hurt you the way I hurt Sara. There's one glaringly obvious difference between then and now. I never loved her the way I love you.'

'But—but what about Gray? Have you handed in your resignation already?'

'That's why I wanted to speak to him, for confirmation I would still have a job with the Demons next season so I know I have something to offer you other than another dead-in-the-water career.' He'd been honest with Gray about what had happened, risking their friendship over the betrayal, but he was a father too and he'd understood his motives. Right before he'd told him to move his butt and get back to work before face-off.

Goal!

As they turned to face each other and confront the situation, the celebrations around the arena stalled the response he'd been waiting to hear all day. They were so locked in that moment, intent on finally resolving their status, neither even turned to see who'd scored. Although they did share a smile when the announcement came that Anderson had put the Demons ahead.

'I guess our jobs are safe for another season, huh?' He cracked a joke because he was afraid those three words he'd waited a lifetime to say had come too late. This wasn't Hollywood, there was no guarantee they'd just run titles and walk off into the sunset because he'd broken out the 'I love you' speech.

Charlotte was stunned by the news that he'd given up a new job and a move to London all for her. 'You really mean it?'

'I really mean it.'

He grabbed her hand and placed it on his chest. A definite ploy to stop her from thinking straight when that solid muscle beneath her fingers brought back memories of their night together, exploring each other's bodies until she'd known every inch of him.

'Do you feel that? My heart is pumping with adrenaline, waiting for you to tell me that you want to be with me and Alfie.'

'You were, are, the best thing to ever happen to me. I didn't know what living was until you two came along.'

She could tell how much he'd struggled, trying to combine parenthood with everything else. The worry lines were etched deeply on his brow and she dared to move closer to test the theory this wasn't the same man who'd planned to run away from her when the going got tough.

'I love you, Charlotte. I still want that fresh start but this time I want it with you. No secrets, no pretending I know what's best for everyone else, just open and honest discussion about what we want, or where we go, as a family.'

'A family?' She needed someone to pinch her and prove this was real, not a dream conjured up by her broken heart.

'You. Me. Alfie. Together. For ever.'

'I couldn't think of anything more perfect.' She wound her arms around his neck and snuggled in close, willing to risk everything she had for a chance of happiness.

Somewhere far away the final klaxon sounded and declared the Demons play-off champions, but it was Charlotte who felt like the real winner now they'd both shaken off the shadows of the past for a future together.

EPILOGUE

'How did it go?' Charlotte hadn't been able to settle all afternoon, waiting to hear how Hunter's meeting had gone with Alfie's teacher.

It had been a whirlwind of a year for all of them and she hoped it hadn't affected his schoolwork. There'd been the move into the cottage and getting used to living together as a family and the rushed wedding when they'd decided life was too short to waste any more time. It was a lot for a young boy to deal with all at once.

And her.

That parental guilt she'd worried about all along had well and truly kicked in but she wouldn't be without either of them for the world.

Hunter sat on the end of her desk. 'It went great. Mrs Patterson said he's top of the class for reading and maths.'

She could stop sweating now she'd been reassured his new stepmother wasn't responsible for a decline in his grades. He didn't appear unhappy with the new arrangement, he was as good as gold for her. She simply worried constantly about his well-being. It was taking a lot of will-power not to become a helicopter parent. Especially when she might be in danger of upsetting the family dynamic again.

'I'm so glad. He's been through a lot.'

'To quote his favourite teacher, "He's a happy, well-adjusted little boy."'

Hearing that made her well up because it was so important to her. Plus she was a tad hormonal these days.

'I'm sorry I couldn't make it in time. My appointment overran, otherwise I would've been there too.'

'I know, sweetheart. It's fine. You were there for his school play when I couldn't make it. That's part of the reason we make such a good team. There will always be at least one of us there waving pom-poms for him.'

It was true, they were a great team in all aspects of their lives. Gray had been only too happy to sign them both on for the new season and when the office next door to hers came onto the market Hunter had been able to set his own private practice up too. They shared the parenting as much as they could, with a little help from the O'Reillys every now and then.

'Where is he?'

'With his grandparents. They suggested we might like to go out to dinner or something while they babysit tonight.'

'Or something?' She hadn't missed the fact he'd locked the door on his way in. A clear indication they wouldn't make it out in time for dinner.

His cheeky grin said he had more than food on his mind too. 'Are you finished here?'

'For now. I need to write up a few progress reports for Gray but I can do that before the next match.'

'I can't believe it's play-off season already. That means a certain one-year anniversary. Perhaps we should celebrate?' He waggled his eyebrows. As if she needed reminding what they'd got up to this time last year. They'd done a lot more since.

'We can celebrate but it'll have to be minus the alcohol.' The news she'd been hiding was bubbling to the surface.

'You're not feeling sick again, are you?' He reached out to feel her forehead.

'I have a confession to make. I had an appointment today but as a patient, not a doctor.'

'You're scaring me now. Why didn't you tell me there was something wrong?' He scrambled off the desk and took her hand, his concern touching.

'I wanted to confirm my own diagnosis first. I think we're on our way to starting our own little hockey team.' She moved his hand to her belly, which was apparently full of more than Hunter's maple syrup pancakes.

'You're pregnant?' His eyes were like saucers as his slack jaw gradually widened into the happiest, sexiest smile she'd ever seen. She hadn't known men could get the pregnancy bloom too but he was beaming from the inside out.

'*We're* pregnant. I expect you to be with me in this every step of the way.' As happy as she was at the news too, there was a little trepidation at what the next few months had in store.

'Don't worry, there's nowhere I'd rather be than right here.' He placed a soft kiss on her belly to confirm they were in this together.

This baby was a new beginning for all of them. One they all deserved.

* * * * *

MILLS & BOON®

MEDICAL ROMANCE™

THE ULTIMATE IN ROMANTIC MEDICAL DRAMA

A sneak peek at next month's titles...

Just can't wait?
Buy our books online before they hit the shops!
www.millsandboon.co.uk

Also available as eBooks.

MILLS & BOON®

Why shop at millsandboon.co.uk?

Each year, thousands of romance readers
find their perfect read at millsandboon.co.uk.
That's because we're passionate about
bringing you the very best romantic fiction.
Here are some of the advantages of
shopping at www.millsandboon.co.uk:

* **Get new books first**—you'll be able to buy
  your favourite books one month before they
  hit the shops

* **Get exclusive discounts**—you'll also be
  able to buy our specially created monthly
  collections, with up to 50% off the RRP

* **Find your favourite authors**—latest news,
  interviews and new releases for all your
  favourite authors and series on our website,
  plus ideas for what to try next

* **Join in**—once you've bought your favourite
  books, don't forget to register with us to rate,
  review and join in the discussions

Visit **www.millsandboon.co.uk**
for all this and more today!